Nina Singh lives just outsid[...] her husband, children, and a [...] Yorkie. After several years i[...] she finally followed the advice of family and friends to 'give the writing a go, already'. She's oh-so-happy she did. When not at her keyboard, she likes to spend time on the tennis court or golf course. Or immersed in a good read.

Jenny Lane (she/they) writes contemporary stories with queer characters ranging from middle grade to adult. Their stories are queer, whimsical, heartwarming…and always end with a happily-ever-something. There is nothing Jenny loves more than a fire pit, an ocean view, and a good book to read—but they will settle for any combination of these three. When she isn't writing or reading something, she works as a librarian and advocate for literacy.

Also by Nina Singh

Their Accidental Marriage Deal
Bound by the Boss's Baby

If the Fairy Tale Fits… miniseries

Part of His Royal World

Winter Escapes miniseries

Prince's Proposal for the Canadian Cameras

Her Fake Wedding Date in Sicily
is **Jenny Lane**'s debut title.

Look out for more books from Jenny Lane.
Coming soon!

Discover more at millsandboon.co.uk.

RESISTING HIS CINDERELLA RIVAL

NINA SINGH

HER FAKE WEDDING DATE IN SICILY

JENNY LANE

MILLS & BOON

First published in Great Britain 2025
by Mills & Boon, an imprint of HarperCollins*Publishers* Ltd,
1 London Bridge Street, London, SE1 9GF

www.harpercollins.co.uk

HarperCollins*Publishers*, Macken House, 39/40 Mayor Street Upper, Dublin 1, D01 C9W8, Ireland

ISBN: 978-0-263-39685-0

08/25

MIX
Paper | Supporting
responsible forestry
FSC™ C007454
FSC
www.fsc.org

This book contains FSC™ certified paper
and other controlled sources to ensure responsible forest management.

For more information visit www.harpercollins.co.uk/green.

Printed and Bound in the UK using 100% Renewable Electricity
at CPI Group (UK) Ltd, Croydon, CR0 4YY

RESISTING HIS CINDERELLA RIVAL

NINA SINGH

MILLS & BOON

For my children.
For taking me to places I would never think to go.

CHAPTER ONE

HE WAS GOING to have to start all over. From square one.

Matteo Talarico slammed his laptop shut and stared at the Roman skyline outside his window. The Emmanuel Monument stood magnificently tall and grand against the setting sun in the horizon. A year ago, he would have never guessed that he'd have to give up looking at that view. Give up the office and the building that held it.

It was gone. All of it. Liquidated. The family's holdings set up on the auction block like discarded remains. After all these years, it had taken one man's folly to bring it all down. That man being his father.

Stefan Talarico had ruined the business his own father, Matteo's grandfather, had started and nurtured all those years ago. To make matters worse, he'd done so in the most clichéd way imaginable.

He'd let himself be duped by a beautiful woman.

Like a true mark, his old man had fallen for the false compliments and pretty—ultimately fake—platitudes simply because they'd been uttered through pretty, pouty lips.

Matteo rubbed his forehead and tried to clear his head. The negative and angry thoughts churning through his head for the past couple of years, ever since that woman had entered his father's life, did nothing to better the reality he was facing. Decades of consistent business growth and success only to have it end with such chaos and loss.

Tala Industries, a name synonymous with high-end luxury condominiums and deluxe commercial real estate, was on the brink of complete bankruptcy.

Whatever it took, he would see the woman pay for what she'd done. If he could ever find her.

First things first, Matteo had to come up with a plan to rebuild Tala Industries from the ground up. One brick at a time. If only he knew where to start.

His cell phone vibrated on the desk behind him and he groaned. He was getting so tired of answering calls from creditors and business scavengers alike. But the contact that appeared on his screen told him that the call was from neither. Though probably not all that much better.

He clicked on the icon to answer his lawyer's call. "Aldo. Please tell me you're calling with some good news," he said, though that was highly unlikely and they both knew it.

"Well, in a sense, I think I might be."

Now that was curious. "In a sense?"

"My office received a call earlier this morning pertaining to you. From the islands."

"Which one?"

"Sardinia. Cagliari to be more precise."

Matteo wracked his brain but came up with nothing in response to the news. He didn't know anyone in the town of Cagliari. Or in any part of Sardinia, for that matter. He could count on one hand all the times he'd visited the Italian island south of the region of Tuscany. "And?"

"It turns out you had a distant relative who made her

home there. An elderly distant cousin. On your mother's side."

The other man's use of the past tense told him whoever this great distant cousin had been, she was now gone. But what did it have to do with him? Aldo seemed to be taking his sweet time getting to the point. "Go on," Matteo prompted.

"She passed on last month. At the youthful age of ninety-eight. She didn't have any direct family of her own, it turns out. But apparently often talked fondly of a little tyke who visited her once or twice decades ago."

Huh. Matteo had zero recollection of any such visits. Though that wasn't surprising. His parents traipsed all over the Italian landscape when he was growing up, occasionally bringing him along. More often, they left him behind with the household staff.

Aldo continued, "She listed you as an inheritor of part of her estate. An estate attorney from a small office in Cagliari notified us that we'll be receiving the paperwork later this week."

He knew better than to get his hopes up in response to this unexpected news. After all, what kind of inheritance could a long-lost spinster cousin of his beloved mother possibly be able to afford him? In all likelihood, this phone call was probably just going to result in yet one more nuisance to-do item added to his already chaotic life presently. She'd likely left him knickknacks and collectibles he'd have to try and figure out what to do with.

"As far as I can tell based on the phone call," Aldo was saying, "you've inherited a patch of land."

Matteo straightened, his attention sharpened. Land.

"She left me property? That could be worth something."

"It appears so," Aldo answered. "Like I said, I don't have a lot of the details just yet. We shouldn't get ahead of ourselves."

Matteo clamped down on the frizzle of excitement now traveling up his spine. Aldo was right. For all he knew, the phone call might have been referring to nothing more than a parking spot.

"Also, there's just a slight caveat."

Matteo pinched the bridge of his nose and resisted the urge to curse out loud. Of course there was. Even this small crumb the universe was throwing his way had to be too good to be true. The way his luck was going so far, he wouldn't expect anything less.

"What's that?"

"Turns out you'll only be getting a part of the property. The other, more substantial part houses a small bed-and-breakfast establishment. The hotel and the land it sits on have been bequeathed to someone else."

Matteo inhaled, his mind quickly processing the information. A bed-and-breakfast sat on part of the property. So it was definitely larger than a parking spot or something similar. All right, he might be able to work with that.

"Who?" Matteo asked. Another long-lost relative perhaps? What were the chances there'd been more than one out there that he hadn't known about?

"I don't have that information yet. Perhaps when the paperwork finally arrives we'll get more details."

Right. Nothing to do but wait. Matteo had somehow found himself in yet another holding pattern.

"Contact me as soon as the documents arrive," he instructed the lawyer. The other man agreed, then ended the call.

Matteo refocused his gaze on the horizon, staring at the distance in the direction where Sardinia, the island in question, would be located. The amount he knew about Sardinia could fit into a thumbnail. He wracked his brain to summon any kind of memory about his long-ago visits but nothing came to mind.

Still, he'd just been presented with a parachute, one that might set him on a direction toward some kind of recovery. One he would have to diligently pursue.

After all, what choice did he have?

Mariana Renati took another large sip of her double espresso and savored the rich, chicory taste. The caffeine was much needed this morning. Not that such wasn't the case most days, but today in particular she needed all the energy she could summon.

He was due to arrive later this morning.

The elusive long-lost son of a long-lost cousin. The man she'd been trying to get a hold of for the past month and a half on Anna's behalf. Only to have her emails go unanswered until it was too late.

The old woman had simply wanted to connect one last time with someone she could call family.

Sure, he'd been apologetic at the end when he'd finally answered her messages. Had told her of his sad, sorry excuse of being busy at work with changes to the family business. Yada yada.

She could guess the truth. Whoever Matteo Talarico was, he had no interest in connecting with a distant elderly relative until he'd heard about what was in it for him.

"Mari, are you back here?"

Roberta's voice sounded from the front of the storage room. She'd been found. Was a few minutes of peace while drinking her morning cup too much to ask for? Today of all days?

She clamped down on her frustration. Rather unreasonable of her to be frustrated at one of her trusty and loyal employees.

That thought gave her a moment of pause. To think. She actually had employees. Roberta and her twenty-something son, Miyko, were in charge of the front office and check-ins/checkouts. Three other born-and-bred Sardinians rounded out the janitorial and cleaning crew. A revolving group of part-time employees made up mostly of college students or bored adults rounded out the staff. It wasn't as if Mari had had anything to do with their hiring. Roberta and Miyko had been a fixture here since Mari had arrived on the island four years ago. The others had mostly been hired alongside her when she'd been brought aboard. Anna's years-long volunteer association with the local university procured the part-time student help.

Still, they all reported directly to her. A fact that had her occasionally riddled with anxiety and self-doubt at the responsibility on her shoulders. Last night she'd woken up no less than three times with her heart racing and covered in perspiration. Twelve people depended on her for their very livelihood now. She'd never felt such a weight on her shoulders.

Which was why this upcoming meeting with this Matteo Talarico was so vitally important. Now that it was finally happening.

But first, she had to go see what Roberta needed.

"*Scusa*, Mari," Roberta began when she reached her side. "The guest from last night, he is asking assistance with the bikes."

Mari could easily guess which guest she was referring to. The man was a regular who checked in every June and always overstayed his welcome. He was from the mainland, with some kind of familial tie to the island. Honestly, Mari couldn't guess why he made the yearly trip or stayed so long. He seemed to be utterly miserable every time he was here.

With a resigned sigh, Mari set her cup down and rose from her lounger chair. She'd done a routine check of all the bikes yesterday evening before wrapping up her nightly chores and retiring sometime after midnight.

"He insists you be the one to help him," Roberta added.

That checked out. The man had also insisted yesterday that she check the espresso machine as something seemed "off" to his apparently highly discerning taste buds. Never mind that her barista was an expert at handling the machine and making a top-notch beverage.

"I'll be right there," Mari answered and took a final swig from her mug. When she arrived at the portico attached to the hotel where they stored the bikes, she found Signore Gio standing hands on hips, a glaring scowl on his face.

"There you are," he said when he saw her approach.

"*Buena sera*, Signore Gio," Mari answered with as wide a smile as she could muster. It wasn't easy. "What seems to be the issue?"

He pointed to the bikes. "These chains all need to be oiled. They're unacceptably dry. How am I supposed to take any of these to ride on the path in the condition they're in? Not a single one is rideable at the moment."

Mari knew without a doubt they weren't that dry. She oiled them weekly. Every Monday, in fact, the day there was the least demand for bikes. Oiling them more often than that would be completely unnecessary. But Signore Gio simply didn't seem to feel complete when he didn't have something to complain about.

Of course, Mari wasn't going to bother explaining any of that to the man. No, she wasn't about to give him what he wanted—an argument. Or a chance to berate her intelligence or competence, as he was wont to do.

Little did Signore Gio know, she had plenty of experience with such scenarios. And people like him. No, strike that. She'd in fact dealt with much worse.

Instead, she increased the wattage of her smile and gave him a friendly nod. "I'll get on it right away, Signore Gio. Which bike would you prefer? I can start with that one."

He looked ready to argue before he gave a dismissive wave of his hand. "It hardly matters. I'm already delayed for the morning. Just get them oiled already and I'll come back after having a cup of coffee."

"Of course," Mari said, fake smile still in place. Poor Esmerelda, she was on espresso and beverage duty this morning. She would have to deal with the ornery old goat for the next few minutes at least.

Mari was oiling the chain on the last bike when she heard footsteps behind her. She sucked in a deep breath as she finished, steeling herself for the second unpleasant encounter of the morning with Signore Gio.

"Ah, you're back. Choose any bike you like," she said, rising and admiring her work as she wiped her hands on a white rag. A smear of black grease marred the terry towel surface.

But when she turned around, forcing yet another fake smile, the man standing before her was most certainly not Signore Gio.

No, the man who'd just walked up behind her didn't resemble Signore Gio in any way. First of all, he had to be at least two decades younger. Tall, imposing, with dark hair and eyes the color of the Sardinian horizon late at night above the cliffs, he looked like he might have stepped out of a cologne ad in an international magazine or embarked from a yacht. For all she knew, he just might have.

Actually, upon further consideration, the two men did indeed have one thing in common. A very displeased expression directed her way. Her current visitor looked about as disgruntled as her previous one had been. Though this one seemed to wear the scowl better.

Mari knew why Signore Gio was upset. But what was up with this guy?

Despite his displeased expression, it was hard to ignore the absolute magnetism of the stranger. Tall, dark and most definitely handsome, the man was the type who no doubt made women swoon.

Not her, however. She had no use for a handsome face. Not anymore.

"I'm looking for a Signora Mariana Renati," he announced, not bothering to introduce himself. "I asked the lady out in the garden, but she brushed me off. Rather rudely, I might add."

He had to be referring to Roberta. She was the only one who might be tending to the flowers at this time of day. And she did tend to get rather frustrated and impatient with any interruption during her gardening time. As if there weren't close to a million other details around the hotel that needed attention. But it was hard to deny Roberta the pleasure she received in tending to the flowers. Still, it wasn't acceptable to be less than hospitable to any of their guests.

"Apologies. I'll be sure to speak to her."

He gave her a dismissive wave of his hand. "Right. So this Mariana person, where might she be?"

"Actually, you've found her." Mari reached her hand out and then snapped it right back upon seeing that the towel hadn't eradicated all the black goo from her skin. "That's me. I'm Mariana."

But who in the world was he? Unless… It couldn't be. Matteo Talarico wasn't due to arrive until much later this afternoon!

He lifted a dark eyebrow. "Do you and your mother have the same name or something?"

What the devil was he talking about? "Uh…no. Can I help you with something, Signore…?"

He ignored her question, his eyes narrowing on her. She'd never seen a man look so handsome while looking so displeased. There probably wasn't much that could make this particular man look anything less, Mari figured.

She gave herself a mental thwack. Enough already. She had to stop lingering on how attractive he was.

"Do you mean to tell me that you're *the* Mariana Renati? The only one?"

Honestly. What was there to be so confused about? "The only one around here. Now, what can I do for you?"

The scowl on his lips transformed into a crooked smirk. Then turned into some semblance of a smile, though it held zero humor.

"Oh, I get it," he said, crossing his arms on his chest in front of the well-tailored shirt he wore.

"Get what?"

"You can't possibly have much experience running a food cart, let alone a hotel. You look like you're barely out of school."

What in the world? "I'm not sure how my age is any of your business." At this point, given his attitude, Mari was past caring who he was. Even if it meant losing a potential future guest. The man was beyond rude. Bordering on boorish. No guest was worth that. Not after what she'd already endured. "You haven't even told me who you are."

"Matteo Talarico."

Mari couldn't suppress her gasp. Well, wasn't this a fine state of affairs. Now that he was finally here, Mari would just as soon ask him to leave. To think, she'd been harping on how good-looking he was just a moment ago. The words he was throwing at her were far less than pretty.

Had she somehow offended this man in the past and forgotten? That didn't seem likely. Matteo Talarico wasn't the kind of man a woman forgot.

"Honestly, is there like some kind of underground club or something? Do you lot meet regularly and discuss individual strategies?" he continued, making no sense whatsoever.

What in the world was he getting at? Did he mean business strategies? If so, she could hardly see why such a thing might bother him so much.

"I honestly have no idea what you're talking about. Nor why you're being quite so rude. Mind if I ask why?"

The smirk widened and he shook his head. "I have a question for you first."

Mari took a deep breath, tried to summon some patience. Fine. She would bite. If only to get to the bottom of all this. "Go ahead," she said, gesturing with her palm up. "Ask away. And if you're still wondering about my experience, I grew up working in a restaurant. Then went to school for hospitality and spent a couple of years in the field before I got to Sardinia. I've worked here about four years. About half of that time as manager."

Not that she owed this man any kind of explanation. So why was she compelled to be giving him one?

"It appears you're not doing a very good job."

"Of all the—"

"Between the rude employee who greeted me. Then there's the guest in the lobby currently complaining about your watered-down espresso and the lack of adequate bikes."

He actually cut her off! Mari's jaw fell. Granted, those weren't the ideal first impressions she would have had greeting him. Still, he was being unreasonable and jumping to all sorts of conclusions about her competence. "Would you like me to explain any of that to you?" she asked, though she had a hunch what his answer was going to be.

He shook his head. "No. I had another question in mind. How exactly did you manage to bamboozle my mother's cousin into handing the hotel over to you?"

Mari felt the blood drain from her face as his words hit their mark. *How dare he!*

Several beats passed where she could do nothing but stare at his face, his baseless accusation hanging heavy in the air. The breath seemed to have left her lungs. Someone else accusing her of duplicity. Honestly, what was it about her that made men think she could be pushed around with baseless allegations? Did she give off some kind of invisible aura? Was there a hidden sign about her that read "Kick me, I won't fight back"?

No! Not anymore. She vowed long ago that she wouldn't put up with it. This Matteo Talarico had no right to stride in here in his fancy tailored shirt, his shiny polished shoes and killer good looks to try to test that vow after all this time.

Lifting her chin, she breathed deeply through her nose. "I have no idea what you're talking about. Anna asked me months ago when she first fell ill to contact you. Which I did. Repeatedly. You never bothered to respond until she was gone."

That comment seemed to hit the mark. A muscle twitched ever so slightly along his jaw. "She wanted you to have the land adjacent to the hotel. Said that you were a successful businessman who would know how to put it to use."

"Yet she gave the hotel itself to you. An inexperienced novice who worked for her for less than five years. Doesn't that sound the slightest bit 'off' to you?"

That settled it. She'd had more than enough. "I think you should leave, Mr. Talarico."

"We have things we need to discuss."

"We can discuss them through our solicitors. Goodbye."

He appeared ready to argue. Mari held her breath for the length of time it took him to finally dip his head in a nod.

"Fine. I'll go. For now," he added before she could take a breath of relief.

"By the way," he tossed over his shoulder as he turned away toward the door. "You have a dark smudge on your face. Right cheek."

CHAPTER TWO

HE SHOULD HAVE done this first.

Instead of making a beeline straight to the hotel to go and find her, he should have taken the time to do exactly what he was doing now. Taking just a few minutes to gather his thoughts. And getting some rest after a busy travel morning. But he'd blown it.

What had gotten into him? He never operated on emotion.

Not that it was any kind of excuse, but the combination of jet lag, utter disappointment at his father's recklessness and the crushing weight on his shoulders to keep some small part of Tala Industries afloat, the small number of staff who still depended on him for their livelihood. It had all brewed together into a raging storm within his core. So he'd taken it out on the one person on the planet who might be able to help him with what he hoped to accomplish.

What an awful first impression.

If he was being completely honest with himself, he'd have to admit that laying eyes upon Mariana Renati had come as a bit of a surprise. That certainly hadn't helped to temper the way he'd reacted to her. He hadn't been expecting someone quite so...*striking*. It was the first word that came to mind. Even grimy with a smudge of grease on her cheek, Matteo had been struck by the extraordinary hue of her eyes, the way her hair fell in loose tendrils around her rosy cheeks. How lush and red her full lips were.

Upon finding out she was *the* Mariana Renati, the inheritor of the hotel, his suspicions had simply taken over. Still, he should have reined in his reaction.

If only he had come here first. The beachside ristorante slash bar he was seated at offered a perfect view of the crystal-blue water of Poetto Beach. Framed on one side by the looming cliff known as the Sella del Diavolo, the Devil's Saddle, the scene could have been lifted from a Renaissance painting. Matteo vaguely recalled the legend behind the name. Something about a biblical battle where the devil himself was knocked off his demon steed and dropped his saddle onto the side of a mountain, breaking a bite-shaped chunk off the cliffside. If anyone were to ask him, the landmark looked more like a large piece of brownie with a bite taken off the top. The Devil's Bite Mark might have been a more suitable name.

His meandering thoughts were interrupted when the petite waitress in a black miniskirt and crop top placed a sweaty bottle of ale on the table in front of him.

"Grazie," he said, not hesitating to take a long, refreshing gulp. He was already starting to feel less out of sorts. Only, the easing of his ire served to bring about the rising tide of guilt.

He'd really been out of bounds back there with Mariana Renati. Matteo cringed inwardly as he recalled his childish taunt as he was leaving about the smudge of grease on her face. How utterly petty of him. If he had to be further honest with himself, he'd have to admit that part of his frustration had involved the wayward thought that she looked rather cute, unaware of the blemish below her greenish hazel eye and shapely dark eyebrow. Or how much he had to resist the urge to reach over and rub the smudge off her face with his finger.

Well, that was enough of that. Things were complicated enough between him and the pretty manager without adding an inconvenient dose of attraction to the mix.

So he'd taunted her about it instead.

As if his thoughts conjured her, Mari appeared a few feet in front of him on the beach, lugging a large beach umbrella under one arm and the leg of a long lounge chair hoisted on the other shoulder.

That had to take quite a bit of strength.

So she was physically strong as well. It wasn't lost on him that the way she'd stood up to him back there proved no small amount of inner fortitude. She'd actually kicked him out!

Mariana was accompanied by a portly elderly woman in a bright floral swimsuit.

The petite waitress reappeared at the table. "Can I get you another?" she asked, pointing to the nearly empty bottle of ale. He'd been thirstier than he thought.

"Not just yet," he answered, his gaze still focused on Mari as she thrust the sharp end of the large umbrella into the stand. Matteo couldn't help but be impressed. She got the handle in several inches.

"Actually, I was wondering if I should go help with setting up that umbrella," he said.

The waitress followed his gaze and let out a small chuckle. "No need. She'll have it up in no time. That signorina is a pro. Mari does three or four a day for her guests."

Mari. The use of the affectionate nickname wasn't lost on him. It appeared the pretty hotel manager had endeared herself to at least one member of the staff at the eatery across the road from her business.

And he had to accept that the hotel was indeed hers. Though he had every intention of changing that fact first chance he got. If he got his hands on the hotel and the land it sat on, he could begin the process of rebuilding Tala Industries. The building could easily be turned into a condo complex with some renovations, guaranteeing a steady flow of income as soon as the units were ready to rent. The land would serve as collateral for the funds he'd need to start the process. The small patch he'd been granted himself wouldn't be enough to secure any kind of loan. No, he needed all that had been bequeathed to Mari. In return, he would guarantee she was compensated handsomely as soon as he could pay her. Somehow, he was going to have to convince her that his ideas would be a win-win for them both. That was the goal, anyway.

He'd just have to go about it in a better way than barging into her place of business and acting angry and confrontational.

It had just come as such a shock when he'd first laid eyes on her. He wasn't expecting someone like her to be the manager in question. Though he could see how wrong he'd been on that score. Between the way she'd handled him earlier and the way she was competently setting up a spot for her elderly guest on the beach, there was more to the woman than met the eye.

Never judge a book by its cover and all that. He wouldn't

make the mistake of underestimating her again. Still, it was rather odd that his mother's cousin had bequeathed the hotel to an employee. Quite the inheritance for someone who wasn't blood. Mari may have impressed him, but he would still fully get to the bottom of exactly what she'd done to be granted such an inheritance. So help him, if there'd been any kind of duplicity involved, he would make sure to address it.

He was getting rather tired of those who would cross a Talarico.

Regardless, Matteo would have to at least pretend to be amiable.

"Actually, there isn't much Mari can't do," his server added with no small amount of admiration clear in her voice.

Matteo was beginning to get that distinct impression of Mari Renati himself.

Try as she might, Mari just couldn't get this morning's fiasco out of her head. Her mind's eye kept replaying the conversation—or rather, the altercation, to be more accurate—with Matteo Talarico like a film loop over and over.

The nerve of that man. She knew the type all too well. Privileged, successful, used to getting his own way. Men like him expected the world to kneel at their feet. Well, she certainly wasn't about to. No one would hold such power over her ever again. A flush of shame washed over her that she'd ever let it happen in the first place.

Her only excuse was that she'd been young and naive when she'd begun dating Trevor. At first, she'd been both surprised and honored that someone like him would even notice her, let alone want to pursue her romantically. His well-heeled family made no secret of the fact that they thought Mari was well beneath someone like their son. It didn't take much for Trevor himself to reach the same conclusion.

She pushed the thoughts away and made herself hop off the trip down memory lane. Matteo Talarico was the one to thank for the ride.

"I don't know why you bother cleaning this pool," Roberta's voice sounded from across the patio as Mari fished yet another black fly out with the long pole netting.

"It's not like anyone ever uses it," she added a moment later. "Not with a world-renowned beach right across the roadway."

Mari bit back the snippy response that formed on her tongue. Roberta was very good at critiquing her, but Mari chose to believe that it came from good intentions. Still, after this morning's unpleasantness, she just didn't feel like hearing any more about just how inadequate she was.

"Be that as it may," she began in as smooth a voice as she could muster, "the pool should be kept clean in case anyone does want to use it."

Roberta's response was a loud "hmph."

"Shouldn't you be at the desk?" Mari inquired. It was past noon and typically the time their guests began to trickle in. "Miyko should be preparing for the afternoon's aperitif with the chef."

"I'm getting there," Roberta answered with a dismissive wave of her hand. "Though I'm not sure why you're wasting time out here. You could be tending to the guests yourself."

And what exactly would that leave Roberta to do? She was thinking of a tactful way to ask that question when a rich, deep voice sounded from the screen door that led to the hotel foyer.

"Sorry to interrupt, but there was no one at the desk."

She'd only heard it once before but there was no mistaking it. *He* was back. A strange and unfamiliar shiver ran down the length of Mari's spine.

Honestly. What was it with her physical reaction to the man?

It was bad enough he'd shown up earlier when Signore Gio was complaining; now he'd caught them with an unattended front desk.

Mari caught the netting pole just in time before it dropped out of her hand and fell into the pool. As disoriented as he was, she might very well have followed it into the water. That would have been just the icing on the cake. First she argues with him with bicycle grease smeared on her face and then gives him the pleasure of watching her fall into a pool fully clothed.

Thank the deities above she hadn't given him that satisfaction.

She didn't bother to look in his direction. "I'm afraid we're all booked, Signore Talarico. You will have to find other lodgings."

She glanced up just long enough to see him thrust his hands in his pockets. She didn't dare look at his face. No doubt he was glaring at her. What did he want anyway? Was he here to chide her some more?

"We're booked?" Roberta piped up. "News to me. I thought that Swedish family canceled just this morning."

Damn it, Roberta. For once could she have picked up on a cue?

"I think it's more that I'm not welcome here," he answered the other woman.

"Why? What'd you do?" Roberta wanted to know.

Mari gripped the pole in her hand tight enough that her knuckles turned white. Looked like she wasn't going to be able to ignore Signore Talarico's second unwanted visit of the day. And it was unwanted, wasn't it?

What a silly thought. Of course it was.

Setting the netting down, she swiped her hands down her shorts, resisting the urge to wipe her face in case she hadn't gotten all the grease off. She had, hadn't she?

Enough with the self-questioning already.

"Roberta, please go tend to the desk, as I'm sure we'll have guests arriving. I'd hate for them to be greeted by an empty chair, just like Signore Talarico here."

Roberta stood there a moment longer, her gaze shifting from one of them to the other. If Mari didn't know better, she might have said the older woman appeared amused. Finally, she threw up her hands and made her way to the pathway that led to the front door of the hotel.

Mari glared at Matteo from across the pool as soon as Roberta's shadow cleared the gate. "I believe I was very clear that any further communication between us would need to go through third-party channels."

He bounced once on his polished heels. "Look, for what it's worth, I'm back here to apologize. I was incredibly rude earlier. And you had every right to make me leave."

Huh. She hadn't seen that coming. He didn't seem the type to apologize often. This had to be some kind of act.

"I am genuinely sorry for my behavior."

Mari crossed her arms in front of her chest, not ready

just yet to accept his remorse. For all she knew, his words weren't even sincere. Maybe he was just embarrassed.

Still, she was begrudgingly tempted to welcome his apology as he gazed at her with those dark eyes and sensually set mouth.

"You would have every right to ask me to leave again. But I'd really wish you would hear me out. We have a lot to talk about. Do you know how long it takes to have an attorney draft even the simplest note and how much they bill for it?"

"Some things are worth the money. Avoiding you certainly would be worth any amount."

He grimaced and clasped a hand to his chest. "Ouch. I suppose I deserved that."

"You absolutely did. For the record, what exactly were you accusing me of?"

He shook his head. "I was wrong to accuse you of anything. Mea culpa."

Mari felt a softening around the hardness in her chest. She wanted to curse herself for it. It shouldn't be that easy for him to douse the flame of her ire so quickly. No doubt that charming smile of his and those smoldering good looks proved quite effective at soothing feminine anger. Well, she wasn't about to let it work on her.

"Fine," she bit out. "You've said your apology. Now if there's nothing else for the moment, I have things to do."

He didn't get the hint. Just stood staring at her as if studying an unfamiliar object he couldn't quite discern.

Well, that made them somewhat even. She wasn't quite sure what to make of him either. Except to note that her heart was pounding in her chest and her cheeks felt flushed.

And it had nothing to do with the late June heat.

* * *

She was a hard worker. He had to give her that. In fact, it appeared like she was the only one who did do any kind of work around here. Maybe that quality of hers was what drove his relative to bequeath her with such a large inheritance. But plenty of people throughout the world worked hard without being granted an established hotel for their efforts, for heaven's sake. The old woman could have simply gifted her with a sum of money and a guarantee that she could continue her employment.

"You have to admit," he began, though she wasn't even looking at him any longer, "it's a strange way to distribute her assets. The established hotel to an employee. The smaller plot of land adjacent she gives to blood kin. You can't blame me for being somewhat curious."

She stopped her chore to send an intense glare his way. "Is that how you were behaving earlier today, then? Curiously?"

"Look, I said I was sorry. It just took me by surprise. Usually, assets as grand as hotels are left to family members."

The intensity of the glare grew. As did the reddish hue coloring her cheeks. The strain of her chore had her skin glistening in the sun with a sheen of sweat. Her hair was a mess of curls atop her head, a few tendrils escaping out of the tight knot to wisp about her shoulders. Under any other circumstances—say, if they'd run into each other at a function or in any piazza—he might have asked her out. She was certainly attractive, curvy in all the right places, lush lips perfect for kissing.

And that was quite enough of that. He had absolutely no business appreciating how kissable her mouth appeared. So not what he was here for.

The woman found him disdainful, for heaven's sake. As made evident by her next words. "I don't suppose that it might have ever occurred to you that Anna might have considered me as family?"

Well, when she put it that way. "You know what I mean. Typically, blood ties trump all others."

She nodded once. "Right. I think I might know what blood ties you might be referring to. Like blood relatives who pay no attention to notices alerting them that their family member is ill? Who don't respond right away or make any kind of effort to come be by their relative's side before the end? To hold their hand and offer words of comfort and love."

She had him there. If he had to guess, Matteo would say that Mari had done all the above and more.

"You speak the truth, of course. I should have made more of an effort to respond to your messages and find out what was going on with Anna. It's been something of a tough year and I've been dealing with a lot." Like the loss of a generation's worth of corporate development, not to mention name recognition. Thanks to his father.

Mari didn't seem impressed with his excuse. If looks could kill, he might have been dead and buried by now. She began to gradually pull the long pole out of the pool and carried it to a shed behind her. Matteo got the distinct feeling he'd just been silently dismissed.

Ha! She wasn't going to get rid of him that easy. Several moments passed while she remained in the shed. He was beginning to wonder if she was going to try and wait him out. That would leave him with very few options. He couldn't very well corner her in there. That would be downright creepy.

And he certainly wasn't about to partake in a game of "come out, come out, little pretty." A sigh of relief escaped his lips when she finally reappeared out of the shadows of the small space.

"You're still here," she declared.

He'd never met a woman who managed to charm him while being downright annoyed with his mere presence. Maybe it was the cute crop bathing suit top she had on over loose-fitting gym shorts. Maybe it was the way her tanned skin had him imagining how it might feel to the touch.

Matteo swallowed a curse. There he went again.

What was wrong with him? The answer was obvious. He'd been without female companionship for too long. When was the last time he'd been on a date? The fiasco with Tala Industries had taken up all his time and energy for the past several months. All for naught. Had to have been way too long ago, by the look of things. Otherwise, he wouldn't be thinking of this woman in anything but an adversarial way, especially considering how angry she was with him still. His apology had done zero good, it appeared.

"Will you leave if I were to say I accept your apology?" she asked.

"It would certainly help to make me feel better. Though I doubt you'd be saying so with any kind of sincerity."

"Lies can be sincere," she answered with a small smile.

Matteo honestly had no idea how to respond to that. "Don't you think we need to have at least some sort of conversation about all this? I'll be the owner of the land right adjacent to this hotel that you happen to own."

Land that was absolutely useless to him unless he could

get this woman to agree to give up ownership of what she'd been bequeathed.

"Are you saying we'll be neighbors?" she asked, walking around the length of the pool and past him toward the colorful garden between the patio area and the reception lobby.

"At the least. Don't you want to know what ways I'm considering developing that land?"

That was a bluff. There was really nothing to develop the empty space to. Another hotel right next door would be redundant, the strip had plenty of restaurants already and food service wasn't particularly his forte. He needed the building and the land it stood on for collateral. Everything Tala Industries owned was already fully leveraged or liquidated.

No, for what he wanted to do with what he'd been given he would need her full cooperation.

At the moment, she seemed anything but cooperative. He would just have to see what he could do about that.

CHAPTER THREE

As much as she hated to admit it, Matteo Talarico was right. They did need to talk. Mari felt the weight of his presence behind her as she walked out of the patio and made her way to the flower garden that separated the pool deck area from the front lobby.

She'd chosen to come this way on purpose. Being in this space always served to soothe and calm her. The rich colorful flowers, the floral scent that drifted in the air on a soft breeze. The little patch of land between the patio and the building could always be counted on as a small oasis of tranquility. Sometimes, when one of those mid-sleep panic attacks struck, she even came out here in the middle of the night.

Funny, the garden's soothing effect didn't seem to be working quite so well at the moment. Mari's pulse was still racing. She could still feel heat burning in her cheeks. Something about this man had her reacting physically in ways she couldn't explain, nor did she like.

It made absolutely no sense. Yet her body didn't seem to want to listen to reason.

"Wow," he said behind her. She turned around to find him staring at the flower bushes, an expression of marvel on his face. "This place is something else."

All right. That was a point in his favor, albeit granted

unwanted. She might not have taken him as the type of man to notice and appreciate a well-tended garden.

"This was Anna's masterpiece. She spent hours and hours out here. Until...until she couldn't. We're trying to keep it intact as best we can. Roberta's taken over its care. She's the older woman you saw in the lobby when you first arrived."

"It's like its own little oasis."

That was a rather charming way to describe it. Charming was also a good way to describe Matteo this time around. The man had the looks of a cologne ad model and despite their first rather tumultuous meeting, she had to admit he was beyond charismatic.

If only he had introduced himself as the prince charming type upon meeting. And therein lay the issue. If she were being honest with herself, she would have to admit that a great part of her ire with Matteo was that his words had hit rather close to their target. Maybe she really did have no business trying to run this place. Had Anna even been in sound mind when she'd asked to change her will to hand the hotel to Mari? What if she hadn't been? What if this place failed after all these years and it was due to her incompetence?

Breathe. Just breathe. Nice and deep.

"I barely remember her," Matteo said, tugging her out of her thoughts. His gaze returned to her face. "I'm surprised she remembered me."

Mari nodded. "She did. Even as her mind started to go toward the end. She spoke of you occasionally. Said you were precocious and curious as a child. Wandered around this place like you owned it."

He flashed her a charming grin. "I still get that from people. A lot."

"Color me shocked," she said, inserting as much sarcasm into the words as she could.

"So, she did all this, huh?" he asked, gesturing around to the bounty of flowers that surrounded them.

"Yes. We have a lawn service for maintenance. But other than that, this was all her doing."

He thrust his hands into his pockets, an action she was beginning to see was rather an ingrained habit for him. His eyes focused on her once more.

"I regret not visiting more. And it's inexcusable that my parents eventually stopped visiting altogether."

He wasn't going to get any kind of argument from her on that score.

"On top of discussing our respective inheritances, I'd love to hear more about her. Please, let me buy you dinner later tonight. Maybe in the piazza?"

The offer took her by surprise. Surely, she wasn't even going to entertain the thought.

Before she could answer, Miyko appeared from around the pathway. Dressed in a colorful romper complete with a bright purple ascot around his neck, he blended quite nicely with the surrounding flowers. His face, however, was anything but cheery. It took a lot to irritate her first assistant, and he was clearly irritated. She didn't have to grasp at straws to guess as to why.

"He's asking for you again," he said, pausing midspeech to look Matteo up and down before turning back to her. "In the lobby. Refuses to tell me what the issue is. I promise I tried to get it out of him."

Mari rubbed her forehead and cursed inside. Great.

Now she would have to contend with Signore Gio again on top of everything else. To make matters worse, Matteo was here to witness it all this time. More proof of her incompetence in the form of a dissatisfied guest.

"I don't suppose you can tell him I'm busy and convince him to let me go find him later?"

Miyko tilted his head and thrust his fists onto his hips. "What do you think? I tried that in the first place."

It was worth a shot, though she'd known the attempt would be futile. "All right, I'll go see what he wants."

As expected, Matteo followed them both down the path to the front lobby, where a rust-faced Signore Gio stood glaring at the doorway.

"What can I help you with this afternoon?" Mari asked, her voice friendly and accommodating. Though a lot of good that would do. There really seemed to be no way to placate the man. She knew the exact day and time he was due to check out. She was counting the minutes. The day couldn't come soon enough. Then she wouldn't even have to think about him again until next year.

But that wasn't the case this morning. Today she was going to have to work to appease Signore Gio yet again. This time with an audience that included the one man she really didn't want witnessing her struggles with a disgruntled guest. He'd already judged her once and found her lacking, apology or not.

Signore Gio crossed his arms in front of his chest. "The temperature in my room is quite uncomfortable. I'd like it much cooler. It's as hot as a Turkish bath in there."

"I see. Did you try lowering the climate adjustment gauge?" She wouldn't put it past the man to skip that logical step before seeking her out simply to harass her.

Signore Gio rolled his eyes so dramatically she wondered if it would give him a headache. "Honestly. Of course I did. What kind of dolt do you take me for?"

Mari figured he really didn't want her to answer that question. "I had to ask."

The man shook his head slowly with lips pursed. "No, no you really didn't."

Mari resisted the urge to glance in Matteo's direction. He probably found her getting tongue-lashed by Signore Gio quite entertaining.

"Why don't you give me a chance to change and I'll run up and take a look at it myself."

"It's the least you can do," Gio said. "And I'd prefer if you came up right away. Rude of you to ask me to wait."

Rude? He had just called *her* rude? Of all the hypocritical…

Mari mustered all her patience and took a deep breath before speaking. "I understand you're unhappy with the temperature in your room, Signore Gio. We will make sure it gets resolved. If I can't figure it out, I'll have an order sent to the maintenance service right away. But first, I'm going to go at least throw a T-shirt on. It will only take a moment."

"No."

The simple word took her aback. *No.* Even for Signore Gio it seemed rather harsh. Cruel even.

No acknowledgment or consideration of her request whatsoever. As if her thoughts or feelings on the matter meant absolutely nothing. As if she herself meant nothing. Like it was okay to treat her as insignificant, a mere cog in the machine to be ordered around according to his whims.

Treating her just as too many others had in the past.

At least with Signore Gio, it wasn't personal. Except that it was. It would always be personal. How could it not be?

Mari spent several moments trying to figure out what to say. Words seemed to escape her. And then she felt a gentle touch on her elbow from behind. So slight, she might have imagined it. But then she felt his heat behind her and she knew it was real. Matteo.

If she didn't know better, she might guess that he was touching her as a show of support. Boosting her confidence. That was unexpected.

But darned if it didn't work.

Matteo standing behind her gave her just the nudge she needed to snap out of her shock and stupor. Inhaling deeply, she straightened her spine and lifted her chin.

She chose her words carefully, apologizing politely. *"Mi dispiace,"* she began in Italian. "The thermostat issue hardly constitutes an immediate emergency. I will be up to your room as soon as I've thrown a shirt on, signore."

She locked eyes with the older gentleman and didn't so much as blink.

After several beats passed, Signore Gio appeared ready to argue. Mari preempted him with a cross of her arms over her chest. She was done fighting but she would stand her ground. It would just take some more practice. And Signore Gio was certainly giving her plenty of opportunities to practice.

The older man's lips tightened and his skin flushed a deep pink. Mari half expected him to stomp his feet. Finally, he pivoted on his heel and turned to walk back to the hotel. "Do not take more than five minutes," he demanded as he walked away.

Mari finally released the breath she'd been holding and allowed her shoulders to droop in relaxation. Though she'd have to deal with him again in a few short minutes, at least this was one small battle won.

For now.

Plus, she had a more immediate concern. Matteo remained standing behind her, touching her still. The gentlest of touches, just at the base of her elbow. Yet it was enough to send currents of electricity through her arm and up her spine.

What was that about? Why was she physically reacting to his touch? Whatever the reason, it wasn't a good one.

She stepped away and turned to face him.

He began a slow clap. "Bravo. That was handled beautifully."

Silly. But she felt a jolt of pleasure run over her skin at his compliment. "I've had plenty of practice over the years."

He lifted a single eyebrow. "Oh?"

She really shouldn't have said that. "Well, I should get going. Don't want to make Signore Gio any crankier than he already is."

"That's a pretty low bar," Matteo said, turning to stare in the direction Signore Gio had just walked.

"Don't I know it."

"Would you like company when you go to his room? I could come with you."

The offer took her by surprise. Hard to believe this was the same man who'd stormed into the portico this morning to accuse her of swindling a little old lady. This newer version of Matteo Talarico was throwing her off in all manner of ways. As tempted as she was to take him up on his generosity, she really didn't want to face Signore Gio by herself, especially if his thermostat issue wasn't going to be an easy fix.

But she was the manager here. Actually, as of a few months ago, she was even more than that. She was now the owner of the establishment. How would it look if she couldn't handle a simple maintenance request without an emotional support buddy by her side?

"Thank you, but that won't be necessary," she answered. "I'm a big girl. I can handle it myself." She gave him a small smile before turning toward the stairway.

"I have no doubt," Mari heard him say as she walked away.

At least one of them was sure.

"Well, that didn't take terribly long."

Matteo was still in the lobby when Mari made her way back downstairs from Signore Gio's room. Her stomach made an unexpected little flip upon seeing him. Yet another unwelcome physical reaction to him. No denying that it was anything but excitement. Which made no sense at all. She wanted to be rid of the man, for heaven's sake.

"That's because Signore Gio was adjusting the thermostat for the hot-tub on his patio and not the temperature-control dial for his room."

"Huh. Did he have the decency to apologize for his mistake?"

Mari couldn't contain her chuckle. "On the contrary. He said we shouldn't have dials for each that look so similar. Or that we should have marked them more clearly. Never mind that there's a clear picture of a hot tub above one of them."

"I see. You have your hands full with that one." He bounced on his heel. "So you never answered me," he said a moment later.

"I'm sorry, I seem to have forgotten the question."

"I asked if you'd let me take you to dinner."

As he said the last word, Mari's traitorous stomach made a grumbling sound so loud she wondered if the beachgoers beyond the path might have heard it. If Matteo heard, which he must have, he was polite enough not to mention it.

"I usually just ask chef to prepare me a tray that I take up to my room."

He tilted his head. "Well, as exciting as that sounds, would you at least consider dining with me instead? We could head to the piazza."

Exciting. He had no idea just how overrated Mari found the notion of excitement. How hard she'd worked to achieve the kind of life that let her relax for a couple of hours in the evening before bed with a quiet dinner and a good book.

No. She'd had quite enough excitement in her previous life.

"Why?" she asked.

"Why should you come to dinner with me?"

She shook her head. "Why are you asking me to?"

His lips settled into a small smile. "Well, partly because there's a lot we need to talk about."

"What's the other part?"

"To give me a chance to at least partially make up for the way I behaved this morning. It's the very least I can do."

That was true enough. Mari surprised herself upon

realizing she was actually considering taking him up on his offer. She hadn't been to the piazza in ages. It was a glorious evening, a perfect night to enjoy a meal under the stars in one of the many open-air trattorias the center offered.

So many reasons to say yes. One very big reason to say no. She could fall so easily for the charms of this man. A complication she didn't need in her life at the moment, if ever. Considering how much time they were sure to have to spend together in the coming weeks until this whole estate thing was settled, saying no to him right now was the most sensible path.

Though she really had worked up an appetite dealing with Signore Gio. And chef was preparing Milanese tonight for dinner, a dish she wasn't particularly fond of.

To his credit, Matteo stood waiting patiently for a response. Not a hint of frustration that she was taking too long to answer.

"It's just one dinner," Matteo finally nudged, his smile still slight and friendly. He glanced at his watch. "My flight to Rome doesn't leave for another five hours. You'd be doing me a favor not letting me spend the time meandering the streets of Cagliari by myself and eating solo."

A hint of something shifted in her chest, something she refused to acknowledge as disappointment. "You're flying back tonight?"

He nodded. "Only because I didn't plan very well. Most of the rooms on the island were booked. And the hotel I usually stay in in Rome has a suite on standby for me."

Right. Matteo Talarico was the type of man luxury hotels reserved suites for. In other words, he was completely out of her league. Which was a ridiculous thought anyway.

After all, he was attempting to apologize to her. The last man she'd been involved with was completely unfamiliar with the concept. Trevor was much more talented in the art of gaslighting her into believing that everything that went wrong was her fault. Silly of her to even compare the two men, really.

"So what do you say?" Matteo asked again.

As if to completely mock her once again, another low grumble echoed from the vicinity of her stomach.

This time, Matteo didn't hide his amusement. He released a low chuckle and winked at her. The wink was what finally did it. The last of her resistance seemed to crumble like a collapsing wall.

"All right. But only because I've worked up an appetite."

He clasped a hand to his chest in exaggerated horror. "You wound me. I thought it was my charm that finally convinced you and not your hunger pangs."

She begrudgingly returned his laugh. "Actually, there's another reason."

That head tilt again, as if he couldn't quite figure her out. Well, she could say the same of him.

"What's that?" he asked.

"For Anna. You aunt must have had some kind of faith in you that led her to bequeathing you part of her estate. Despite not having set eyes on you as an adult."

Mari had a lot to thank Anna for. The least she could do was give her partial heir a few minutes to hear him out.

She could only hope she wouldn't regret it.

CHAPTER FOUR

MATTEO FELT AN unreasonable amount of relief when she finally agreed to his offer of dinner.

"I'll just be a minute. Let me freshen up a bit and grab my bag."

"Sure thing," he answered, walking over to the small love seat at the center of the lobby and sitting down. "Guess I'll just loiter in your lobby a little longer."

Mari studied him up and down, as if sizing him up. Again.

She tapped her chin, as if coming to a conclusion. "We can't have our guests thinking we have a loiterer. Even one as well dressed as you are."

"I imagine that wouldn't look good."

She nodded. "It wouldn't. What if they jump to the wrong conclusion that we weren't prepared for a reservation and had you waiting all this time for a room?"

"Good point." The way she was always thinking about her responsibility to this place kept impressing him. For someone so relatively young with limited experience, she fit the role well.

Well, that was neither here nor there. He still had a goal here. He'd be willing to compromise, even offer her the opportunity to stay in her current roll. Win-win all around. But the end game couldn't change. He needed her to relinquish her part of this estate.

"Why don't you come down with me? I won't take long to get ready. Just going to brush my hair out and freshen up a bit."

"All right," Matteo answered, wondering if the moment implied some kind of marker between them, a development of some kind of trust. She led him past the check-in desk, through a small office that housed two wooden desks that faced each other and past a narrow hallway to a steel door that opened up to a narrow stairway that led down. They were descending to the deepest caverns of the Hotel Nautica.

Finally, they reached a door with a number panel lock. Mari quickly entered a combination and the door swung open to the inside. He followed her into a small apartment furnished with two love seats that faced a colorful hanging tapestry on the opposite wall. A small kitchenette to the side divided the living space. No television. No end tables. Yet the apartment still exuded a sense of coziness and comfort.

"I'll just be a minute," Mari repeated and walked through a doorway Matteo assumed had to lead to her bedroom. Surprising, really. She could have her pick of living quarters in this hotel. From what he'd seen online, some of the suites were downright ritzy with ample space and personal patios sporting luxurious hot-tubs. Yet she'd chosen to live in a small, unassuming apartment deep in the basement.

He studied the space while he waited. She'd certainly made the best of the limited area. The walls were painted a cheery light green, and a three-tier shelf against the opposite wall housed several potted plants. A postage-stamp-sized window sat high on the wall bordering the ceiling and offered a surprising amount of natural light for this time of day.

More than what he did see, Matteo was struck by what was missing. Not that he was looking for clues, but there was nothing here that offered any kind of information about who Mariana Renati truly was. The only photographs on the walls were pictures of various famous landmarks around Cagliari, including the Devil's Saddle cliff. A couple of grand churches. He strode over to a smaller framed photo by the plant shelf, the only photo that featured any people in it. Mari stood in the center smiling between an older woman and the man who manned the desk downstairs. The woman had eyes the same shade as his own. She had to be Anna, his mother's distant cousin. They stood in the garden of the hotel.

Nothing in here gave him any kind of idea about where Mari came from. How she found her way to Sardinia, of all places. He had no doubt she was American; the accent was unmistakable. If he had to guess, he would say she'd made her home in New England a good number of years. Not that he could tell from anything in here. Like she didn't exist until she arrived in Sardinia.

Matteo gave himself a mental shake. Honestly, why did it matter? He didn't need to know anything about Mari Renati aside from what it would take to convince her to turn over her share of this property to him.

He didn't need to know her life story, for Pete's sake. There was no reason for him to be so curious about her.

He heard her bedroom door open behind him, then turned to find Mari already ready to leave.

"That was fast."

She shrugged. "I am rather hungry. And I figured you didn't want to be kept waiting."

Matteo took a moment to study her. She'd unclipped her hair and it now hung in soft, thick waves over her shoulders. A bright red sundress showed off the bronze tan of her skin. She'd added a dab of color to her lips but as far as he could tell she wore no makeup.

Fetching.

The untoward thought echoed through his head without warning. But there was no denying that Mari was a very attractive woman. He'd dated far more glamorous women, women who spent an inordinate of time and mass amounts of money prepping for the simplest of outings. Mari had taken less than ten minutes and he was downright struck by how attractive she looked in a simple red dress and open-toe sandals. Toes that were painted a neon blue color that matched a stone ankle bracelet she wore above her left foot.

That settled it. He must be hungry too. Or perhaps jetlagged still. Clearly, he wasn't thinking straight. When had he ever noticed a woman's toes before?

"Matteo?" she asked, a curious smile on her lips. "Did you want to get going?"

Great. He'd been caught practically gawking at her.

"More than ready. Let's go," he said, extending his arm in a gesture to have her lead the way.

A moment later, they were on the sidewalk in front of the hotel. He followed her onto the paved pathway between the steel gate and the beach.

The businessman in Matteo immediately made several more observations on top of the ones he'd already noted. This really was the ideal place for an establishment such as the one he had in mind. On a busy public path and crowded beach. The location offered the perfect opportunity for anyone looking for an ideal relaxing Italian residence. With Rome a fast plane ride away, a person could be certain to enjoy the best of what Italy had to offer. Island sights and beaches and the sightseeing opportunities of one of its major cities. It was a wonder Tala hadn't ventured to this part of Italy already. His mind reeled with the possibilities running through his head, all the ways a luxurious condo building would thrive in such a place. But first he had to convince Mari to relinquish her ownership.

If only Anna had left the entire property to him solely, he could get started right away. On top of giving him another chance to rebuild what his father had destroyed by bankrupting them, this project could give Matteo a true opportunity to create something from the ground up by himself. A chance to finally prove himself by saving them from the disaster his parent had thrust them all into.

Mari snapped him out his thoughts. He wasn't sure if he'd heard her correctly.

"What was that?" he asked.

"I said, if we walk somewhat quickly, we should catch the coming bus and not have to wait for the next one in twenty minutes."

Bus?

"We're taking public transportation?" he asked, belatedly realizing he'd been blindly following her off the pathway and down the residential street behind the hotel.

She didn't bother pausing, glancing at him sideways.

"It's the most economical and most convenient way to get to the piazza."

Matteo didn't bother to try and recall the last time he'd taken a public bus anywhere. The answer was never. The closest he'd ever come was a party bus his friend Gus had rented for his bachelor stag activities in Toronto to take them from casinos to clubs and back to their hotel. So not the same.

"It will take us right to the harbor, and it's a quick walk to the piazza from there."

"I see. Couldn't we just call a car?"

He couldn't interpret the smile she sent his way. "We're almost there. The bus will get here by the time you arrange for a ride. And I don't know about you, but I could use a walk in the fresh sea air."

She paused a moment before asking, "You do walk occasionally, don't you? Or do you mean to tell me you take cars whenever you need to go somewhere."

"Of course I walk." That was true enough. He wasn't going to specify that most of his walking was done as a warm-up preceding a punishing run on the treadmill in a dedicated room of his penthouse apartment full of gym equipment. The fact was, she was right that he typically took a car service whenever he needed to travel within the city. It was simply a matter of efficiency. Interesting that she had him figured out in so many small ways.

A moment later, they were crossing a busy intersection to reach a covered stand smattered with various film posters and advertising flyers. A handful of other people stood waiting, including a young woman gently nudging a stroller back and forth, as well as a harried-looking man in a business suit and messenger bag scrolling frantically on his phone. The Devil's Saddle framed the skyline behind them against the backdrop of crystal-blue sky dotted with puffy white clouds. If he were to pick any day to walk, this wouldn't be a bad one to choose. And he certainly couldn't ask for better company.

The last thought gave him pause. If he were to examine it closely, despite having just met Mari, he was beginning to genuinely enjoy being around her. She was the type of person who seemed to bring a certain joy out into the world surrounding her.

"Let's go," Mari said behind him, taking him by the forearm and tugging him across the street. In his distraction, he hadn't even noticed the neon sign of the stick figure walking on the streetlight. Nor had he noticed that a large bus with wide glass windows was rapidly approaching from the other side. "I don't want to miss it. Most of the drivers are friendly and cordial but some of them can be complete—" The last word was cut off by the noisy brakes of the bus as it came to a stop. Though he could guess the general intent of whatever she'd said.

Matteo dashed behind her, skirting a revving motorcycle who'd stopped too far past the white crossing line. Honestly, he didn't understand her panic. If they did miss the bus, they could in fact go ahead with his preferred option of hailing a cab or calling a car service. But darned if he didn't get a small rush of adrenaline running past Mari to make it to the stop before the bus arrived. As if he were back to being a small boy competing in a lawn race with one of the staffers he'd spent too much time with as a child.

They needn't have worried.

By the time they got there, the young mother was struggling to lift her baby out of the stroller and fold the contraption. The driver dramatically huffed in his seat. The man clearly fell into the latter category Mari had been referring to earlier.

"I'm sorry," the young mother said in a heavy Eastern European accent. "Sometimes the strap gets stuck."

"May I?" Matteo asked her, gesturing to the stroller.

She nodded, stepping back. He didn't bother trying to unclasp the belt the little tyke was secured with, opting instead to lift the entire contraption and carry it up the stairs.

He could have sworn the chubby-cheeked infant smiled at him when he set it down in front of an empty seat and held it securely until Mama arrived.

He looked up to find Mari smiling at him too.

Three stops later, their mode of transportation had grown increasingly crowded. Matteo wasn't about to complain. Mari sat next to him, her arm brushing against his. The flowery scent of her shampoo tickled his nose. It reminded him of the garden they'd been standing in earlier today.

Was that really just this afternoon? He'd felt like he'd lived a month since arriving in Cagliari this morning. And he felt like he'd known the woman next to him much longer than less than a day. Something about Mari evoked a sense of familiarity he couldn't quite explain. He really wished they'd met under different circumstances. Though truth be told, she wasn't the type of woman he would normally expect to find in his orbit. No, his tastes usually ran more cosmopolitan. Definitely not the kind of woman who took a bus into town and cleaned debris out of a pool after sparring with a grumpy old guest at her hotel. The way she'd stood up to the man had been downright impressive. His last romantic relationship had been a short yet heated entanglement involving a French model.

Not that he was thinking of Mari in any kind of romantic way. They were… Well, he couldn't quite say what they were just yet. Fate had thrown them together in a rather unusual way. And right now, she happened to be the one thing standing in his way of obtaining a much-needed goal. He wasn't going to forget that one pertinent fact.

Despite the alluring scent of her hair under his nose.

As if mocking him for the thought, the bus chose that moment to hit a rather significant bump and jostled her up against him. Matteo resisted the strong urge to wrap his arms around her shoulders and hold her there.

She smiled at him awkwardly and shifted back to rest her side against the wall.

"This is our stop," she said a moment later, rising out of her seat.

Matteo followed suit and they exited the bus onto a busy sidewalk. The harbor across the street was dotted with boats both small and large. A massive cruise ship sat docked in the center, dwarfing the other watercraft.

"The plaza will be busy," she informed him as they began a leisurely walk down the street. "Looks like a cruise just came in."

"It never ceases to amaze me how colossal those floating hotels can be built," he said, taking in the sight of what had to be a three-thousand-cabin ship at the least.

"That's exactly what they are," Mari responded as they continued to make their way down the busy and noisy street. "And they need just as much staff to keep the guests happy as the major high-star hotels."

"You sound like you speak from experience."

"I do, as a matter of fact," she answered without elaborating further. There was a story there. One she wasn't willing to tell him. Yet.

They turned the corner and the sidewalk became even more crowded. Loud groups of teenagers entering and exiting cafés, couples holding hands strolling, young and old alike. Families with small children. It appeared the piazza was a draw for all manner of Sardinians this time of day.

"Quite a popular place," he commented, letting her lead the way.

"It typically is this time of year. And this time of day."

It was easy to see why. The center of town seemed to have something to offer everyone. Souvenir shops as well as high-end fashion stores. Fast-food pizzerelli diners as well as fine-dining restaurants with uniformed waiters. And everything in between. Compared with the big cities like Rome and Florence, this seemed more intimate. Cozier.

Maybe flying into Cagliari wouldn't be such a chore after all. He could see himself visiting often once he got the resort established and running.

"I didn't expect it to be quite so…modern," Matteo said, though he wasn't certain he'd reached at the right word. He'd been expecting a small village with a quaint-and-cozy town. Not this bustling and busy community with designer clothing stores and gourmet restaurants.

"Don't be fooled," Mari said. "Cagliari has a lot of history. As does all of Sardinia. These buildings here might be new, but just beyond the center are churches and cathedrals that are centuries old."

Her voice held no small amount of pride. She spoke

quite fondly of her adopted homeland. While here he was, planning on setting stakes in this locale with a business he'd be running, and he knew so very little about the island and the town that would house it.

No doubt about it, he was going to need Mari's help to get said business off the ground. So she would have to be a willing participant. He got the feeling that was going to take some work on his end. He would have to give her an incentive to cooperate.

First thing first, he had to establish a rapport between them. Which would hopefully lead to gaining her trust.

And hopefully it wouldn't take long. Matteo had some trusted staff he'd like to move over to the new site and keep gainfully employed without interruption.

Before long, they approached a circular rotary with a tall statue looming in the center. Clearly depicting some kind of regal figure, judging by the crown on its head.

"What an interesting display," Matteo said. "What is that statue supposed to represent? And why is it wearing all that colorful garb?"

Her response was a hearty chuckle. "You really do need a basic lesson on Cagliari's history, don't you?"

"I guess so. What do you suppose we should do about that?"

We. The word hung between them so small yet so powerful. Matteo scrambled for something else to say. How presumptuous of him. As if his lack of knowledge about the island and village were any of her concern.

But perhaps the bigger question was, why was Matteo even thinking about Mariana Renati in such a way, as if they were some kind of team?

Probably because he wanted it to be the truth.

CHAPTER FIVE

WE.

Mari really wished he hadn't said what he'd just said. And that he hadn't used that particular word. Only, part of her was maddeningly pleased that he had. Which made zero sense whatsoever. In no way, shape or form would she and Matteo ever be considered any kind of "we." At the most, they would simply be neighbors.

"So, care to start my first lesson, then?" he asked, his gaze still focused on the fifteen-foot-tall statue. "Starting with who this gentleman is exactly?" he added a moment later.

Mari forced herself to return to the topic at hand. It was all too easy to lose her focus when she was around this man. "That's King Carlo Felice," she answered, her gaze following his.

"Huh. And did he like to dress in extravagant colors or something?"

"I'm sure he did. Being a king and all. But the reason his statue is dressed up is because it's a tribute to our soccer team. The Cagliari Calcio recently won the Serie A cup. The last time that happened was several years ago. I wish I could have been here for all the celebrations. There were fireworks, a grand festival, hundreds of people lined the streets."

He turned away from the statue then to look at her, one eyebrow raised. "You weren't here then?"

She shook her head. "I was still back in the States, hadn't moved to Sardinia yet."

The lone eyebrow remained lifted. "You seem confused?"

He shrugged. "It's just hard to believe that you've been here such a short period of time, given how acclimated you seem to be to the town."

Acclimated. Is that how she sounded? Funny, there were still some days when she felt every bit the outsider here in this part of the world, despite her Italian heritage and devotion to the place.

"How long have you lived here exactly?" Matteo asked.

"About four years, give or take."

"So Anna hired you not long after your arrival."

"Pretty much."

They'd drifted backward away from the statue and close to the traffic circle. A moped cycle blared its horn at them as it passed. Looked like neither one was paying attention to their surroundings. For his part, Matteo appeared genuinely interested in learning more about her. Or how she'd come to be a Sardinian resident, anyway.

Not that she could look too deeply into that. The man was just naturally curious. Or he was simply making conversation. Still, aside from Anna, Mari couldn't recall the last time someone had displayed any kind of interest in her whatsoever.

Except for Trevor, whose betrayal had been sharp and painful. He'd deserted her when she'd needed him the most.

So he knew that much more about Cagliari now. About one of its princes and its football team. An initial lesson in the Italian island's history. As interesting as that was, what he really wanted to know more about was Mari's story. Exactly where had she come from? What had brought her here? Sure, Sardinia was a lovely island, Cagliari a vibrant city with a rich history. But he wanted details about Mari's history.

And why was he so curious about her in the first place?

A curiosity that was maddeningly inconvenient. He wasn't in Sardinia to make friends. Least of all to make a friend of the one woman who was standing in the way of all his plans.

After gazing at the statue a few more minutes, Mari turned to him with a small smile. "Ready to move on?"

Right. They were here for dinner after all.

He held his arm out in front of him. "Lead the way. I am but a devotee in your wake following you where you take me."

"Wow."

"A bit much?"

She nodded, her smile growing wider. "Just a tad. Seeing as I'm merely taking you to grab a bite to eat."

They started walking around the statue past the circular roadway toward a wide hill. "Although," Mari continued, "very few meals in this part of the world would be categorized as a simple bite."

"More so than the mainland?" he asked.

"Oh yes. Italians in general like to linger over their meals. But Sardinians in particular make dinnertime an all-out event."

"Then I say we get started."

They began making their way up the hill past pizzerellis with long lines out front and charming small boutiques.

Scattered in between were tourist shops full of small fixtures and colorful magnets in the window.

"I didn't expect it to be quite so…commercial," Matteo said.

"Parts of Cagliari absolutely are," Mari answered, her breath on a slight hitch. The hill was steeper than it had appeared from the square by the statue. Matteo felt a bit out of breath himself, though he was loathe to admit it. "But wait till we get to the top. The gardens and architecture are straight Renaissance Italy."

Before Matteo could reply to that, a sudden blur darted at them from the opposite direction, headed straight for Mari. The helmeted figure showed no signs of slowing down. Her gaze fixated on Matteo, she wasn't going to see him coming.

"Look out!" Matteo barely got the words out as he reached to grab her about the waist and yank her out of the projectile's way. She landed against him, their bodies slammed together. "Skateboarder."

"Uh, thanks," she said, blinking up at him with those sparkling hazel eyes he was growing so familiar with.

It took a second for Matteo to find his own voice. Her scent drifting to his nose, the warmth of her seeping through his clothing. She made no effort to move out of his grasp, and heaven help him, he couldn't seem to loosen his grip on her.

"*Scusa!*" The kid's voice echoed behind them as he continued barreling down the hill. He didn't sound all that sorry.

"They think it's a thrill to skateboard down the hills," Mari said, her eyes still fixated on his. How had he not noticed before how dark her eyelashes were? Or the way her eyebrows arched so perfectly, just a shade lighter than her hair?

Get a grip.

What in the world was wrong with him? Waxing poetic on a crowded hill about a woman's eyebrows. Maybe that cliché about apples falling from trees might actually apply to him. How easily he was distracted by a pretty face. Just like his old man.

Unacceptable. He made himself release her and managed to step half a foot away.

Mari blinked a couple of more times, then straightened the hemline of her dress. "It's a wonder no one has gotten seriously hurt," she added a moment later.

"I get it," he answered as they resumed their walk uphill. "Any teen worth their salt would want to skate down such a tempting landscape. Though maybe that particular one could have chosen a less crowded time."

Despite his words, he felt a modicum of gratitude for the kid. His daring ride had given Matteo a chance he wouldn't have expected to get. A reason to hold Mari in his arms.

Just. Stop.

Shaking off yet another wayward thought, Matteo followed in her wake.

"We're almost there," she told him over her shoulder.

A few moments later, to his surprise, she turned into what could only be described as a narrow alleyway.

Where in the world was she taking him? They'd passed by numerous fancy-looking restaurants on their way here. But apparently they'd be eating in a small hole-in-the-wall away from the main road.

Finally, Mari stopped in front of a glass door with metallic lettering. *Andiamo's.*

"Not too many people know about this place," she told him as he held the door open for her. "The chef likes to keep it that way. He's not in it for the tourist dollars. Just wants to practice his craft and cook for people he knows will appreciate the food."

Huh. Now that was a novel concept as far as Matteo was concerned. Imagine dedicating your life to a craft and then not being incentivized to make money off your hard-earned skills. Matteo gave a mental shrug at the thought. To each his own. But most of the world didn't work that way.

"A secret for the locals?"

As soon as they stepped inside, myriad aromas tickled his nose. Spices. Tomato sauce. A sweet scent that reminded him of fresh oranges off the tree. The restaurant was most definitely not what he was expecting. It was like stepping into a space/time continuum. They'd entered through a small door off a narrow alleyway. But somehow the inside of the establishment surprisingly vast. Tall ceilings, a wide dining area and a long hallway across the room that seemed to stretch farther down to another part of the establishment. A long wooden bar to the side sported glass shelves packed with dark wine bottles and other spirits.

"You seem surprised," Mari said, a small smile hovering on her lips.

She wasn't wrong. In fact, so far his visit to Cagliari had held one surprise after another.

"This was most certainly not what I was expecting when we turned into that alleyway."

She nodded, flashing him a wide smile. "It's almost magical, isn't it?"

"That's one way to describe it." Another might be to call it an optical illusion.

"Wait till you taste the food. Talk about magical."

"How in the world does the owner keep this place a secret from the tourists?"

"It's in the best interest of the locals to keep the information to themselves."

A slim, tall woman dressed in black slacks and a form-fitting black vest over a white T-shirt approached them, her smile directed at Mari.

"*Bella*, how lovely that you are back. One of the tables in the back okay, as usual?"

"That sounds lovely, Luciana. *Grazie*." She turned to Matteo, then made quick work of introducing him to the hostess. They followed her down the hallway for what seemed like an inordinate amount of time. This place really was an optical illusion. Or maybe Mari was right, there was some type of ancient European magic involved.

As silly as that sounded, Matteo found himself entertaining the thought just a tad longer than reasonable. The illusion only grew stronger when they finally reached the end of the hallway to step out into an outdoor seating area that could only be described as a vast, colorful garden. Bright green bushes and citrus trees ripe with fruit lined the perimeter. Lush, thick grass covered the ground under their feet. The early evening sky cast mild, gray shadows over the landscape. Luciana led them to a round table and another server immediately appeared with full glasses of icy water and plastic-covered menus. She greeted him with a smile and Mari with a few words in Italian.

"You seem to know the staff here well. And you said only locals really know about this place."

"Yes," she answered, taking a sip of her water.

"I take it, then, you spend a lot of time in town?"

She nodded, taking a bite of a piece of bread and swallowing. "Any chance I get. The square reminds me of Faneuil Hall back in Boston. And the rest of the piazza could be the North End, Boston's version of a Little Italy."

So he'd been right about her being a New Englander. "Boston, huh? That's where you're from?"

Another nod. "I grew up in the North End. In fact, my parents owned a place just like this. Only much, much smaller in scale."

"Why'd you leave?" He was surprised at the question as soon as it left his mouth. But he couldn't help the nagging sense that there was a story there. One he was uncharacteristically curious about.

She looked away, but not before Matteo registered a flash of pain behind her eyes. "It was time to move on to new things. I managed to land a job aboard a cruise ship, which brought me here. And I ended up staying."

That explained the remark she'd made earlier when they'd walked by the big ships. The rest about her was still a big mystery, however. One he desperately wanted to unravel for some reason. "Do you miss it? The States? Your home?"

"Yes and no," Mari answered, taking another bite of her baguette. Clearly she wasn't going to expand on that rather cryptic response.

Matteo wasn't going to push. To any outside observer, they may have appeared to be having a pleasant conversation between two friendly acquaintances, but the reality was that Mari was choosing her sparse words very carefully and giving nothing away. She was guarded, the walls around her nearly tangible. He reminded her of a fawn licking its wounds in solitude.

Was she wounded, then? Had someone hurt her?

That thought had his blood boiling in a way he didn't want to examine.

Mari pulled one of the menus from the center of the table closer to her, began studying it. Clearly an attempt to change the topic. He had no doubt she knew the offerings by heart, given her familiarity with the place.

A server appeared with a tray of antipasto and silently set it down with a smile.

Before he could reach for a morsel of food, Matteo's phone dinged with a message. Glancing at the screen, he bit off a curse.

His father.

"Excuse me," he told her, rising from the table. "I need to take this."

The conversation with his father went about as well as expected. The man was apologetic and regretful. He must have spent another restless night taunted by all the bad decisions he'd made recently. But what good was any of that doing them or Tala Industries? None.

By the time Matteo returned to the table, he was beyond agitated, hoping the upcoming meal would serve to soothe his frazzled nerves.

"You look like you want to throw a plate. We can leave, if you'd like," she offered.

Matteo shook his head. "Not a chance. I'm famished and this food looks great. My father occasionally needs to get things off his chest, is all."

"Like what?"

Matteo inhaled a deep breath. It wasn't often he spoke of his father, but he found himself wanting to with Mari.

"First he neglected the company, leaving me one hundred percent of the responsibility, and then he let himself be swindled out of most of our wealth. All to please a woman he barely knew. And when it was all gone, so was she."

"Oh, my."

"His reaction to the loss of my mother. In his grief, he sought to find a replacement for her. But he managed to find a con woman instead." The words seemed to be pouring out of him, as if they'd been sitting on his tongue, waiting for the right ears to hear them.

"Matteo, that's dreadful. Your poor father."

Somehow, it didn't surprise him that she'd found sympathy for his foolish papa. He hadn't quite managed to summon the same toward his parent within himself.

She reached for him then, covering his hand with hers. Her palm felt soft, warm against his roughened skin. The contrast sent an unfamiliar sensation through him.

He didn't know how much time passed with the feel of her hand against his before they were interrupted. Two people, a man and a younger-looking woman who appeared to know Mari, approached them after entering the dining room. The young woman smiled politely as they made their way over. The man, on the other hand, looked less than pleased, his gaze shifting from Mari, over to Matteo, then finally resting on their joined hands atop the table. The sight clearly made him unhappy judging by the man's instant frown.

Mari definitely noticed the look as well, as she quickly

pulled her hand away and tucked a strand of hair behind her ear.

Whoever this man was, Mari cared what he thought.

A bolt of disappointment sheared through Matteo's gut. Along with another sensation he didn't care to examine.

CHAPTER SIX

SHE REALLY SHOULD have been more prepared to run into someone she knew while at Andiamo's. So it was rather inexcusable that she was caught quite so unprepared and scrambling for words as the two newcomers to the dining room approached their table.

But why did it have to be those particular two? Almost anyone else would have been better. Antonio Giraldi, a professor at Cagliari University, accompanied by one of his American students from Colorado. Catherine was a sweet young lady who had never been anything less than charming to Mari, but she also never passed an opportunity to spread gossip and innuendo.

As for the professor, well, Antonio had expressed his interest in getting to know Mari better more than once. Antonio was always a gentleman and never pushy. Nice enough to look at with a pleasant personality. But Mari had never felt so much as a hint of romantic attraction toward the man in return. Such a shame, really. Being attracted to the professor would be so much more convenient. Antonio wasn't the type of man who would hightail and run when the going got tough like Trevor had. Or the way her mother had decades earlier.

Matteo, on the other hand, struck her as if he very well

could be the type who would do just that. After all, he'd thought the worst of her initially, hadn't he?

Not that it mattered. The man was only here for a few more hours.

"Mari?" Antonio asked as they drew closer, his gaze alternating between her and Matteo. Out of reflex, she yanked her hand away out of Matteo's. Both men clearly noticed the hastened action. Matteo tilted his head and Antonio's eyebrows rose half an inch. Luckily, Catherine was too busy closing in on her for a hug to seem to have noticed.

"Mari! So nice to see you here," the other woman exclaimed, throwing her arms around Mari's shoulders. "Who's your friend?" she asked, her eyes fixating on Matteo as soon as she stood. Catherine's expression held no small amount of feminine curiosity.

Mari somehow found her voice enough to make quick introductions. Matteo stood to shake the professor's hand and flashed a dazzling smile to Catherine, who in turn looked as if she may swoon in reaction.

"I didn't realize Anna had any kin in Italy," Antonio offered, his eyes still assessing Matteo as he sat back down. "Or any at all, for that matter."

"Did you know her well?" Matteo asked.

Antonio nodded. "Fairly well. Anna was a regular fixture in town. Stopped by the university often to bring baked goods or meals to the students. Volunteered her time too. Assisting foreign students get acclimated to the town."

"We all loved her," Catherine added with a solemn nod of her own.

Mari noted the rosy flush of the young woman's cheeks.

She seemed to have trouble tearing her gaze from Matteo's face. Who could blame her? The man was strikingly handsome. More than a few female heads had turned in his direction as they'd made their way to the restaurant earlier.

Mari couldn't help but compare the two men before her now. Antonio had classic features that bore tribute to his Roman ancestors. He would be described as attractive by any standard. Crystal-blue eyes, blondish hair with streaks of chestnut brown. A professor of history, his intelligence shone clear in his eyes. He was dedicated to his students and to his chosen field. All that a woman could want and ask for, really.

Just not her.

Her gaze fell to Matteo. In looks, he was the complete opposite of the other man. Dark hair, charcoal black eyes and rugged, sharp features. He was a good three inches taller than Antonio. And while the professor was fit and toned, Matteo clearly had the type of physique that was evidence of hard work and what had to be a punishing fitness routine.

Her thoughts were interrupted by the sound of someone clearing their throat. She couldn't even tell who had done it. Mari snapped her gaze away from Matteo's face. In her dazed distraction, she hadn't even noticed the lull in conversation.

Oh god. Had she been staring at Matteo while the others looked on?

Finally, Antonio broke the silence. "Well, I guess we better head over to our table." He sounded less than enthused about doing so, however.

Catherine nodded in agreement. "Yes, I offered to buy Professor Giraldi dinner in exchange for his gracious offer to assist me with my essay. I'm having the most difficult time writing this one."

Antonio gave her shoulder a reassuring squeeze. "In your defense, it's a rather daunting subject. The influence of ancient Phoenicia on Italian Renaissance art."

"That does sound quite daunting," Mari agreed. "Yes, well. We should let you two get to it, then," she suggested.

Antonio pursed his lips. "Right, then. Guess we'll see you Thursday, Mari."

"I'll be there, as usual."

It was only after the two had walked away that it occurred to her that her statement might have sounded rather rude. The thought was horrifying. What in the world was wrong with her? Something about Matteo was throwing her off and had her acting uncharacteristic and foreign. First getting caught just staring at the man, then making it clearly obvious that she wanted to be alone with him at dinner.

Wait a minute.

That was almost as horrifying as the last thought, in that it was absolutely true. She *did* want to be left alone with Matteo, had grown frustrated and impatient with the interruption of Antonio and Catherine stopping by their table.

Absolutely unacceptable. She hardly knew the man. And that was the problem in itself. Just how badly she would like to change that. She wanted to know him. In all manner of ways.

What a mess.

"What's Thursday?" Matteo asked, cutting into her disturbing self-revelations. "If you don't mind my asking."

It took a second to register what he was referring to.

"Oh, I volunteer at the university. Facilitating a group

study once a week to assist the American students with their Italian. There are several dozen here for the summer, studying abroad for extra credit."

Matteo leaned his forearms over the table. "That's very kind of you. To donate your time in such a way."

"It was Anna's idea."

"Anna is sounding more and more saint-like the more I hear about her."

"She was indeed. I think you would have liked to have known her."

"I'm beginning to realize how true that is. It's truly my loss that I didn't get a chance to make more of an effort to meet her. I'll regret that going forward."

"It wasn't all one-sided. She had regrets too."

He narrowed his eyes on her. "What do you mean?"

A tender spot reserved for Anna rose to the surface of her chest. "Anna told me she wished she might have tried harder to reach out. Both to you and your mother."

At the mention of his parent, Matteo seemed to wince ever so slightly. So slight she might have missed it. He glanced to the side before returning his attention to her. Whatever emotion it was that had been triggered at the mention of his mother, he seemed to have shaken it off.

"She was lucky to have you there with her."

"There was no one else. But I could argue that I was the lucky one."

He flashed her a knowing smile. "I bet you would, Mari."

As tired and jet-lagged as he felt, Matteo really should have suggested they end the evening after dinner and that he finally get some rest. But he didn't want this time with

Mari to end. There was so much more he wanted to ask her. Not just about the hotel and Anna, but also about her past. What exactly had brought her here? Why were there no clues about her previous home in her current one?

What was the deal between her and that professor?

Not that any of it was any of his business. Particularly that last question.

Still, he was trying to come up with an excuse to suggest prolonging the evening a while longer when she luckily took the matter into her own hands.

"I should probably walk some of this off," she said, gesturing to the now-empty pizza platter sitting in the center of the table and the various other mostly eaten dishes surrounding it. As good as Mari had said this restaurant was, her words hadn't been able to do the place justice. The roasted branzino was so fresh he would guess it had been caught just this morning. The pizza and vodka-sauce-soaked homemade pasta had both been works of culinary art. All of it followed by a melt-in-your-mouth limoncello cake with mixed berry drizzle.

"It will have to be a very slow walk. After all that food."

She nodded solemnly. "Really slow," she agreed. "Especially seeing as we're going further uphill." She pointed toward the ceiling.

Matteo released a low groan, only half joking.

Mari laughed at his reaction, her eyes twinkling with amusement. "It will be worth it. The view from the top of this hill is breathtaking. Trust me."

"I do trust you," he told her, the words surprising him as they left his mouth at how true and correct they were. A rather surprising turn of events. Not to mention unexpected and quick.

He didn't often put his trust in others so easily.

He'd already shared more about his father with Mari than anyone else ever. And he'd met the woman less than twenty-four hours ago.

Not like he knew anything about the woman really. Yet, he'd shared one of the most personal, shameful parts of his past with her just now at dinner. A part he'd rather hide from the world. As of yet, the business world knew Tala Industries' financial troubles only to be the result of poor management and fiscal irresponsibility. No one had yet scratched the surface to uncover that the source of that mismanagement had been due to his father's arduous interests that had him falling for a con woman. The news reports that would be generated if the truth was uncovered made Matteo shudder.

Thinking of Tala triggered a reminder of why he was here in the first place. Instead of pouring his soul out to Mari about his father's mistakes and their tragic results, he should have been gently proposing taking over the hotel from her. But at the moment, he couldn't seem to bring himself to even broach the subject. The evening and dinner were much too pleasurable. He didn't want to mar the experience in any way.

"Let's start that walk, then, shall we?" he said, signing the bill and standing. Suddenly, he found he was eager to get outside into the fresh air, his mind in need of clearing.

As they made their exit, they passed the table where Mari's friends sat with their heads over a tablet. The gentleman, Antonio, snapped his head up and gave them an intense perusing stare as they passed by, and Mari waved. The young lady flashed a wide smile, her eyes landing square on Matteo.

Mari turned to him as soon as they stepped outside, a knowing look in her eyes.

"What?" he asked.

"I get the feeling I'm going to get a lot of questions about you when I step into the classroom on Thursday. From Catherine."

"Just Catherine? Antonio looked plenty curious himself about what you were doing having dinner with me."

The gentle smile on her face faltered. "Yes, well. Antonio can ask too, I suppose."

They began walking toward the main pathway. Matteo found he couldn't stop himself from asking the next question. "Is it his business to know?"

It took Mari a moment to answer. "Who I choose to have dinner with is my business and mine alone. I don't have to answer to anyone."

Anymore. The word may have been unspoken but it was as clear as the evening sky.

As relieved as Matteo was about her response regarding the professor, he felt that same tug of ire in his chest. Someone had clearly hurt Mari. He'd suspected so but now he had no doubt. It really was none of his business. How many times did he have to remind himself of that fact since meeting her? So why was he so vexed and angry about it on her behalf?

"Do you want to talk about it?"

"About Antonio? He's a close friend."

It was hard to tell whether she'd intentionally misinterpreted his question. And even harder to guess exactly what she meant by "close."

Again. None of his business. Like she'd said a mere

moment ago, whom she chose to spend time with was her business alone.

He would just have to keep reminding himself of that too.

What had she been thinking? There'd been absolutely no reason for her to suggest prolonging this evening by asking Matteo to take a walk with her after dinner.

She was no doubt going to regret this come tomorrow. Though acting on impulse had worked out pretty well for her more than once in the past. Like the series of events that had led her to Cagliari in the first place.

Something told her that impulsiveness when it came to a man like Matteo wouldn't work out quite so well. Not for her, anyway.

They made their way up past the shops and restaurants until the road narrowed and the modern structures gave way to older resident buildings and a cobblestone road.

A few minutes later, they'd reached the grassy area Mari considered one of her favorite places on the island, if not the entire world. High atop the hill, with a breathtaking view of the skyline in the distance, the park had to be the most relaxing spot on the planet. Rosemary bushes that framed its perimeter lent a subtle scent of the herb, adding to the ambience.

"Wow. That's quite a view," Matteo commented. "And it sort of smells like we're still in the restaurant."

"Very observant. Here, I'll show you." She led him to the nearest bush and plucked a few leaves and popped them into her mouth.

Matteo stared at her as she chewed. "Those are edible?"

She nodded. "Unless, for some reason you have an aversion to rosemary."

"This is rosemary?"

"Yes. It grows wild throughout the island," she answered. Then seemingly without thinking, she raised her hand to his mouth to offer him the rest. His eyebrows rose about an inch, leading her to realize exactly what she'd done. Before she could snatch her hand away, he reached for it, gently wrapping his fingers around her wrist. Then his lips were on her palm, taking the remaining leaves into his mouth. A bolt of lightning shot through her core at the contact, leaving a scorching heat in its wake. Several heavy moments passed where neither one of them spoke, the world around them seeming to disappear. She could only stand still and watch as he slowly chewed, his eyes locked on hers, his warm hand wrapped around her skin. So intimate. Lifting her hand to his mouth had come as naturally to her as bringing the leaves to her own lips to taste.

The thought brought yet more heat to her center. She imagined those lips on hers, the way he would taste right now with the rosemary leaves upon his tongue. How it would feel to taste him.

Just stop.

Mari gave herself a mental shake and pushed the illicit thoughts away.

Finally, she somehow found the wherewithal to come to her senses and gently pull her hand away. Matteo sucked in a sharp breath. Was he as affected by what had just happened as she was? Did he even notice the charged air between them? Maybe she was imagining all of it.

Struggling to find her voice, she finally managed to

tear her gaze away from his and motion to the horizon. "Wait till you see the view from up here. Follow me."

Without waiting for an answer or a reaction, she turned on her heel and walked to the other end of the park to the rock wall ledge that overlooked the majestic scene beyond. She could sense Matteo less than a foot behind her. He audibly gasped when he reached her side. The stunning buildings and structures of the town below them spread out toward the brilliant blue of the ocean. Just beyond the water was the looming rocky Isola de Cavoli, a small island within boating distance. She could only imagine Matteo's reaction at seeing all this. The first time she'd come upon this view, she'd felt as if she'd walked up to a massive painting that had somehow come to life.

"It's like nothing I've seen before," he said next to her, the awe in his voice sharp and clear.

She could say the same.

"You haven't seen anything yet. Just watch, the sun's about to set."

Matteo draped his forearms over the rock wall and crossed his wrists. Mari found herself studying him from the side, hoping he wouldn't notice. He seemed wholly focused on the scene before him. All sharp angles and dark features. The way he was postured as he watched the sun begin to set, everything about the man screamed masculinity. Against this backdrop, he might have stepped right out of a cologne ad in some high-end magazine. She made herself look away before he turned and caught her staring. How horrifying that would be.

When she'd first sent those emails to the mysterious relative Anna had told her about, it hadn't even occurred to her that she'd be standing next to him after dinner one night fighting a wholly inconvenient physical pull unlike she'd ever felt toward any man.

Several moments passed in silence, as they simply watched the explosion of colors before them. A brilliant shade of red with streaks of dark orange. The pole lights around the park began to light within moments of the sun's descent. The brightest stars began to twinkle above them.

Matteo turned to her, his smile wide. "Thank you for bringing me here. It's been a while since I was able to simply stop and appreciate my surroundings."

His words brought an inordinate amount of pleasure to her heart. Then she noticed the deep sorrow in his eyes. His father. He'd mentioned earlier in the restaurant that his parent had been a source of turmoil in his life.

"Do you want to talk about it?"

He gave a casual shrug of his shoulder but a wealth of emotion washed through his eyes. "It's a common enough story. My father didn't know what to do with his grief after the loss of my mother. So he left himself open to be used by the first woman who showed him any interest." Matteo continued staring off into the distance as he continued. "A woman who happened to be the furthest in resemblance to my mother as imaginably possible." He released a small chuckle that held no mirth. "That might be the funniest part in all of this. He thought he could replace his wife of thirty years with the likes of *her*." The last word held so much disdain, Mari felt as if she might be able to touch it in the air.

Matteo gave a shake of his head. "Enough of all this sad talk. No need to mar what's been a highly enjoyable evening so far, is there?"

As far as changing the subject, it was a rather effective attempt. She wasn't going to push. Heaven knew, she didn't really want to discuss the parts of her past that had brought her so much pain either.

"Let's head back toward town. We'll take another way down."

He lifted an eyebrow. "Oh?"

She smiled at him. "There are some girls I'd like to visit. I stop by to see them whenever I come here."

"Girls?"

"A few boys too."

His eyebrows furrowed in confusion. The man really was good-looking when he was perplexed. And at all other times too, actually.

Mari chuckled at his expression. "You'll see." Taking his arm, she led him to the other side of the park to the stone stairway that led about halfway down the hill to her intended destination.

"Right there." She pointed to a small alcove off to the side. Nestled under the overhanging branches of a downy oak tree was a five-foot-tall structure complete with pet beds and a tall scratching post. Bowls full of food and water sat at the grassy base. "Good. Looks like most of them are here."

Matteo shifted his gaze from the sight before him, to Mari's face and back again. "Kittens. Your boys and girls are kittens. They're who you come to visit when you come here."

She nodded. "That's right. They're all complete sweethearts."

One of those sweethearts, perhaps the smallest of the litter, jumped down from her ledge and made her way to where Matteo stood. She nestled her nose against his ankle, purring softly.

"She likes you," Mari announced.

"Huh." Matteo stared at the little feline as if he was seeing a cat for the very first time. Then he bent down and picked it up, brought her up to his face. "Hello, little one."

"That one's called Dante," Mari informed him.

He brought the kitten closer to his face and rubbed his cheek against its soft fur. Dante meowed with clear contentment. Mari had to look away, the image of Matteo handling a small cat with such gentleness and affection doing something to her center that felt both alien and raw.

How did he manage to look so masculine and rugged snuggling a small kitten to his chest?

"I don't think I've ever held a kitten before," he told her, nuzzling Dante some more. "I've only ever had dogs growing up. Much bigger than little Dante here."

Inexperienced or not, he certainly seemed to know what he was doing, holding Dante like a fragile piece of glass, nuzzling against his whiskers softly. Even though the kitten looked like a tiny toy in Matteo's large hands, Matteo seemed to be a natural at handling it.

"Just FYI though, Dante can be a little temperamental."

Even before she got the last words out, the little rascal let out a surprisingly loud screech and jumped out of Matteo's hands. It landed deftly on its feet. Along the way, he swiped a sharp claw against the top of Matteo's hand. The resulting scratch was immediate and angry. Matteo barely noticed, fixated on the kitten now at his feet who had just jumped out his arms but seemed intent currently to climb back up his leg.

"I think he's telling you he'd like to go back to bed now."

Matteo bent and picked Dante up once more.

Mari stepped over to them and studied the ragged scratch on the top of Matteo's hand. "Uh-oh. Might want to watch yourself for any strange symptoms."

He lifted an eyebrow in question. "Symptoms?"

Mari wrangled a serious expression over her features. "You never know with outdoor animals. Wouldn't want you coming down with rabies. Or something worse."

He grew a shade paler. "Worse than rabies?"

She nodded solemnly. "I mean, rabies is bad enough. Agonizingly painful and the symptoms come on instantaneously."

Matteo grew a shade paler at her words. She just couldn't do it to him any longer, worrying him in such a way. "I'm only teasing you, rabies is considered nonexistent in Sardinia." Still, she couldn't resist adding, "Fleas, on the other hand…"

Matteo paused in his handling of the furry creature he held. "What?"

Mari could barely suppress the laughter hovering in her chest or the twitching of her lips. She knew for a fact each of these cats was tended to with proper medication and administered all necessary preventatives.

Matteo gave her a stern look. "Ha, ha. Very funny."

Walking back to the structure, he gently placed the squirming feline on one of the empty beds. The tiny creature let out a squeaky meow in protest at being put away but then snuggled into the soft material and promptly closed its eyes. The image struck Mari in a part of her she hadn't acknowledged in a long time. She'd vowed not to acknowledge that part of her after Trevor. And had no business doing so now, especially because of the man before her. Still, the way Matteo looked right now, gently handling the kitten with such care and affection, had the coldness within her core beginning to melt.

Oh, she really had to be careful here. Mari made herself look away when Matteo gave the tiny cat another soft scratch under its chin. But the picture remained hanging in her mind like a portrait. She recalled the way Catherine had looked at Matteo back at the restaurant, all the feminine stares that had been directed at him as they'd walked up the hill and climbed the steps. The man had a scorching appeal and if she wasn't cautious, she might very well get burned.

CHAPTER SEVEN

MORNING ARRIVED MUCH too early the next day. Or perhaps Mari just felt that way because she'd only recently drifted off to sleep. A restless sleep at that. Thoughts of Matteo had kept intruding on her attempts to reach slumber. The expression on his face as they'd watched the sunset together. Funny, she'd seen the sun setting from that vantage point countless times since she'd arrived in Sardinia, but the view last night had seemed almost magical.

Even against such a dreamlike backdrop, the hurt in Matteo's voice when he'd spoken of his father had resonated deep within her core. She had to wonder if he'd gotten a chance to grieve for his own loss due to having to deal with his father's behavior. Heaven knew, she was still grieving the loss of her own father. Losing Papa had caused a wound in her soul that would never heal. At least Matteo had another parent to share the pain with, despite their clearly strained current relationship. At least Matteo's other parent hadn't abandoned him, unlike Mari's mother.

Now, it was hard to reconcile the man who'd held Dante gently up against his chin with the one who had arrived yesterday morning with all that bluster and insult. The first impression he'd given her of himself had been almost reproachful, with the way he'd accused her of taking advantage of Anna.

Perhaps that first version of Matteo was the preferable one. She was far too attracted to the version from last night.

There were definitely layers to the man she wouldn't have guessed upon meeting him that first time. The way he'd held little Dante so gently in his large hands replayed like a movie in her mind. How would those hands feel against her own skin? What would it feel like to have him nuzzle his cheek against hers that way?

Whoa, boy. She gave herself a mental thwack. Thoughts like that were nothing but dangerous for her sanity. Fantasizing about a man was entirely a foreign concept for her. No reason to start now.

Only there was, wasn't there? The reason happened to be six feet tall, devastatingly handsome and happened to have spent the night in her hotel.

So close and yet so far.

Great, now she was waxing poetic. How utterly pathetic of her.

Mari rubbed a palm down her face. Enough of that. She had an establishment to run. Signore Gio would no doubt demand some of her time after she'd been gone all last evening. And there was something pressing on today's schedule, she was certain. What was it? For the life of her she couldn't recall.

She didn't have it in her just yet to retrieve her phone from the bedside and call up her calendar. Whatever was on her itinerary would become clear soon enough. Mari would tackle it right after she took a shower and downed perhaps a pitcher of Esmerelda's espresso. Maybe she'd run into Matteo in the dining area. Was he up already? How had he found his room? Hopefully, it had been to his liking. It wasn't one of the hotel's high-end suites but was cozy enough with a striking view of the beach and ocean. Maybe he was at his balcony staring at the view right at this moment.

Stop that! Stop thinking about him already. Sure, the two of them seemed to have made some sort of connection yesterday at dinner and then during the walk afterward. But last evening was just…a brief interlude. Who knew when the man was going to be back in Sardinia. He was just here to look into the parcel of land Anna had left him. Then he'd go back to his life in Rome and would probably not even bother to visit the island again.

He'd go on with his life and she would have to go on with hers. Funny, forty-eight hours ago, that prospect would have been just fine with her. She was more than content with her current lot in life. She lived and worked in paradise. Her job was fulfilling, and she was good at it. A volunteer gig at the local university brought her into contact with diverse and enigmatic young students from all over the world. Sure, she missed Anna and would do so forever. But she was lucky to have had the older woman in her life to begin with. Anna had been more family to her than the blood kin who'd made her final days in Boston the nightmare that she'd had to run away from four years ago.

As far as a love life… Well, she couldn't even go there. Not in her mind and not in reality. Getting over the way Trevor had treated her was going to be a lifelong endeavor. She'd thought he'd loved her, that he would stand by her. Instead, he'd dumped her and ran when her life was thrown into turmoil by her uncle. He'd never come out and said so, but Mari had seen the suspicion in Trevor's eyes when her uncle had made his accusations. She could tell he'd begun to realize that what his parents had been saying about her being beneath him might be true, after all. Trevor had never actually admitted to believing her uncle's lies. She might have even respected his decision to walk away if he had.

Instead, he'd taken the easy way out. Told her he couldn't handle the turmoil in her life.

Too complicated. Those were Trevor's exact words. Like the possibility of being charged with a crime was nothing more than an inconvenience.

Mari scoffed out loud. He'd been right, hadn't he? He'd simply walked away rather than help her deal with it all.

Thoughts of those dark days threatened to shadow her spirit for hours if she entertained them at all. Instead, she made herself focus on the melodic birdsong faintly echoing from outside her window and the soft crashing waves of the ocean that one could hear if their ears strained enough. Several deep breaths later, she tossed the covers aside finally and scrambled out of bed.

The steamy hot shower served to jostle the remaining lingering unwanted thoughts from her mind and she felt lighter and calmer as she made her way downstairs to the lobby.

Miyko stood at the front desk and gave her a scrutinizing look when she approached.

"You were gone late last night," he said, his gaze roaming the length of her. "For you anyway," he added. "You're usually in bed by nine at the latest."

She ignored the speculative comments. He was clearly

fishing for information about her time spent with Matteo. She had no inclination to give him any. "Good morning, Miyko. And how are you today?"

"Bene, grazie," he answered. *"E tu?"*

"Bene. Though I'll be much better once I get some of Esme's espresso."

Miyko's eyes followed her as she headed toward the coffee bar. "Well, don't take too long. The rep from the excursion company is due to arrive within half an hour."

Mari paused in her tracks. A curse escaped her lips. That was the engagement she'd been spacing on. They were due to experience one of their excursion offerings firsthand.

"Oh, and I won't be able to accompany you, after all. Mama is not feeling too well. I'll have to stay here and man the desk."

"Is Roberta okay?"

Miyko waved his hand dismissively. "She just overindulged at dinner last night. Chef made his rich and heavy lasagna."

Mari's concern for the older woman was quickly displaced with frustration at what her absence would mean for her schedule today.

"I can hardly go by myself. They've made accommodations and prepared food for at least two people."

Matteo chose that moment to step out of the elevator. Miyko's eyes lit up with mischief at the sight of him.

Mari could just guess where his thoughts had led. *Oh no.*

"You don't have to, Mari. I have an excellent idea."

He nodded in Matteo's direction.

It had been a while since Matteo had needed a cold shower in the morning to start the day. That's what happened when a man's dreams overnight kept featuring a dark-haired, doe-eyed beauty who had him thinking wicked thoughts about her all night.

Knowing she slept only a few floors below made the yearnings all that much stronger. So close yet so far.

Sitting on the edge of the comfortable mattress in a damp towel around his waist this morning, Matteo wondered if he'd stayed under the cold spray long enough. A lingering heat still curled at the base of his center. More than once last night, he'd fantasized about what it would feel like to kiss her, to hold her in his arms. What her reaction might be if he found his way to her room and knocked on her door. Would she let him in, greet him with bated breath and longing the same way he longed for her?

Not that his wayward thoughts were any of Mari's fault.

No, it was all his doing that he couldn't get her out of his mind after they'd returned to their respective rooms last night. They were mere acquaintances who'd just met. But last night might have been one of the most picture-book-perfect evenings he'd spent with a woman. Even riding on a city bus with Mari was somehow notable and romantic.

If only circumstances between them could have been different. If only he wasn't here to see about acquiring control of the hotel and the land it sat on.

A surge of guilt made him wince internally. Such a useless emotion, guilt. A luxury he couldn't afford. He had a business to rebuild and right now, this hotel was the only clear path to begin that endeavor.

How utterly troublesome that he was so attracted to her.

Last night should not have happened, he shouldn't have enjoyed it so much. He'd meant to at least broach the subject of taking over the hotel from her, yet he'd never gotten around to it. That was unacceptable. Right now, he should be back in Rome at his office trying to figure out what his next steps should be.

Had he really been playing with a kitten? The dull ache of the small scratch at the top of his hand was proof that he indeed had.

More importantly, had he really shared so much about his difficulties with his father and about the loss of his mother? It was as if someone else had entered his body and discussed all those things with Mari.

By contrast, he knew next to nothing about her. He had no real idea about her past. What had driven her from the cobblestoned sidewalks of Boston to the shores of Sardinia? What exactly was her story?

She certainly didn't seem inclined to share the way he had. Well, no more. From now on, whenever he interacted with Mari, he would be a closed book. Just like her.

If he was smart, he'd try to avoid her altogether until the next flight back to Rome this evening. In the meantime, he had to get dressed and find some breakfast and much-needed caffeine.

Stepping out of the elevator into the lobby moments later, he sensed Mari's presence before he saw or heard her. So much for trying to avoid the woman for his sanity's sake.

The employee who manned the front desk—Miyko was his name?—flashed him a curious smile. Mari's focus was on the other man, shooting daggers at him with her eyes.

"I think Signore Talarico should join you today, Mari," Miyko was saying.

Join her for what exactly?

He was about to direct the question out loud to Mari but her expression had turned downright murderous. He could practically see steam rising out of her. Her ire was directed straight at her employee. If looks could kill, the man would be growing cold on the tile floor right about now. Miyko, for his part, didn't seem to notice Mari's discomfort. In fact, he appeared to be enjoying himself.

Miyko crossed his arms in front of his chest and directed his next comments to Matteo. "You see, Mari and I were supposed to go on an introductory excursion by one of the hotel's outside partners. A limo ride to the harbor, followed by a sail on a pirate ship to a tiny island with a historic lighthouse. They're trying to sell us their services."

Huh. What did any of that have to do with him?

Miyko continued, answering that very question. "Turns out I can't go. I have to stay here and man the desk. You should go with Mari in my place."

Mari's eyes grew wide. She stepped over to the desk. She cleared her throat nervously before beginning. "On the other hand, the two of you could go. And I can stay here and mind the desk."

Miyko shook his head slowly. "That makes no sense. We need to see how the excursion might be experienced by both our male and female guests."

Mari sucked in a breath. "But I'm sure Signore Talarico has other things he needs to do. I'm guessing he's much too busy to waste away the day with such things."

Ouch. Matteo was trying hard not to be offended at just how strongly Mari felt about not going on this little trek with him.

"Actually, I'm totally free until my flight later this evening."

Mari's jaw fell as she turned to him. She seemed to be scrambling for what to say next as she worked her jaw up and down.

"I've never been sailing on a pirate ship before," he added.

That was true enough. He was more than a little curious about that leg of the trip in particular. It wasn't as if he had anything better to do before his flight. And he was rather curious about what else the island had to offer after the experiences of last night.

Right. As if that's the only reason, a faint voice teased him from the back recesses of his mind.

Matteo pushed it away before it could grow any louder.

Matteo tended to keep a spare pair of swim trunks in the bottom of his carry-on luggage. He'd never actually needed them until today. Good thing too. He didn't think Miyko's clothing would fit him very well. And there was no doubt the other man would have offered to let Matteo borrow a pair. He seemed very intent on making sure Matteo was able to go on this excursion with Mari.

Mari, on the other hand…

Sure, Miyko was absolutely playing him as some sort of pawn. The game seemed to be forcing Mari's hand and trying to embarrass her. Maybe it was some kind of employee/boss power play. Or maybe Miyko was just a mischievous trickster who liked to watch others squirm in discomfort.

Or all of the above.

Whatever the case, Matteo didn't see a way to back out of the trip now after he'd already said yes. Besides, he really did want to go.

"I'll just go get my things," he said, ignoring the look of utter defeat on Mari's face.

What was so wrong about the prospect of spending the day with him anyhow? After all, they'd had a good time yesterday together, hadn't they? Why did she look horrified at having to be with him again?

Silly question.

The answer was the same reason that he should have declined the offer to go. Hadn't he himself just a few moments ago upstairs in his room decided that last night had been a mistake? Hadn't he vowed to stay away from Mari because of how attracted he was to her?

His resolve sure hadn't lasted long. About the length of time it took him to get downstairs and lay eyes on her again.

Well, if he was going to spend the day with her, he definitely had to be more careful about exactly where his thoughts led.

Miyko glanced at his watch. "Yes, go get your things, Signore Talarico. The car should be arriving in a few minutes to pick you two up."

Just like that, it was a done deal. Matteo nodded. "I'll be right back."

She was already at the curb when he made his way back downstairs, standing in front of a sleek, black sedan so highly polished that the sun reflecting off its surface had him squinting. She looked as if she'd rather be anywhere else.

She also looked lovely. In the short period of time they'd been apart, Mari had somehow pulled herself together as if she'd had hours. Her hair sat in some kind of complicated-twist bun atop her head that left several delicate tendrils loose, framing her face, the loose hair blowing against her skin in the soft breeze. She wore a colorful printed wrap dress that hung to her curves in all the right ways. The amber hue brought out the golden tone of her tanned skin. On her feet were delicate sensible sandals with straps that wrapped around her ankles and showed off her neon-painted toes.

Great. Now, he was noticing her toes again.

She looked like a picture out of an advertisement for European island living. Except for the scowl on her face.

Matteo went from feeling offended to amused. She really was feeling put out about this whole thing. Would Miyko see a dock in his pay? Was Mari the petty vengeful type?

Perhaps her vengeance would be directed at Matteo for accepting the invitation.

His amusement grew. No other woman had ever had him guessing and wondering about them quite so before. Mari felt like a puzzle he needed to figure out.

A driver emerged from the other side of the car and greeted him in Italian. An older gentleman with a friendly smile and crisp uniform, he looked straight out of central casting if the director needed an Italian chauffeur.

He opened the back door for them and Matteo motioned Mari inside. With a loud, resigned sigh, Mari sat inside the car and scooted over to the other side. She flashed the driver a friendly smile along the way. Something told Matteo that would be one of the few smiles gracing her lips today. With a low chuckle, he joined her inside the car.

His amusement faded quickly once he sat down in the car seat next to her. The sedan wasn't quite as roomy as it looked from the outside. A tinted glass partition separated them from the driver in the front seat. So they'd essentially be alone together, in tight quarters for who knew what amount of time. He really should have asked more questions about this excursion.

"How long before we get there?"

"We're heading to the other side of the island. It's about a two-and-a-half-hour ride," she answered, sounding not terribly happy about it.

Okay. That wasn't so bad. He could do a bit over two hours. He could ignore the sheen of her skin, the scent of her berry shampoo, the urge to brush one of those wayward tendrils off her cheek.

But then she shifted to place her bag by her feet and her bare knee brushed against his leg. The contact had heat shooting through his thigh and then higher. Matteo gripped his fingers tight against his palm to keep from reaching for her, rubbing his hand against that tempting, tanned and shapely knee.

Mari seemed unaware of the slight contact. And why wouldn't she be? It was barely a whisper of a touch. Yet it elicited a physical reaction within him that he felt deep in his core.

So maybe he was wrong about being able to handle over two hours alone with Mari in the car. They'd barely been in the back seat for a full minute and already he was hyperaware of how attracted he was to her.

Matteo watched out the window as the buildings and hotels of the city gave way to rural, grassy hills and rambling fields. The first part of the ride passed mostly in silence, except for the soft notes of the Spanish guitar music the driver had piping through the vehicle. Matteo had half a mind to ask him to switch to another playlist. Something about the notes brought to mind slow dancing closely with a partner, and the atmosphere felt too romantic for comfort.

Mari's next words definitely reset that vibe.

"Did you itch much last night?" she asked him. "I don't see you scratching."

That question was definitely not romantic in the least. "Itch? Why would I itch?"

He remembered then the way she'd teased him yesterday about handling the kitten. "Ha, ha. Very funny. I don't have fleas."

She shrugged. "We can only hope. Sometimes it takes a day or two to manifest their symptoms." Her tone was serious enough, but Matteo didn't miss the small tug at the corner of her mouth to keep from laughing.

"I don't have fleas," he repeated. But darned if he didn't feel a slight itchy sensation along his skin below his left knee. No way he was going to give her the satisfaction of scratching at it. He was positive it wasn't any kind of insect bite. Mari was just getting back at him about agreeing to go on this trip. The chances he had a fleabite were astronomically low.

Weren't they?

"You know," he began, turning in his seat to fully face her. "I don't think Dante infected me with bloodsucking parasites, but if I went back there and the little critter tried climbing up my pant leg, I'd lift him up again."

She raised a delicately arched eyebrow. "Is that so?"

He nodded. "Yes. In fact, there's nothing about yesterday that I'd do any differently."

Whoa. He hadn't meant to utter such a double entendre. Surprisingly, he meant what he'd just said. Mari sat staring at him, her mouth agape now. His words or their meaning were not lost on her.

Scrambling to fill the heavy air and just to have something to say, Matteo pointed out the window at the field they were passing, not even certain what he was looking at.

"Those have got to be the funniest-looking dogs I've ever seen."

Mari blinked up at him, confusion flooding her features at the sudden change of topic. Eventually, she moved her gaze to where he pointed.

A chuckle escaped her lips as soon as she did. "Those are not dogs, Matteo."

Matteo squinted, turning his head, but the vehicle was traveling too fast to get another good look. "What were they, then?"

"You need to get out of the city more," she told him, amusement dancing in her dark eyes.

"Why?"

"That's what sheep look like when they've been shorn of their wool."

"Huh. Who knew? I guess I do need to get out to the country more often."

Mari's' chuckle erupted into all-out, full-on laughter. Matteo found it was impossible not to laugh along with her.

And just like that, the tension between them broke. As if it had never been there.

It was really too bad that she was going to have to fire Miyko as soon as they got back to the hotel. She'd never actually agreed to go along with any of this. Though, truth be told, Mari probably could have fought harder to say no.

Frankly, she'd been surprised that Matteo had even agreed so readily to come along. Miyko hadn't even tried to persuade or bamboozle him the way he'd done with her. Go figure. Mari would have absolutely pegged him as more of an eighteen-hole-golf-followed-by-cocktails-then-dinner-party type rather than the sort who'd be interested in a pirate-themed daylong boating excursion.

Matteo Talarico had managed to throw her one curve after another since he'd arrived on this island. She was done trying to figure him out.

Well, now that she was here, she may as well try and enjoy herself. Plus, she had to admit it—Matteo made her laugh. She couldn't remember the last time she'd said that about a man. Or that she'd done much laughing at all, for that matter.

Now, as the car came to a stop at the marina, Mari exited the car and took a moment to ground herself. It was going to be a long day, spent mostly alone with Matteo. The warm glow of the sun, along with the soft breeze drifting off the water, served to further temper her mood. This wasn't so bad. Maybe Miyko would be keeping his job after all. Matteo joined her by the side of the car, stretching his arms up toward the sky. She caught a peek of a toned and tanned stomach as his T-shirt lifted at the waist. She sharply tore her gaze away. If this day was going to go smoothly at all, she had to stop doing things like that. Like noticing his taut stomach. Or the way the warm sun brought out the lighter streaks in his dark hair. Or how enthusiastic he looked at the moment.

Right. She was going to stop all that. Starting now.

The driver came over and explained the exact time and spot that someone would be back to pick them up. Matteo shook the man's hand and she didn't miss that he slipped a couple of bills into his palm in the process.

Mari bid the driver goodbye as another couple of gentlemen approached them with wide smiles and greetings in Italian. Her accent when responding must have given her away as an American because they immediately switched to flawless English.

"Welcome to you both!" said the blond one with the bright hazel eyes. "I'm Franco and this is Stavi. We're your tour guides. Are you ready to start your adventure?"

Mari nodded, though she was far from certain.

CHAPTER EIGHT

THE DAY COULDN'T have been better suited for them. Stepping out of the vehicle, Matteo took a moment to take in his surroundings. The sun shone a bright golden yellow, reflecting off the soft ripples of the water. Boats and ships of all sizes dotted the square dock. Nautical flags surrounded the larger Italian il Tricolore atop the three-structure building. The soft breeze occasionally gave way to a stronger gust that sent the aroma of the sea drifting in the air.

An adventure. That's what the tour guide had called it. Sure, he was trying to sell this outing to Mari so she'd offer it at her hotel to her guests, but Matteo could see how the excursion would be a popular draw to tourists and locals alike. Look how readily he'd jumped on the chance to go. He didn't often act on impulse. But saying yes this morning had definitely been impulsive.

Maybe it was meant to be that he be here. When was the last time he did anything just for the hell of it? Just to enjoy himself, have a little fun? Even the party-like events he often attended were business related.

Maybe this entire week was meant to be. Fated somehow. The call from his lawyer. Then traveling to Cagliari.

Meeting Mari.

Maybe he was meant to know her. To get a touch of some lighthearted fun that included watching a sunset atop a majestic hill, petting a soft-furred kitten, sailing on a pirate ship. All in the company of a beautiful woman who seemed to draw out a side of him he hadn't known existed.

Too bad it was all so temporary. Too bad she was no doubt going to dislike him when he finally confessed as to his real motives.

The idea sent a sinking feeling in his chest. It bothered him that Mari would think less of him at some undeniable point in the future.

A blur of motion caught the side of his eye, pulling him out of his unpleasant musings. He looked down to see a small child approaching the two of them. A girl dressed in a colorful frock, carrying a basket. She held it up to Mari, then swung it in his direction. "Fig!" she exclaimed. *"Per te,"* she added.

A frazzled petite blond woman was fast on her heels. *"Scusa,"* she said, in a flustered tone. "She's very excited about the figs she picked at her grandfather's garden. I'm sorry she's intruded."

"That's all right," Mari immediately answered, reaching inside the offered basket. "I'd love a fig, *grazie.*"

The mother gave Mari a relieved smile. "You've made her very happy." She glanced from Mari's face to Matteo. "Do you two have any of your own?" she asked, just as Mari took a bite of the gifted fruit. She sputtered at the question just as its exact meaning registered in Matteo's head. The mother thought they were a couple who possibly had children. No wonder Mari appeared near ready to spit out her fig.

They both immediately began denying the woman's assumption in unison.

"Oh, we're not—" Mari began, mumbling through her mouthful.

Just as Matteo shook his head, saying "No, that's not…"

The woman seemed to realize her mistake, though her expression was one of tickled amusement. "Ah, I see," she said, gathering her daughter about the shoulders and turning her around. "Pardon my mistake."

Matteo watched the two figures walk away, wracking his brain for what in the world he might say to Mari next. She had to feel as awkward as he did.

He cleared his throat before beginning. No sense in ignoring the proverbial elephant between them. "It's an innocent enough mistake on her part."

Mari quickly nodded. She was clearly at a loss, too, for she simply held up the fruit in her hand. "Want a bite? It's quite fresh."

She immediately dropped her hand before waiting for an answer, her cheeks flushing a ruby red. Yet another innocent remark that was actually quite loaded. Mari clearly came to the same realization as soon as she'd said the words.

Matteo did his best not to groan out loud. The thought of reaching for her hand, pulling the fig up to his own lips, taking a bite from the spot her lips had just touched had lightning bolts shooting up his center.

Blessedly, Stavi chose that moment to announce that their transport boat had arrived to sail them to the bigger ship farther out at sea.

"We'll be serving some light refreshments on board," he told them. "To stave off your hunger until lunch on the beach later."

Lunch on the beach. That sounded…quite romantic. Matteo had to suppress yet another groan. He gave his head a mental shake, focusing on the here and now. They were boarding a boat. Mari was taking her shoes off and handing them to Stavi, who placed them carefully in a plastic container. Then he reached his hand out to her. Matteo didn't even think of what he was doing; if anyone was going to help Mari onto this watercraft, it was going to be him. Taking her hand and gently wrapping his other arm around her waist, he gently guided her onto the first step. There was nothing for it, the woman felt natural in his arms. Touching her felt natural, innate. As if he'd been doing so his whole life. As if he never should stop.

He could only hope Mari didn't notice how his hands lingered about her waist, how he hesitated letting go of her.

Once Mari was on board and had moved onto the seat, he followed her lead and took his own loafers off and handed them to Stavi before boarding himself. The other man gave him a knowing smile as he descended onto the boat, followed by a quick blink of an eye.

Matteo wasn't going to try and interpret what any of it might mean.

Mari settled into the plush leather bucket seat portside and pushed her sunglasses farther up her nose. The feel of Matteo's palms against her skin through her thin dress had her senses tingling. Good thing he had been holding her; she'd nearly lost her balance at the unexpected contact. She tried to take her mind off how good it had felt to be held by him by concentrating on the spectacular view.

Not a cloud in sight, the sky was a brilliant blue that could have come off a paint palette. A gray mountain loomed far ahead in the distance, the water clear and deep beneath them. A picture-perfect scene, really. As much as she liked Miyko—well, most of the time she did—sitting here with her employee would not have held the same appeal. As loathe as she was to admit it, doing this with Matteo by her side made it more exciting, more thrilling.

As if they might have been a real couple like the young mother on the dock had assumed.

Now, that was dangerous territory better left unexplored. But it didn't mean she couldn't take this as the opportunity it was. Nothing said she couldn't enjoy herself today. She'd dare to say she deserved some lighthearted fun.

The only problem was, it was starting to become quite difficult to view the man with her in any kind of lightened way.

As soon as Matteo sat down next to her, Franco appeared with a tray laden with fresh fruit, crispy crackers and thinly sliced meat. Along with two very large bright orange cocktails.

Aperol Spritzes. She had to be careful; those always tended to go to her head.

"An aperitif," Franco said, setting the tray down between them, then walking away.

"Something about all this seems so familiar," Matteo began.

"Oh?"

"I think my parents and I might have gone sailing off this very marina all those years ago, during that visit to Anna I mentioned earlier."

Mari lifted her glass and took a sip of her Aperol Spritz, savoring the orange citrus flavors and mild effervescence against her tongue.

"You mentioned traveling with your parents when you were much younger." She got the impression those family trips had eventually stopped for some reason.

He nodded. "Yes. When I was really young."

As much as she didn't want to probe, Mari's curiosity got the better of her. "Not when you grew older?"

Matteo's lips tightened. He looked off into the horizon, squinting against the bright sun. "The trips didn't end. I just wasn't included anymore. Not after about the age of six. Or maybe it was seven."

Definitely not the answer she'd expected. "You weren't?"

He shook his head, his gaze still focused on the horizon. "Once I grew old enough, I was simply left behind at home while they wandered the world. I was still young but old enough to interpret the implications behind my exclusion."

"Implications?"

"I was in the way. They wanted their privacy, without a third party."

Mari tried to wrap her mind around that statement but found she simply couldn't. He wasn't a third party. He was their son.

She couldn't even imagine it, being viewed as an intruder by your own parents. Mari didn't have a mother she could compare such an experience with, but she couldn't imagine Papa ever thinking of her in such a way. Of course, there'd been times when she'd worn his patience, particularly as a teen. But Mari had never once questioned whether her presence was wanted by the single parent who was raising her.

Matteo continued, "I was sent to a boarding school in Switzerland where I spent most of my days until attending university in the States. Wasn't home much, or when I was there, my parents were usually away. I spent the time with the house staff."

Mari's heart began to grow heavy at the thought of a

small Matteo wandering the halls of his large Roman villa by himself. "Not even during summers and holidays?"

Matteo released a chuckle that sounded anything but amused. "Particularly not then. They were too busy enjoying each other's exclusive company."

Now she pictured him wandering those same halls during Christmas or Easter, an even glummer image. With no one to celebrate with aside from employed strangers. She wondered how many of those employees couldn't wait to end their shift and go back to their own lives, their own families. Leaving behind the little boy in their care for the next person on the rotation.

She couldn't quite come up with an adequate response. Matteo continued, somber eyes still fixated ahead. "My parents were very much in love. Right up until the very end." Another empty chuckle. "Doesn't sound like the kind of thing a child would be forlorn about, does it?"

Mari could easily understand how a child might have felt unhappy in such a household, when the two people who were supposed to love you the most in the world only had room in their hearts for each other.

"Any child in your circumstances would understandably feel excluded from their parents' lives, Matteo. I imagine it must have felt very lonely for you growing up."

The way he stiffened next to her had Mari wishing she could suck the words back. The already strained smile across his lips further tightened. Matteo clearly didn't appreciate the thought that she might pity him. Little did he know, pity was the furthest notion from her mind.

"Yes, well. Water under the bridge. Taught me some valuable lessons, anyway."

"What kind of lessons?" she prodded. What possible

lesson could be learned from having your parents view you as a nuisance who had to be sent away because they were too into each other to deal with their only child? Despite not having a mother, Mari had never felt unwanted or unloved by the father who'd raised her as a single parent.

She'd had no idea how lucky she was until his loss.

Matteo shrugged, narrowed his eyebrows, as if weighing his answer. "Falling in love that deeply isn't healthy. My father fell apart when he lost my mother. Became an entirely different man. One I hardly recognized. He went from a successful, shrewd businessman to a gullible patsy craving affection. A man who fell for the first con that came his way. No love is worth that."

"I see."

"And it certainly doesn't make sense to bring any children into the world if you're not interested in spending any time with them. Why even bother?"

Mari had to suck in a breath at the harshness in his words. His beliefs about parenting aside, Matteo's entire view about love and affection was that it made a man weak. That it wasn't worth the potential hurt an all-consuming love might cause. Such a shame, really. The man had so much to offer the right woman. Maybe even a woman like herself.

Not that she had really been entertaining such a nonsensical notion.

Had she?

Technically, she was on duty. This excursion was officially a business trip. So that Mari could make an informed decision about whether or not to offer this tour company's services out of the Hotel Nautica. She needed to be shrewd, observant, taking in all the details so that she could help her guests make informed decisions. Which would have been exactly how she would have behaved if the original plan to attend with Miyko had held instead of being here with Matteo.

She really had no business enjoying herself quite so much.

But it was so hard to keep her imagination at bay. So hard to keep from pretending this was some kind of romantic date. Silly of her, really. This was completely Miyko's fault. Of course, she wasn't really going to fire him. Mari would be lost without Miyko and Roberta. Still, he deserved at least a stern lecture about inserting himself in other people's lives.

In all fairness to Miyko, however, he wouldn't have appreciated the outing nearly as much as Matteo seemed to be. Mari had to wonder when he'd let himself take a day of freedom just to have fun. The things he'd told her about his father's behavior and the resulting struggles with the family business should serve as a warning that the man was at a pivotal moment in his life. Starting any kind of relationship was probably the last thing on his mind. She'd say the same for herself. She was still finding solid ground after leaving Boston. Losing Anna had come as yet another blow.

Their conversation when they'd first boarded had cast the briefest shadow over their ride. But now that they were enjoying the refreshments, the earlier lightness seemed to have returned to Matteo's eyes. That lightness grew into clear excitement as they approached the ship. The vessel looked like something out of a swashbuckler novel. Complete with wooden mast, skull-and-crossbow banner and the bust of a mermaid decorating its bow.

"Wow," Matteo said, excitement laced in his voice. "That's quite a replica. I feel like I'm about to go plundering and pillaging with my mateys."

Truth be told, she was rather impressed herself. Sardinian history was rife with pirate tales. Here they could playact at one. It wasn't the only thing she was tempted to playact at.

How easy it would be to imagine they really were a couple, romantically spending the day together. Looking forward to an amorous night.

She couldn't succumb to the temptation of her fantasies, however. Her desires had to remain in check. But, heaven help her, they were so close to the surface as she followed Matteo off the transfer boat, then let him lead her onto the narrow ramp to board the bigger ship. He did that thing again where he guided her by holding her at the waist. The ironic thing was, rather than steadying her, the feel of his hands on her seemed to have the opposite effect. It was throwing her off-balance. She stumbled a step and came perilously close to slipping off the edge and splashing into the water.

"Steady there," he said behind her, his breath warm against the back of her neck. "It isn't time for the swimming part yet."

He was so wrong. She was swimming all right. Her head was swimming with all matter of untoward thoughts. Like how it might feel to turn around and plant her lips on Matteo's, right here in front of these two strangers. How that warm breath might feel as their mouths met. It was a ridiculous idea. And a dangerous one.

Hadn't she sworn years ago after her experience with Trevor that she'd fight any and all attraction to a man like Matteo? It simply wasn't worth it. Trevor had simply walked away from her when things had gotten messy in her life. Just as her mother had decades earlier when she'd walked away from her husband and daughter. Mama had complained more than once about the pressures of raising a child and being a wife while running a business. Then one day she'd simply left it all behind.

But Matteo was making it harder and harder to keep her vow with each passing minute. All these years she'd thought she was being steadfast and true to her ideals. When the true reality was that she simply hadn't been tempted to any degree before. And Matteo happened to be one solid mass of temptation.

"Guess I need to find my sea legs still," she said, blessedly reaching the deck. He was fast on her heels, jumping on board right behind her.

"Off to the islands," Franco announced once they were situated.

"I'm going to head below deck to freshen up a bit," Mari told the three men, desperately needing some time alone to gather her thoughts. Her attraction to Matteo had reached inexplicable levels. She needed to collect herself. The excursion hadn't even really started yet and she was already out of sorts fighting how drawn she was to the man and thwarting off thoughts of kissing him.

She took her time in the phone-booth-sized privy. Splashing cold water on her face, Mari reminded herself of all the reasons she had no business thinking of Matteo as anything more than a blood relative of Anna's who would be in and out of her life in a matter of days. When she finally got herself under some semblance of reasonableness, she made her way back up to the deck.

"Ah, you're back," Matteo said. The sight of him now had all her reassurances rushing out her head. He'd taken his shirt off and stood between their tour guides bare chested, muscular and tanned.

"Just in time," he added, a mischievous smile framing his lips.

Mari found her voice, forcing her gaze away from his bronze skin. "In time for what?"

He pointed to Franco and Stavi. "They're having us walk the plank."

Time certainly flew when you were having fun.

As often as he'd heard that cliché throughout his life, Matteo couldn't recall ever having a firsthand experience to prove it. The day was proceeding in a blur of activity.

Now at the small destination island, he and Mari were encouraged to jump off a wooden plank about eight feet high into the water. Well, he himself needed no encouragement. Mari, on the other hand, needed a bit more prodding.

After the initial shock of the deep plunge, Matteo lost track of time again. He had no idea how long they'd been swimming and treading water and simply enjoying watching the birds and small fish that obliviously swam near the two interlopers within their waters.

Just as he was about to start to prune, Stavi used a bullhorn to tell them lunch was ready. He and Mari swam ashore to find a picnic blanket spread over the coarse sand. A basket full of sandwiches, pasta and crisp vegetables awaited them along with two bottles of rich Toscana chilled just right.

He let Mari pull the food out while he uncorked the wine.

"I don't know how you'd say no to this as part of your excursion offerings, Mari. These guides sure know what they're doing."

She blinked at him before nodding, her gaze drifting over the elaborate spread. "I'd say."

As much as he was enjoying himself, something about Mari's demeanor was scratching at him. She seemed distracted, not fully present. Probably worried about all the work awaiting her upon her return. If he was smart, he would be plagued by the same exact concern. The reality that awaited him back in Rome was going to be a colossal drain of his mental resources.

Yet, the only thing distracting him from all the fun was the way Mari looked in the swimsuit she wore. It was beyond modest by any means. A crop top of some sort coupled with boy shorts. But the fabric hugged her skin in such a way that Matteo was certain he'd be seeing that swimsuit in his dreams for countless nights to come.

As well as the woman wearing it.

Matteo made himself focus on the food before them. Getting all this out in a dinghy had to have taken quite a bit of effort. Mari sat staring out toward the sea, chewing quietly on pieces of the baguette rather than actually taking a bite of the sandwich itself.

"A lira for your thoughts? You appear to be a thousand miles away."

Her gaze snapped back to his face and she swallowed the morsel of food in her mouth. "Oh! I was just thinking what Miyko might say about coming to an agreement with the tour company. It can't be solely my decision."

Matteo put his sandwich down. So, he'd been right. She

was focused on the business aspects of this outing. Here he was, salivating over the way she looked in her swim attire while truly enjoying her company. And she wasn't even entertaining any thoughts of him.

Served him right. Mari was the smart one. The one focused on what mattered.

He should take a page out of her book. In fact, Matteo was skating perilously close to the thin ice his father had fallen through. Allowing himself to be distracted by his attraction to a beautiful woman just because they happened to be out on an adventurous field trip together.

Mari was probably taking mental notes of exactly what food had been served and the labels on the wine. He'd leave her to it. Let her concentrate on her decision-making.

The rest of the meal passed in mostly silence. With the occasional trite and quick comment about how fresh the vegetables were or the fruity taste of the wine. Soon after, Franco appeared to bring them back to the ship.

On to stage two.

"We'll sail now to the other side of the island," Franco was saying. "To see the abandoned lighthouse. It's a beautiful structure that offers a bird's-eye view of the ocean and other islands nearby."

"Sounds great," Mari answered, as they both helped pull the picnic blanket up and folded it.

Before long, they were back on the boat and back in dry clothing. Mari stayed below deck again as they sailed to the other side. Most likely jotting down notes about the excursion. She'd probably forgotten Matteo was even up here.

That was just as well. No matter that it left an empty sensation in the hollow of his gut. His problem, not hers.

Eventually, a tall, white-bricked columnar structure

that seemed to reach the clouds slowly came into view. Mari finally appeared just as Franco approached from the portside. He explained the lighthouse had been there for close to half a century and had weathered all manner of storms.

Mari joined Matteo where he stood at the deck. Stavi was already lowering the dinghy that would take them ashore. When it came time to hop on, as much as Matteo told himself he should keep hands off, he couldn't seem to help it. Mari appeared hesitant about stepping onto the wobbly plank, so he helped her to board. As a compromise, he made sure to only hold her hand this time. They reached the sand within a few minutes.

"Follow that pathway between those two bushes. It will take you up to the entrance to the lighthouse."

Mari snapped her head in Stavi's direction. "Wait. You're not coming with us?"

The other man shook his head. "Franco and I have much to do back on the ship. One of us will be back in no time to pick you up. Enjoy the scenery." He pointed to the lighthouse and then up toward the sky. With that, he steered the dinghy around and started back toward the ship.

Mari stood staring after the small boat as it sailed farther away. She looked more than a little apprehensive.

"If you'd rather not, we can skip the lighthouse visit. Just walk around the island. I see some pretty flowers."

She bit her lip, considering, then slowly shook her head, turning to face him. "No. I have to go. I need to be able to explain the details for any guests who might ask if we make this one of our offerings."

That made sense.

Still, he wasn't about to let her go up there alone. What

kind of gentleman would that make him? What if she missed a step and slipped? She'd seemed off-balance all day. Missing her sea legs, as she'd explained earlier.

He'd be flattering himself if he thought it had anything to do with him.

They walked about half a mile that had to be one straight hill. Not so much as an acre of level ground. The base of the lighthouse appeared in front of them after what seemed like an inordinate amount of climbing.

"Is all of Sardinia this hilly?"

Mari took a moment to catch her breath before answering. "As a matter of fact, a lot of it is. There's a theory that native Sardinians live longer because of all the cardio exercising climbing various hills to get anywhere."

The sheen of sweat forming on his forehead gave credence to such a theory, Matteo figured. To think, he'd always tried his best to stay fit and made an effort to work out daily. Yet this was the second time he'd felt winded climbing up a hill since he'd arrived on the island. It had to be the higher altitude.

It was as if she'd read his mind. "It's a bit different than a gym full of equipment."

Was she making fun of him? The slight twitching of her lips at the corners said that was a distinct possibility.

"I've only been here a couple of days, still getting used to the climate and terrain. Plus, I've never had any complaints about my stamina," he added a moment later, then realized exactly what he'd said.

Mari's jaw fell open. As much as he wished he could take the words back, he had to admit to being at least a little pleased at her shocked expression.

Several beats passed in complete silence.

Finally, she ignored his loaded statement and instead pivoted on her heel, then strode to the wooden door. "It looks completely deserted. Like no one's been here in ages."

Her tug on the door proved useless. It didn't so much as open a crack.

"Here, let me try," he told her. Grasping the doorknob, he pulled as hard as he could, putting his entire back and legs into the effort. Not that he was trying to prove anything about how physically fit he was. Absolutely not. That would be childish and silly.

His efforts eventually proved fruitful. The door eased open with a loud groan to reveal a dark circular area. A winding staircase loomed large in the center of the room. A glance up high didn't even offer a glimpse of the top. The lighthouse was simply too tall and much too dark.

"Yet more climbing," Matteo commented, then gestured toward the steps. "After you."

Mari pursed her lips in hesitation but gingerly made her way to the stairs and began to climb. Shafts of dust drifted in the air. Matteo counted about a hundred steps before he gave up and just followed Mari to the top.

When they got to the watch gallery, he couldn't deny the effort was worth it. Crystal-blue water as far as the eye could see met a bright clear sky on the horizon. The large cruise ships dotting the surface of the ocean appeared deceptively small from this distance.

"Wow," was all he could think of to say. Mari seemed at a loss for words also. It was as if they'd stepped into a celestial work of art, staring at it from above. Matteo lost sight of how long they stood there, simply admiring the amazing scene before them. The clouds above shifted slowly across the sky.

Finally, Mari turned and removed her sunglasses. "We should probably head back. I've seen all I need to see. I think our guests would be delighted to have this as an option on their itinerary."

"No need to run it by Miyko after all?" Matteo asked as they made their way off the gallery and began the descent back down the stairs.

She shook her head. "I have no doubt he would agree. That view alone up there makes it worthwhile."

Matteo might have argued that walking a plank and pretending to be a pirate were top contenders as well. Particularly for the youngsters. Or those young at heart. Did he qualify as the latter?

His childhood years weren't ones he would relive or revisit. He'd spent too much time alone, particularly during off-school days when his friends were back home with their families while he'd been left to wait out the time until classes resumed.

His parents were fortunate to have found each other and for the years they'd had together. But they'd had no business being parents.

Like he'd said to Mari earlier, it didn't make sense to start a family or have a child if one didn't have the ability to nurture and love them. What if Matteo was cut from the same cloth? He didn't want to disappoint a child the way he'd been disappointed repeatedly growing up.

Matteo gave himself a mental shake. Why was he dredging up all this now? The past was the past. He turned his attention back to the steps.

"I think you should definitely hire Franco and Stavi,

if you ask me," he told Mari, following her down the staircase.

"Yeah, well. I'm still getting the feel of this whole business decision-maker thing. My father made it look so easy."

He didn't get a chance to ask her to elaborate. An inkling of unease skittered along the surface of his skin. Something was off about their surroundings. The air grew darker the farther down the steps they went when it should have been the opposite. It was also noticeably quieter than when they'd made their way up several minutes ago. Mari noticed it too, her pace slowing. A glance below showed nothing but pitch-black darkness at the ground level.

"The door must have swung shut due to a gust of wind," Matteo explained. He reached for her, taking her hand in his. One misstep and they were sure to tumble down several feet. As enticing as the idea of having Mari sprawled over him was, a perilous fall down a steep stairwell wasn't exactly what he'd have in mind.

"Just go nice and slow. Watch your step."

He heard her humph. "I can't watch anything. It's dark as midnight."

"It's a figure of speech."

"Right. Sure." Her voice shook on the last word. Matteo realized she wasn't being snappy. Mari was genuinely anxious. He gripped her hand tighter in reassurance.

"Relax. We'll be down to the bottom and out of here in no time."

The second part of that statement turned out to be a big, fat lie.

CHAPTER NINE

"WHAT DO YOU mean the door won't open?"

Matteo did his best to summon an even, non-alarming tone before he answered her. After all, Mari's voice held enough alarm for the both of them.

"It appears to have slammed shut. Hard enough that it's jammed now. It was much easier to push it open from the outside."

Pulling it open from inside, on the other hand, was proving rather difficult, especially given the inability to see in all the darkness. He pulled his cell phone out of his pocket and tapped the screen. Zero bars. "There's no cell reception here."

"I doubt there is on the entire island."

"There goes plan B. At least we can use the flashlight function." Setting the light on, he studied the bolt on the door. Yep, it was definitely jammed.

"Maybe if we both try to open the door together?" Mari suggested.

Matteo shrugged in answer, not that Mari could see him do so in all this blackness. Her form was barely more than a shadow.

"We can try," he answered. "But there's barely enough purchase on the small lever for me to get a firm grip. We'll never get more than two hands on it."

He could practically hear her trying to think through for a solution. Mari really didn't like being stranded. Not that he found it a joyous development himself, but Mari seemed overly anxious. It's not like they would be stuck here for days.

He wasn't even going to voice that idea out loud.

"Maybe if I hold on to the lever and you hold on to me," she suggested.

"It's worth a shot, I suppose." Maneuvering behind her, Matteo wrapped his arms around her middle, trying desperately to ignore the intimate nature of their positions. In any other universe… No, he wasn't going to complete that thought.

"Tell me when," he told Mari.

"Okay. Now!"

Matteo gave her a good yank. But the effort only had him stumbling backward, his hands still wrapped around her middle.

"I need a better grip," she told him. "Let's try again. Harder this time. Hold me tighter."

Matteo bit out a silent curse.

"Did you say something?" she asked.

"Just that I hope this works," he lied.

They didn't fare any better this time around.

"Let's just give it a few minutes," he suggested. "Stavi said they'd be back in no time. Maybe it hasn't been as long as it seems."

"That's not very specific though, is it? I mean, what exactly did he mean by 'no time'? We had to have been up top for at least half an hour. Shouldn't one of them be back by now?"

"They might be on their way at this very moment, Mari."

The light from the small device next to them cast shadows around her face. She looked ethereal, breathtakingly lovely with the small amount of light highlighting her sharp features. And wasn't this a time to be noticing how enticing she was.

"Maybe we should go back to the top and try yelling for them."

"I don't think that's a good idea. I consider it lucky that we didn't take a tumble on the way down. Why don't I go up alone? You wait here."

She immediately shook her head, her swaying hair swinging shadows along the stone walls. "I'd rather not stay down here by myself."

"I guess our only option is to hang tight, then. Give the guides a few minutes."

Even in the dim light, Matteo could see just how unexcited she was at that option. He didn't see much of a choice.

Mari must have come to the same conclusion. With a resigned sigh, she walked over to the nearest wall and leaned her back against it, crossing her feet at the ankles. In the tight space, he could smell the gentle fruity scent of her shampoo mingling with the tropical, coconut aroma of the lotion she'd applied while they'd been on the boat. It wasn't hard to imagine her sun-kissed skin even in the darkness.

He realized she was saying something. So deep in his thoughts of how her skin smelled, he hadn't even heard her words.

"There it is again," she said, her voice a high pitch. "Did you hear that?"

He hadn't. He hadn't even heard *her*.

"There's something in here with us!" That time he definitely heard her. The next moment, she had flung herself at him.

He wasn't prepared, hadn't really seen her coming, studying the ground for whatever it was she'd been referring to. He heard his cell phone go skating along the ground, then hit the wall. They both went toppling backward. Matteo hit the ground but barely registered the impact. Just like he'd imagined, Mari was sprawled on top of him. It took a moment to find his breath, though it had nothing to do with the physical hit he'd just taken. His breathlessness had everything to do with her.

"It's just the wind. We're alone, Mari."

"Oh." Her voice came out in a whisper, her breath hot against his chin. She made no effort to move off him, and he made no effort to take his arms off her.

The small light from his phone flickered once, then went completely out. The only sound now was her soft gasps. His body responded immediately as heat curled through his core and shot through his every cell.

"Matteo?"

The way she said his name turned the heat to scorching hot. He couldn't even be sure which one of them moved first. But in the next instant their lips were joined.

Matteo thrust his hands through her hair, pulling her closer. He'd never be able to get her close enough. Never be able to get enough of the way she tasted, felt against the length of his body.

Finally, a small voice of reason cried out in the back recesses of his brain. Though it would be so easy to continue kissing her, tasting her, pulling her ever so closer to him, Matteo knew he had to stop.

This wasn't the time or the place. With more strength than he would have guessed he possessed, he reluctantly let her go.

More.

The single word echoed through Mari's mind, emanating deep from her very soul. They'd always been headed here, hadn't they? Even that first day when he'd approached her, full of bluster and innuendo, deep in her core she'd known she was being faced with an attraction that was going to take her by surprise, sweep her off-balance. That she was powerless to stop it no matter what she'd vowed all those years ago about falling for someone again.

She'd just refused to admit it to herself. Until now.

Now there was no denying what her senses were crying out for. More of Matteo Talarico. The taste of him, the heat of him. The way he made her feel even when he wasn't touching her. The feel of his fingers thrust through her hair.

It was all so much better than she'd imagined. And oh, how she'd imagined. Even as recently as when they'd had lunch together on the beach.

She'd lied to him back then when he'd asked her what she'd been thinking of. Mari very well couldn't have admitted that it was this very thing that ruled her thoughts. She couldn't tell him that it was him on her mind. Kissing him. Being held by him. Who knew that the very thing she'd been fantasizing about would be happening just a few short hours later? But this was much better than any fantasy. She wrapped her arms around him tighter, pressed farther against his length. She would never be able to get enough.

Not like this.

Mari couldn't even be sure which one of them had spoken the words. But they flooded her mind like torrents of ice water splashed over her skin. This wasn't the time or the place.

"Mari," Matteo's voice sounded in her ears, speaking the words as if he'd read her mind. "This is not the time. And not the place. Not like this."

Heat rushed to her face as the shame flooded her. Thank heavens one of them had the sense of mind to say so. He was so very right. That didn't make pulling away from him any easier. The darkness made it hard to read his features. Mari couldn't decide if that was a good thing or not.

With trembling fingers, she rubbed her tingling lips. "Oh, my…"

"It's not that I don't want—"

She cut him off, couldn't listen to such words right now. "I know, Matteo. I'm not sure what just happened."

"I'm pretty sure I know," he countered, running his hands up her shoulders. "But when we're finally together, it won't be in a dark and damp basement."

When. He'd said *when.* As if it was a certainty, this thing between them.

Her mind began scrambling for the words to acknowledge his assumption, her heart pounding in her chest. But there was another pounding sound ringing in her ears, drawing her attention, coming from outside her head. Actually, the sound was coming from outside. *Outside.*

"I think someone's here finally," Matteo said, his breath hot against her face.

Right. Someone was at the door, knocking. That was what that noise was.

Mari wasn't sure whether to feel relieved or frustrated. Or both.

"We should probably go and answer," Matteo added gently. She realized with no small amount of shame that she'd made no effort to remove herself from his embrace. Not that he'd made any kind of effort to let her go either.

Scrambling for some sense of grounding, Mari pulled her arms from off his shoulders. Her lips tingled and she traced them with trembling fingers. The action didn't seem to be lost on Matteo. His eyes grew darker with heat. They were never going to answer the knocking at this rate.

"We really should get that," she prompted.

Still, it took several moments for either of them to move. When she finally managed to pull herself off him, Matteo slowly straightened and adjusted his collar. Mari's fingers itched to reach out and run her hands through his tousled hair. She resisted the urge. Matteo looked every bit a man who was just interrupted. Mari shuddered to think how her own state of disarray might appear. It wasn't going to take much extrapolation to figure out what might have happened in here between the two of them just now.

Whoever was at the door would undoubtedly put two and two together pretty quickly.

A few short seconds later, the door swung open with a loud squeaking noise. Light flooded through the doorway, framing Stavi in the frame.

The man gave them a sheepish shrug. "*Scusa*, Signora, Signore. We may have made a mistaken assumption."

"What kind of assumption?" Matteo asked, making Mari stifle another groan. She could only guess. Did Matteo have to make him spell it out?

"Well, we figured maybe you would appreciate some time alone in here together." Stavi looked off to the side; he didn't look particularly chagrined. More amused, actually.

Mari did her best to keep a lid on her emotions. It wasn't easy. "I'm not sure what would lead you to believe we'd like to be stuck here for so long. We left the gallery a while ago. It's dark and damp down here."

Stavi's eyebrows drew together, his lips tightened. His entire expression read "the lady doth protest too much." Mari dropped her gaze down to the floor, a rush of heat flooding her cheeks. She could only imagine the deep red color they would appear. Why did people keep assuming they were a couple anyway? The mother at the pier, these tour guides. Even Miyko was intent on throwing them together on this tour.

Stavi gestured to them to step out, speaking as she strode past him. "I hope this doesn't mean we won't get the contract."

This time, Mari did groan out loud. As far as what the last hour might mean, the contract wasn't even in her top ten.

By the time they made it back to the marina and met their chauffeur, Mari's heart had steadied somewhat. But not by much.

The events of the last few hours seemed like something out of a dream, as if they hadn't even happened.

But they had. She had kissed Matteo. And she could

have—probably would have, even—gone much further if not for the interruption.

After they'd gone a few miles, Matteo turned to her with a tight expression. "Look, Mari. About what just happened back there, I don't really know what to say. Only that this island seems to have triggered some kind of romantic impulse in me. And you're a very attractive woman."

Ouch. Despite the compliment at the end, Mari wanted to shrink into the seat at his words. He was basically telling her that their kiss was nothing personal. Nothing really to do with her.

"No explanation needed," was all she could come up with to say. Matteo cursed under his breath.

She tried not to let the disappointment of his words show on her face and turned to look out the window. The evening was growing dark; stars slowly began to twinkle in the royal blue sky. Of course, Matteo regretted what had happened back at the lighthouse. As he should. As she herself very well should. But her foolish heart was apparently much more pliant than Matteo's. Deep down, she had to admit the truth. Because the fact was, she didn't regret kissing him. Not one small bit. Oh, there was no doubt it had been a mistake. A colossal one she should have been smart enough to avoid. But that didn't make her want to take it back. She liked that her mouth had had the pleasure of tasting his.

What did any of that say about her? About the woman Mari had become when she hadn't even noticed? Ever since he'd entered the picture of her life, it was as if she'd become someone else in that short period of time. Someone who wantonly kissed a man in a deserted lighthouse and then didn't even feel the need for remorse despite the circumstances.

Matteo would be gone within hours. Mari had no clue when she would see him again. If ever.

She couldn't fathom he would come back to visit just to check on a small plot of land unless he chose to build a residence there. And why would he do that? His life was in Rome.

The rest of the ride consisted mostly of silence. Mari leaned her head back against the seat, feigning sleep. No words were going to do anything to alleviate the awkwardness between them, so why try at any kind of conversation?

In a matter of hours that felt like months, their car blessedly pulled to a stop in front of the Nautica. All Mari wanted right now was to scrub the day away in her phone-booth-sized shower and crawl into bed. Then she would somehow try to forget the events of the day. The evening sky had now grown dark navy. How late was it anyway? She got a clue to the answer when Matteo cursed again, louder this time, after glancing at his watch.

"What's the matter?"

"That little delay back there set my schedule back just enough that I don't think I can make my flight back to Rome tonight."

Oh no. A conflicting mishmash of both disappointment and joy warred within her chest. Matteo might not be leaving tonight, after all. But that was only going to be delaying the inevitable.

"Not unless by some miracle the flight has been delayed," he added, rubbing a palm down his face. The idea of having to spend another night here was clearly taxing him. Mari would try not to take that personally also.

"We can check at the front desk."

They entered the lobby to find said desk being manned by Lisette, one of the students from the university who covered during odd shifts or when the hotel was short-staffed. Like tonight when Miyko had already worked a full shift and Roberta was under the weather. Mari released a sigh of relief. At least something had gone her way tonight. She really didn't have it in her to deal with Miyko's teasing comments or knowing looks at the moment.

"Any issues, Lisette?" Mari asked, hoping fervently that the answer was no and that Signore Gio in particular had had a quiet evening.

"None. Just one message. Analisa asked me to tell you that she plans to call you in the morning. It's about the gala next week."

Analisa was the president at the university. Though what the woman needed to talk to her about regarding the annual fundraiser ball was lost on Mari. The event was going to be sad enough this year without Anna's presence.

After brief introductions, Mari made her way to the computer monitor and called up the airline site. The screen loaded information on upcoming flights. Nothing appeared to be delayed.

Matteo bit out another curse. The pirate cruise must have had an effect on him. He was swearing like a sailor all of a sudden. Or maybe he was just growing more comfortable in her presence. She didn't have the time or sense of mind to analyze that possibility just now.

"Looks like I'm stuck here another night," he said above Mari's shoulder.

Stuck.

His use of that particular word struck Mari harder than it should have.

"Guess I'll need the room again," he added a moment later.

Lisette's head snapped up, confusion etched across her face. Mari knew what was coming. She came perilously close to uttering a curse herself, her mind scrambling for a fix before the other woman made the announcement. "But there are no free rooms, Signore. We are full this evening." She motioned to the door behind her. "We've taken the liberty of moving your bags to the storage room. Miyko led me to believe you would be checking out this evening."

Matteo blinked at Lisette, then turned to her and blinked some more. Mari could practically visualize his trying to process the ramifications. "You mean I have to try and find another place to stay? Isn't there anywhere I can room here? A utility closet?" He pointed to the same door. "That storage room, perhaps."

Sure. Either of those options might make sense if he was okay sleeping upright. They were both barely bigger than a phone booth.

There really was only one other option, other than tossing Matteo out on to the street. Which, truth be told, did hold a certain appeal.

She spoke quickly, before she could change her mind, hoping against hope that she wasn't making yet another colossal mistake given what had almost happened between them at the lighthouse. "You can stay in my suite."

CHAPTER TEN

MATTEO WASN'T SO sure how wise this was. But it wasn't as if he'd had much choice.

Following Mari into her apartment with his bags in tow, he thought of all the other options. Maybe he should have chosen to just wander the streets until morning.

Standing across the room by the door, Mari sent him a soft smile. "I know the place is rather small. But it's just the one night. Hopefully you can find a way to make yourself comfortable."

Hardly likely. But not in the way she might think.

Mari continued. "I'm sorry, I know it's not quite what you're used to."

Here she was actually apologizing when she was gracious enough to let him spend the night in her apartment. She could have easily sent him on his way, told him to bide his time at the airport. Or anywhere else.

In a previous life, he might have been tempted to take advantage of the situation. But not now. Not with Mari. With Mari, he was going to do his best to remain the utmost gentleman until this trial of a night led to morning.

"Please don't apologize," he said, setting his bags down by the kitchen counter. "This is more than hospitable of you. I'm the one who should be sorry about the inconvenience."

Mari glanced off to the side, as if unsure what to say.

They were walking on proverbial eggshells. As if they were barely more than strangers forced to share a small space for the night. As if he hadn't been holding her tight against his chest, tasting her while she straddled him just a few hours ago.

"You should probably take the bed," she told him. "You're much too big for the—"

He wasn't even going to let her finish that sentence. "Absolutely not. The couch is fine. I am not going to kick you out of your own bed, Mari."

"But—"

He held a hand up before she could argue any further. "Don't even bother, it's out of the question. Like you said, this is only for one night."

She nodded once. "Right. Let me get you a pillow and some covers, then. I'll be right back."

Matteo watched her stride to her bedroom and rubbed a hand down his face. Eyeing the couch, he had to acknowledge just how small it indeed was. Barely more than a love seat. But he would make do, even sleep sitting up if he had to.

Something told him he wasn't about to get much shut-eye anyway. Not with knowing Mari was just a few feet away.

She returned carrying an oversize pillow and thick knit cover. "Well, good night, then," she said, handing him the items.

"Good night."

Mari offered a small smile before heading into her bedroom and shutting the door. By the time Matteo slipped on his nightwear, turned off the light and got under the blanket, he couldn't hear her rustling around behind her door any longer.

His mind wandered to all sorts of unwanted places. Was she asleep already? Was she a light sleeper? What did she wear to bed? Did she like comfortable pajamas or something basic like shorts and a T-shirt? Or a skimpy nightie? His breath hitched and then stopped altogether at the next option—maybe she slept wearing nothing at all.

With a self-aimed curse, Matteo tossed to his side a bit too forcefully. In the process, he flung out his arm and smacked it against the center wooden coffee table. A loud thud echoed through the room at the contact followed by another even louder one as the table toppled over.

Mari's door flung open another moment later. "Is everything all right? What happened?" she asked, flipping the wall switch. Bright light bathed the room. She held her hand against her chest.

Matteo sat up, cursing himself silently. "Nothing. I just appear to be uncharacteristically clumsy these days. I'm sorry I woke you."

Well, on the bright side, at least a couple of his earlier questions were now answered. Mari wore an oversize, long-sleeved shirt and baggy gym shorts that hung low on her hips. Matteo's eyes fell to her shapely tanned thighs before he shut them tight. How in the world could a woman look so sexy wearing the most casual attire? When he opened his lids, he made sure to focus on her face.

Her gaze traveled over him to the upended table, then back to where he sat on the sofa. A determined look washed over her features.

"That settles it. You will be sleeping on the bed, and I'll sleep out here."

His answer to that was simple. "No."

She slammed her hands on her hips. "I will crawl over you and struggle to push you off if I have to."

That particular image had blood shooting to various parts of Matteo's body. Mari's eyes grew wide as she realized what she'd said, and a slight flush of pink spread across her cheeks.

"Mari, I'll be fine out here," Matteo insisted, though the mess on the floor said otherwise.

Mari released a loud sigh. "Look, this is silly. We're both adults. I have a wide bed. Let's just share it and make sure to stay on our respective sides. You can do that, can't you?" She threw out the last statement like some kind of challenge.

Matteo wasn't about to admit that it just might be a challenge he could very well fail.

Maybe this wasn't such a great idea.

Every cell in Mari's body was fully aware of the man lying on his side with his back to her less than a foot away on the mattress. She'd clearly misjudged the size of said mattress. It seemed much smaller now with Matteo atop it. In fact, her entire room felt much smaller with him in it. She could barely make out his shadow in the darkness. The lack of a visual seemed to add to their closeness somehow. Why had she never thought to plug a night-light in? Did she have any in the house anywhere? Perhaps she should go look.

"I'm keeping you awake, aren't I?" Matteo's voice sounded through the darkness. "Just by being here. I should leave."

Mari threw her arm over her eyes. So much for pretending slumber.

"That's not necessary. Besides, it's not just you." Maybe

just like 95 percent or so. But she was telling the truth. There were actually other things on her mind keeping it from shutting down for the night.

"Oh? How's that?" Matteo asked.

Mari sucked in a deep breath. She shouldn't have said anything. Should have just offered Matteo warm milk or something and gotten some for herself. Instead, she'd opened the door to further conversation. And she couldn't seem to stop.

"At the lighthouse," she began, seemingly unable to stop herself. Then she couldn't seem to come up with more to say. Several beats passed in awkward silence.

"Yes?" Matteo finally prompted.

"I'd like to explain."

"Mari, you don't have to say anything."

"No. It's not… That isn't what I mean." If he was referring to the kiss, heaven knew there was no way to explain *that*. She wanted to explain her reaction at realizing they were stuck with the door jammed.

"Then?"

"The way I panicked. When we couldn't get out. That isn't how I am. I mean, now. And before I wasn't either." Mari stifled a groan of frustration. Now she was just jumbling her words. There was no use. "Never mind. Forget it."

Matteo turned to her in the darkness. "Please go on, Mari. I want to know. Before what?"

Before her life was completely altered in ways she would have never expected. Suddenly, she wished fervently that she'd never opened this can of worms. Where to even start?

"Tell me," Matteo prodded, his voice soft and gentle, barely more than a whisper.

"I'm not sure where to start, really," she admitted. "I just wanted you to know that the way I panicked, when we were trapped. I wasn't always like that."

"What were you like?"

"I was clearheaded. Calm. The type of person who looks for solutions rather than panicking. I'd like to think I'm back to behaving that way again. Though you wouldn't know it from my reaction to the jammed lighthouse door this afternoon."

"Mari, don't think anything of it. I certainly didn't. You behaved as many people might under such circumstances."

"That's just it. There was a time when I would have kept a cooler head. I thought I'd worked my way back to being that person again, here in Sardinia."

"Tell me," he repeated.

"Everything changed when I lost my father. It was rather unexpected. I wasn't prepared."

"What about your mother?"

She scoffed. "She walked out when I was barely a teen. I came home from middle school one day and she just wasn't there. All her things were gone. It was just Papa and me after that."

"He was a good father."

"The absolute best."

She couldn't even be sure why she was getting into all this. The past was the past. But now that the words were flowing, she couldn't seem to pull them back.

"I was barely twenty when I lost him," she continued. "Attending Boston College, not too far from home in the North End."

"The North End," Matteo supplied. "Boston's Little Italy."

She nodded, not that he could really see her. It really was cave-like dark in here. She'd never actually realized before just how black the nights were in her room.

"I came home weekends to help in the restaurant," she told him. "A restaurant I'd been groomed to take over since I was a child."

"What happened?"

Mari sucked in a breath as the memories washed over her, painful and cutting. In the darkness, the scenes played before her eyes like a sad movie. "My father was an excellent parent and a skilled chef. But he wasn't the best planner. He left us vulnerable."

"Vulnerable how?"

"My uncle swooped in like a vulture. All too ready to take over an established business he had no hand in creating or nurturing over the years. A business I was trained to take over when the time came."

"He pushed you out?"

If only that had been the extent of it. "First he tried to tell me I couldn't handle it. That I didn't have what it took to run a restaurant. I pushed back. Told him that I had to try. When that didn't work, he tried a much more cunning way."

"What was that?"

Mari took a deep, shaky breath before she could continue. "A wealth of earnings went mysteriously missing. He accused me of stealing from the restaurant, which wasn't technically mine yet."

Mari heard Matteo's sharp intake of breath next to her. She made herself continue. In for a penny and all that. "He had enough contacts in Boston PD who believed him. He threatened to have me prosecuted if I didn't simply walk away."

"Mari, I don't know what to say."

"No number of employees or neighbors or business contacts were enough to vouch for me. It was my uncle's plan from the moment he heard of my father's death if I didn't succumb willingly. And it worked."

"So you left."

She gulped past the painful lump in the base of her throat, forced herself to continue. Too late to stop now. To her surprise, she found she didn't really want to. "Yep. Walked away from the restaurant, college, the only home I'd ever known."

"Do you think he really might have pulled it off?"

"I don't know. I was scared and alone."

"There was no one at all you could turn to for support?" he asked.

More painful memories assaulted her. "I was seeing someone, but he turned out not to be the person I thought he was."

"In what way?"

"He was from a well-known, established Brahmin family. A family who couldn't really see me as one of them. When the ugly business with my uncle went down, he found he agreed with them."

"Please don't tell me he believed your uncle's lies."

"He never came out and said so. But I think at least a part of him did. In any case, he wasn't going to risk being associated with someone who might be prosecuted. Or worse, depending on the outcome."

Another long sigh echoed through the darkness. "Do you think your uncle would have gone through with it?"

"I simply couldn't risk it. By then I'd lost Papa, the man I thought I'd spend my life with, and my future taking over my father's dream. I couldn't take any more chances."

"I see."

"I had fantasies of returning one day and making him pay for all his deceptions. After a while, it just didn't seem worth it. I'd found another home with Anna, after all."

Matteo stayed quiet for the longest time. So long, Mari embarrassingly wondered if he might have actually fallen asleep on her. Finally, she heard him suck in a breath before speaking. "Don't ever doubt yourself, Mari. Especially not for being human. Anyone would be impressed with all that you've accomplished after being blindsided by someone who should have been looking out for you. And then abandoned by the man who should have had your back."

She sniffled, then rubbed a palm over her nose. "Thank you for saying that."

"It's true. And something tells me you would have gotten there with or without meeting Anna."

She wanted to argue that. Anna had quite literally saved her. But suddenly exhaustion simply overtook her.

Mari couldn't recall the exact moments after her unexpected purge of emotion. Or even the exact moment she'd fallen asleep.

When she opened her eyes next, the room was lit up with a bright ray of sunshine pouring through the high window.

And she lay curled up tight against Matteo in his arms.

This really was no time to dillydally. After having been away from the Nautica all day yesterday, Mari really needed to get downstairs and see to her duties, starting with greeting all the guests who were due to arrive today and checking the status of various operations that kept the place running. Instead, here she sat in a thick terry bathrobe barely dried off as Matteo took his turn in her small shower. It was hard not to imagine him in there, the way his large frame would take up the entire space. His body tight in the small quarters.

The body that was snuggled up against her most of the night.

If she were a different kind of woman, she might throw caution to the wind, throw her robe off and march back in there with clear invitation, duties and consequences be damned. Heat swirled in the pit of her stomach as a flush rose to her cheeks. No strings, no attachments. After all, the man was leaving today for who knew how long. Which should have been a relief yet somehow had her feeling hollow and disheartened.

What might Matteo's reaction be if she did barge in there? She had a hunch he wouldn't turn her away.

And then what?

Mari gave her head a brisk shake. The reality was, she simply wasn't that kind of woman. The other reality was Matteo's impending departure back to Rome. All of which meant her best course of action right now was to get up off her mattress, stop her useless imaginings and get downstairs to tend to her responsibilities.

Ten minutes later, that's exactly where she was headed. When she arrived at the front desk, Miyko and Roberta were both there. Both of them snapped their heads in her direction, Miyko's left eyebrow rose so high it stood an inch above his glasses frame. Roberta was giving her the side-eye with a knowing look.

Mari was so not in the mood. "Not one word. From either of you."

"But Mari," Miyko began, stopping abruptly when Mari lifted her palm up.

Walking behind the desk, she pulled the main office laptop over to her to check the flight status of impending guest arrivals.

"Has anyone arrived early?" she asked.

Miyko huffed before answering. "Not yet. Has a particular somebody left yet? You know, after spending the night in your apartment."

Roberta chuckled softly behind them.

Mari released a resigned sigh. Apparently she had no hope of avoiding the proverbial elephant in the room.

"Matteo simply needed a place to stay for the night, Miyko. There really is nothing more to it than that."

"Hmm, pity."

Mari was going to ignore that. "He's getting ready to leave for the airport as we speak."

"Too bad he wasn't given a reason to stay."

Before Mari could come up with a response to that ridiculous statement, the lobby doors slid open and a familiar face strode in. Analisa Mangiani, president, University de Cagliari. A petite woman with a perky disposition, Analisa had risen in the ranks from professor to dean to president in an impressive short span of time. All well deserved. Mari just now recalled Lisette mentioning the other woman would be calling. Looked like she'd decided to stop by instead.

"Mari, *buongiorno*. How are you, dear?" she asked after acknowledging the others.

"Fine," Mari answered. "What a pleasant surprise. What brings you here this morning?"

"I love this part of the city. The beach, the cliff, the pathway. Gave me an excuse to come."

"What did?"

"I wanted to talk to you about the international student gala next week."

Mari hadn't had a chance to think about the annual event given all that was happening here at the hotel. Every summer around this time, the university held an extravagant ball in honor of all the American and other foreign students who were attending for special programs during the summer weeks. Officially, it was a party for the students and faculty who taught them, but the real intent was that it worked as a fundraiser aimed at the often well-to-do parents. With auctions, raffles and mild asks for donations, the yearly event was usually a successful moneymaker. One in which Mari always felt underdressed and out of place. This year would be no different, no doubt.

"What about it?"

"Well, I wanted to tell you in person. We want to add a small ceremony."

"Ceremony?"

Analisa nodded. "In Anna's honor. For all that she's done for the university and students over the years."

Mari felt an unexpected sting behind her eyelids. The thought that Anna was being posthumously honored by the university she cared for so much touched a central part of her soul. She would have been beyond honored indeed. "That's really lovely of you, Analisa. I know she would have appreciated it."

"It's no less than she deserved," the woman answered.

"We'd like to present a gold plaque to hang in the lobby or anywhere else you deem fit."

"We would be thrilled to display it. Thank you."

"And you would be the one I present it to at the gala," Analisa added. "I can't think of anyone more appropriate."

Matteo chose that moment to exit the elevator and stride into the lobby. He approached the desk, his eyes firmly focused on her until he finally reached them.

"Good morning," he said to the room in general.

Everyone but Mari returned his greeting. She couldn't seem to find her words. Her skin automatically heated, her body recalling the way his arms had felt around her.

He was leaving.

Matteo turned to Analisa with a polite smile. Mari finally found her senses.

"Matteo, this is Analisa Mangiani. She's the president at the university."

After introducing her, Mari explained the reason for the other woman's visit.

"Lovely to meet you," Analisa told him with a pleasant smile and delicate handshake.

"Matteo is a distant cousin of Anna's," Mari explained.

Analisa's eyes grew wide and her jaw fell. "Anna's cousin? Really?"

Matteo nodded in response. Mari could sense what was about to happen and simply couldn't process how she felt about it.

Analisa confirmed her guess with her next words directed at Matteo. "Well, as Anna's kin, you simply must attend the university gala next week when we'll be honoring her. Consider this a personal invitation from me."

CHAPTER ELEVEN

One week later

MATTEO EXITED THE car and adjusted the collar of his tuxedo shirt, an unfamiliar sensation of nervousness swirling in his midsection. He hadn't spoken to Mari since he'd left Cagliari a week ago, aside from a simple text asking if they might arrive at the university gala together, to which she'd surprisingly answered yes.

Funny how the fates had him back here when he was convinced a week ago that he was walking away for a good, long time. At least until he figured out how to proceed. The time he'd spent with Mari had been nothing short of paradigm shifting. His entire plan, to find a way to have her give up ownership of the Nautica, was now in question. He'd made his mind up upon awakening with her in his arms that morning after she'd poured her heart out to him the night before.

She was the rightful owner. And she was good at managing the hotel. Where that left him, he had no clue. Considering that his own circumstances, and that of Tala Industries, hadn't changed, the situation posed nothing short of a reset. He had to find another way to reestablish the family business. How exactly he was going to do that was a mystery.

Unfortunately, he was still no closer to a solution seven

days later. Which begged the question, why was he even here? He didn't have time to indulge in attending fancy parties.

But he knew very well why, of course. This party gave him a chance to see her again.

A text appeared on his phone as soon as he walked through the sliding double doors.

I'll be down in a minute. Sorry for the wait. Just finishing up.

The woman really couldn't help apologizing for no reason. Besides, something told him she would be worth the wait. He wasn't wrong. When Mari appeared moments later from the hallway that led to her apartment, Matteo had to remind himself to breathe.

A shade of red he couldn't recall ever seeing before, her dress hugged her curves in all the right places and brought out the subtle auburn highlights in her hair. Rimmed in black, her eyes sparkled like jewels. Her rich, thick hair sat atop her head in some kind of complicated knot with a few tendrils escaping to flow softly against her cheeks.

He wasn't sure what he'd been expecting but she'd exceeded anything he might have imagined.

"What is it?" she asked after several beats of silence when he couldn't seem to get his mouth to work. "I never know what to wear to this thing. Do you not think this works?"

Matteo had to release a breath before answering. "Oh, it works. It works very, very well." Try as he might, he couldn't seem to keep his eyes from traveling over her entire body, down to her strappy shoes.

Mari's mouth opened into a small O and a pink flush spread over her cheeks. He really shouldn't have said what he had. Recovering, he cleared his throat and held out his elbow. "Shall we?"

She blinked several times before taking his arm and following him out to the car. In a manner of minutes, they were approaching the tall iron gates of Cagliari University. A uniformed guard approached their vehicle, asking for their credentials before letting them through. Moments later, he was leading Mari through a large set of wooden doors opened for them by more uniformed attendants and into a grand ballroom with a glittering chandelier dangling from the high ceiling. The party appeared to be in full swing with an orchestral band playing beyond a high-gloss dance floor.

Mari's hand tightened on his arm. Matteo realized she was tense all over, her lips a tight thin line.

"Large crowds make me nervous," she admitted, ducking her head as if embarrassed.

He didn't get a chance to answer as they were immediately approached by a tall gentleman wearing a dark suit and wire-rimmed glasses. He looked somewhat familiar.

"Mari! You're here finally." The man faltered on the last word as his eyes landed on Mari's hand on his arm, then on Matteo's face. His smile instantly faded.

"You're here, too," he added rather solemnly.

"You remember Professor Antonio Giraldi?" Mari said just as Matteo placed who the other man was. The professor they'd run into that night at dinner. He'd looked equally as disappointed with Matteo's presence then as he did now.

"Of course," Matteo said, reaching his hand out, which

the professor barely touched in a poor excuse for a hand-shake.

"Can I get you a drink?" Antonio asked Mari, as if Matteo wasn't even there.

"We've just arrived, Antonio," Mari said with a pleasant, friendly smile. "Still getting our bearings."

"Of course," the other man answered, finally deigning to glance in Matteo's direction only to give him a withering stare. "Save me a dance, then?" he said, his eyes returning to Mari and lingering on her much too long before finally turning and walking away.

Matteo had never felt a stronger desire to punch another man in the face. Ridiculous really. It wasn't as if he had any claim to Mari. They weren't even here with each other as some kind of date. Simply together in Anna's honor to accept her posthumous award.

All that aside, he'd be damned if Mari danced with anyone but him tonight.

Mari tried in vain to quell the shaking in her middle as she glanced about the ballroom. All the usual suspects were here, which included several of Sardinia's most well-endowed families and the top scions of business. As nervous and out of place as she usually felt at this event, tonight Mari was particularly fraught with anxiety. Maybe it was the prospect of having to go up on stage and accept Anna's award.

She was only fooling herself. Her nervousness had more to do with *him*. Matteo.

She'd almost turned him down when he'd texted to suggest they arrive at the ball together. But what possible reason might she have given to do that? Tell him how right she'd been about the butterflies in her stomach that appeared when he was near her? Or how she hadn't been able to get those hours they'd spent together out of her mind?

No. It was better to forget all that anyway.

All she had to do tonight was graciously accept Anna's honor, make the rounds with polite small talk. And do her best to ignore the effect the man at her side was having on her.

Easier said than done.

It didn't help that all eyes appeared to be on the two of them, with more than a few pairs of female peepers locked on Matteo in particular.

"Hey, try to relax," he said beside her now. "If you want, I can come up with you."

She blinked at him in confusion.

"When you accept the plaque," he clarified.

As far as she was concerned, that was a foregone conclusion. "I assumed we'd be accepting it together."

To her astonishment, he lifted his hand to rub the back of it gently along her cheek. "I'll come up with you, but you'll be the one speaking and accepting the honor, Mari. It's more rightfully your place to do so."

The depths behind his eyes and the solemnity of his words held so much meaning, Mari wasn't quite sure what to make of it.

"I have no doubt you'll know exactly what to say," he added a moment later. "Now, let's get that first drink, shall we?"

With that, the subject was changed before she could think of the right questions to ask. How did he keep doing that to her anyway? Making her lose her train of thought, barely managing to find the right words to say to him.

Tonight, maybe it had something to do with the way the man looked in a tailored tuxedo that fit him like a glove. The way the dark fabric brought out his bronze skin and dark eyes. How she could see the muscles of his toned arms under the fabric of his sleeves.

It was more likely all of the above.

Mari accepted the flute of champagne he handed her with no small amount of gratitude. As much as bubbly went to her head, she was going to need the liquid courage to go up on stage when Analisa asked.

As if her thoughts had conjured her, the other woman strode over to them with a wide smile. "There you are. Ready to do the honors?"

Mari tightened her grip on the flute as a wave of panic surged through her. Already? She wasn't anywhere near to being ready, had barely had three sips of the champagne. And she certainly wasn't about to slam the rest of the glass down her throat. That would only lead to a different set of issues later on in the evening as the bubbly went to her head all at once.

A sensation of warmth appeared at the base of her spine. Matteo had placed his hand on the small of her back. His heat traveled slowly up her body, soothing her as it spread.

"You can do this," he said softly against her ear.

The words and motion catapulted her back several days to the moment in the lobby when he'd wordlessly lent her much-needed support as she was being chastised by Signore Gio. He was doing it again now, just as effectively.

The man had some kind of magic touch she couldn't explain. At the moment, Mari was more than grateful for it.

"Would you like me to come up wi—"

Mari didn't even let him finish the sentence. "Yes, please. Absolutely."

Depositing her glass on a nearby tray, she moved toward the stage following Analisa and making sure that Matteo was fast on her heels. Accepting the plaque and her quick speech of thanks had tears springing in her eyes as she recounted Anna's many contributions. The moment passed in a blur, but before Mari knew it, she was nodding in acknowledgment to a loud round of applause. Finally, she made her way back down on wobbly legs. Matteo held on to her arm the entire time. Or maybe she'd been the one holding on to his. Mari couldn't even be sure. Analisa gave her a tight hug at the base of the steps, then ascended them herself to announce the dancing portion of the evening.

"I could certainly use the rest of that champagne now," she told Matteo, beyond relieved that part of the evening was over.

Matteo tipped his head toward her. "You've more than earned it and I will be honored to get you a fresh glass. I only ask one thing in return."

"What's that?"

"That I be granted the added honor of dancing with you after."

Matteo knew he was asking for something he shouldn't want.

But he wasn't about to pass up the opportunity to dance with Mari. Not when he had no idea if such an opportunity would ever arise again. Watching her up there as she spoke about Anna, the way she pushed past her apprehension, the words of appreciation so sincere and heartfelt, he wanted to take her in his arms and kiss her as soon as she was done. He'd settle for swaying with her in his arms.

"I have a better idea, in that case," she began and his heart stopped that she was about to turn down his request. Time seemed to stop until she finished the statement. "I think we should skip the champagne and head straight to the dance floor."

The surge of sheer pleasure at her words made him feel like a besotted teen who'd just asked the prettiest girl in school to prom. Without another word, he led Mari to the dance floor and took her into his arms. The urge to snuggle his face into her hair was almost unbearable. The way she felt up against him, the fruity scent of her hair, her smooth skin. His senses were on overload. Slowly, they began to move in sync to the soft notes of the slow ballad. They may as well have been the only two people in the ballroom. Or even the entire planet. The song came to an end and Mari made no move to step out of his arms. So he simply continued holding her, swaying with her until the next one came on.

Three more songs played but Matteo had lost all sense of time. To him, the music had become one long melody. The two of them hadn't even stopped moving in between the changes.

"Looks like the band is taking a break," Mari said, her words pushing through his hypnotic state. There was no other way to describe it.

"Right," he said, reluctantly letting her go. "I guess we should finally go get that drink now."

"I think I'd rather get some air, if it's all the same with you," she countered.

"I think that's a great idea." He could use a good dose

of night air himself. Maybe it might help him to pull his thoughts and senses together.

Though he rather doubted it.

They made their way outside and kept walking until they reached a majestic fountain in the middle of a grassy rectangular garden. The shimmering lights of the city below framed the scene like they were in some kind of divine work of art.

Funny, he'd never realized before coming to Cagliari the breathtaking views a city built on so many hills would afford.

"You were perfect up there," he told her, just to have something to say.

Mari stared out into the flowing water of the fountain. "I'd be hard-pressed to recall exactly what I said even. Despite having rehearsed multiple speeches, I still wasn't quite sure what the right words would be."

"You picked the right ones."

She turned to him then, her eyes darkened with appreciation. And, heaven help him, with longing. She shifted ever so slightly closer, her head moving toward his. It was his undoing, the head tilt. Before he knew it, his lips were on hers, her arms wrapped around his shoulders. She tasted like the freshest fruit and the sweetest honey. Every inch of her felt right up against him. Time became a continuum. As did their most intimate moments spent so far together—the embrace in the lighthouse, waking up with her in his arms that morning in her room, slow dancing with her moments ago. He knew then without a doubt that he wanted more of those scenes. So much more.

"I'm glad you came back," Mari said, her breath hot against his lips. Her words sent arrows of pleasure through his heart as the feel of her shot lightning bolts through his core. She sounded like a woman who might have missed him while he'd been gone.

"Me too. For what it's worth, I think I'll be coming back more often."

She tightened her grip on him then and he thought he might die from the pleasure of it.

"And staying longer when you do, I hope."

"Is that an invitation?"

She nodded against him. "An open one. Do you think you'll accept?"

Like he had any choice in the matter given all the sweet ecstasy he was feeling at the moment. He wanted to find the words to answer her, but his mind was a scrambled mess. Nothing but the pleasure of tasting her registered. Were they secluded enough out here to take things any further? He wanted desperately to find out.

The question was answered in a frustrating negative a moment later. A spattering of voices sounded from behind them as a group of chatting and laughing students rounded the garden and drew closer. Mari pulled away and made to step out of his embrace. With great reluctance, he finally let her go, though it was downright painful to do so.

"We should probably head back inside," she said, breathless. The students had joined them at the fountain, now fully engrossed in their own giggly conversation.

"That does it," he announced once they'd stepped back into the ballroom. "I'm getting both of us that drink finally."

"You have no argument from me," Mari answered, flashing him a sweet, rather shy smile.

Matteo resisted the urge to take her hand and drop a

kiss on the inside of her palm. He had every intention of doing so later tonight when he finally got her alone again. Along with myriad other things he would love to do to her. All of which involved much more privacy than they were afforded at the moment.

Making his way to the bar, he nearly groaned out loud when he was intercepted. The president, Analisa, stepped in front of him before he could pretend not to see her and ditch the distraction.

"We're so glad you joined us this evening," she said with genuine warmth. "Anna meant a lot to this place. Happy to have her kin join us here as we honor her contributions."

"Happy to be here."

"Mari usually comes with Anna. It would have been hard for her to attend alone."

Except she probably wouldn't have been alone for long. Matteo could think of at least one besotted professor who wouldn't have left her side. He pushed the thought aside.

"It's clear Anna meant a lot to her," he supplied, wishing this conversation was over already so he could get back to the subject of all this talking they were doing.

Analisa nodded. "The feeling was mutual. Mari arrived in Anna's life just at the right time. Made sure all of Anna's affairs were in order."

A flash of unpleasant suspicion shot through his gut. Matteo chose to ignore it. Analisa wasn't saying anything about Mari that wasn't completely innocent.

Still, he couldn't stop from asking the next question. "How so?"

Analisa shook her head in solemn sincerity. "As soon as Anna got the terrible news about her condition, Mari was at her side constantly. Taking her to all the medical treatments, spending time with her. And as if that wasn't enough, she made sure to make all the right appointments regarding the hotel and that all the right paperwork was filed to ensure the Nautica continued to run without any hiccups. And that the university was taken care of as well."

Shadows began to shift behind Matteo's vision. Appointments. Paperwork. Affairs put in order.

Matteo tried to brush off the feelings of dread that invaded his soul. He was simply being paranoid. Analisa was simply explaining all the ways Mari was a devoted companion to Anna during her final days.

Only… It was all rather convenient, wasn't it? Upon examination, facts were facts, after all. All the evidence seemed to point to one feasible conclusion.

He bit the inside of his lip to keep from cursing out loud, hard. What a gullible fool he was. Exactly like his old man. He'd been so blinded by his attraction to her that he'd missed what was so blatantly obvious. Mari was there to make sure Anna signed all the documents she would need to determine whom her primary beneficiary would be. For all he knew, she'd held Anna's hand in hers to ensure the right line was signed. The one that gave her ownership of the hotel.

Thwarted in her takeover of her father's business, she'd managed to find a substitute.

Looked like the apple didn't fall far from the tree, after all. Matteo had fallen for the charms of an attractive woman who had led him to believe all that she'd wanted him to.

Like father like son.

CHAPTER TWELVE

MARI COULD SWEAR she was floating on air. The pleasure of Matteo's kiss still burned against her lips, the taste of him lingered on her tongue. If they hadn't been interrupted, she wasn't sure where things might have led right there by the fountain. Though part of her was relieved, more of her was frustrated that they hadn't gotten the chance to see where the kiss may lead. The night was still young, however. All sorts of possibilities still remained.

First and foremost, she was going to ask Matteo to dance with her again. Then later, she planned to ask him back to the hotel with her. For a nightcap. And hopefully much, much more.

Exhilaration and excitement pumped through her veins. Now that she'd made the decision, she knew without a doubt exactly what she wanted.

She wanted Matteo.

She traced him approaching from the other side of the room. Funny, he wasn't holding any flutes. Was he that anxious to dance with her again that he'd forgone the refreshments? A feminine thrill surged through her at the thought. Her feet automatically moved toward him to meet him closer to the dance floor. Then she stopped dead in her tracks at the sight of the expression on his face.

Something was terribly, terribly wrong.

"What's the matter?" she asked when he reached her side, afraid of what the answer might be. "You look as if you'd like to smash a fist through a wall."

"Very astute observation, Ms. Renati. But that's just one of your qualities, isn't it?"

Mari could only blink in confusion. "I don't understand. My qualities?"

He was practically glaring at her. "That's right. Among many. Astute, opportunistic, cunning. I could go on."

Was he really talking about her in such a way? The fury in his eyes directed toward her clearly told her he was.

It took a moment for the accusations to fully register. When they did, Mari's own ire bubbled and tipped over. How dare he!

She took a deep breath through gritted teeth. "I have no idea what you're on about, but we are not having this conversation here."

"That's where you're wrong," he threw out. "We're not having this conversation at all. There's nothing to talk about." With that, he pivoted on his heel and strode out of the ballroom. Mari had no choice but to chase after him.

She reached the circular driveway to find him waiting on the chauffeur who soon appeared with the car.

They'd ridden about a half a mile when she couldn't stand the loaded silence any longer.

"Stop the car, please," she pleaded with the driver. She had to get out into the night air. She was going to be sick.

They pulled up in front of the concrete steps of a grand church. Mari fled the car as soon as it came to a stop. The building was one of her favorites here in town. Renaissance architecture and stone statues of cherubs along the tall ascending steps. Right now, none of that beauty so much as registered as she sucked in much-needed air.

"Are you about ready?" his deep voice eventually sounded from behind her.

No. She wasn't ready. Not for any of this. What in the world had gotten into him that he was treating her this way all of a sudden?

Steeling herself, she turned to face him. "Don't you think you owe me an explanation for the way you're behaving? Is that too much to ask?" she demanded to know. Funny, she recalled making a similar inquiry of Trevor all those years ago. When he'd told her he was done with her, that her life had gotten too messy and complicated for someone like him to deal with.

"I have a question for you first," he threw out, his eyes still dark with anger in the glowing light of the streetlamps.

"Fine, you go first, then." Anything to get this godforsaken night over with. To think, she'd been looking forward to extending it. To actually spending the night with him. Now, she didn't even recognize the man who was looking at her with such disdain.

"You said you came here to Sardinia after being accused of theft."

Mari's heart pounded harder in her chest. The conversation had taken a turn she would have never seen coming. Where exactly was he going with this?

"That's right. By my uncle. What's your question?"

He slammed his hands into his trouser pockets. "Was it really a baseless accusation? Or did you actually do it?"

This couldn't be happening. Mari couldn't believe the

words Matteo had just so angrily thrown out. Didn't he realize they could never be taken back?

Perhaps she'd heard them incorrectly. Maybe the loud roaring echoing in her ears had muddled what he'd said.

But that was wishful thinking. Still, she couldn't keep from wanting to be certain. "What did you just ask me?" Her question came out raspy, strained. It was a wonder she'd managed to speak at all. "Did you really just ask if I was a thief?"

Matteo swallowed before he spoke. "You're not answering the question."

So she had heard him right. A stream of ice flushed under her skin. The roaring in her ears grew louder. How was any of this happening? Mere minutes ago she was kissing this man with her arms wrapped tight around him.

Now, he was accusing her of the very same ugliness she'd been subjected to before she'd left the States to start a new life. And here she thought she'd overcome her past. Had even let her guard down enough to open her heart to the man who was currently stomping on it.

"Still no answer? Then how about you tell me whether it was Anna's idea to hand over the hotel to you," Matteo bit out, his lips a tight angry line. Lips that had been passionately on hers before whatever had caused him to ask her questions so offensive and hurtful.

Where was this coming from? Mari ultimately didn't really care what the impetus might be for all that was happening right now. All that mattered was Matteo had come to the conclusion that she was dishonorable. Worse, that she might be a thief. All without giving her the benefit of the doubt, or so much as giving her a chance to get to the bottom of his anger.

Reflexively, she straightened her spine until she stood rod straight. "That's because I refuse to dignify the question with a response."

The line of his tight lips turned into a smirk. "How convenient for you."

She might have laughed at that statement if it wasn't all so tragic. For some reason, all these years later, she stood confronting baseless accusation. Her mind grappled for a reason. Had Matteo somehow run into someone from her past back in Boston? Someone who had believed the vicious lies her uncle had spewed back then?

If that was the case, why wasn't Matteo back at the university with her right at this moment, discussing what he might have just heard? If he had any faith in her whatsoever, if he trusted her even a little, they'd be calmly discussing all this over two flutes of champagne. Instead, he was out here firing wounding questions at her. Questions he should have come to the answers to on his own.

But perhaps she'd given him too much credit as her heart had grown tender for him. Perhaps she should have seen that he was not all that different from Trevor after all.

No. In fact, Matteo was worse. Her ex simply hadn't cared enough to see past the lies.

Whereas Matteo was all too quick to believe them.

She really was quite the actress. Matteo watched as Mari swung open the car door and fled through the sliding doors of the Nautica without so much as a glance behind her.

For one insane moment, Matteo had the urge to jump out of the car and run after her. To demand the answers she refused to give him. His hand was on the door handle, gripping tightly on the verge of flinging it open, when he finally came to his senses. Chasing after her would be pointless. He'd only be chasing after something he wasn't going to receive: the truth.

But he had received it, hadn't he? Her silence was answer enough, wasn't it? Mari couldn't even give him the respect of saying in words what was so obvious. She hadn't been able to give him a denial. Or even so much as an excuse. He might have even been able to work through forgiving her if she'd offered even so much as that little of a crumb. She hadn't given him anything. After he'd let his guard down and trusted her.

After he'd fallen for her.

Yep, he really was a blind, besotted fool. To think, he'd entertained thoughts of coming back to the island regularly to visit her. He'd even considered asking her to come with him back to Rome, maybe even long term.

He'd considered asking her for so much more. He scoffed as he recalled how he'd rehearsed just this morning how he might approach her about rebuilding his business with her by his side. As partners. And as lovers.

Thank the gods he's been spared from doing so. Hard to believe he'd been so close to making such an enormous mistake. Served him right for believing for even a moment that a true relationship might be in the cards for him. He'd just come way too close to succumbing to the same weakness his father had. He'd seen firsthand over the years how falling for someone could make a man weak and vulnerable.

Why in the world had he even thought to risk it?

Well, lesson learned, and it had been learned well. He wouldn't soon forget what he'd been taught.

He had some decisions to make and some work to do. Now that his focus was back where it should be, he would figure out how to rebuild Tala and throw himself wholly into making the company successful again. And he'd get to the bottom of exactly how much Mari had intervened in the drafting of Anna's final will. He would get his answers one way or another. Whether Mari supplied them or not. He'd given her a chance and she'd blatantly thrown it away.

Letting go of the door handle, he motioned for the driver to continue on once he'd seen that she was well past the front desk and through the hallway leading to her apartment.

Time for him to go home as well.

She hadn't slept a wink.

Images from last evening outside the church had played like a tragic movie over and over through her head as she'd tossed and turned all night, tears threatening to spill with each passing moment. To her credit, miraculously, by the time the dawn sun appeared outside her window, she hadn't shed a single one. Though the resulting headache from the strain of keeping them at bay combined with the lack of sleep now had her dreading the day ahead.

But she had a job to do. And she would do it.

Her resolve was tested almost immediately when she reached the lobby. Signore Gio stood at the front desk, his arms crossed tight in front of his chest. He and Miyko appeared to be in the middle of some type of stare-off.

She had no doubt why the man was here. To see her. She hadn't even had any coffee yet, her eyes still stung and her headache was pounding harder against her temples by the second.

Mari didn't bother to stifle her groan. Not this morning, not after what she'd endured last night. If Signore Gio was here for yet another fight, then for the first time ever, she was going to give him one. Too bad, actually. The man was due to check out in about forty-eight hours.

She didn't even try to wrangle her usual fake smile.

"What can I do for you?" she asked. No preamble, no good-morning greeting. Not today.

For the briefest second, Signore Gio startled and a surprised look washed over his features before he resumed his usual scowl.

"It's impossible to sleep in the room you've assigned me."

"Why is that?"

"There's a bird, right outside my window. Chirping nonstop as soon as the sun rises. Awakens me at the crack of dawn."

Mari didn't bother to ask why he'd be bringing the matter up now, a mere two days before he was scheduled to leave. "And what exactly am I supposed to do about a bird, Signore Gio?"

He shrugged. "That's your job to figure out, isn't it?"

That was it. She'd had it.

Inhaling deeply, she turned to Miyko. "Miyko, why don't you go get yourself some breakfast."

They both knew he wasn't a breakfast partaker. But he didn't argue. Whatever Miyko saw in her facial expression must have told him better than to try. With a simple nod, he darted toward the kitchen.

Mari turned back to the man at the desk, making sure

to keep her voice steady. "Signore, I do a damn good job of keeping this place running and profitable. Most of our guests gush about their stay as they're leaving, and they write glowing reviews about us online. My employees seem to have no complaints either." She paused to take another deep breath. "I'm not sure why *you* are so discontent with our lodgings and with me in particular and frankly, I'm beyond caring. I know for a fact this is a topnotch hotel and I'm very good at running it. If you're so disappointed with us year after year, I'm going to have to insist that you do not return. Not next summer. Not. Ever."

The man's mouth fell open before she got the last words out. Then he blinked at her. Once. And again.

Mari fought back the panic that perhaps she'd gone too far. But indeed, she in fact couldn't find it in herself to care. Whatever the consequences, so be it. Signore Gio had picked the wrong morning to test her this time. And was that the sound of someone clapping slowly in the not-too-far distance?

Signore Gio began to stammer. "I...uh ...well, there's..."

She cut him off. "In fact, I'd be happy to issue you a refund for your expenses so far and there'll be no charge for this stay. Just as soon as I make a note that any future reservation you try to make will not be honored." With that, she pivoted on her heel and pulled the laptop over to call up his file.

"I have no one," the man blurted out before she could so much as push a key.

It was Mari's turn to blink in confusion. "I beg your pardon?"

Signore Gio cleared his throat, his gaze trained on his

feet. It took several moments for him to speak again. "I said, I have no one," he repeated.

"I don't understand."

"My wife is gone. And my daughter refuses to speak to me. She's somewhere in America. New York, I think, now."

Okay. What did any of that have to do with her and the Nautica? "And the two of you are estranged?"

He swallowed. "Yes. She's upset with me. Has been for years."

It didn't take too far a stretch of the imagination to believe that statement. "Why is that?" Mari asked, merely because she wasn't quite sure what else to do.

"Because I disapprove of her husband and told her so. She's never forgiven me."

The realization dawned on her all at once. Signore Gio wasn't disgruntled, he was simply lonely. And he had a very odd way of addressing his loneliness.

Mari rubbed a palm down her face. At least now she knew the source of all his complaints. It had nothing to do with her. "Would you like to have an espresso with me, Signore Gio?"

The man blew out a breath and nodded slowly, looking relieved. Mari pushed the laptop away and walked to where he stood. "Let's go get that cup of coffee. I think we could both use the conversation."

He nodded once more, then followed her silently toward the kitchen.

Mari counted the beats until her blood pressure resumed a normal rhythm. Regardless of Signore Gio's misplaced cries for attention, every word she'd just said about the hotel and her running of it were 100 percent the truth.

Now that she'd had to defend herself, the reality was crystal clear. She did have what it takes to run this place and make it successful.

Matteo thought she'd acquired the Nautica via deceit and not because she deserved it. Well, he was wrong. Just like her uncle was wrong when he'd tried to convince her that she wouldn't be able to take over the running of the restaurant.

She knew better.

CHAPTER THIRTEEN

Three weeks later

MATTEO SLAMMED THE laptop shut and flung the printout of the latest spreadsheet across the room in disgust. The numbers just kept getting bleaker and bleaker. And he was no closer to a solution as to how to keep the business operating before his suppliers and contractors began terminating their services. His father had liquidated every account he possibly could, put their biggest assets up as collateral for bank loans. Both personal accounts and those of the business were completely dry. Each day there was less and less lira to pay off the bills that continued uninterrupted.

Though he was regarding the old man much less harshly lately. Matteo had proved in Sardinia just how easy a mark he himself would have made under the right circumstances.

With a harsh curse, he stood to stare at the view outside his window. The gray cloudy sky and wet mist settling over the piazza matched his mood to a tee. There he went again, thinking about her. And doubting himself. Had he been overly harsh back there when he'd found out the truth?

Maybe he could have given Mari a chance to explain herself.

What good would that have done? All the surface facts pointed to a very unflattering picture of Ms. Renati. First, she's accused of stealing by her uncle. Then she conveniently inherits a hotel from a frail old woman she met just a few short years before. What are the odds of such scenarios happening under nonsuspicious circumstances? No, the picture was clear and damning. He was only second-guessing himself because he was a fool who still dreamed about her at night. Who wanted to believe she deserved the benefit of the doubt when all the evidence said otherwise.

A nagging voice echoed in the back of his mind, saying most of that evidence was rather weak and circumstantial.

Enough!

He had work to do. The best course of action right now was to figure out how to keep Tala Industries afloat. Once that was taken care of, he would look further into exactly what had gone down between Anna and Mari. He wasn't about to let it go until he had all the answers about whose hands the Nautica had ended up in after Anna's passing.

An hour later, after staring at a laptop screen that kept blurring in his vision due to his lack of focus, Matteo finally threw in the towel. He'd have to change his original plans around. There was no hope of moving forward with anything else until he found out what he was desperate to know.

Pulling out his phone, he clicked on the number for his lawyer. After a brief greeting and the regular pleasantries, Matteo asked the question that had been eating away at him for the past three weeks.

"What can you find out about the property in Cagliari and the adjacent hotel?" he asked, tapping his gold ink pen against the surface of his desk.

"What do you want to know exactly?"

"Anything you can uncover."

"I suppose I can contact a few colleagues on the island. See what they can tell me about the place."

"I'd appreciate it, Aldo. Give me a call when you know more."

The call didn't take long to arrive. Four hours later as Matteo was poring over yet more dismal figures on yet another spreadsheet, his phone lit up with his lawyer's picture. He snatched it up before the second ring.

"What have you got, Aldo?"

"Well, information on the Nautica was surprisingly easy to come by, actually. Turns out more than one financial firm had washed their hands of the place."

"How so?"

"Your elderly cousin was making some bad decisions toward the end of her career as hotel owner."

"What kind of bad decisions?"

"Let's see." Matteo could hear the shuffling of papers through the tiny speaker and the clicking of a keyboard. "She went heavily into debt, made some really bad decisions and then took out loans against the property to try and rectify her mistakes. The place was about to go under and be auctioned off to settle her debts. I can send you the specific numbers if you'd like."

Huh. All that was very interesting, but nothing so far had given Matteo any kind of answer about Mari. "What turned it around?"

"Well, according to the files, the place seemed to start turning a profit again about three and a half years ago. The lawyer in Sardinia seemed to think the turnaround had to do with a change in management."

The final three words landed like hammer blows through his mind.

"Your mom's cousin seems to have handed over the reins to someone much more competent around that time."

Matteo closed his eyes and released a deep breath. Three and a half years ago. That meant the change in management Aldo was referring to was none other than Mari herself. She'd taken the Nautica from the brink of near bankruptcy to a profitable operation. All while Anna was alive and well and still sole owner. Before she'd gotten sick.

That only meant one thing. That if it wasn't for Mari, the Nautica would be in the hands of the highest bidder. And an elderly woman, a blood relative of his, could have very well ended up in the street.

Mari had saved the Nautica. And in the process, she'd saved Anna from losing the home she'd loved and lived in her whole life. Mari had put in the work and that work had made all the difference. No wonder Anna believed she deserved to own the place. Anyone in their right mind would.

"Was there anything else?" Aldo was asking, but Matteo barely heard. He thanked the man through a haze of mind fog and clicked off the call.

Finding out the truth had taken one phone call and he'd had the answers less than an afternoon later.

Answers he would have easily obtained if he'd only given Mari a chance to give them. Only one question now remained: What, if anything, was he going to do about what he'd learned?

Matteo slammed the pen against the desktop so fiercely

it formed a divot on the highly polished surface. He'd certainly been right about one thing back in Cagliari. He really was a fool.

No. No. No.

She refused to let the tears fall yet again. Slamming the skimmer into the pool a bit too hard, Mari barely noticed when the resulting splash hit her square in the chest. Given that it was pouring out, the extra water hardly made a difference.

She skimmed the surface of the pool, ignoring the fact that it was already spotless. It had been three weeks already. Time to get over what had happened with Matteo and move on with her life.

Miyko or Roberta could deal with him if he ever found reason to return. In the meantime, the plot of land he owned sat empty and unused. Under other circumstances, she might have suggested all manner of ways that land could be put to use for guests of the Nautica. For instance, as a paddleball court. Or they might even build a cover or roof over it and install billiard or ping-pong tables. All ideas she had planned to run by him at some point before he showed his true colors.

Instead, it was now past time to forget Matteo even existed.

Right. As if it were that easy. As if she could simply flip a switch. As if her mind didn't replay every moment she'd spent with Matteo, including the soul-crushing ones that last evening when he'd accused her of manipulating Anna—again—without even giving her a chance to explain Analisa's statements.

Well, that pretty much told her all she needed to know about him, didn't it? He was just as bad as Trevor. Or her mother, for that matter. And somehow, this betrayal hurt so much worse than Trevor's ever had. Which made absolutely no sense. She'd been ready to marry the former if he'd asked, the way he'd led her to believe before she'd lost Papa. While Matteo had barely been a bump in the road of her life. Only, the bump had upended her entire existence and teased her with the type of man she might have fallen in love with.

The word knocked her cold. *Love.* But there was no denying. In the short time she'd known the man, she'd somehow fallen recklessly in love with him. Mari nearly toppled into the pool as the shock of it fully hit her. Then she wondered if she should jump in anyway, just to punish herself for being so foolish.

Well, that showed her, didn't it? Another lesson learned. As far as she was concerned, she had no business even contemplating love or romance. Not ever again.

She'd been ready to give her heart and body to a man who couldn't even bother to let her explain the error of his suspicions. Ha! It was bad enough he had those suspicions in the first place.

"You do realize it's raining?" Miyko's distinctive voice reached her from across the pool. She'd been so deep in thought, she hadn't even noticed his arrival. Sporting a poncho-like raincoat that barely reached his bare knees, he made no effort to hide his annoyed smirk. Mari figured Roberta must have sent him out here to check on her.

"Yes, in fact I do."

"Yet you're still cleaning the already spotless pool that no one will be using anytime soon."

"Someone might want to swim in the rain."

Miyko merely shook his head. "You need to talk to him," he said several beats later.

She decided to feign ignorance. "Is one of the guests asking for me?" she asked, knowing fully well that wasn't whom Miyko was referring to. "I'll be there in a minute."

Miyko slammed his fists against his hips. "I don't mean one of the guests and you know it."

"If you're referring to that…that…" She spluttered to come up with the right words but nothing matched what she was feeling. "That man who owns part of this land, I have nothing to say or hear from him. Ever. Please don't bring up his name again."

To her surprise, Miyko's features softened and he gave her a sympathetic smile.

"Come inside, Mari. I think you could use an aperitif."

"Now? Why?"

"Because I would like one, and we need to have a long-overdue chat."

Something in his voice and the set of his smile told Mari she shouldn't dare argue. Swiping the moisture off her face, she set the skimmer down and followed Miyko inside.

When they arrived at the dining room, a pitcher of citrus spritz and two frosty glasses sat waiting for them in the corner table.

Though she was near to soaking wet, unlike Miyko, who was smartly taking off his raincoat, Mari figured she didn't want to risk irking him by asking him for a delay while she changed.

"Look," he began once they'd sat down and he began pouring the drink into their glasses. One of the Nautica's regular servers appeared with a tray of antipasto and fresh bread before making themselves scarce. "I'm going to do most of the talking, capisce?"

Despite his insufferable attitude and overall haughtiness, Mari couldn't help but feel touched. He'd gone through the trouble of setting all this up. Roberta had probably had something to do with it as well.

"Sure thing," she answered, taking a sip of her drink.

Miyko set the pitcher down after filling his own glass. "I don't know what happened between you two, but you haven't been the same since the night of the gala. And whatever it is, I think you need to clear the air or it's going to continue eating you up inside."

"I don't think that's a good idea."

He leaned his elbows on the table. "I see, so your plan is to run from this also. Just walk away. Again."

His words gave her pause. "Also? Again? What's any of that supposed to mean?"

"I know what happened to you back in Boston," he declared without any kind of preamble, as was his style.

The statement hardly came as a surprise. For all of her good qualities, Anna wasn't exactly immune to sharing juicy information when it meant having an avid audience at her whim.

"That has nothing to do with this."

Miyko's lips tightened. "From where I'm standing it most certainly does."

Okay. She would bite, if not simply out of curiosity. "How do you figure?"

"You walked away then too. Just as you are now."

She shook her head in argument. Miyko had no idea what he was talking about. "I had no choice. I had to leave."

"Didn't you have a choice?"

"What in the world was my other option?"

"You could have stayed and defended yourself." He plucked an olive off the tray and tossed it in his mouth.

Mari leaned back in her chair, allowing Miyko's words to sink in until they settled deep into her soul.

She wasn't about to say it out loud, but she had to admit he was right. She owed it to that scared twenty-year-old she'd been back in Boston to stand up for herself this time.

Even if it meant facing down the man she'd foolishly fallen in love with, who very well might not believe her.

CHAPTER FOURTEEN

MATTEO'S PHONE LIT up and sounded the ringtone of his assistant. He had half a mind to ignore her. She was probably just relaying another urgent message from another partner who demanded to be paid already.

But ignoring his problems wasn't going to get him anywhere. He clicked on the screen to answer.

"There's someone here insisting to see you," the elderly woman explained without bothering to say hello.

Matteo glanced at his calendar app on one of the monitors on his desk. The hour was empty. "Do they have an appointment?"

"No, but she insists she isn't going to leave until you see her."

A germ of optimism formed in his gut. Was there even a slight chance?

"Shall I call security, sir?"

Matteo rose from his desk and strode to the door. He braced himself before opening it, not daring to hope. Standing behind it, being glowered at by his assistant, was no other than Mariana Renati herself.

Despite the anger in her expression, his chest filled with joy at the sight of her.

He stepped aside and gestured to his office. "Come in."

Mari shot him several daggers with her eyes before

brushing past him through the narrow doorway. Even now, despite the circumstances, a rush of heat flushed through his core as soon as her body came in contact with his.

"Please cancel my calls until further notice," he told his assistant, then took a deep breath before stepping inside and shutting the door behind him.

Mari was pacing with intensity in front of his glass wall. His heart ached looking at her. Dressed in a casual loose T-shirt and denim jeans, she looked even more beautiful than he remembered. And oh how he'd remembered. The apology sat burning the tip of his tongue but for the life of him, he didn't know how to start.

She had every right to call him a rat bastard and then simply walk away. It would be no less than what he deserved.

"I have a few things I need to say to you," she said, finally coming to a stop. "And you need to hear them in person."

"I didn't think you'd want to see me again." A sharp ache originated at the base of his spine and shot upward. Now that he'd said the words out loud, he realized just how much they hurt.

"I didn't. I mean, I don't. You don't deserve to have this conversation, but I do. So we're having it."

He leaned a hip against the side of his desk. "I won't interrupt."

She nodded once briskly. "Good," she said, then rammed her fingers through her hair before going on. "I ran into Analisa a couple of days after the gala. She mentioned what the two of you talked about. Then I managed to put two and two together and figured out why you changed so drastically that night. It's because you thought the worst about me."

Her voice quavered on the last few words and the angry mask fell away for just a brief moment. What he saw underneath the fury tore his heart to shreds. Hurt. Matteo swallowed past the lump that suddenly formed at the base of his throat and scrambled for words knowing full well that none could come close to undoing the damage he'd caused.

"I have no excuse." That was the absolute truth. Only that he'd been colored by his dad's folly and his own insecurities. "If it's any consolation, it didn't take long for me to figure out just how wrong I was." But by then, it was already too late. He'd lit the match and set everything on fire.

Mari didn't even seem to be listening. He could hardly blame her. He had no right to expect her to hear him. Not after the way he'd treated her.

"Anna figured I needed the Nautica much more than you ever could. You were the heir of one of the biggest corporations in all of Italy. How did none of that occur to you?"

Well, when she put it that way.

She wasn't even going to mention the fact that she'd literally saved the hotel from financial disaster. Wasn't even going to throw that accomplishment in his face. If he didn't feel like an absolute heel already, that was enough to have him feeling lower than the belly of a reptile.

"Mari, there's nothing I can say." *Sorry* would ring so hollow it wasn't even worth uttering the word. "Just know that I would do anything to take back that night. To somehow start over. But I know that's not possible."

She crossed her arms in front of her chest. "That's right. There really is nothing you can say or do. And I've said all I needed to."

Without another word, she made for the door and didn't even bother slamming it after her. Simply walked out of his office.

And out of his life for good.

Matteo sat staring at his wall for so long after Mari left, he barely noticed when the shadows of early evening began appearing. His mind replayed the scene with her over and over like a stuck film loop.

He'd made some mistakes in his life, but nothing compared to the mess he'd made with the one woman whom he'd fallen for. He wasn't even going to bother to deny it. He'd fallen for Mari Renati and he hadn't even realized while it was happening.

But none of that mattered. Because she was gone.

Unable to stand his own company any longer, he made his way outside and wandered along the piazza. His stomach grumbled a complaint, making him aware of the fact that he'd missed both lunch and dinner. But food was the last thing on his mind right now.

Wandering aimlessly for an hour did nothing to clear his head. The images continued to mock him. Mari's grimace of pain as she'd confronted him. The look of utter disappointment flushing her face.

Well, she wasn't any more disappointed in him than he was. Because that wouldn't be possible.

The evening had grown fully dark by the time he finally looked up to realize exactly where he was. Turned out, he'd ended up outside his father's flat. Pulling his key card out, he let himself in through the front door.

The lamp in his father's office was still on, spilling soft light out into the hallway.

He'd been avoiding his father, afraid of saying something he might regret and couldn't take back. He scoffed internally at that. If only he'd been as cautious when it came to Mari.

He walked in to find Stefan typing away at his laptop. His father gave him a surprised look of joy upon seeing him.

"Matteo. This is a pleasant surprise."

"Hello, Papa."

His father went immediately to the bar and began pouring two glasses of his favorite Chianti.

"What brings you by?" he asked, handing him a glass of the rich red wine.

"I'm not sure exactly," he answered honestly.

"Aldo called. Said he's been trying to get a hold of you. You're not answering your phone and you're not in the office."

"I was otherwise occupied," Matteo answered, his mind still numb. Why exactly had he come here, of all places?

"No matter, he's on his way here. So it works out that you're here, too. Convenient coincidence, huh?"

"Why is he coming here?"

Stefan shrugged. "Says he has something urgent he needs to tell us. Wanted to do it in person."

The announcement slowly began to permeate through Matteo's emotionally fogged mind. There had to be a pressing reason Aldo was making a house call.

But he had other things on his mind at the moment.

His father was putting on a brave face, but Matteo saw through the surface mask. "You still miss her, don't you?" he asked bluntly, not realizing what he was going to say until the words had left his mouth. "Mama."

Stefan did a double take, set his wineglass down on his desk and sat on the leather love seat a few feet away. "Of course I do. I miss her every day and will for the rest of time."

"Enough that you risked everything to find her replacement in another woman. One who said all the right things."

"I never sought to replace her, son. That wouldn't have been possible. I only wanted to attempt to fill the large hole she'd left in her absence."

Funny, his father had felt a gaping hole in his life, and it hadn't even occurred to him to try and get closer to his son to help alleviate his pain.

"Was it worth it? We lost everything."

His father hesitated and Matteo wanted to fling his wineglass against the wall. How could the answer not be an immediate "no"?

He bit down on the harsh words at the tip of his tongue and gave his father time to answer. It took a while.

"The time I had with your mother was the greatest gift life could have given me. I don't deny that I made mistakes after she was gone. But I can't be sorry for trying to find even a semblance of such a love again. I'm only sorry that my actions caused you harm."

Matteo could only nod, studying his father's weathered face. He saw now that he could have given the man some grace. Stefan was still deeply grieving. He'd been a vulnerable old man who'd had the misfortune of crossing paths with the absolute wrong woman after losing his beloved wife.

Along those lines, maybe he should have given himself more of an opportunity to grieve as well. But dealing with his father's failings was easier than facing his own pain of loss.

Minutes passed as they both stood staring at the floor. For the life of him, Matteo didn't know what to say. But perhaps words didn't need to be spoken. Perhaps it was enough that they were finally together, acknowledging the loss that had shattered both of them.

The ringing of the doorbell sounded through the air.

"That will be Aldo," Stefan said, rising to get the door.

Their trusted lawyer appeared behind his father moments later. Stefan poured another Chianti and handed it to him.

"What brings you here?" he asked as the man took his first sip.

"I come bearing good news."

Matteo felt his shoulders drop a good three inches. He didn't think he could handle any more upheaval in the span of twenty-four hours.

Aldo continued, "Interpol contacted the Italian authorities to inform them of a ring of heists throughout all of Europe. Turns out the woman who swindled you out of your money was part of a larger crime ring. The major players have been found and arrested."

Stefan's eyes grew wide. "What exactly does that mean?"

"Most of the money was deposited in various Swiss bank accounts. The funds are all frozen at the moment, but we should be able to recoup some, if not most, of your losses sometime in the future." He held the glass up in a toast.

It took several moments for Aldo's words to sink in. When they did, Matteo felt the weight of a hundred earths suddenly lifted off his back. Miraculously, the nightmare was coming to an end.

He stepped over and shook Aldo's free hand hard enough that the man's feet shifted beneath him. Then he turned and enveloped his father in a tight bear hug.

"I have to go!" he said, making his way out.

"Go where?" his father asked behind him.

"To an island."

Now that his company woes were being resolved, he had other more pressing business to attend to.

"There's a guest requesting an umbrella be set up on the beach," Miyko announced the moment she made her way to the desk. It was barely nine in the morning. No one went to the beach this early. She hadn't even had her coffee yet.

Mari blew out a puff of frustrated air. "Great, another demanding guest to take the place of Signore Gio." Just when she'd cleared the air with Signore Gio right before he checked out.

"They've been waiting quite a while," Miyko continued. "I'd get to it if I were you."

"Can't Carlo do it?" she asked.

"It's his day off," Miyko answered with a wave of his hand. "You have to do it."

Mari didn't bother to ask why the task fell to her if Carlo couldn't. Miyko had made it very clear from the beginning that he refused to tackle any kind of beach duty. So much for a relaxing cup of espresso before she started her day.

With a resigned sigh, she went to the storage room to get an umbrella and lugged it across the bike path to the beach.

Only to find it empty. No one was there.

Was this some kind of joke? She was ready to turn around and give Miyko a piece of her mind for childishly pranking her when she noticed it.

A blanket had been spread out a few feet from the water. Was that where she was supposed to install the umbrella? Where was the Nautica guest who'd requested it?

She dropped the umbrella and approached to take a closer look. What she saw only added to the confusion. At least three dozen roses had been spread out on the blanket. In the center was a basket overflowing with breakfast pastries and a capped pitcher of something that appeared to be a mimosa.

What in the world?

Then she figured out what she was looking at. Someone had clearly planned a romantic gesture and had obviously put a lot of thought into it.

Her eyes stung at the realization. Whoever had done this must be head over heels in love to go through all this trouble. Would that ever be a fate she would experience? To have someone love her as much as this person loved whoever he was about to propose to?

Doubtful. As painful as it was to admit, she didn't see it happening. She'd been burned twice already, and wouldn't take a chance again anytime soon. It didn't help that she'd probably be yearning for Matteo Talarico for the rest of her days.

A shadow slowly began to appear behind her and Mari took a moment to compose herself before turning around, hiding the foolish tears she was barely keeping at bay.

"This is lovely," she said over her shoulder. "I'll get your umbrella set up right away."

"That won't be necessary."

That voice. She had to be imagining it. Her yearning for Matteo now had her hearing voices that couldn't possibly really be there.

"Mari." She heard her name spoken softly behind her and squeezed her eyes shut tight. She didn't dare turn around, because then she might see that this really was all a mirage. This couldn't really be happening.

Matteo couldn't really be here.

"Please turn around. I've traveled all night to see you."

Swallowing past the brick in her throat, Mari slowly shifted around in the sand.

No mirage. He was real. Matteo was really standing here, before her on the beach.

"Please forgive me," he said, reaching for her and brushing a soft finger along her cheek. "I don't think I can go back to the life I lived before I met you, darling."

Mari's mouth went dry, the ground beneath her feet shifted. If she could sink into the sand and curl into a ball without embarrassing herself, she would do it.

Instead, she sucked in a fortifying breath, then immediately shook her head. His words were oh so tempting, and Mari wanted so badly to embrace them. But she just couldn't risk it. She couldn't risk letting this man tear her heart to shreds again. She wouldn't be able to survive it a second time.

"I have to go," she said, making her way past him. But he stopped her with a gentle hand on her elbow.

"You would be more than justified in walking away. I can only vow that I'll spend the rest of my life—of our lives—doing everything I can to make my foolishness up to you."

Mari's heart pounded against her ribs hard enough to have her shaking. Or maybe she was shaking because she wanted so much to reach for him, to plant her lips against his and taste him the way she'd longed to ever since she'd stormed out of his office that day in Rome.

Every waking minute.

Matteo gently took her hand in his, rubbed a finger along her palm. She couldn't have pulled away if she wanted to.

"My behavior that night had nothing to do with you, Mari. Please try and understand."

She most certainly was, trying that is. And as much as she wanted to take his words at face value, the reality was that he'd hurt her. Deeply.

Matteo used his free hand to ram his fingers through his hair. "I'm making a mess of this, I know."

"Maybe I should do the talking, then," she suggested with a bravado she didn't quite feel.

His gaze bore into hers. "Please. I owe it to you to listen to every word you want to say."

Very well, then. It wouldn't be too difficult to find the words. After all, she'd had internal rehearsals of such a conversation between them every day since she'd last seen him. Gulping a sharp breath, she began, "Your first reaction that night was to believe the worst. Your next reaction was to simply leave."

He tightened his grip on her hand, didn't interrupt her. Good thing, too, because if she didn't get this out all at once, she may never be able to. "The way you thought the worst of me and then walked away hurt more than anything I've had to endure in the past. Not my uncle's duplicity or the way I'd been betrayed all those years ago. I need to be sure I can protect my heart from that ever happening again. I don't think I can survive it if it did."

He forcefully shook his head. "Mari, you won't have to. I'll do anything to convince you."

"Maybe you can start by telling me why."

Matteo closed his eyes tight, tilted his head upward. "You came along when I least expected it. And you swept me off my feet. I didn't know how to handle the possibility that you might not be exactly what you are. So I foolishly took the easy way out. It was easier to do that than admit you'd broken through all my defenses."

Mari could only listen, reminding herself to breathe. In. Out. In. Out.

He continued, "I know it's no excuse, but I didn't have the best examples of an authentically loving relationship to serve as a guide. Not growing up. And not as an adult. But I'm hoping you can teach me. There is no one else who can. Or who I want to learn from."

Maybe she was the foolish one, because she believed him. And heaven help her, she could already feel the fortified walls around her heart beginning to crumble. The scent of him, those dark eyes that had haunted her dreams, feeling his hot breath against her skin. Her resolve began to melt like an ice cube dropped into hot liquid. Try as she might, she didn't have the strength to resist much longer.

"You'll spend the rest of our lives making it up to me,"

she affirmed, her voice trembling. She would expect nothing less.

He cupped the back of her neck, dropped a gentle kiss against her temple.

"That's right, *mi cara*. Starting this very moment."

As his lips brushed hungrily against hers, she believed him without a doubt.

EPILOGUE

Eighteen months later

SHE'D BEEN GONE for over half an hour already. Matteo peeked another glance at his watch and resumed his pacing. As much as he'd wanted to go with Mari, and as badly as he wanted to haul himself over to the restaurant now, this was something she had to do on her own.

He'd be sure to be there for her afterward.

The sounds of early evening Boston traffic echoed around him. His first time in the city and it didn't disappoint. A steel drum band played a bouncy rhythmic tune across the square. The archway he waited under was lit up in brilliant lights like the rest of the city in preparation for the upcoming holidays. All in all, a fairly magical scene.

Matteo fingered the velvet box in his pocket yet again, trying to imagine her reaction when he finally presented it. He'd been waiting for just the right moment and thought tonight would be it. But if she took any longer getting back, he might have to rethink his plans.

Just when he'd decided he couldn't take the waiting any longer and had to go check on her, he saw Mari strolling toward where he stood. Was it his imagination or did her steps seem lighter than they had when she'd walked away to her personal mission almost an hour ago?

"You're back." He stated the obvious as she grew closer. By way of an answer, she wordlessly launched herself into his arms. He wrapped her tight in his embrace and waited in silence.

He wasn't going to ask how things went. She would tell him what she needed to, if she needed to at all. He was merely here for support. And currently, for comfort.

Several beats passed before she finally pulled away with a sniffle. He planted a soft kiss against her lips.

"I got what I came here for," she stated, nuzzling her face against his chest. Her words were muffled when she spoke again. "A much-needed apology. He seems genuinely remorseful."

Matteo remained silent. This was her moment to share as much as she wished. "And now I'm done with that part of my life for good," she announced, pulling away and tilting her head up to look at him.

He lowered his head to kiss her deep and long. When it was over, they were both panting for air.

"On to new beginnings," she said, her smile wide and full of affection. For him. It still floored him how lucky he was to have found her, that she had forgiven him.

"New beginnings, huh?" he asked.

She nodded once.

"In that case…"

Reaching for the velvet box, Matteo kneeled before her and pulled it out of his pocket. "Please do me the honor of starting the next chapter of your life with me. As my wife." Popping open the lid, he held it up to her to reveal the sparkling emerald cut stone on a tricolor band made of the finest Italian gold.

Mari's eyes grew wide and her jaw dropped open. She

clasped her hands on her mouth and stood still, simply staring at him. For one insane moment, Matteo thought she might be wavering with her answer, that he'd read everything all wrong these past several months.

Finally, she pulled him up and threw her arms around his neck, a happy giggle reached his ear. Matteo blew out a breath of sheer relief as Mari did a little jump for joy as he held her tight.

"Is that a yes, then?" he asked needlessly.

"Yes, my love! Absolutely and wholeheartedly yes!"

And as several bystanders cheered and clapped for them, under the sparkling lights of the decorated archway, he slipped the equally brilliant ring on her finger.

He could hardly wait for their new beginning together.

* * * * *

If you enjoyed this story, check out these other great reads from Nina Singh

Prince's Proposal for the Canadian Cameras
Bound by the Boss's Baby
Their Accidental Marriage Deal
Part of His Royal World

All available now!

HER FAKE WEDDING DATE IN SICILY

JENNY LANE

MILLS & BOON

For Meaghan

When they ask me my favourite part, it's always you.

CHAPTER ONE

Mia

MIA KNOWLES STARED at the ornately carved wooden box, perched precariously on her lap, as though it contained the answer to all her problems. In reality, it held the itinerary for her best friend's wedding of the century at Mia's family's resort, the newly renovated La Piccola Barca, on the Sicilian coast. From the welcome dinner that evening, to the endless parade of chartered yachts, beachside activities and lavish nights out on the town, the event was sure to be memorialized in wedding magazines for years to come.

And Mia was going alone.

Which was *fine.* She had to do this. She *wanted* to do it. This was, after all, her best friend's wedding. And she had promises to keep. Promises she and Cate had made to each other when they were twelve years old, running along the beach in front of Mia's summer house in the Hamptons.

Or the promise she'd made two months ago, when she'd told Cate she was bringing a date to the wedding. When Cate's sister, Beth, had broken up with Mia six months ago, Cate had been more upset than both of them put together. Having a date had been a small white lie to prove she was over Beth, but months later she still didn't have someone to bring with her to Sicily.

Much to Mia's parents' chagrin, the social media influencer they'd tried to set her up with had quickly lost interest when she realized Mia had no interest in splashing her face in the news anymore.

And then there was yet another promise she'd made to her father before boarding the plane this morning. She was supposed to use this trip to boost her family's name. La Piccola Barca was their newest resort, and this was an opportunity to revitalize their brand. Mia had lots of ideas on how to improve her family's image—but her ideas, centered around philanthropy, were not what her father wanted to hear.

Mia was really good at keeping her promises to other people, not so good at keeping the ones she'd made herself. Promises like standing up to her family and asking for what she wanted. So, she'd told her father yes and watched her mother smile in approval.

Mia shoved the memory away. "What have you gotten yourself into now?" she whispered under her breath as she stared at the box.

The box didn't answer.

The last time Mia was with Cate, they'd both been in thin cotton tank tops, singing karaoke in a private booth while on vacation in Miami. But as she sat in the back seat of the black town car, something told her this week wasn't going to hold any of those private moments with Cate that she'd always treasured.

And that was because her best friend had gone and fallen in love with Noah Brewer. And when you marry into a multimedia mogul's family, appearances had to be kept up. Mia suspected that was the reason her parents had offered the use of their newly renovated resort in Sicily to Cate and Noah for their extravagant affair.

"Mia, sweetheart," her father had said over brunch last month as he sopped up a sunny-side up egg with toast. "This is what we expect from you. Go to the wedding, chat with the guests, remind them that the Knowles family is still here. You know I'd go, but I have the meeting with the board at the end of that week. Can't miss it."

Her older brother and sisters would be at the meeting, too. The Knowles children all knew their places, and Mia's role was catching the eye of the paparazzi and media. When Mia was nineteen, they'd spotted her and Cate partying on spring break and the video went viral. Instead of her father being embarrassed, he had latched onto this angle for keeping the family relevant and smiled approvingly at her for the first time she could remember.

Mia would do anything to see her father smile at her like that again. Smiles he usually reserved for her siblings. So, she would go to the wedding, play her part and build up trust until the time was right. And *then* she would ask to work on some of their philanthropy projects. But she *wouldn't* get caught up in a planned scandal, or get photographed by the paparazzi. She was determined to leave all that behind.

Mia gently set the box next to her and bit the edge of her lip. *Think, think, think.* She needed a plausible excuse for why she had not brought a date to the wedding. Last-minute work trip? Food poisoning? She couldn't tell Cate the truth—that she'd lied in a panic. Her best friend didn't need to spend this week worrying if Mia still had a broken heart. Cate needed to focus on her wedding. On Noah.

"Just one more moment, Miss Knowles. We are almost there." The chauffeur smiled at her kindly from the rear-view mirror. No doubt mistaking her sigh for travel weariness and not the low-level panic creeping up the back of her skull.

As the car slowed, Mia took in the glowing white buildings of La Piccola Barca in the distance. From here, it didn't look like much, but Mia knew the real view was from the water. La Barca, as it was becoming known, was nestled into the edge of a cliff on the Sicilian coast. Every suite had a view of the sparkling sea, not to mention there was a private beach, luxury spa and five-star cuisine. It was the perfect spot for a Brewer to marry a Richards and get the attention they deserved.

As the car reached the main entrance, her breath caught in her throat. Being here, actually arriving at La Barca, made all of this wedding business real.

Mia took in the expansive lobby and the wide windows open to the sea beyond. It had been years since she'd been on a relaxing vacation. She'd spent the last eight years in school working toward her philanthropic dreams, determined to do something with her status in life. And she knew this wasn't exactly a vacation, but there was something about this place that felt like an adventure was just waiting to happen.

When the front desk staff let her know the family's suite wasn't quite ready, she waved off the apologies before ambling along the gleaming white marbled corridor looking for Cate. The resort wasn't huge like some of her family's other resorts—it had a certain sense of charm. And if her memory was correct, her favorite place would be just around the corner.

It was just off to the right—an airy room filled to the ceiling with shelves of books. Their heavy leather spines and art climbed the walls, beckoning Mia to come inside.

She needed to find Cate. There was an itinerary to keep,

but surely, she could sit for a minute and catch her breath. She ducked into the room and ran her fingertips along the book edges. The wide windows on the far side of the room were wall-to-wall blue, the ocean staring back at her as if to say *What on earth are you doing in there when you could be out here?*

Mia was about to leave when she heard the flutter of a book page being turned in someone's assured fingers. A woman was sitting in a corner. Her back was to Mia; she was facing the sea. She had books and papers and a neat, shiny laptop spread out in front of her as she worked in smooth silence. Watching her work was like watching a synchronized swimmer.

She had warm brown skin and her hair lay down on her shoulders in soft curls. Her suit, which made her legs look a million miles long as it clung to her thick waist and round curves, seemed out of place for a resort by the sea, but somehow it felt right. Mia wanted to take a step closer and see more of this woman.

Mia wasn't the type to check out strangers. She didn't have the desire for casual relationships that were doomed to fail before they began. Her relationship had fizzled with Cate's sister, Beth, last year when they tried—and failed—to do the long-distance thing. At least that's the reason Beth gave her over FaceTime. The awkward ending had led to even more tension between Mia and Cate's family. Something she was desperate to repair at this wedding. The last thing she needed was to get all hot and bothered by a hotel guest when she was in Sicily, thousands of miles from home.

The woman clicked at something on the computer and reached for her phone before it even started buzzing. When she answered the phone in French, her tone was clipped and polite. And somewhat familiar.

Her voice grew tense, but not loud. She spoke in an even tone and tapped her pen absently on the paper while she talked. Mia couldn't help but creep closer as she tried to parse out where she knew that voice from. She grabbed a random book from the shelf and sat in a chair near the windows.

The woman stood and began crossing from one area of the room to the next, careful to keep her voice quiet. She'd abandoned the jacket of her tailored blue suit on the chair. A soft blush camisole with thin straps clung to her shoulders, and Mia wondered where she could find one for herself. This woman was every bit the confident, well-spoken, no-nonsense businesswoman she wished she could be.

A tingle of a memory raced up Mia's spine. She knew this woman. If only she could remember her name.

The woman let out a low growl into the phone and, with one last word, smashed the end-call button. As soon as the call disconnected, she deflated like a gorgeous hot-air balloon coming down to earth and she draped her arms loosely around the chair.

"Come on, Eliza. Don't cry." She closed her eyes and shook her head, as if she was trying to rid herself of the emotion. "Not here. Not now. Just fix this."

Eliza. Eliza Brewer. As in the new CEO of Brewer Media Enterprises. Cate's future sister-in-law.

A dozen distinct moments zipped through Mia's memory. Fundraisers, parties and social engagements where Eliza Brewer was just off to the side, smiling politely next to her father at every event.

Annoyance pricked Mia's skin with the vivid memory of a few years ago when Eliza had treated her with cool disinterest at a party. And then, just two months ago, she'd helped Mia with a—situation—when she was working a fundraiser. A thrill ran down her spine at the memory of that night.

Part of her wanted to comfort Eliza, who was clearly upset about something. But Eliza Brewer wasn't the type that would appreciate being comforted.

Eliza turned abruptly and jumped at the site of Mia, clutching a book.

"I don't speak French," Mia blurted out as she rose from her chair. Their last encounter had been just as awkward. *Remind her how immature and uncultured you are compared to her, Mia. Great.*

Eliza cocked her head at Mia in confusion. "What?"

"I promise. I didn't understand any of it." Mia gestured helplessly to the phone still clutched in Eliza's hands.

Eliza's eyes went wide as she took in Mia. "Don't worry about it," Eliza murmured.

Mia was weary from travel; her brain was as rumpled as her travel clothes. But her body still turned to liquid as Eliza's eyes roamed over her.

"Still, I'm sorry." Mia's voice was gentle as she took a step closer.

"No, it was my mistake." Eliza's warm eyes went cold, and she hurried to the desk, where she began stacking her papers and placing everything into a large bag. She made eye contact with Mia again and Mia wanted to die right there, the icy stare freezing her in place. "I shouldn't be having business conversations where someone like you could walk in."

Eliza

Eliza knew better than to be working somewhere where it could get back to her brother. He made her promise to enjoy Sicily, and his wedding, and not overdo it with work. Her mother had also not so subtly hinted that she would have a wedding date if she just "tried to loosen up a little." However, since she took over for her father, there was no such thing as *out of office*.

If she learned one thing from Elijah Brewer growing up, it was that business came first. For the last ten years, Eliza had adopted the same work ethic. The business came before personal hobbies, before friends, before sleep. And, just like her father, it also came before relationships.

Her father had learned that the hard way. Her mother left them when Eliza was only ten. It wasn't a mistake she was going to make for herself.

So she'd hidden herself away in the spot she thought she'd most likely be left alone. The gorgeous—and blessedly empty—library off the lobby.

She'd only gotten in that morning and despite her suite being spacious, with sweeping views of the ocean and the craggy rocks of the Sicilian coastline, she couldn't work there. It was too quiet and too closed off. So she'd trudged to this—not so secret—space and prepped for the upcoming merger. Her brother didn't have to know.

But now Mia was staring at her, a smattering of freckles across the bridge of her nose still making her look like she didn't have a care in the world. Her mouth formed into an O with a gasp of surprise.

Mia, who was a few years younger, and always the life of the party, wasn't afraid to be herself. Eliza and Mia weren't friends, but they often found themselves at the same events. Eliza envied the easy way Mia could move through a crowd. Eliza knew every party was a chance to make connections, impress her father and broker deals. So far, it had worked. She was just over thirty and was already the CEO of her family's company. It was worth the long nights, worth giving up any idea of a serious relationship, worth being serious. But right now, Eliza had to bite the inside of her lip to keep a smile from twitching across her lips.

If anyone could ruin her focus this week, it was going to be Mia Knowles.

"What are you doing here?" Eliza worked to keep her voice cool. Mia's face scrunched in confusion. And damn, that was cute.

"I'm the maid of honor." She said it like it was some kind of VIP pass to any location at the resort.

Eliza took a step closer and waved her hand across the room. "No, what are you doing *in here*? Shouldn't you be down by the pool, getting massages and sipping wine and taking a helicopter tour of the island?"

Mia quirked one adorable eyebrow at Eliza. "Helicopter tour?"

Eliza shrugged and let her eyes rake over Mia once more. "I don't know what people do for an entire week in a place like this."

A faint blush bloomed across Mia's cheeks, highlighting her freckles. Eliza knew she was being rude, but she couldn't help it. Her default mode was all-business, thanks to her upbringing. She couldn't just rush off to the pool for drinks in the middle of the day.

Mia cleared her throat and tucked a stray lock of hair behind her ear. "I just arrived. I was looking for Cate, actually. Shouldn't you be out there, too, Eliza?"

The way she said her name made the hairs rise up along Eliza's arms.

Eliza narrowed her eyes at Mia. *Touché*. But she wasn't going to tell her that. She didn't plan to spend this week doing any of the activities mapped out in the tiny wooden box she'd received as best woman from her baby brother. Of course, she'd attend the mandatory family events like the dinners and receptions, but she had no intention of hanging out with her kid brother and his fiancée—or any of their friends—longer than was required. It's not like anyone wanted her there.

Eliza was at her best behind a desk, in a boardroom, on a conference call. It was what her father had raised her for since birth. Her brother had the charisma. Eliza had the MBA and had spent her entire life training for her new CEO position.

She was ready.

"I was just on my way, actually. I think they're all down by the pool." Eliza knew they were down by the pool. Her brother had texted her twice, and she'd ignored both messages. But Mia didn't need to know that.

"Oh. Okay." Was that disappointment in her tone?

She was about to speak; she wet her lips and parted them when a loud squeal erupted from the other side of the room.

Cate Richards, her soon-to-be sister-in-law, stood in the doorway with her arms thrown wide. "Mia! You're here!"

She ran to Mia and they embraced in a warm hug, rocking back and forth. It was exactly the kind of hug Eliza had been trained never to give in public. Never to give at all, come to think of it. It made something twist in her stomach.

"Oh, Mia. This place is gorgeous. It's like your family pulled something straight out of my dreams and brought it to life here."

Mia waved her off and held her at a distance, taking her in.

"You look gorgeous. I'm glad I'm finally here," Mia said.

"You look…sober. Come on, let's get you settled and

head down to the pool. There are some people I want you to meet."

"Sounds good. Eliza? Are you coming?" Mia turned back and her warm hazel eyes gleamed with an invitation. Eliza got the feeling Mia wasn't just being polite. There was a curiosity in her stare that Eliza hadn't felt in a long time. She really, really wanted to follow them. Her phone vibrated on the table, a reminder that she had work to do.

"Eliza, you should join us. It's gorgeous down there," Cate insisted.

Eliza thought about it. Maybe she could. Maybe once, here at a private resort, in the middle of the sea, maybe she could slip for a moment. Maybe she could try to figure out why Mia's smile was something she wanted to chase down.

"I can see you're thinking about it," Cate said kindly. She really did like her future sister-in-law. And she was from a good family. It made sense in all the important ways. But more than anything, she was happy her baby brother was marrying someone he loved. One of them should have the chance at finding love—and with Eliza's schedule and high expectations, it wasn't going to be her. She couldn't hurt someone the same way her father had hurt their mother. Better to stay single.

"Maybe this will persuade you. Mia is bringing some kind of mystery date to the wedding. And I want to hear all about it. Who is she?"

Mia froze and smiled weakly. Eliza's heart sank. Of course, Mia had a date. It made all the sense in the world. This was for the best. The last thing Eliza needed was a distraction. She'd focus on work, just like her father expected, and let her thoughts of Mia go.

Eliza nodded in clipped politeness at both of them and began gathering her items once more. "Well, hopefully

I can join you soon. I just need to clean up here and get changed. But if not, I'll see you tonight for sure."

"Were you working?" Cate frowned at the laptop in Eliza's arms. "Please tell me you weren't working."

"She wasn't," Mia blurted out. "I wandered in here looking for you, and she was reading."

Why on earth was Mia covering for her? And she was terrible at it, too. It was an obvious lie to everyone, but Cate was too kind to point that out.

"Well, anyway. Drinks. Pool. Mystery date. Let's go."

"Okay," Mia said. "It was nice to see you again, Eliza."

And as Eliza watched them walk out the door, she gave herself to the count of three to be disappointed before returning to her laptop.

CHAPTER TWO

Mia

MIA WAS GOING to come clean about her nonexistent date as soon as they got to the pool. But the rest of the wedding party was already in the water splashing, chatting and listening to music. Noah thrust something frozen and pink into Mia's direction, and her ex, Beth, was staring at her from behind large sunglasses. So Mia went into charming party mode, abandoning her plan.

Mia had swallowed her embarrassment down and looked for courage at the bottom of her Bellini.

And now she was going to have to conjure that confidence again for the evening's events. There was a dinner, where everyone would have their dates and their fancy outfits and questions about her family. Mia didn't have a date. Or her family there to back her up.

But she had an amazing dress.

She smiled in the bathroom mirror and waited for it to reach her eyes. Her extroverted side was going to dazzle tonight. Her parents would surely hear about how well she'd done working the room.

She *needed* some confidence.

But most of all, she needed to find a way to say *I'm enough on my own*. To Beth, to her parents, to herself.

First, she had to get through this dinner and come clean to her best friend. She chose a spectacular emerald green dress for tonight's soiree. Her parents had offered to send her a new wardrobe for the week, but Mia had found this one all on her own.

This dress made her feel alive. It hugged all the right places and made Mia feel like she was in charge of her own life, if only for one night. The neckline was a modest sweetheart, with just the slightest hint of cleavage, and although Mia worried it was too much, it made her feel too good to take it off, like sexy green armor. She pulled her hair into a sweep of curls, added a delicate silver bracelet and dotted her favorite perfume just behind her ear.

There were many balconies on her family's suite at the edge of the property, but this one was her favorite. To her left, the sea rippled out in waves. The sunset's sherbet hues reflected in the ripples and sparkled like a smattering of diamonds. But to her right, the hills of Sicily swelled around each other like the soft curves of a body.

There was an olive tree orchard, just like the one she ran through as a child when her family visited Sicily before their lives changed, and her father became obsessed with status and the next big resort launch. Before her mother became obsessed with appearances and turning their family into a household name. The steady rows of perfectly spaced trees, thousands of years old, bearing fruit for generations, grounded Mia in the moment. She wasn't going to forget who she was, or what she wanted, even if she had to fight for it.

Her phone dinged with a message, pulling her back into the moment. It was from her father.

Have fun tonight, Mia. Please say hello to the following families. I look forward to your report in the morning.

Below his text was a picture of his favorite notepad, scrawled with names in his writing. Mia bit the edge of her lip and nodded once to herself.

Right. She had a job to do.

She repeated the names to herself as she crossed the property and braced to enter the party.

The terrace overlooking the Mediterranean Sea swirled with life all around Mia. Elegant floral arrangements adorned the terrace in bursts of white and yellow and pink. A canopy of twinkling lights hung high above them, allowing a view of the stars and the full moon across the water.

Tables and chairs dotted the terrace with crisp white linens and a scattering of fresh fruits and blossoms. Each place setting contained a handwritten menu card detailing the courses for the night. There was fish, and then some more fish and finally fish. Mia turned the menu over in her hands and sighed. She would kill for a slice of pizza right about now. She absently wondered if she could sneakily order room service later. Or escape to town for some street food tomorrow.

Probably not. There was a lot to do.

She let her hand trail over the blossoms and inhaled the sweetness of the bougainvillea and jasmine. At least there were some good things about tonight. A gentle sea breeze caught the hair at the nape of Mia's neck and her skin prickled. Almost as if she was being watched. She glanced around the space, but everyone was politely conversing as the servers expertly wove through the crowd, distributing champagne and appetizers.

Mia scanned the faces of those around her; there had to be someone her father would want her to talk to. But every time Mia glanced around the open space, the only person making eye contact with her was Eliza. Her eyes bored into Mia's with heated consternation and Mia couldn't look away. There was an electricity between them crackling under the surface from their encounter earlier that day. Mia took a step toward her, seeking more of this spark she couldn't seem to shake.

"Well, if it isn't Mia Knowles." Chad's floppy brown hair had grown into a calculated swoop since their high school days, but Mia would know that voice anywhere. He blocked her path and grinned down at her. Chad had made her days at Greenwood Prep…well, not hell exactly, but unpleasant. And of course, his family was on her father's list. "Not surprised to see you here, attached to Cate's hip, as always."

Mia steeled herself. "Chad, always a pleasure." She smiled and channeled the confidence and charisma her parents expected. This is why she was here. Keep the Knowles name in other people's mouths.

His practiced smile made his left dimple pop. "What have you been up to? It's not too late to come to law school with me."

"I just graduated, actually. Public administration and business." Mia thought of the long hours she'd put into her degree for the last two years. The one her mother had called a waste. She'd learned so much and now had actual concrete ideas to strengthen her family's philanthropy work. There were so many potential opportunities to give back to their community. She just needed to figure out how to tell her father her ideas.

"That's cute, Mia. Maybe your dad will let you throw

more parties like this one. The food is great." Chad's smile was condescending and wolfish as he tossed an arancini into his mouth.

Angry tears prickled the edges of her eyes. This was all anyone would see. It was all Eliza had seen that morning. The baby of the family—only good for getting dressed up and socializing.

She scanned the party, looking for an out, and once again found Eliza. Her eyes seemed to go right to the core of Mia. She felt exposed, laid bare. They hadn't seen each other in two months, but with one glance, one brief conversation in the library this afternoon, Eliza had stripped everything away and obviously saw the same Mia her father saw: an unserious girl who talked too much and wasn't good for anything but a party. Eliza broke the stare first, shaking her head and looking away when someone approached her.

Who did she think she was? Well, Mia was going to show her. She'd do as her father wished, but she would do it her way. There wouldn't be Party Girl Mia tonight. She was going to be polished, poised and reserved. Hopefully word would get back to her father that she could be taken seriously.

But as the evening continued, Mia felt more and more out of place. The only thing people wanted to talk to her about was her social life and what they thought they knew about her from the latest magazine article. Mia had ideas, dammit. She had a vision for her family's company. She had ideas for philanthropy, but all most people wanted to know was if she had a recommendation for a place to eat while they were here.

"Mia, darling girl, come here." Cate's mother held out a hand and gestured to Mia. Finally, a friendly face at the party. Her silver bob shone in the evening glow. Cate's mom had high cheekbones and delicate hands. Mia had always been afraid she'd crush her if she squeezed too hard.

"Hello, Mrs. Richards."

"Oh darling, we were devastated when you and Beth ended things." Mrs. Richards sighed, clearly sad for her daughter.

"Yeah, I guess we're just better as friends." Mia said the words she'd rehearsed in the mirror.

Mrs. Richards tsked. "She was so broken up about it, too."

Mia almost choked on her drink. Beth had been anything but sad over FaceTime. She had been clinical, precise and unfeeling.

"We were quite shocked, actually. To hear you weren't ready to settle down." Mrs. Richards scanned the open space with her discerning eyes before landing back on Mia with one raised brow. "Cate said *you* were bringing someone. Where is she?"

Mia knew when Beth broke up with her, it might make things challenging for the rest of her family. But she and Cate had agreed to not talk about how Beth had broken Mia's heart. She had no idea that Beth had spun the story to make Mia look like the one who didn't want to be together. Mia felt a fresh wave of pain from the lie, leaving her adrift in sadness and frustration. She wanted to float far away from Mrs. Richards, from Beth, from every memory they shared. Fine. Beth could manipulate the past however she pleased. Mia didn't want to have anything to do with it. Not anymore.

In a moment they were going to all find their seats for dinner. Mia knew she would be at a table with Beth and, no doubt, Beth's new girlfriend. The thought made her stomach turn. Not with jealousy, but with white-hot embarrassment that she'd lied about a girlfriend of her own.

"Excuse me, I just need to check on something." Mia didn't wait for Mrs. Richards to respond. She pivoted and walked toward the balcony as she blinked back hot tears.

The moon hung low across the water, reflecting out in long streaks of white across the sea. Mia leaned over the edge of the banister and looked out across the waves. She needed a plan, and she needed one fast. There was no way she was going to keep telling Cate that someone was coming. She needed to come clean.

"Do you make a habit of barging into people's private spaces?" The voice was low and smooth, like silk on the back of Mia's neck. The confident tone made something stir in Mia's stomach. She wished she could capture it, drink it down, give a bit to herself. "Or is that just something you do for me?"

Eliza

Eliza shouldn't be talking to Mia. She should have been out at the party, mingling, making good impressions. This wedding was a business opportunity more than anything else, and she'd been distracted all night.

Mia glowed in the evening moonshine. The emerald green of her dress set her hair on fire and made the casual freckles along her collarbone stand out in contrast. The slight curve of a sweetheart neckline drove Eliza wild. She wanted to know what was just beyond that dip.

That's what Mia Knowles was. A walking contrast. Her quiet confidence, her cutting words. Her girlish freckles, and the delicious way that dress clung to her hips. Eliza couldn't help but stare. Eliza walked away, just to breathe, to get ahold of herself. Over on the secluded lookout, the music and the party and the chatter from the guests were dulled. Her father's constant observation to make sure she did everything *just so* couldn't find her here.

But then Mia had gone and followed her. Had she followed her? Mia looked startled and kind of annoyed. She did that thing where a small line formed between her brows. Eliza spent the last fifteen years learning how to keep her face perfectly still, to not give herself away at a business meeting. But there was something honest about Mia. Eliza felt as though she could read her every thought with one look.

Still, she shouldn't be talking to her now, in the darkness of this cliff's edge. Mia had a girlfriend. Or at the very least, a wedding date, which was more than Eliza could say for herself. Just like her father, she was attending this wedding week on her own. Her father told her that she would have to make sacrifices in life if she wanted to be successful. They all had to make choices. And Eliza chose work.

Mia huffed, and it was so adorable. Like an angry kitten. "Sorry, I didn't know you were here. I can go."

"Wait—" Eliza leaned against the rail, her black tuxedo jacket unbuttoned, revealing the silky bodice underneath. She didn't miss the way Mia's eyes quickly darted down and back up. *Well, that's interesting.* Eliza dipped her voice low, "I thought this was your thing. Parties. So, why, Mia Knowles, are you hiding out?"

Mia rolled her eyes and it hit Eliza square in the chest. Eliza thrilled at the idea that, for whatever reason, she could rile Mia up.

"Not you, too." Mia leaned over the edge of the railing. The sea breeze made her hair dance as something floral and delicate mixed with the sea salt in the air. Eliza wanted to tuck that lock of hair behind Mia's ear and get a better look at her face.

Instead, Eliza walked closer, mirroring Mia's lean, resting her elbows on the railing. "Oh, come on. I've seen the headlines. Hell, Mia, I've approved them for publication. You and Cate. My brother. You are always in the spotlight." *In the very best way*, she didn't add.

God, how many times had she reviewed picture after picture of Mia for the who's who pages? Hundreds? But none of the images were as stunning as Mia now, anger in her eyes, a bit undone. So alive.

"You think you already know who I am, so nothing I can say is going to change that," Mia said coldly.

"Mia?" a voice called out from somewhere behind them.

Mia swore under her breath before she pushed off from the balcony and turned to leave. Good. Eliza should let her walk away. If she cared about Mia at all, she would disappoint her now in a small way, instead of a disastrous way later.

But before Eliza knew what she was doing, she grabbed Mia's wrist and pulled her toward the edge of the terrace. Mia gasped, her eyes wide in confusion as Eliza caged her against the wall, and hid them behind a curve of a rock.

"You're out of view," Eliza whispered. "If you don't want to be seen here, this is the place to hide."

Eliza was making all of this up of course, but dammit, she didn't care. She would say anything if it meant thirty more seconds in this space with Mia. She held her thumb at the pulse point on Mia's wrist as it beat wildly beneath her. She should shove her hand into her pants pocket before doing something really stupid.

"I *can't* hide," Mia hissed. Her breaths came out heavy and her eyes flashed with heat.

There you are, Eliza thought. Eliza had the wild urge to move her thumb back and forth right over Mia's bracelet, but resisted. It was too damn much.

"I need to be out there. I promised my father I'd—"

"Your father?" Eliza cut her off. Eliza knew what it was like to have expectations put on you. She knew how hard it was to say no to family. Hell, sometimes she was the one demanding her own brother behave a certain way.

Mia blinked and shook her head. "You wouldn't understand."

"Try me." Eliza let out a breath and leaned in close. She thought of all the things her own father made her promise and all the things she didn't get to experience growing up. Mia's breath caught and Eliza realized she would give anything to know the meaning of that one sound.

Trust me. Tell me.

"Mia, what are you—" The surprised voice cut off with a short gasp. "Oh, um, I'm so sorry. I didn't realize…"

Eliza's back was to whoever had stumbled in on this moment. Eliza squeezed her eyes shut as she placed the melodic voice. It was Cate. Her future sister-in-law. Eliza froze in place, waiting to see what Mia would do next.

"Cate, wait—" Mia rushed out. She broke eye contact with Eliza and called, "This isn't…"

Mia tugged away from Eliza's hand, her bracelet catching on Eliza's jacket cuff.

"Mia, wait, your bracelet—"

Mia's bracelet snagged, pulling Mia stumbling into Eliza. Eliza caught Mia and steadied her, but not before a small black button popped free and landed on the ground. Mia leaned down and scooped it up before grabbing onto

Eliza again, more carefully this time. She pulled her out of the darkness of the edge of the balcony.

"Come on, help me explain this," Mia said.

The two stepped from behind the rocks, Mia looking annoyed and Eliza feeling like a kid who'd been caught with their hand in a cookie jar.

Cate's brows knit together and she frowned, looking back and forth between the two women. "Mia? Is this what you wanted to tell me?"

"What?" Mia squeaked.

"Mia! Oh my God. Of course." Cate brought her fingers to her lips as a small laugh bubbled out. "Why didn't I see this before? Eliza is your wedding date! No wonder you've been so secretive."

"Cate, just hang on a minute. Eliza isn't my wedding date. She's—" Mia glanced helplessly at Eliza. Panic and frustration flashed across her face.

"Oh. My. God." Cate rushed over and swept Mia into a hug. "She's your girlfriend? Of course she is. Wow! No wonder you were nervous to tell me. This happened at the Fieldings' fundraiser a few months ago, didn't it? You were both there. Oh, this is just so unexpected. I love it." Cate let out a little squeal. "Does Noah know?"

Eliza couldn't speak. She needed to clear this up. At some point, Mia's actual wedding date was going to show up and Eliza would look foolish. But Mia wasn't correcting her friend. She seemed too stunned to speak. Her mouth kept opening and closing.

Cate clapped her hands together, letting them know she'd decided. "Okay, I'm going to find Noah. If he knew about this already, I'm going to give him hell." She kissed Mia's cheek and rushed off, leaving them stunned on the balcony.

Eliza turned to face Mia. "I have a feeling I made the situation worse. Your girlfriend is going to be pissed, isn't she?"

Mia closed her eyes and fidgeted with her fingers.

"There isn't a girlfriend," Mia said as her shoulders slumped. "And now there is a big mess I need to untangle."

There isn't a girlfriend. That tiny spark of hope set Eliza on fire as a terrible, terrible plan formed in her head.

She couldn't for the life of her think of a reason someone like Mia Knowles would have any trouble getting a girlfriend. Unlike Eliza, who had a million reasons she couldn't date someone and would only end up disappointing a partner with her lack of emotional availability and her busy schedule.

But something with an expiration date? A few days of fun in a luxurious resort and, perhaps most importantly, being able to help someone like Mia Knowles? A tiny spark of something that felt a bit like hope filled Eliza's chest.

"Or," she said casually, as if this didn't matter to her at all, "we don't untangle it."

Mia crossed her arms and narrowed her eyes at Eliza. "Excuse me?"

Eliza shrugged and leaned back against the railing. She could afford to be confident now. "My brother thinks I'm just a boring workaholic. And my mother has been breathing down my neck to date someone." The edge of Eliza's mouth tugged into a smile. "And you seem to have invented a mysterious girlfriend. So maybe we don't untangle the mess. We could tell everyone we're dating. Win-win."

Mia raised her brows and dammit, it was charming. Mia Knowles had a thousand expressions using eyebrows and freckles alone, and Eliza wanted to figure out what each one meant. "You don't have to do this. You don't even like me. I'm sure she hasn't told, like, *everyone* yet." But even as she spoke, Mia took a step toward Eliza.

"You sure about that?" she asked. "Come on, one week. It will be easy. I'll be working, you'll be busy being maid of honor. We pretend to be a couple at a few dinner events and the wedding reception. No big deal."

Eliza's heart pounded beneath her camisole and she hoped Mia couldn't see how nervous she was. Mia stepped close.

"One week," Eliza murmured. "And then we make something up about a breakup."

She braced for the inevitable no, pressing herself back against the wall.

"One week," Mia said. She slid her palm against Eliza's. "You've got yourself a deal." Her skin felt like silk and fire all at once. Mia Knowles was going to pretend to be Eliza's girlfriend. For one week.

This was going to be a disaster.

CHAPTER THREE

Mia

MIA READ OVER the scrawled numbers on the slip of paper in her hands for the third time before knocking on the door to Eliza's room. Last night, Eliza had pressed the page ripped from her planner into Mia's palm, and whispered, "Call me tomorrow and we can work out the details."

But Mia had called twice. It was only nine in the morning and Eliza was already ghosting her. So now she was knocking on her door. They needed to talk.

The door cracked open, revealing Eliza, in dress pants and a silk tank top, her hair in perfect curls. Mia stood awkwardly in her yellow bikini, covered with a sundress and strappy sandals.

"Oh, wow. You look really nice," Mia blustered. "I mean, professional. In the pants." She gestured at Eliza's outfit and bit back an embarrassed groan. Why did she always get so flustered around her?

Eliza offered her a gentle smile, the way someone might smile at an inquisitive child. Mia fidgeted under her stare.

"I'm sorry, but I'm working right now. This is why I asked you to call." Eliza's words were brusque. "Look, I'll call you later and we can meet up to make a plan."

"I *did* call you. Twice. But the boat leaves in an hour,"

Mia said. "If we don't talk now, we'll be talking on the boat with ten other people."

Mia didn't add that one of those people was her ex-girlfriend.

Eliza blinked at her and pressed her lips together before raising one perfectly manicured brow. "What boat?"

"Didn't you read the itinerary? Cate and Noah chartered a yacht for us today." Mia fidgeted with the edge of her bag strap. "Well, not for *us*, for the wedding party. I figured we should arrive together. It will make our story a bit more plausible."

Eliza's eyes went wide as she shook her head. "I don't… boat." She looked back into her room with regret. "I wasn't planning to go."

Mia hoisted her bag higher onto her shoulder and bit the edge of her lip. Nerves swirled in her stomach. She didn't want to keep up this charade alone. "Oh. Okay. That's fine. I can just tell everyone you're busy. With, um, work. It's work, right?"

Eliza huffed out a breath and frowned. A small line appeared between her brows and Mia had the urge to smooth it out. She wasn't used to seeing Eliza unmoored, and she didn't like it one bit. "Please…don't tell my brother I'm working right now. Just… Come in, okay?"

Mia counted the minutes on her phone as she sat in the wingback chair of Eliza's sitting area. Five minutes later, Eliza emerged from her bedroom with her hair neatly tucked under a wide-brimmed hat and wearing soft linen pants. A black swimsuit strap peeked out at Mia from under Eliza's shirt, making Mia's brain slightly fuzzy.

"Let's get this over with." Eliza spoke with the efficiency she probably used when staring down a large to-do list at work.

Mia didn't want to change Eliza. She didn't want her to feel like she couldn't be herself. But she wanted to see how hard she could push her to open up. Mia knew under that hard exterior there had to be some kind of softness.

She leaned forward and tugged on the wide brim of the hat. Eliza's eyes went wide and it made Mia want to do it again.

"Let's have some fun." Mia winked.

The morning sun sent sparkles dancing across the azure ocean, but all eyes were on Mia and Eliza as they boarded the impressive yacht, looking like a mismatched pair of socks.

"I was worried you'd leave without us," Mia called into the morning air.

Cate laughed and waved to her from the deck of the yacht. "We almost did. Get up here!"

"Welcome to *Amore Mio*." An older man with a barrel chest covered in a white polo held out his hand. He had a thatch of dark brown curls and laugh lines crinkled his eyes as he helped Mia cross onto the boat. "I'm Captain Marcello. My crew and I will take excellent care of you today."

"It seems you already are," Mia said with a broad smile. "Thank you for waiting for us."

"My pleasure, signorina." He turned to Eliza, who did not take his hand and boarded the boat with confidence and the air of someone who just wanted to get this over with.

The ship was a substantial sixty feet at least, and as they made their way to the front they found fresh fruits, pastries and, yet again, fish, laid out in a massive charcuterie spread. A bar sat off to one side with a young man in a crisp blue polo waiting to serve them.

Beth sat in a lounger at the edge of the deck. Which Mia expected. Of course Beth would be there. She was part of the wedding party. But her girlfriend wasn't with her, which Mia had to admit was a bit of a relief.

"Remember," Cate said as she held up something alcoholic and fruity. "This is a relaxation zone. A time for us to unwind away from our families before things get hectic this week."

Everyone collectively nodded and whooped while Noah scooped Cate into his arms and carried her off somewhere secluded as they prepared to leave the harbor.

Two of Noah's groomsmen gathered near the bar, already ordering drinks. Eliza wandered over to the edge of the deck, leaning over the railing and staring out into the cerulean water, her ridiculous wide-brimmed hat obscuring her face.

Mia's stomach swooped. She thought she was going to spend today relaxing, but one look at Eliza and her entire body felt like a firework about to go off. She dropped her bag near a chair, abandoning her book and sweater, and headed to the edge of the deck.

"Hey," Mia said gently, not wanting to spook Eliza. "Is now a good time to figure some things out?"

"What is there to figure out?" Eliza stiffened, but then forced her shoulders to relax. "We're on a boat. We…do boat things."

Beth shuffled a few feet away, clearly trying to listen in on their conversation. Like hell was Mia going to let that happen.

"Yes, but we're going to have to do them as a couple," Mia hissed into Eliza's ear. She glared at her meaningfully and Eliza sighed.

Eliza slid her hand into Mia's and squeezed. "Come on,

babe," she said over her shoulder. Mia followed her gaze to find several people watching them. "I want to explore this boat."

Eliza kept Mia's hand in hers and led her up a series of stairs to the top of the yacht. It was windy up there, loud in a way that centered her and calmed her nerves. Eliza dropped her hand as soon as they were out of view. Mia leaned over the railing and frowned. Had she done something wrong?

"I'm already messing this up, aren't I?" Mia sighed. "I'm sorry, I've just never done this before, and I want to be good and I… I don't know how."

Eliza's frown deepened and she huffed out a breath. "Mia, you aren't doing anything wrong." Eliza grabbed Mia's shoulders and Mia felt it everywhere. The slight brush of her thumbs on the edge of her bikini strap, the firm pressure of her palms against Mia's cool skin.

"You're just saying that." Mia sighed. "I know how to *turn it on* when it's expected. I know how to charm a room and be the life of the party, but for some reason, I'm off my game. And you're giving up so much to be here. I know you wish you were working."

"For the record, you're making me say this." Eliza's voice shifted into what Mia imagined she sounded like in a boardroom. "You are Mia Knowles. You are smart and creative and brave. You have a master's degree. And I know what I signed up for. My work won't suffer, because my work *never* suffers. And this?" She gestured vaguely between the two of them with her free hand. "This is going to be fine."

The words rushed over Mia like a burst of sunlight peeking through clouds. Eliza must have noticed she was touching Mia with no one watching, because she removed her hands quickly and cleared her throat.

"You know about my master's?" Mia asked.

"Oh." Eliza shifted her eyes and looked away. "You mentioned it at that party a couple months ago. And I think my brother told me. Anyway—" she squared her shoulders and smiled "—we don't need some scheme. We just tell the truth as much as possible. So, let's go downstairs and wow them at breakfast. We've got this."

But ten minutes into breakfast, Mia realized she did not totally have this. And neither did Eliza. For all her confidence, when Noah asked his sister why they bothered with separate rooms, she practically spit her mimosa across the table. And while Eliza always seemed in control, this morning her leg danced under the table in a slight tap with each new question.

"I'm just saying." Noah shrugged and took another bite of his omelet. "I'm sure we can move you into the same room."

"That's not necessary," Eliza said with a shrug. "We didn't want to draw attention to us and take away from your big day."

"I'm staying in the family suite," Mia blurted out. As if that explained everything. She felt every bit the stereotype of a spoiled heiress that she was working so hard to combat. "My parents insisted."

"And I know Mia likes her early-morning runs." Eliza shrugged and took a sip of mimosa. "She needed at least one night of rest."

How on earth could Eliza know that? Did something about Mia scream runner?

"Mia, you went for a run?" Cate pouted. "But this is my wedding week. Relaxation only!"

"Running is relaxing. For me."

The conversation shifted into a debate of the best trails to run, then the best golf courses to play on, and Mia turned to face Eliza. Eliza's deep brown eyes stared back at her.

"How did you know?" she mouthed at Eliza. "About the running?"

"I saw you," she murmured noncommittally. Eliza leaned in close, her breath hot against Mia's ear. It tickled her neck, and she laughed despite herself. Mia didn't turn. She didn't dare move an inch. Eliza's nose ran along the shell of her ear and she wasn't sure if it was an accident or an act. Either way, she reminded herself not to get too carried away.

"You saw me?" Mia's voice was barely a breath. She grasped her water glass, but it was sweating and her fingers slipped.

"Running along the beach this morning. Do you always run barefoot?" Eliza said the word *barefoot* like it meant naked. And it might as well have the way Mia shivered.

Eliza

When Noah asked Eliza to be his best woman, she figured her duties would include standing beside him on his wedding day and giving a toast. She was good at giving speeches and rarely minded being scrutinized by groups, so she'd said yes.

There was also the fact that she loved her baby brother more than anything in the world. Even if she hadn't always done a good job of showing it. Especially in the last few years. But upon her arrival in Sicily, she'd been gifted an ornate wooden box with five days' worth of events for the wedding party outlined on heavy white paper inside.

She'd planned to skip every single one. Her father made sure she understood how demanding her new role as CEO would be—and she intended to make him proud. She'd been working eighteen-hour days. Sometimes longer. And just because she was in Sicily for the week, that didn't mean the work stopped. Even now, there were a million tasks she was ignoring to be here.

It was around four o'clock that morning that she bolted upright in bed. She'd forgotten to send notes to her administrative assistant before falling asleep. She *never* forgot to send notes before going to sleep. How could she have been so irresponsible?

It's not like she could make this up later. Promising to fake date Mia meant she had to attend this barrage of events. Her pulse raced, and it took another twenty minutes of tossing and turning to admit sleep would not happen if she didn't get some work done first.

She'd pulled herself from the bed, made a cup of coffee and thrown open her windows. The sky was the perfect shade of dusky gray blue you only see when night meets morning, and the world was calm. It was Eliza's favorite time of day. When the world was still and her brain had space to spread out. The breeze billowed the curtains, calling her to the window.

And there, down below, a mile away, a woman was running on the beach, right where water met sand. A fire-red ponytail dark in the moonlight swished back and forth. She couldn't see her face, but it had to be Mia. Seeing her doing something she clearly loved, something just for her, had made Eliza's whole chest ache.

And now that woman was lying next to her on a lounge chair, after the world's most awkward breakfast. Eliza could count eleven freckles along her waist from behind her sunglasses.

Mia had been ridiculous at breakfast, blushing beautifully whenever Eliza got within six inches of her. After that, the entire bridal party had spent the rest of the morning swimming and looking at the sea life around them.

Eliza spent the morning trying not to focus too much on Mia. The way her hair fanned out behind her in the water like fireworks. The way she'd blow out a long string of bubbles when she spotted sea life, as if she couldn't contain her joy. How water would bead across her chest when she pulled herself up on the ladder.

It was hard to reconcile the woman running on the beach with the woman Eliza had sat beside at breakfast. Surely, the awkward, blushing woman couldn't be the same as the confident one so in her element running along the shore? But it didn't matter now; they'd made it through the meal and the swimming afterward. What was much more pressing now was Mia laid out on her lounge chair, her sundress and towel discarded on the deck beside her. Eliza named each magazine category she oversaw, in alphabetical order, to keep her from saying something stupid.

Mia pulled her hair to one side and sighed. Twelve freckles. There was one on the slope of her shoulder near her neck. Eliza's throat went dry.

The second Noah and his friends had convinced a steward to let them try out the Jet Skis, Cate sat up straight and pointed a finger between the two of them.

"Okay, Mia. Spill it. How did the two of you get together?"

They'd successfully avoided this topic all morning and Eliza had foolishly assumed they would have time to work this out before they had to answer.

"Yeah, Mia. I'm sure there's a story there." Beth sat in the shade under the awning. Her words were saccharine sweet as she clicked a button to turn the page on her e-reader and frowned. "Why don't you tell us all about it?"

Eliza didn't miss the way Mia stiffened at Beth's words. She knew they had a history, but she didn't know how the two had ended things. She added it to the list of one million things she didn't know about Mia Knowles, but was determined to find out.

Mia turned her head toward Eliza and her eyes went wide. She was up to something.

"Go on, babe, tell them." Mia smiled at Eliza and bit her tongue between her teeth. "It's so much better when you tell it."

Eliza ignored how cute Mia looked with her tongue poking out. Mia Knowles was trouble. But when Mia crinkled her nose, Eliza rolled her eyes and said without thinking, "I've always had a thing for Mia."

"What?" Cate's voice was a high squeak.

To Mia's credit, she didn't balk. Her eyes narrowed and she pressed her lips together in a smile.

"Of course. Look at her. She's amazing. But it was two months ago that we finally talked." Eliza didn't realize she was going to tell this story until it was tumbling out. "You were right, Cate. It was at the Fieldings' fundraiser. Mia helped organize the donor recognitions. She was so…competent. She had this clipboard and kept biting her pencil. It was the hottest damn thing I'd seen in my life. So I made sure we bumped into each other and I offered to help."

Eliza's cheeks were on fire as she looked Mia in the eyes and said, "And I haven't stopped falling since."

Mia's gaze turned heated and her eyes went wide for a moment before she schooled her features. Eliza was in trouble. She knew it. Because Mia remembered. She remembered that night, too.

And Eliza was terrified Mia might know that she was actually telling the truth.

CHAPTER FOUR

Mia

MIA'S STOMACH FIZZED with anticipation as a candy-apple-red cable car came careening around the bend. It swayed back and forth from the momentum as a worker grabbed onto the rail and pulled it to a crawl. Exploring Mount Etna had been on her bucket list for as long as she could remember, and the impending cable car ride was a nice distraction from the butterflies in her stomach at the idea of seeing Eliza again today.

Of *pretending* again today.

"Do you want to ride with us?" Cate said, gesturing toward the car. "Noah and I don't mind."

The rest of the party had already climbed into the earlier cars, but Mia stalled as long as she could. Not because she was scared, but because Eliza hadn't shown up yet. Maybe she would not come at all.

But just then, a town car pulled up. The driver quickly rounded the front of the car and opened the passenger door, revealing a pair of long legs, then wide hips, and finally a waist that curved in slightly. Mia's throat went dry.

"Oh, good. She made it." Noah seemed just as surprised as Mia felt. "We'll see you up there, okay?" And with that, he and Cate jumped into the waiting cable car.

It was one thing to pretend to be together while people were watching. It was another to be trapped with Eliza Brewer for fifteen minutes as they ascended a mountain with nothing to talk about. Because Mia was not going to bring up the bomb Eliza had dropped yesterday on the yacht when she mentioned the Fieldings' fundraiser.

Mia had spent the last two months trying to forget the night that ended in disappointment. She'd been so excited when Mrs. Fielding had approached her with an opportunity to get involved. The weeks she'd spent working on the team and preparing for the fundraiser behind her parents' backs had been exhilarating. She'd shoved that night—and the woman who was the one bright spot of her evening before it fell apart—deep down in a locked box of her heart.

Mia had worn a simple black dress with a suit coat and had kept her hair up and out of her face in order to stay focused the entire afternoon. Her weeks of hard work had paid off. Donors had seemed happy, champagne had been flowing and, so far, her parents had not noticed that Mia had been working at the event instead of attending it.

In a few moments, she would change into something more acceptable for a Knowles, tug her hair down and join her family.

She would show them her work, her involvement. Her father was going to be impressed. This was going to work. He would have no choice but to allow her to support the family's philanthropic efforts. He would have to give her a rightful spot in the company.

She had bitten the edge of a pencil, a terrible habit she needed to break, and checked the last name off the list before dropping her clipboard on the table. She had glanced around the hall and noticed her parents chatting with another couple across the room. Panic had filled her chest as they began walking. If her parents saw her like this, well, her secret would be out.

Mia had dashed toward the room where she had stored her second dress and quickly removed the silver-sequined number from a garment bag, nearly tripping in her hurry to pull it up her body. Her elbow had banged against the edge of a chair as she had attempted to pull up the zipper.

No matter, she had decided—she would just finish it up in front of the mirror.

Once she had adjusted the dress, she had attempted the zipper again. But the zipper had been stuck, leaving her breasts exposed in the front. She was going to have to walk out of this room with a wardrobe malfunction to flag down someone on the staff. With her luck, someone would catch it on camera, and the only thing her family would remember from this night would be how Mia Knowles had been in the news again.

"No, no, no," she had muttered as she desperately tried to reach the zipper behind her. "Come on, stupid zipper."

She had tugged again, to no avail. The zipper had been caught on itself, and no matter how hard she tugged, it hadn't budged. Tears had pricked her eyes. How had she thought she could pull this off? If she couldn't change, then she would have to put her suit back on, and that wouldn't do for her father.

She had searched the room for something she could use to zip the dress. A hook maybe? The edge of a hanger? The door had clicked open, and Mia had frozen, casting her eyes downward. She hadn't wanted anyone to see her with half her chest hanging out.

"Oh! I'm so sorry, I thought this was the restroom." The woman had averted her eyes. Mia had waited for her to leave, but she had taken a step closer and said, "Hmm… looks like you could use some help. May I?"

Mia had nodded. "That would be great. Thank you, it's just… I can't let my parents see me like this. I'm not supposed to be working, but I was working, and now I'm not going to be able to go out there," she had rambled. "I'm supposed to be out there, dazzling people. But I can't do that with…" Mia had made a vague gesture at her chest.

"You're going to have to turn around."

Mia had finally looked up, noting the amusement dancing in the woman's eyes. Mia let out a small gasp. *Eliza Brewer.* Eliza was the older sister of Noah Brewer, a friend from college. Thankfully, she hadn't seemed to recognize Mia. That would make this exchange ten times more embarrassing.

Mia had done as she was told and had held still as Eliza gently swept Mia's hair from the back of her neck and to the side. Her cool fingers had made Mia shiver as she had tugged the zipper up the last three inches.

"Thanks," Mia had said with relief.

"Of course," Eliza had replied. "I'm—"

"Mia, darling, there you are." Her mother's voice had rung out in the space as she had barged into the room and stepped toward Mia. "What on earth are you doing in here?"

"Mother, hello." She had looked at Eliza, silently asking her to keep her secret. Eliza had nodded once.

"She was helping me out with a wardrobe malfunction." Eliza had held up a button and gestured toward an empty spot on her blouse. Mia could have sworn the button had been there just a moment before. And then, Eliza had winked.

It wasn't until two months later—yesterday on the

yacht—that Mia realized Eliza had known it was her the entire time. Or, at least, she'd put it all together since then.

It appeared Eliza Brewer's job in life was to keep saving Mia from embarrassing situations. She'd spent the week after the fundraiser remembering the feel of those fingers on her spine. And grateful that Eliza hadn't told her mother all the secrets she had spilled. But that memory was no longer a secret moment Mia could pull out sometimes when she was lonely. Because she shared that memory with Eliza. Her girlfriend. *Fake* girlfriend.

Mia's stomach pitched as she realized the unfair advantage Eliza had in this situation. Eliza Brewer had a way of sweeping in and fixing things for Mia. And that was the last thing Mia needed. She needed to accomplish something on her own. So, yes, Eliza was objectively attractive. And yes, she made Mia's stomach go all warm inside. But Mia didn't need a girlfriend to save her. Mia didn't need anyone.

Especially not a CEO with the kind of business skills that would put any of her work to shame. She needed to stand out to her parents on her own.

Mia blinked back into the moment and realized the worker was holding the door open with a frown.

"After you." Eliza gestured with one hand to the cable car.

Mia huffed and climbed in the small space, taking the bench seat on the right. Eliza slowly placed one foot on the swinging car, as if testing its soundness, before climbing in and perching on the bench across from Mia. Their knees knocked together and Mia mumbled a half-hearted "sorry" as she struggled to get out of the way.

"Sorry I'm late. Just a second," Eliza said in a tone that revealed nothing. She held up her finger before returning to her phone. She typed rapidly for several seconds before smashing one last key with a flourish. "Thanks, had to get that one sent out."

The morning sun reflected off the windows in the cable car, making Eliza look bright and fuzzy along the edges. Mia sat tentatively on the opposite side. She scowled. "Why did you help me?"

"I'm sorry?" Eliza didn't look up from her phone, scanning over something new.

"At the Fieldings' fundraiser. You zipped me up and then disappeared. I didn't think you knew who I was." There was a hint of accusation in her tone. And Mia wasn't sure why. Eliza had been so kind. But maybe that's what bothered her most. Eliza had a reputation for being brutal. Being honest to a fault. So, why had she treated Mia differently?

"Oh." Eliza's eyes went wide for a moment with realization. "I guess... I mean, I assumed you wanted to be alone."

"With my mom? Yeah, right." Mia was pouting. "I would have gotten the zipper." She needed Eliza to know that she didn't need rescuing. She didn't need *her*.

Eliza sighed and finally shoved her phone in her bag. She crossed her legs, letting her shorts ride up the edge of her thigh, exposing a delicious strip of skin. *Don't get distracted, Mia.* "You just seemed really nervous. Like there was all this—" she gestured with her hands "—fizzing around inside you. I just wanted to help."

"I guess that makes sense," Mia said, deflated. "I just... I don't like to rely on other people. I need to prove I can do things on my own."

"It was fine. Really. I know you like parties and big

scenes and being the center of attention. I was just doing my part to get you back where you belonged."

And there it was. What she'd already known. The world whooshed by underneath them as they steadily climbed the mountain. Eliza wasn't *helping* her. Eliza just saw a party girl when she looked at Mia. Not an equal or a professional. Eliza saw Mia exactly like the rest of the world saw her. Well, that was fine. They didn't need to be friends to get through this week. They just needed to put on a show.

And if that's what Eliza expected, that's what Mia would deliver.

Eliza

Eliza rubbed at her temples again as she kept her eyes on the floor of the cable car and not the ground a hundred feet below. The memory of her phone call with her father this morning was still looming in the back of her mind as she tried to work through Mia's words. He didn't even have the time to knock on her door and sit down with her to talk things over, but he'd called her just as she was about to leave for this ridiculous hike around an active volcano. All to help a woman Eliza wasn't entirely sure liked her.

A woman who didn't even want her help.

A woman Eliza had tried her best to forget about after that stupid fundraiser two months before. Eliza had seen her across the room, biting that damn pencil, and something had unlocked inside her. She thought she'd found a kindred spirit. Someone else who was working just as hard as she was. Maybe someone who had the same pressure. Someone she could relate to.

She hadn't meant to follow Mia into that empty room,

but when she'd found her in there, cursing in front of the mirror in a million sequins, she'd been at a loss for words.

"I'm sorry I didn't properly introduce myself that night," she said again. She sighed and set her bag to the side. "But I'm not sorry I helped." She finally lifted her face, just enough to make eye contact with Mia sitting across from her. There was heat in Mia's glare and Eliza felt it everywhere.

"When I took over as CEO, I knew there would be social obligations. And I'm fine in office meetings, or in the boardroom. I can present in front of a hundred people. But dressing up and being social…that's hard for me." God, this was embarrassing. Admitting to Mia she had flaws. Mia would probably end this right now.

But Mia's expression went soft at the edges as Eliza's words fell away. Mia was glamorous and Eliza was never going to really be a part of that world. Even with her auburn hair pulled back into a braid and ridiculous hiking pants that hugged her legs, Mia Knowles was a breathtaking distraction. But a distraction nonetheless. One Eliza couldn't let get in the way of her career.

And definitely not someone she wanted to let down when she inevitably chose her career anyway, just like her father had done to her mother. "I'm not good at making friends."

Mia leaned forward, about to speak, when the cable car hit a transition pole and lurched before clunking back into place. Mia hummed under her breath and leaned back.

Eliza blew out a steady breath. Not that she was afraid of heights. She was fine with tall buildings; it was just the instability of it all. The cable car was so tiny and the hundred-foot plummet below them felt so imminent. And the

entire space smelled deliciously like Mia. Like wildflow-
ers and citrus. Like sunshine.

Mia recovered and plastered on a smile, but it didn't
reach her eyes. "Lucky for you, Ms. Brewer, I am excellent
in front of a crowd. Leave this week to me. Just follow my
lead, and I'll have the paparazzi after us in no time." She
picked at her nails and recrossed her legs. "That is what
you want, right? What you expect? For your family to see
you happy and enjoying life?"

Eliza absolutely did not want that. Especially when it
posed a risk to Mia. But she *did* want her mom and brother
to seeing her dating someone, enjoying the week. And Mia
seemed to have decided. She was about to argue with her
when the cable car swung backward, her stomach plummeting with it. And then the pulley halted. They'd stopped.
They were hovering above a volcano with nothing but rock
below and…they'd stopped.

Eliza gritted her teeth and huffed out her nose in an attempt to quell her panic.

"Eliza?" Mia's voice was distant. As if she were under-
water. Or maybe Eliza was.

"Did we stop? Why did we stop?" Hesitancy crept into
her usually calm voice. The ground was so far away and
the cable car was so, so small. And getting smaller by the
second. She slammed her eyes shut in an attempt to disas-
sociate. What if it never started again? What if they were
stuck forever? What if the cable snapped?

A cool palm pressed gently onto Eliza's knee. "It's okay.
You're okay. Someone probably reached the top, and they
had to slow us down." Mia's voice was soft. But Eliza's
pulse thundered in her ears.

The cable car lurched again and Eliza knew for sure

they were falling. Then there came a gentle thud as Mia's body settled next to her.

"Get back on your side!" Eliza screeched. "The weight imbalance. Move back."

Mia shushed her and put her hand on her knee again. "Is this okay?" she asked.

Eliza nodded. And then Mia's thumb moved slowly back and forth. Eliza could hear her exaggerated breathing. "With me, Brewer. Come on. In through her nose, out through her mouth." Mia breathed again and Eliza mimicked it.

After what felt like hours, the cable car lurched once again and Mia's hand was gone as quickly as it had appeared. She maneuvered back to the opposite side and smiled softly at Eliza.

"Sorry, you just seemed really worried."

"Where did you learn to do that?" Eliza asked. It was a technique she'd learned in therapy years ago. The slow breaths, focusing on what she could hear and feel around her.

"Panic attacks," Mia said simply. "I get them sometimes. It used to be worse, but they're not as bad now."

Eliza nodded, amazed at how openly Mia could share something like that. Eliza could barely share how she liked her coffee, let alone details about her mental health. Her father had always taught her she needed to hide her weaknesses, lock them away. Emotions, good or bad, didn't serve anyone in business.

She wanted to tell Mia about her own anxiety, how she worried she wasn't good enough. For her job, for her father, for a girlfriend. How she feared she'd just disappoint someone by choosing her work the same way her father had always done. That's why she was cold. That's why she didn't make friends.

"Mia, I—"

But they'd made it to the top. Whatever bubble they existed in suspended above the mountain was bursting.

Mia cleared her throat and folded her hands into her lap. "Right. You don't have to say anything. Just do your best to pretend you're in love with me and I can take care of the rest."

Before Eliza had a chance to respond, the door slid back on its track and Mia dived out of the cable car, making it swing. Eliza stood slowly and carefully stepped out into the much cooler air. She took a deep breath, grateful she was back on land, but wondering why her head was still spinning.

"Come on, Eliza, everyone is waiting for us." Mia slid her hand into Eliza's and pulled her close. "And they're all watching," she murmured close to her ear. Mia's warm breath traveled along her neck and sent a shiver along the shell of her ear.

Right. Mia promised to put on a show. And damn, she was good at it. She tugged Eliza close, stood on tiptoe and pressed a kiss to Eliza's temple. "Now giggle," she demanded.

Eliza spluttered out a confused laugh that sounded a lot more like a snort.

"I can work with that," Mia mused.

They spent the morning on a guided hike around the craters of Mount Etna. The earth beneath them seemed to tremble with anticipation as they explored, walking over hardened lava juxtaposed with small plants shooting up from the ground in defiance.

Eliza was sure she'd fall at any moment. But Mia was

confident and competent, asking the tour guide questions, cracking jokes and doting on Eliza whenever someone was watching. Her fingers would brush the back of her hand, or she'd wink. She even leaned in close, squished their bodies together and took a selfie of them with the island stretching out behind them. Eliza would do anything to get a copy of that photo.

"Told you I could turn it on," she whispered in Eliza's ear. It was such a stark contrast to the Mia from the first dinner. The nervous and awkward Mia that Eliza found so endearing. This was Mia Knowles, exactly as the world expected her to be.

Eliza clasped onto Mia's hand like she was afraid she was going to get lost. She barely said two words. When they'd stopped for water and a rest, Noah sat down next to Eliza on a large rock. The island spread out below them in a stunning tableau.

"You know," he said leaning in close. "This might be the first time I've seen you without your phone clutched in your hands like a lifeline."

Eliza huffed. "Yeah, well, wedding week and all that," she said, trying to hide her annoyance.

"It's a good look for you, that's all I'm saying."

Eliza and her brother had been close once. She was the one who would help him with homework after school, and she turned up music and held dance parties to distract him when their parents were fighting. She had been his person before she moved in with their father and was told it was time to grow up—and time to stop doting on her brother. She'd been so desperate for her father's approval, she'd complied.

Eliza wasn't close to anyone now. This was maybe the longest conversation she'd had with Noah since he was in high school. Guilt tightened around her ribs when she realized that was more than ten years ago.

"You look more like *you*, less like Dad 2.0."

"I'm not Dad 2.0. Don't say that." The words were out of her mouth before she realized what she was saying. The worst part was her brother wasn't wrong. She *was* like their father. Which was why she was supposed to keep people at a distance. She'd just wind up hurting Noah more. She sighed. "I didn't mean… I just…"

"It's fine." Noah stood and nodded toward Cate. "I'm going to check in with Cate. Are you still coming dancing with us later tonight?"

Eliza's feet ached, she felt a headache coming on and her to-do list was a mile long. She couldn't afford to go out dancing tonight. She couldn't really afford any of this. But her brother was talking to her. He *wanted* her there. And the hope in his eyes crumbled all her defenses.

"I'll be there," she said.

"Be where?" Mia asked, walking up behind Eliza and rubbing her shoulders through her jacket. The touch at once calmed her annoyance and sent a new surge of something through her body instead. Something that felt a lot like comfort and desire all wrapped into one.

"Dancing. Somewhere." Eliza made a mental note to check her itinerary when she got back to the room. And then she'd work for a few hours. And then she'd finish work when they got back, no matter what time it was. "I mean, I'm not dancing, but I'm…going. I guess."

"Oh, this is going to be fun," Mia said, a twinkle of something mischievous in her eyes. Eliza felt a low tug in her belly when Mia shimmied her hips. "I'm going to get you on the dance floor, Eliza Brewer. Just you wait."

CHAPTER FIVE

Mia

AT THIS RATE, Mia was never going to get to Cate and Noah's co-ed stag night. She'd been on the phone with her parents for less than five minutes, but each question left her feeling increasingly unsteady. She wanted a bath and a good book, not a night out dancing.

"How is Mount Etna this time of year?" Her mother preferred Europe in the fall after the tourists were gone.

"It was beautiful, Mom. You'd love it." The panoramic view of the cerulean sky as it dipped into the sea and the vast lava deserts weren't the only things that made Mia's breath catch in her throat during the hike. There was also the way the tiny furrow between Eliza's brows would disappear, for just a moment, as if she was just learning how to have fun.

"Mia?" Her father's tone implied that this was not the first time he'd said her name. "Where are the pictures? I didn't see any posts on social media."

Mia immediately put her dad on speaker and toggled to the photo album on her phone. She had to swipe past three selfies with Eliza before finding something she could *actually* post that would work for her father.

"I was going to add it tonight," she lied. "I need time to make a story out of it."

"Good, good." Her father did not know what she was talking about, thank goodness. "Make sure you use the hashes so people find the resort."

And there it was. She was waiting for her dad to bring this up, and it had taken less than seven minutes. Her dad knew next to nothing about social media and marketing, but he knew Mia was good at getting attention. He hadn't called to check on her, then; he'd called to make sure she was doing her part.

"Of course, Dad." She bit the edge of her thumbnail and stared at the last image from the day: Eliza gripping the edge of the cable car seat as they made their way back down the volcano. She looked very annoyed in the photo, her lips in a thin line as she stared directly into the camera. Mia loved it. And she knew she'd never, ever post it.

"Listen, I have to go," Mia finally stated. "We're going out tonight and I need to meet up with Cate."

"Have fun," her mother said.

Her father added, "Pictures, Mia. Videos. Hashes. Do something helpful."

She said her yeses and I-love-you's and hung up the phone. Cate was her best friend. She wasn't going to use the biggest day of Cate's life to bring notoriety to her family. No matter what her father asked.

It had been a long time, maybe years, since Mia had felt useful in her day-to-day life. But maybe Mia could be of some use to Eliza. Eliza kept sneaking looks at her phone and biting the edge of her lip throughout the day. Mia knew nerves when she saw them. She knew *stress*.

If she was really dating Eliza, she'd stop the nervous

habit by biting Eliza's lip and dragging her tongue along the seam until Eliza couldn't remember the time of her next meeting.

But this wasn't real. She knew Eliza was only doing this to convince her brother she wasn't only about work. Mia was a temporary escape for Eliza. And Eliza was doing Mia a massive favor—saving Mia from her lie about a wedding date, or potentially a really sensational scandal that would set back any progress she'd made with her father.

It was better this way. A simple arrangement for the week. She'd see how much she could pull out of Eliza in the time she had. Mia was determined to make that furrow disappear again, if just for a moment.

"Mia? Hello?" Cate waved a hand in front of her face and giggled as Mia blinked back at her. "Wow, you must be thinking about someone else right now."

A knowing smirk crossed her friend's face. Mia's cheeks felt hot. What had she missed?

"What was that?"

"I said, did your dad listen to your idea?" Cate asked as she added another layer of mascara to her lashes. "About the Knowles Foundation? I'm sure he would listen if you just—"

"I don't want to talk about my dad tonight." Mia's chest felt tight as she pushed away the words *Knowles Foundation*. She ignored the memory of her father canceling her request for a meeting. She wasn't sure how to get through to him.

Maybe she should just take out an ad in one of the Brewers' magazines: "Heiress Tells All!" Except it would be about her wanting to do more philanthropy work to expand her family's name. She doubted that would get her father's attention. Maybe he would be happy to know she was making connections with a certain CEO of Brewer Media Enterprises?

She was *not* going to tell her dad about Eliza.

"No, she'd rather talk about Eliza," Beth murmured. She'd been doing this all day. Little side comments about Eliza. If they were designed to frustrate Mia, it was working. But there was a little thrill that she'd somehow managed to get under her ex's skin.

This was the most time Mia and Beth had spent together since before their breakup. Looking at her now, Mia could see the woman she had thought she loved hiding somewhere beneath the scowl. Beth was smart and kind and practical. Above everything else she was practical.

When she'd FaceTimed Mia to break up with her, she'd used data points and given specific, excruciating details of why they weren't a good fit. At the time, Mia had been crushed. But with some time and some distance, Mia knew Beth had been right. Not because of anything Mia could help, but because she and Beth just weren't *right* for each other.

"Beth, stop." Cate narrowed her eyes at her sister. "You promised," she mouthed.

Mia knew she wasn't supposed to see that last part. Maybe Beth didn't like seeing Mia with someone as serious as Eliza Brewer. You didn't get much more serious than the CEO of a multimillion-dollar company who, according to Mia's quick internet search, had never had a serious girlfriend.

By the time they arrived downtown, Mia already felt pleasantly tipsy, just the right amount of fizz running through her. Noah and his groomsmen were already spread out in multiple booths at the back of the club. This place was too small, too intimate, for a separate VIP area like the clubs she visited back home. Mia loved the freedom that came with the tiny island of Sicily. No one seemed to care who she was or what she was doing. She hadn't seen one camera flash in three days.

She spotted Eliza sitting in a booth next to her brother, Noah. Her hair was pulled back for the first time, exposing her neck and creating a delicious curve to the slope of her shoulder. Mia felt the annoying urge to run her fingers along it while they danced. She wondered how far Eliza would take things for the sake of the ruse.

Eliza looked up, catching Mia in a stare, but Mia couldn't make herself look away. "Dance?" she mouthed, tipping her head toward the dance floor. If Eliza said yes, then Mia would enjoy the night. She'd see where things might go.

Eliza shook her head slightly and looked down at her drink. Maybe she was embarrassed. Or maybe she was in the middle of something. It was fine.

"Mia!" Cate threw both arms up the air, each one holding a shot. "There you are. Hold this." She handed one shot to Mia and then clinked her glass against Mia's.

"To you and Noah!" Mia shouted over the crowd. She was about to take the shot when Cate stopped her.

"To you and Eliza!" she countered. They took the shots and Mia felt the burn all the way down. "Seriously, you two are adorable. She keeps staring at you."

"Really?"

"Oh, wait. Nope." Cate squinted at something behind Mia. "She's back on her phone. And frowning. How do you deal with that? Noah wants to throw the phone into the ocean."

She desperately wanted to turn back and see if it was true. Eliza was in a nightclub. On her phone. Probably with work. Before Mia could intervene, Cate tugged her arm and then they were on the dance floor, surrounded by a sea of moving bodies and music Mia couldn't quite place. One song. And then she'd find Eliza.

But before the song was over, there was someone at her back, a nose bending toward her ear. "You didn't come over to sit with me."

Eliza. She smelled like mint and sugar and limes. Her breath left a trail of goose bumps on Mia's neck. Mia leaned her head back, but didn't stop moving to the beat.

"You didn't want to dance," she lilted. She moved her hips. Did she just imagine the low growl that came from Eliza's throat?

"You're supposed to be my girlfriend." Eliza put extra emphasis on the word *girlfriend*, as if Mia could miss the annoyance coming off her in waves.

"I guess there's only one option then." Mia turned abruptly, wrapped both hands around Eliza's wrists and tugged her farther into the dance floor. "You'll have to stay and dance with me."

Eliza

When Eliza saw Mia disappear into the sea of dancers, she didn't think. She just stood. Quickly. She tucked her phone into her back pocket as she strode toward the dance floor, as if there was some kind of hook in her stomach she couldn't ignore. The idea of Mia dancing with someone else turned her inside out.

But now Mia was so close, smelling like sweat and citrus and slightly floral. It was driving Eliza wild. She was in so much trouble. Eliza tried to keep her expression neutral, but the steady thump, thump, thump of her pulse under Mia's fingertips no doubt gave her away.

The music shifted into a new song. Mia backed away and whisper-shouted, "It's fine. We don't have to—"

The bass kicked in and everyone shouted, moving in closer all around them. Eliza couldn't resist anymore. She didn't want to. She could let go. For five minutes. What was the worst that could happen?

She reached around Mia's lower back and pulled her close. Her body pressed into Mia's seamlessly. Everything about Mia was easy and smooth. It was the simplest thing in the world to press against the swell of Mia's breasts and look into her eyes.

"I thought you couldn't dance?" Mia asked. Her voice was all breath.

"I said I didn't dance, not that I couldn't dance." Eliza pinched Mia's hip playfully, making her yelp.

"Think you can outlast me on this dance floor?" She smirked.

No. It had been years since Eliza danced with someone. Maybe longer.

"I was made for parties, remember?"

But Mia didn't need to know that Eliza had next to zero game on a dance floor or otherwise. This was just like the boardroom. Never show your cards. Close the deal.

"Oh, Mia." Eliza leaned down involuntarily, just inches from Mia's mouth. "I can outlast you anywhere."

Mia's eyes darkened, her pupils blown wide. She began moving faster. Her hands were everywhere; her hair was everywhere. Eliza's heart was in her throat and she did her best to keep up. Every time Eliza got a grasp on her, Mia would turn or spin, press her back against Eliza's front.

Eliza threw her head back and laughed, lost in the beat, lost in the moment. She just wanted more.

"You know…" Mia threw her arms around Eliza's neck and smiled wickedly. "You don't seem to have convinced your brother."

Eliza immediately turned toward the back corner booth. Mia cupped the side of her face and brought her attention back to Mia.

"Eyes right here, Brewer." Mia's stare was molten hot and Eliza melted beneath it. She was practically jelly in Mia's arms. Mia could make her into anything she wanted. "Cate says you're staring at your phone more than you're staring at me. I think you need to keep up your end of the bargain."

The words were like a splash of cold water. A flush of something close to anger ran down her spine. Her brother, and her mother for that matter, were so quick to judge when she worked. They didn't understand. They *couldn't*. They had no idea the pressure she was under. Not to mention she wasn't sure how to act when she wasn't *on*, when she wasn't *working*.

"Listen, I never said I was going to stop working." Her hands dropped helplessly from Mia's waist. She stopped swinging her hips. She looked down.

"Hey," Mia whispered in her ear. Eliza shouldn't have tried to dance. She shouldn't have tried at all.

"Hey," Mia said again, more fervently. "I've got you. I've got this. Stay here with me. For five minutes. Show them you don't have to be all about work. You can set some of it down with me, Eliza. I can help."

Eliza wanted to believe her. She wanted to believe this was more than a panicked agreement made two nights ago. But she couldn't trust Mia. She barely knew her. Fingers brushed along her shoulder and her entire body shivered in response. She wanted it to happen again.

"Show them," Mia demanded. She raised her brows and leaned in even closer. There was a spray of summer freckles across the bridge of her nose. Another one below her left earlobe. She smelled like sweat, and heat, and everything Eliza Brewer shouldn't want. Everything she couldn't have.

She bumped her nose against Mia's. A question. Mia nuzzled slightly back and shrugged. "Yes," she said. "Why not?"

Eliza didn't want to answer that question. There were a million why-not's, but there was also Mia's perfect pout right at mouth level. She closed the distance between them and brushed her parted mouth over Mia's. It wasn't even a kiss. Their bottom lips barely touched.

It was practically nothing at all.

Still, fireworks went off in Eliza's chest. It was as if the room was simultaneously silent and moving in fast motion all around them. It was ribbons of color, vibrating, pulsing movements, and Mia's mouth quirked into a half smile.

"Do it again," Mia said against her mouth. "Kiss me. It's okay."

Eliza was the one to lean in this time. She took her time running her fingertips along Mia's arm, up her shoulder, into the space at the back of her neck. This was a terrible idea. It would probably end in disaster.

Eliza kissed Mia again.

CHAPTER SIX

Mia

USUALLY AFTER A night out dancing, Mia woke up completely drained. It was too much peopling for her. Too much being *on*. But last night was different. Seeing Eliza let go, just for a moment, made the crowd and the press of bodies completely worth it.

Eliza made it completely worth it.

Mia woke with the sun and ran five miles before she was scheduled to attend the Wednesday-morning brunch. She even scheduled an indulgent massage for later that morning to ease some of her sore muscles.

Cate and Noah's extended families now filled the resort and Mia promised she would be there for the morning brunch on the beach. She'd meant to talk to Eliza about it the night before on the way home from the club, but embarrassingly, she'd fallen asleep as soon as they'd gotten into the car. Eliza had to jostle her awake off her shoulder, coaxing her out of her dream, gently murmuring "Mia" into her hair.

God, Eliza was so *good* at all of this. She really knew how to put on a show. A very convincing show. If Mia closed her eyes, she could still feel the brush of Eliza's tongue on her bottom lip, seeking entrance. If the whole CEO thing didn't pan out, Mia had no doubt she could become an actress.

As Mia approached the private beachside gathering, she searched the tables for Eliza, hoping they'd have a moment to get their stories straight. A long rectangular table with at least twenty place settings sparkled in the morning sun. The crystal goblets of orange juice and water sparkled as the sun broke through the morning clouds. Flowers in oranges, creams and yellows complemented the tablescape with bursts of color in crystal goblets every few place settings.

Mia smoothed out her buttery-yellow sundress and said a silent prayer of thanks that she'd brought more than enough outfits for this wedding. Thankfully, she didn't have to think about the actual wedding day. Her bridesmaid dress had been designed and custom-made months ago.

She spotted Eliza at the far end of the table. Eliza, for her part, was not hiding the wear of the night before. She looked as if she hadn't slept at all. She wore sunglasses and sipped on her coffee. But her phone was suspiciously absent from both her hand and the table. Mia wondered if it had anything to do with their conversation the night before. Before she could figure out exactly where she was supposed to sit, Cate swept her into a hug.

"Good morning, Mia." She leaned in close and smiled conspiratorially at her friend. "I don't know what kind of promise you made her, but she hasn't looked at her phone once this morning." Cate raised a brow and Mia felt her cheeks grow hot.

"I didn't—"

But she had. Hadn't she?

"Whatever it is, keep it up. There's a spot for you next to Eliza. Although I think it's a bit unfair you can't be next to me. Promise we'll catch up later?"

"Of course," Mia said. A pang of guilt hit her stomach. This was her best friend's wedding. And instead of doting on the bride, she was off kissing her fake girlfriend on the dance floor and then falling asleep in her arms. Well, not *in* her arms. Just…on her shoulder.

But she couldn't deny that Eliza seemed calmer this morning. She wore a sleeveless shirt and her hair was pulled up in a simple knot.

Mia sat down next to Eliza and brushed a quick kiss against the edge of her cheek. "Morning," she said softly under her breath. "How did you sleep?"

Eliza stilled for a moment when Mia pulled away. Maybe the brush of lips against her cheek had been too much for morning brunch, but Mia didn't think it was so bad compared to the night before.

"Morning," she murmured. "Sorry, I didn't sleep well."

Eliza sat up and adjusted her place setting. Perhaps she had trouble sleeping because of Mia. Was this fake date arrangement too stressful for Eliza? She already had so much going on.

Mia pushed down her nerves. She could handle a tired Eliza. Hell, Mia often had restless nights when there was a lot on her mind. But last night was blissfully peaceful. She wanted to make everything peaceful for Eliza, too.

A faint buzzing radiated from Mia's small purse. She had it set to do not disturb, so her father must have hacked through the emergency system. It wouldn't be the first time he demanded to be heard. She quickly glanced down at the text message.

Please call me. I know what happened and I'd like to discuss your future plans.

Well, that was weird. A strange thrill rushed through Mia. Had someone told her father about her involvement in the Fielding Foundation? That would be an odd thing for him to text her about out of the blue, but she clung to that hope. Maybe things were starting to go her way after all.

She slipped her phone back into her purse. "That's weird," she said under her breath.

"Now who's on their phone?" Eliza's voice was teasing, but she must have seen something on Mia's face. She leaned in closer. "Is everything okay?"

"What? Yeah, no, everything is fine. It's my father. I'll call him back later." Mia took a small bite of her pastry and let the flaky crust dissolve on her tongue.

"You have just a bit of—" Eliza pointed to her own lip. Mia's cheeks heated as she swiped at the corner of her mouth. "No, wrong side, just…here."

And then Eliza's thumb brushed across the edge of Mia's mouth. The contact sent Mia's stomach plummeting. She was instantly back on that dance floor with Eliza's lips brushing across her own. She composed herself and took a steadying breath. *You're at brunch. With Cate's great-aunt and her grandparents, too. Calm down.*

"Thanks." Mia's words were all breath. Mia wanted to snatch the sunglasses off Eliza's face to get a clear idea of what was running through her head. "You're really good at this."

Eliza cleared her throat and sat up, the moment broken. "I could say the same for you. My brother was beaming this morning. Everyone seems on board with—" she gestured with her coffee cup between them "—this."

As if on cue, Beth dropped into the seat across from them. Her mouth twitched into a not quite frown when she realized who was sitting across from her. Mia had to remind herself, not for the first time, that Beth was the one who broke up with *her*.

"Morning." Mia pushed a chipper tone into her words.

"Mia. Eliza." Beth poured orange juice into a glass and sipped at it. "Did you speak with your father already this morning? He reached out to my parents looking for you, but said he was hoping to speak with you directly."

"I haven't," Mia said. This was weird. Beth and Cate's parents didn't have anything to do with the Fieldings' fundraiser. Unless… A sense of dread pooled in her stomach and her shoulders hunched. A knot of stress was forming somewhere under the surface. "I was going to speak with him after this."

Beth's eyes sparkled with amusement. Mia felt an instant, warm pressure on her thigh. Eliza's hand rubbed gently up and down, grounding Mia in the moment.

"That's smart." Beth set her juice down and glanced between Eliza and Mia. "You know, I have to admit. I was shocked that your parents don't know you're dating Eliza. I figured that they would have met her already."

Mia's heart beat rapidly in her chest. If her parents knew, then someone had told them. It could have easily been anyone here and Mia chastised herself for not thinking this through. If her father found out that she'd gone behind his back and worked with the Fieldings, he would be so angry. Angry for making him look foolish. And angry for stepping out of line.

It was an open secret that the families had a long-standing, unspoken rivalry in the travel industry. When Mrs. Fielding had asked Mia to help out at her annual fundraiser, Mia thought it might have been a joke. But it had turned out to be one of the best experiences of her life.

Foolishly, she hoped that by working with the Fieldings she could show her family how silly the rivalry had been.

Nerves coiled tight in her stomach. Of course, word would get back to her father. She placed her hand over Eliza's and squeezed.

"Mia and I were trying to keep things quiet at first. You know, to make sure we could handle the long-distance part of our relationship. It's not easy to be hours apart." Eliza's hand remained warm and steady on Mia's leg. "As you can see, we seem to be doing just fine."

Guilt pooled in Mia's stomach as she peered up at Beth. Her ex stiffened at the words, her eyes going just a bit wide. No one else seemed to notice, but when Beth's eyes flicked up to Mia's for a split second, there was hurt there. And maybe regret?

Mia didn't hold the eye contact. Instead, she watched Eliza's thumb as it slowly traced circles on Mia's thigh. There was a part of Mia, however small that part might be, that wanted Eliza's words to be true. She let herself think, just for a moment, how nice it would be to date someone that had her back. Someone who believed in her dreams and supported her. She reminded herself that Eliza was playing a role. For a temporary week-long facade. No doubt, workaholic Eliza would struggle with a real long-distance relationship. God, she didn't even know where Eliza lived!

Mia's phone pulsed once in her purse. She nudged her purse open and pulled out her phone. And there it was, just below the message from her father. A Google alert for her own name. She didn't want to click on it. She already knew.

The spinning lights of the club last night weren't the only flashes going off around them. Someone must have taken a photo. She closed her eyes and shoved her phone back into her purse. The credibility she'd worked so hard to build the last few months dissolved around her like sand she couldn't catch between her fingers. She was once again just a photo in a magazine.

And her father had seen it. At least he'd be happy. Mia tipped her head from side to side, trying to work out the stress that settled between her shoulder blades and neck whenever the pressure and expectations from her family became too much.

"I need to get out of here," Mia said. Mostly to herself.

"I've got you," Eliza said with a curt nod. "I know just the thing."

Eliza

Eliza didn't know all the hiding places in this resort, but she knew enough to be able to get Mia alone somewhere and figure out what the hell was going on. Eliza was a fixer. A closer. So, whatever this issue was, she was going to make it go away. And then she was going to make whoever upset Mia pay for it.

She was about to push back from her chair when the clink of a spoon against a glass quieted the group. Her father stood, with her mother by his side, and greeted the guests. Eliza's heart squeezed in her chest the same way it always did when she saw her parents side by side. Even though she was a grown adult, watching them stand next to each other as a united front dredged up all those times in her childhood when they hadn't. She knew this was all for show though, and that next week they would go back to not speaking to each other for years, if they could help it.

They'd been happy once. At least, Eliza thought they'd been happy once. And look at them now. Destroyed by time and money and the obligations of work.

"Good morning, everyone. We're so glad you could join us this week to celebrate our son, Noah, as he gets married."

Eliza watched her mother's neutral face as her father spoke. From the outside, you'd never know that she left him because he didn't spend enough time with his family. They'd agreed to co-parent in an efficient manner and in return, she kept up appearances at social engagements and business events. They were the picture-perfect amicably divorced couple.

But Eliza knew the truth. She remembered holidays her dad showed up late to, or not at all. The recitals and school assemblies he'd missed. The way her mother's face would pinch in disappointment when he sent flowers instead of himself. It made her stomach clench into knots.

"As many of you know, my daughter, Eliza, took over as CEO of Brewer Media last year. And while she's been busy learning the business and following in my footsteps, her brother went and fell in love." Eliza's cheeks went hot and she looked down. He always did this. He was a master at belittling and pushing you all at once; backhanded compliments for her brother and careful warnings for her. She gritted her teeth and forced a smile when she realized everyone was looking at her.

Eliza leaned in close to Mia and apologized. "We can go as soon as he's done."

"No," Mia said, plastering on a smile. "It's fine. We should stay. It's nothing. Really."

Anger flared low in Eliza's belly. She knew that face. Mia's smile was thin, flat and didn't reach her eyes. Her shoulders bunched slightly right where the thin yellow straps of her dress clung to her shoulders.

"Mia, you look like you're about to murder your breakfast roll. So, please, tell me what's going on. You told me last night I could set some of this down. Let me do the same for you."

Something passed over Mia's eyes. Hope, or maybe even more fear. She sighed and closed her eyes, slowly exhaling a breath. "There are photos of us. From the club last night."

The words came out clenched, as if it were painful to say them. Eliza didn't remember photos being taken last night. She just remembered lights and heat and noise. She remembered the salty taste of Mia's neck.

"Are you sure?" Eliza regretted the words as soon as they were out of her mouth. Mia's face flashed with hurt as heat bloomed on her cheeks. She nodded once.

"I have alerts on my phone. And apparently...so does my dad. Or at least, I think he does. He keeps messaging me."

The words sank in and Eliza's stomach pitched. If there were photos of them, then this wasn't some fake dating thing for a week at a secluded wedding they could quietly let go. If there were photos of them, then the world knew. Her mind went back to last night. The flashes. As they kissed. It wasn't just the lights. Someone was in there. And Mia didn't want to be seen.

"I'll fix this," Eliza says.

"There's nothing to fix. It's already done. And it's not like you leaked the photos. It's not like you could know how something like that would set me back years in a plan with my dad."

Eliza knew that feeling better than Mia could imagine. Her dad insisted she keep her image perfect, never showing a hint of weakness. He'd be so annoyed to see pictures of her out dancing when she was supposed to be working. Eliza was supposed to be the responsible one.

Not the one who was out partying. She had clients to impress. Eliza needed to see these photos. And she needed to solve this. Maybe she knew someone and could get them to take it down.

Mia squeezed her hand. "Eliza, it's fine. This kind of stuff happens all the time. I'll be okay. I'll think of something." She was trying to be brave. Eliza wanted to reach out and tuck the strand of hair behind her ears.

She raised her fingers to do it, fake dating scheme be damned, when everyone around her raised their glass and said in unison, "To Cate and Noah." She fumbled for her own glass of champagne that had appeared in the last few minutes and clinked it against Mia's before taking a tiny sip.

Mia sighed and pulled her phone from her bag. "Look. It's not that bad."

Eliza took the phone, unable to tell Mia that she couldn't care less about how she looked in the photo. All she cared about was Mia. But still, she searched for her name. And there, above her family's company website and the article from *Forbes 40 under 40* from last spring was the link to the photo.

Eliza clicked on it without hesitation. And there, front and center, was a photograph of Mia and Eliza in the club. Eliza knew that exact moment. It was just before she sealed her lips on Mia's for a second time. Their bodies were pressed close and Mia was leaning toward her.

God, Mia looked gorgeous. The bright lights made her skin glow and her mouth was curved into a curious smirk. Eliza's hand rested on Mia's lower back and there was no denying the connection between the two of them. Mia was very good at putting on a show. She even had Eliza convinced for a minute.

Eliza was about to click out of the photo. She didn't want to get caught. She didn't want Mia to know how looking at that picture made her feel. But just before she closed the app, the photo credit caught her eye. And the company running the photograph.

It was a subsidiary of Brewer Media. Someone had taken Eliza's photo. Someone had submitted the photo. And someone had approved this photo. And Eliza Brewer was not the one who approved it.

"Come on," Eliza said, standing and dropping her napkin into her chair. "Let's get out of here."

Mia didn't question her. She just rose and silently put her hand in Eliza's, turning her back to Beth, who was now giving them some top-notch side-eye. If Eliza didn't leave right now, she was going to do something she regretted. She was so grateful that Mia trusted her. She pulled her close and they darted away from the beach as Cate and Noah kissed to thunderous applause.

CHAPTER SEVEN

Mia

ELIZA PULLED MIA down a walk and through the private courtyard at the edge of the property. At this rate they were going to wind up lost. Or in the middle of an olive orchard.

"Eliza, slow down."

Thankfully, Eliza listened. She took a sharp turn and ducked into one of the buildings. "Come back to my room with me."

"Excuse me?"

"That's not what I… I just. Can we talk somewhere private?"

Mia's heart thundered in her chest. This was when Eliza was going to end things. End this charade. She was going to tell her it was too much to be associated with a party girl. Mia knew she deserved this. She had been reckless last night. She never should have danced with Eliza in a club, in the middle of town, let alone kissed her. Twice. And then lingered, her fingers toying with Eliza's chain at the back of her neck.

That had been stupid.

"I don't know if that's a good idea," Mia admitted. Her voice was loud and reverberated off the marble floors of the hallway. This part of the resort looked familiar. She remembered the tile, the floor-to-ceiling windows on one side and the cavernous entrance to the resort's spa.

The spa. Her appointment was in ten minutes. In the turmoil of the message from her father, she'd forgotten all about it. The woman at the desk looked up and a broad smile spread across her face.

"Miss Mia," she said in a warm tone. "Welcome back, Miss Mia."

Eliza gave Mia a confused look. But Mia knew this team. She'd been here before the opening. And she'd visited the spa more than once. The sauna was great after her morning run. Not to mention the massage on her calves. She waved and offered a hello in her best stilted Italian.

"Your neck. Your shoulders." The woman pointed at her. "You're so tense. Too much running."

"Oh, no." Mia forced her shoulders to relax, even as she felt the slight pinch. These stressful situations always manifested in her shoulders. Mia didn't have the heart to tell her it had nothing to do with running. "I'm fine. Can I reschedule my appointment? Something has come up."

But the woman wouldn't have any of it. "We have time now. You and your *amore*. We have time. Come. Relax."

Mia desperately wanted some time. She needed Eliza to slow down and think things through. To change her mind about stopping this arrangement with Mia. She grabbed Eliza's hand and pleaded with her eyes.

"You said you wanted to go somewhere private," Mia murmured. "No one will find you here."

Eliza bit the edge of her lip. Mia thought for sure she would turn her down. But then Eliza slid a hand to one of Mia's shoulders and pressed at the knot forming under the surface. God, it hurt and felt wonderful at the same time. Just like everything else with Eliza Brewer.

"You do seem tense. I didn't mean to be selfish. Let's get you a massage. Then we can talk."

Mia breathed a sigh of relief. Eliza's hand trailed from her shoulder down her arm and down to her wrist. She tangled their fingers together and Mia pulled her into the spa.

They were led to a dimly lit room with music playing low. There was a fountain of water babbling in the corner and two white fluffy robes resting on one wide massage table bed.

"Okay, so this must be your room," Eliza said. "I can go wait outside until mine is ready. Or until you're done."

"No," the woman said. "It's no trouble. I moved this to a special couple's massage. You are a couple, yes? So, Mia, you will lay down first, and I will show your *amore* how to release some of the tension in your neck and back. And then you will do the same for her."

Mia knew what a massage entailed. And she'd even done a couples massage in the past. But then, there were had been two beds. And she and her girlfriend had lain side by side while they were given massages at the same time. She'd never had someone else who wasn't a masseuse touch her before. Massage her before.

"Oh, I'm sorry. Maybe there has been a miscommunication. Eliza doesn't… I mean, she doesn't need to—"

"No, it's fine." Eliza's eyes went focused and determined. The way Mia assumed she must look in the boardroom. "I can do this. I'm, um, happy to learn."

"Then I will leave you two to change. Miss Eliza? You can put on a robe for now. Mia, go ahead and lay down on the bed. I will be right back."

As soon as the door closed a giggle bubbled up from Mia's lips. "Eliza. I swear. I didn't know."

"How can you be laughing right now?" Eliza hissed.

"You don't have to do this. We can fake one of us being sick." Mia shrugged and felt the pull in her shoulder.

"No, you're in pain. We can stay. I'll turn around while you get on the bed."

Mia nodded. She wasn't uncomfortable with her body, but she wasn't going to push Eliza. So, as soon as she turned, Mia removed her sundress and her bra and set them both on a chair before lying face down.

"Okay," she said. She closed her eyes and let her body melt into the massage table. "My eyes are closed."

Eliza didn't respond. In the silence, Mia heard a zipper slowly work its way down tine by tine before soft fabric fell onto the floor. She squeezed her eyes shut and tried not to think about Eliza stepping out of her pants. Then there was a soft rustle and an exhale. The camisole. And finally, two quick flicks of some kind of clasp. Mia didn't imagine what kind of bra Eliza wore. She tried to keep her mind blank, until Eliza let out a soft hiss, no doubt as her body felt the cool air hit her now-naked skin.

Mia steadied her breath. "Okay over there?"

"Yeah." Eliza's voice came out all breath. The rustle of cotton and the undeniable sound of Eliza tying the robe around her generous hips filled the room. "Just cold. I'm… decent."

Mia smiled into the bed, but didn't lift her head. God, Eliza was a surprise at every turn. Mia knew this took courage and she didn't want to spook her.

"You don't have to touch me. I promise. I know this is weird. But thank you for doing this."

"Of course, that's what fake girlfriends are for."

At that reminder Mia felt a small clench in her chest. Eliza wasn't calling this off. *Yet.* If they could get through the world's most awkward massage, then maybe they could get through the rest of the week still intact. Mia felt a rush of embarrassment at what was about to happen. Maybe she could convince her masseuse to just demonstrate and not make Eliza Brewer touch her.

"All set in there?" The woman's voice cut through the silence of the room.

"Yes," Eliza said smoothly. As if this wasn't about to happen.

Eliza

When Eliza woke up this morning, there wasn't a world in which she imagined she would have her hands on Mia's shoulders, gently rubbing her thumb into the crease of her neck in order to relieve some tension. And yet, here she was, adding one more moment with Mia to the bank of things she'd have to look back on when this week was over and the charade was done.

She pressed her thumb over the knot and Mia let out a small moan of relief. Eliza lost her goddamn mind.

The masseuse gave her some more pointers and showed her how to access the warmed oil and then left Eliza alone in this room with Mia laid out naked and exposed on the table, only a thin sheet covering her from the waist down and absolutely nothing covering the top.

"You can stop now," Mia huffed out. "I'm so sorry. This is so awkward."

"Don't be silly. You have so much tension." Yep, that was why Eliza couldn't keep her hands off Mia. It was for her physical health. She pressed down on the tendon at Mia's neck and Mia let out another moan that seemed on the edge of pain. "Are you okay?" Eliza's fingers froze in place.

"Yeah. Sorry. It's just stress. I carry it all in my shoulders."

"What are you stressed about?" Eliza asked. She pressed again, more gently this time. Maybe if they talked then they could ignore the fact that neither of them was wearing clothes. "Is it this? Us?"

"No," Mia said quickly. "Yes?" She didn't speak for a moment and Eliza took the opportunity to run her thumbs into the scapula of Mia's shoulders. Mia was like a cat. The more Eliza touched her, the more she relaxed, and the more she talked. Eliza repeated the movement.

"Yes?"

"It's my father. I thought you and I could help each other this week. I didn't want to tell Cate that my date had fallen through. I mean, how pathetic is it that I couldn't get someone to come with me to Sicily for my best friend's wedding?"

"I don't think it's pathetic. I mean, I'm here alone." At least, she had been alone. Now she was definitely something else.

"My parents tried to set me up with someone. It was a disaster. My dad is very concerned about my image. My family's image."

"So, when he saw that picture of us, he got mad." Eliza should have known. The photo wasn't necessarily scandalous, but she wasn't exactly thrilled to be in the news. In the news of a magazine owned by her company. As soon as her phone was back on, she was going to find out who did this. And someone was going to get fired.

Mia snorted. "Worse. I think he's proud. I don't know. Maybe? He's either mad or really impressed. I'm guessing he just wants more photos." Eliza felt Mia slump into the bed. "The only thing he wants from me is to be in the media. He doesn't actually care about my work. He doesn't care about my passions. Just the tabloids."

Eliza thought back to the first time they met, at the Fieldings' fundraiser. Mia had been so worried about her parents. Eliza had no idea she was under this kind of pressure.

"Mia, I'm sorry. I didn't know." Eliza blew out a breath. Mia was being honest with her. Eliza yearned to confide in Mia, but her father's voice echoed in her thoughts, warning her against vulnerability. Reminding her she couldn't trust anyone.

Eliza couldn't be honest with Mia. She could barely be honest with herself. Swallowing hard, she closed her eyes and spoke in a soft voice. "My father doesn't want me to date at all. He spent his whole life building this company, turning it into something our family can be proud of. Something he could pass down to me. Even when I was younger, he never saw Noah as an option. I've always been the dependable one. And I can't get distracted. I have to stay focused. To make him proud."

"Is this arrangement causing stress for you? Do you need to be working right now? We can—" Mia began sitting up on her elbows, ready to leave the bed. Eliza knew in about two seconds she was going to see more of Mia Knowles than she thought she'd be able to handle. The edge of her breasts and the dip of her rib cage were already in sight. Everything inside Eliza coiled tight, centering low in her belly.

Nope. No.

Eliza pressed her back down and looked away.

"No. It's fine," Eliza said as softly as she could. Mia tipped her head and stared at Eliza, concern and worry in her brow. "Hey. Hey? It's okay. It's going to be okay."

Eliza wasn't sure what she was promising. But she hated seeing Mia like this.

Mia's voice came out low and soft. Timid. "I know you're a private person. But I promise I didn't do this on purpose. And I understand. If you want to end things."

Eliza's heart thudded in her chest. In just a few days, Eliza would go back to New York and this would all be a memory.

She didn't have much time at all.

She searched for what little truth she could give Mia. "I don't *want* to end things." And she didn't, she realized. But she would. She pressed her fingertips down Mia's spine, counting the notches as she went. "We still have two more days. We will get through the wedding. And then we can work out some kind of breakup in a few weeks. Something amicable. Maybe we can just blame the distance."

Mia huffed out a breath into the mattress. "Please, whatever we do, can we *not* blame the distance? It's the reason Beth and I... The reason she—"

"No problem. We can think of something else."

Mia sat up on the bed, wrapping the sheet around her. Eliza reached out without thinking and tugged it up to keep it secure. Mia's breath caught in her throat, filling the quiet space around them.

Eliza had been touching Mia for the last twenty minutes, but the brush of her fingers, through a sheet, had done something else to her entirely. And Eliza knew Mia was affected just as much as she was. She could see the evidence of it as Mia's nipples pebbled beneath the thin sheet.

"You know—" Mia's words were low and dreamy, or maybe that was just Eliza's wishful thinking. "In another lifetime, I think we could have made each other really happy."

It was all just too much. Eliza wanted badly to believe her. Mia already made her happy and she didn't want to burst whatever bubble of happiness they had right now. Eliza didn't think. She just took half a step closer, her mouth mere inches from Mia's soft, pink pout.

"Could you imagine?" Mia murmured. Her eyes were hooded and she kept staring at Eliza's mouth. "An aimless heiress and a CEO? This would never work. Not in this life. I can't believe no one has figured out we're not in love."

"Right," Eliza whispered. She bit the edge of her lip and watched as Mia's eyes dropped there again. Was she thinking about their kiss last night, too? Desire pooled low in Eliza's belly as she realized how close she'd moved to Mia, naked beneath the thin sheet. Her words were all breath. A half plea for Mia to stop her if she didn't want this. "Definitely not in love."

Two soft raps on the door caused Eliza to freeze, her mouth hovering just over Mia's. She cleared her throat and pulled back.

That had been close.

Eliza was suddenly grateful the spa woman returned, instructing them to switch places. She was able to bury her face into the soft sheets and didn't have to continue the conversation that had been interrupted. But when the two women left the spa, she was certain something had shifted. Something she didn't want to admit to.

CHAPTER EIGHT

Mia

MIA STARED AT her phone and willed herself not to read the comments. She had half a mind to turn off her Google alerts, too. She'd tried to call her dad back after the massage, but the call went straight to voicemail. He was either very happy or very upset.

Mia had been a mess this morning. Frazzled and frustrated and coming undone. And Eliza had been right there. Calm and collected. Her phone was nowhere in sight. She'd even dared to put her hands on Mia and press at the knot of tension in her shoulders, working away steadily until it was no more than a sore tender spot.

When it had come time for Mia to return the favor, she had to close her eyes as she rubbed in gentle circles down Eliza's shoulders and then back. Eliza was so lovely, sprawled out on the massage table. Her skin was soft and smooth and pliant under Mia's touch. At one point, Eliza had let out an accidental moan that made Mia lose focus for a moment.

Mia had meant to tell her thank you when they were done, but Eliza had to run off for a meeting. She hurriedly told Mia she'd see her tonight at the sunset beach mixer.

Mia spent the afternoon wandering the property. She

stepped into the olive orchard next door and rambled among the trees. There was so much beauty in the trees, the fields. It renewed her spirit to be so close to nature. When Mia was younger, she'd run through the orchards and scrape her knees and dream of her future. But her mother has chastised her and her father reminded her that it was improper for an heiress to run amok. So now she stuck to treadmills and marathons, and running when she could be photographed and handed a medal.

Mia stretched her limbs in the warm sun and contemplated her future. There was what her father wanted…but what did Mia want? Did she want to be constantly under his thumb? She kept letting him win, even at the expense of her own happiness.

Eliza didn't seem to enjoy the pressure from her father, but she appeared to thrive as CEO. She was confident and charismatic and calm under pressure. She was at her best when her fingers were flying on her keyboard.

But that wasn't Mia.

By the time she'd made it back to her room and showered for the mixer, it was too late to call her parents again. But she was going to tell them. As soon as she got home. She was done with these games. She wanted to pursue a career in philanthropy—with or without her family's support. She'd find a nonprofit to work for. She'd open her own nonprofit. She'd figure it out. Worst-case scenario, she'd wait until she was thirty, and then use her trust fund to do it.

With a start Mia realized the only person she really wanted to tell about this revelation was Eliza. She imagined Eliza's smile when she told her. It sent a thrill down Mia's spine. *Thank you for giving me a massage. Also, I think your fingers are magic because they helped me realize I don't need my dad's approval. And also, will you please let me maybe put those fingers in my mouth?* God, that was unhinged.

But Eliza made Mia a little unhinged.

She sighed and adjusted her cotton dress before heading out of the hotel room. A casual mixer on the beach was much needed after the luxurious brunch this morning and an afternoon in the sun.

When she arrived, Mia realized she'd severely underestimated what a beach mixer for Cate and Noah's wedding would entail. She'd dressed more casually than she should have. Everyone else seemed ready for a fancy dinner, not a beach party. Embarrassment flushed hot in her cheeks. This was exactly the kind of thing her parents would chastise her for. But she was twenty-six, not sixteen. So she decided to fake confidence in her pink shimmery beach cover-up dress and strode over to Cate.

"Mia, you made it!" Her best friend's voice carried through the crowd.

Cate stood near one of the bars, Noah on one side and Beth on the other. Noah wore a dark suit with the sleeves rolled up and Cate was in a floral cocktail dress. Even Beth was in a short black dress. But they were all barefoot. The one part of this evening Mia seemed to get right.

Mia hugged Cate, then Noah, and finally gave Beth an awkward nod. "I definitely did not get the black-tie beach mixer memo," Mia sighed. "I'm going to go change."

"It's fine." Cate waved her hand around, the bright orange-and-red cocktail swirling in the glass. "No one is going to notice."

It wasn't the comfort her friend thought it was. Mia felt even more out of place. She took one step backward, determined to slip into something better suited for the occasion, and bumped into someone. Warm arms encircled her waist and a familiar scent enveloped her as Eliza held her tight. Eliza nuzzled her face into Mia's neck and said in a low voice, but still loud enough for everyone else to hear, "Don't you dare change out of this dress."

She squeezed Mia's hip. The press of her fingers was a reminder of that morning. Her breath on Mia's neck was a memory of the kiss they'd almost shared in the dark, close-quartered spa treatment room.

Mia sucked in a breath of shock and surprise.

"I like you like this," Eliza said again. She let go and backed up to take in Mia's soft summer dress.

Mia felt goose bumps rise along everywhere Eliza's eyes trailed. My God. They had one fake kiss and one almost kiss and Mia's body couldn't contain itself. She worked to keep her composure, but she knew her entire body was flushed.

Eliza wore a fitted suit similar to her brother's. But Eliza had left the jacket open and the top few buttons of her blouse were undone. Mia's gaze dropped to Eliza's deliciously soft stomach and up to the thin line of cleavage peeking out from her blouse. It was the least put together Mia had ever seen Eliza in public. And she liked it. A lot. Mia tugged at the collar of her blouse.

"Speak for yourself," she murmured. "This looks great."

"Um, okay you two. Can you try to keep it together for at least a few hours?" Cate teased with a lilt and a knowing smile.

Beth snorted and rolled her eyes. Mia wanted to say something, but couldn't be bothered. Instead, she turned to Eliza and winked. "No promises," she giggled. Then she looped her hand in Eliza's and pulled her from the group. "We'll catch up with you all later."

Mia needed to get Eliza alone for a few minutes. She wanted to tell her thank you. And she wanted to tell her about her plan. She was going to stand up to her father. And she was hoping that maybe Eliza would be willing to keep the fake dating thing going. Just for another week or so, until after she talked to her parents. Otherwise, they would blame this declaration on the breakup and wouldn't take her seriously at all. And Mia needed them to take this seriously.

"Thanks for covering for me back there," she said, leaning in toward Eliza. She found a cabana a few rows down with loungers facing the ocean. The butter-yellow-striped canvas gave the feeling of privacy.

"Oh." Eliza seemed to take a minute to realize what Mia was referring to. She shrugged. "It's a good dress."

"It's pink and shimmers in the light. Everyone else is in black and white."

Eliza shrugged again, a small smile tugging at the corners. "It's blush. Barely pink. And you look good."

"You think I look good?" Mia smiled and batted her lashes at Eliza.

"Stop. You know you're gorgeous."

Mia felt heat spread across her body and low in her belly. Something in Eliza's eyes told Mia this wasn't just an act. There was a part of Eliza, however small that part might be, that wanted Mia. Mia was tempted to see how far she could push Eliza. How far she could push herself. What would Eliza do when there was no one there to see?

"Whatever," Mia said instead. "I wanted to talk to you. About this morning." Mia was going to tell her all the ways Eliza was wonderful. How much she'd helped. How giving she'd been. It was all on the tip of her tongue.

"It was nothing," Eliza said, brushing the comment aside. "There isn't anything to thank me for. We both knew this week was going to put us in some weird situations."

"Weird?"

"Yeah. You know. Awkward." Eliza raised a brow and mimed massaging. "But I think we convinced the masseuse. That was close."

"Yeah," Mia said softly. Well, someone had been convinced—Mia. God, what a fool she was. Mia swallowed thickly and looked away. Whatever opening she'd thought she'd had with Eliza just a few moments before was gone. Eliza was back to treating this, treating her, like a business deal.

"What did you want to talk about?" Eliza asked. She sat on the edge of a chaise and crossed one leg at the ankle. Grains of sand clung to the bottom of her feet like sugar. Eliza absently brushed them away.

Her business-deal face was on, like she was already closed off.

"Oh, nothing. Just something about my parents." Mia waved it away. She didn't need to trouble Eliza with that nonsense. How could she explain it? Compared to Eliza's father, Mia's troubles with her parents seemed trivial.

"Your parents are here," Eliza said with alarm.

"No. They're not here. They couldn't come. It's just—"

"Are you sure?" Eliza looked beyond Mia.

Mia turned and sure enough, her parents were less than fifty feet away talking with another couple. Her parents. Who were supposed to be in New York. Her parents who told her they couldn't come to this event, but they trusted her to handle everything.

Her parents were here. They didn't trust her at all.

Eliza

Mia's face went from confused to upset and then to schooled, perfect calm in a matter of seconds. Eliza wasn't sure what Mr. and Mrs. Knowles were doing at the mixer, but it was very clear that Mia was not expecting them. And Mia didn't seem to be the kind of person who liked surprises.

That must be why Eliza felt the urge to reach out and put a calming hand on Mia's shoulder. To pull her close and whisper in her ear that she could rely on Eliza. That she wasn't going anywhere. But she didn't want to make a promise she couldn't keep.

"Umm, how do you want to handle this?" Eliza said quickly. They hadn't discussed Mia's parents. At all. Were they in on the fake dating arrangement? Was Eliza supposed to keep the act going, or turn things down a bit? She felt like she was about to give a presentation and had left her laptop and notes back in her office.

"Mom? Dad?" Mia waved at her parents from a distance, catching their attention.

Her dad looked from Mia to Eliza and frowned. Okay, so maybe this was going to be even worse than Eliza had thought. She had no experience with impressing a partner's parents. She barely had experience with her own parents. Once her parents divorced, she spent more time caring for Noah and making sure he was okay than either of their parents. And once she was a teenager, she moved in with her father and he treated her more like an intern than his daughter.

She didn't know what to say or how to act. Panic coursed through her as the two people approached. Her own parents had kept their distance from her and Mia, watching her with distrustful amusement and frustration. But Mia's parents marched over with shock and concern. Eliza needed to prove she was trustworthy.

"Hello. I'm Eliza Brewer, CEO of Brewer Media. It's

so nice to meet you. I'm sorry we didn't tell you we were dating. It's so nice to meet you. I already said that." Eliza clamped her lips shut and thrust her hand out, practically wiggling her fingers waiting for a handshake. "Your daughter is an amazing person."

Mr. and Mrs. Knowles stared at Eliza with amusement. Finally, Mrs. Knowles leaned in and offered Eliza a stiff hug. Mr. Knowles took her hand and shook it.

"Of course, we knew you were dating," he said with a barrel laugh.

The hair went up on Eliza's neck. She knew when someone was lying—and this man had no idea who she was. "Mia told us all about it. Our daughter wouldn't keep something so important from us just to have it come up in the magazines first."

Mr. Knowles had a high forhead, a clean jawline and perfectly manicured fingers that he placed on Mia's shoulder before giving a slight squeeze. Her shoulders pinched up just slightly and Eliza wondered how much of Mia's stress and tension came from years of hunching just like that.

"Of course," Eliza said. "Well, it's nice to meet you. Officially. In this capacity."

Mia's eyes flitted to Eliza's and held her gaze. They seemed to be saying *thank you* and *I'm sorry* and *what a mess* all at once. Eliza tried to push all the sentiments back in her responding smile. *I've got you. You aren't alone. Let me carry some of this.*

Mia's parents settled onto the loungers and Eliza had a growing fear that she was about to be interrogated. Or maybe like she was back in boarding school and a lecture from the dean was imminent.

"Can I grab the two of you a drink?" The words tumbled from her mouth as she rushed to stand.

"Isn't there a server who will do that?" Mrs. Knowles asked as she looked around the space.

"I'm happy to do it," Eliza said. "How about the signature cocktail?"

When Mia's parents finally agreed, Eliza couldn't get away fast enough. She would just give them a few minutes to gather their thoughts. Then she would come back, give them their drinks and Eliza would spend the rest of the night trying to get the Knowleses to like her.

When Eliza approached the bar, her brother and Cate were gone. But another familiar face was leaning on the counter, surveying the scene like a lion looking out over his pride.

"Father," Eliza said in a formal tone. "Nice to see you at one of these prewedding events."

"Oh, don't be like that. I'm here, aren't I? And I'm technically *retired*. The better question is, what are *you* doing here?"

Eliza stiffened at her father's brusque tone. She was used to him putting unspoken pressure on her, but no worse than she put on herself. Eliza shrugged.

"I turned my phone off for the day. I put up an out-of-office notification. It should be fine."

"I am well aware you have an out-of-office response on, Eliza. I've received it three times today."

Bile rose up in the back of her throat. What was her dad doing? He was supposed to be retired. Not sending his daughter work emails from his son's wedding. Still, she couldn't ignore the panic rising in her throat.

"Is something wrong?"

Her father frowned at her. She would have preferred a sneer. This just looked like inevitable disappointment. "Apparently nothing I couldn't take care of." He took a long sip of a warm brown liquid in his glass. "Turn on your damn phone, Eliza."

And then he walked away. Eliza felt like she was five years old. Or she was twenty-five, receiving her preplanned promotion to vice president of the company. She felt like she was seventeen, being told what to major in and where to go to college. She felt like she was fifteen, breaking up with her high school girlfriend because it wasn't part of her father's ten-year plan.

Eliza held her breath, reached into her coat pocket and pulled out her phone. She hated that she was so predictable. He probably knew she still had it on her, even if it was tucked away.

Her phone immediately began buzzing with missed calls, voicemails, text messages and emails. She focused in on her work inbox and made quick work of identifying anything that involved her father.

A few story proofs, a meeting scheduled for next week and there, toward the bottom of the pile, was an email with an attachment. The subject line read Sensitive photos. It was an email from one of their photographers. One of the ones paid to be at this wedding. With six versions of the photo Eliza now knew all too well. Eliza and Mia dancing, Eliza and Mia kissing, Eliza and Mia with their bodies pressed close.

The details of the email blurred together as Eliza tried to make sense of it.

Hey boss, I don't think you want these public, but I couldn't resist snapping a photo of you and your partner at the club. Let me know if need anything else.

Her father wasn't even on the original email. Which meant he must still be monitoring her work email with his old account. Anger burned up in her fast and red-hot.

These photos are great. Please add one to the celebrity
column for tomorrow. If Eliza has time to party, we may
as well get some sales out of it.

Her father. Her father had approved the photo. Eliza
couldn't care less about the photograph. They regularly
included photos of their family at events, especially when
they were with other people society cared more about. And
Mia Knowles was definitely someone people cared about.

But he hadn't asked her. And this time she would have
said no. She knew Mia was weird about paparazzi. She
knew Mia didn't want to be in the spotlight.

The messages went back and forth for a bit. Her father
finally stated he spoke to Eliza and she gave her approval.
A fist clenched around her heart and squeezed tight. He'd
lied to the editor. He'd lied to her. He didn't trust her. Or
respect her.

But above all, her heart hurt for Mia. She had to tell
her that the photograph came from her company. That she
was the reason it went to print. It made Eliza's chest ache.

"Can you put your phone away for five minutes?"

Her mother's voice was a hiss in her ear. Eliza immediately pocketed the phone and sighed. She and her mother
weren't close. When her parents had split, Eliza chose to
live with her father. Noah split time between the two. Her
mother viewed it as a betrayal, but Eliza just saw it as a
practicality. She had a lot to learn and she wasn't going
to learn it from California, where her mother had moved
after the divorce.

"Hello, Mother." Eliza decided to play nice. She was already mad at her father. No need to add more to the mix.
"You're right. It's away. Are you having fun?"

Her mom stared at her for a moment, no doubt stunned by the lack of pushback.

"Maybe that Mia girl is good for you," she finally said, taking another sip of her drink. "Where is she? I wanted to introduce myself."

Eliza turned to look back at the cabana. *Crap.* The drinks. "She's sitting with her parents. I'm supposed to be getting drinks."

"Her parents? Wow, this is serious."

Eliza shrugged. She didn't want to lie any more than she already was.

"Yeah, I guess it is."

"Well, you seem happy. Don't let go of it. Your father and I were happy once. And then we ruined it with animosity and work and not being honest with each other. Your brother seems to have found his match in Cate. Maybe you've found yours, too."

Eliza swallowed back a response. She couldn't explain to her mother, of all people, that the only reason she seemed happy was because work couldn't ruin a fake relationship.

The bartender handed Eliza four drinks and her mother eyed her curiously. "Don't let your father determine what happiness and success looks like for you. His dreams don't have to be yours. And his pressure has no place on your back."

Eliza was used to this kind of speech from her mother, but she wasn't used to it stinging quite so much. She'd usually have a quick comeback like *I like my work* or *I also don't need to define myself by your criteria.* Or even *If I didn't take this on, then it would be Noah. And we both know he'd be miserable.*

Her mother always seemed to forget that Noah's choices and her own choices left Eliza with no choices at all. She took on the responsibilities of the family, the company, so they wouldn't have to. And she'd do it again.

But she didn't want Mia to wind up like her mother. Resenting Eliza and spending the rest of her life regretting the years they spent together. No, not Mia. Anyone. Eliza didn't mean Mia. They weren't dating. So there was no possibility Mia would end up like this.

They just needed to stick to the plan. But first Eliza needed to deliver these drinks. And make it through one more night without kissing Mia Knowles.

CHAPTER NINE

Mia

THIS WAS A bad idea. It was after midnight and she shouldn't be a baby about all this. But she couldn't stay in that suite one more minute. Not after her parents' constant barrage of questions. But now she was in her slippers and had the bathrobe from the bathroom closet draped over her shoulders, which felt a lot like the one Eliza had worn in the spa earlier that day.

She knocked again. "Please be awake, please be awake," she murmured under her breath. She was about to knock a third time when the door cracked open two inches and Eliza's face popped into view.

"Mia?" She blinked a few times, as if she couldn't be sure this was actually Mia standing in front of her. Mia flushed as Eliza's eyes took in her thin cotton pajamas, exposing more than Mia would like. "You're…you're in pajamas."

"Yes, welcome to me having a crisis in the middle of the night. Can I come in?"

Eliza pulled the door back and frowned. "Are you okay?"

"Yes, no. I don't know." Mia paced back and forth. "My parents. They take up a lot of—" she mimed what she

hoped would mean, energy, chaos, enormity "—space.
Even in a three-bedroom suite. And I would normally go
to Cate's room, but she's getting married in two days. And
she'd probably look at me weird considering you're my
girlfriend and I *should* be going to your room. So I did.
Come to your room. And now I see that was a big mistake
and I'll go. I'm so sorry I interrupted your night. You were
probably asleep and I—"

Mia felt the cool pressure of Eliza's hands on her shoulders. She squeezed and slipped them down to her arms
before she squeezed again. "Mia. Breathe. You're okay.
It's okay that you're here."

"It is?" Mia felt a rush of calm come over her. Eliza
wasn't going to turn her away. At least not yet.

"Yes. Of course it is. Why don't you sit down and tell
me what happened?"

Eliza led Mia over to a large couch and Mia curled up in
the corner, the way she usually did at home. Eliza's suite
was spacious, but nothing in comparison to the family suite
she'd fled. This room was warm and inviting, and the sight
of Eliza's blazer draped over the back of the couch made
Mia feel inexplicably safe.

"I just wasn't expecting to see them so soon. I thought
I had more time to get everything together. To get a plan
together."

"What are you talking about?"

"They are insisting on having some kind of official
meeting with me. About my future. And I have ideas. I
have plans. I just don't have it all sorted yet. I'm not sure
how to tell them."

"Tell them what?"

"That I want to do more with our nonprofit work. I want
to start our own version of the Fielding Foundation. Re-

ally build something. Make the world better somehow. I have so many ideas, but the last time we talked they just wanted me to be photographed more. Going to events and charities is fine as long as I am in the light, bringing positive attention to our family name."

"You should tell them."

"I want to." Mia sniffed. "God, my headache is back. This is supposed to be a vacation, not a stress inducer."

Eliza left and disappeared into the bathroom. She emerged a moment later with a glass of water and some medicine. "Take this," she demanded.

Mia sat up and dutifully drank the pills down. She rubbed absently at her neck until, suddenly, Eliza's hands were there, pushing in the exact right spot.

"Here, let me," Eliza said in a hushed voice. Mia didn't have the energy to fight her. And besides, it felt really, really good. So instead, she turned slightly, her back to Eliza, and let herself be touched. With each pass of Eliza's thumb, Mia felt her body go slack. But her body was filled with electricity running from her stomach to her toes and all through her brain.

Eliza was touching her and Mia liked it. She liked it a lot. She wanted to maybe touch Eliza, too. But that was a ridiculous thought. You couldn't just barge into your fake girlfriend's hotel room and make a move on her when you were an emotional mess. No matter how much you wanted to.

"Why did you leave the beach so quickly earlier? Did my parents say something?" Mia asked instead.

Eliza's hands stopped, just for a minute, before continuing. Eliza had dropped off the drinks and made a work excuse within two minutes. Her parents had not been impressed.

"I really did have work business to attend to. I'm sorry I disappeared on you."

"You're allowed to have a job, Eliza. Fake dating me doesn't have to be a full-time gig."

Mia turned just in time to see something pass over Eliza's eyes. Something Mia said had been wrong. She couldn't quite tell, but Eliza seemed lost in thought for a moment.

"Listen, I know this is a lot to ask, but do you think I could sleep here tonight? The couch is fine, I just need like a blanket. I don't think I can go back to my suite."

Eliza's face scrunched up before she said, "You're not sleeping on the couch, Mia. You already have more stress in your neck than anyone I've ever seen. You can take the bed. I can sleep on the couch."

"I am not stealing your bed from you," Mia huffed. Eliza had already done so much for her. And here she was, well after midnight, asking if she could spend the night. This was getting complicated.

"It's not a big deal. I promise."

"It is to me. You're sleeping in your own bed."

"Fine."

"Fine?"

"Yes." Eliza stood and hauled Mia up. With both of them barefoot, Eliza was only an inch or so taller than Mia. She held Mia's eyes without moving an inch and smiled. "We will both sleep in the bed. We're adults. And I don't think either of us are going to win this fight. Maybe this way we can both get some sleep."

"You aren't sleeping either?"

"I never sleep well," Eliza said. "Even if I can fall asleep, I'm usually up after just a few hours, my brain in over-drive."

Mia hmmed to herself and considered Eliza's words. Mia may have stress in her neck, but Eliza's entire life was ruled by it. She wished she could relieve some of Eliza's burden the way Eliza had done for her.

She followed quietly as Eliza led her to the bedroom, pointing out the bathroom, the extra pillows and the toothbrush from the toiletries kit. When Mia finally collapsed onto her side of the massive bed, she sank into the pillows and sighed contentedly.

"Your bed is so much better than mine," she pouted when Eliza joined her on the other side, at least two feet of space between them.

"The beds are exactly the same, I'm sure." Eliza's lips twitched. Mia knew she could get punchy and ridiculous when she was tired. It was better to stop talking now. "Go to sleep."

Mia tried to close her eyes, but her body was all too aware of the warm heat coming from the other side of the bed. She tried her best to keep still, but the nervous energy made her twitch and clear her throat and then sigh.

"Mia?" Eliza's voice reverberated in the darkness.

"Yes?"

"Is something wrong?"

"No. Yes. It's just… I can't get comfortable. I have too much running through my mind and I—"

Mia felt a tug on her arm, and then Eliza was pulling her close, into the crook of her arm. "Is this okay?"

"What are you doing?"

"I don't know," she answered. "When I was really little and I couldn't sleep, my mom would run her fingers through my hair, rub at my scalp. Like this." She trailed her fingers through Mia's curls, giving gentle pressure with each pass. "Is this helping?"

Mia let her body give in. For reasons that made no sense, Eliza wanted to take care of her. And damn, she was good at it. "Mmm-hmm," she murmured. She heated under Eliza's touch. Eliza was warm and gentle. Mia melted into her strong arms and soft breaths and gentle tugs in her hair.

Mia fidgeted a bit more, finding her comfortable spot. "All settled?" Eliza asked.

"Think so."

"Good night, Mia," Eliza said.

Mia placed one arm across Eliza's stomach and closed her eyes. "Good night, Eliza." And then she fell asleep.

Eliza

Sunlight filtered through the gauzy curtains leading to the balcony at the far wall of Eliza's suite. Eliza was struck with a sense of panic that this was the first time she's woken up all week when it wasn't dark outside.

It took her a few moments to realize that last night wasn't a dream. That Mia really did show up at her door and then curl up against her like a sleepy cat. She was still there now, her auburn curls splayed out against the pillow and Eliza's arm.

God, had Eliza really suggested they sleep together? This was getting messy. Too messy. Mia needed her to keep this ruse going and here she was asking her to sleep in her bed. And worse, she hadn't even gotten work done last night.

Mia rolled over in her sleep state and nuzzled into Eliza's neck. Eliza froze. It tickled and it made Eliza feel all kinds of desire. Heat and want pooled inside her. But most of all, Eliza felt an overwhelming urge to roll over, pull Mia in close and never let go. She had been able to provide comfort for Mia. And she wondered, just for a moment, what it might be like to do this every morning.

Mia snuggled in even closer, and Eliza had to fight every instinct in her body to not pepper Mia's jawline with kisses and pull her close. That would be a terrible idea. It would make things even messier than they already were.

Instead, she gently stroked her arm and whispered, "Mia?"

No response. Mia let out a little snore and rolled the other way. So she'd been asleep. That was probably for the best. Eliza untangled her arm from below Mia and sneaked out from her bed. She spent a few minutes freshening up in the bathroom before sitting down at the outdoor table with her coffee and her laptop.

She had no idea if Mia was the kind of person who would be mad that Eliza didn't wake her up to run, but she wasn't about to bother her. Eliza made quick work of her emails. Eliza was damn good at her job. Within an hour she had put out three fires, responded to an ungodly number of emails, set up a meeting with the editor who had listened to her father and mapped out their third-quarter plans.

And she hadn't needed her father to do it. For good measure, she drafted three memos to her teams, copying her father on all of them, directing all questions to come to her specifically and noting that under no circumstances should any photographs of Mia Knowles appear in any publication until further notice.

There. She couldn't undo the past, but she could at least guarantee that little bit of privacy for Mia moving forward. If she didn't want to be in the public eye, then she wouldn't be.

"Morning."

Mia's voice came from somewhere behind her, and Eliza

froze before realizing she'd been in some kind of work trance. Mia set a huge mug of coffee next to the cold, half-empty one next to Eliza's laptop.

Eliza smiled at the cup. "Did I wake you with my typing? Sometimes I get carried away."

Mia giggled. "No, but I'm no longer curious what hyper-focused Eliza looks like." She pointed at the chair opposite Eliza and waited for Eliza to nod before she sat. "I've been up for a bit. I asked you if you wanted coffee twice, but you were like—" she mimed typing "—really into it."

"Sorry, it happens. Thanks for this." Eliza took a sip of the coffee. It was hot and just a bit sweet. "How did you know how I take my coffee?"

Mia sipped at her own. "Well, if the eighty-seven sugar packets on the counter didn't give it away, it might have been watching you at brunch yesterday. You're not so hard to figure out, Eliza Brewer."

Eliza's chest tightened. There was something about hearing her name on Mia's lips that made her want to see what else her mouth could do. "So," she began and cleared her throat, "do you have plans before the bachelorette party tonight?"

Mia huffed. "Unfortunately. My parents want to…" Mia made air quotes and sighed.

"Have a meeting with you?"

Eliza felt a fierce protectiveness come over her. She closed her laptop and stared at Mia across the table. Beyond her, the sea stretched out before them. Eliza could still see the path Mia ran early the first morning. She could still remember watching her as her feet dug into the sand. She was so strong, so confident. Eliza wanted to remind her of who she could be.

"What if you already had plans?" she asked.

Mia blinked. "What did you have in mind?"

"Well, I'm just saying, I'm caught up on work stuff for the moment. Maybe your girlfriend swept you away somewhere without warning. And we lost track of time. Somewhere we can't be found."

"I can't just ignore them." Mia bit the edge of her lip and frowned. "I need them to listen to me. Maybe it's going to be a good meeting?"

Eliza raised a brow in question and Mia huffed. "Fine. I know it's not a good meeting."

"I'm not saying ignore them. Just…delay the meeting. Give yourself some time to calm down. Give yourself some space to figure out what you want to say. Come spend the day with me instead. Let's give you some time to get ready for your big pitch."

A smile spread slowly across Mia's face. "Not ignoring them. Mentally preparing. That makes sense, actually."

"And by the time we got back, it would be too late. Put it off until tomorrow. We have plans tonight anyway. You can't fall down on your maid-of-honor duties. And I'm the best woman and all. We'll be much too busy."

"Very busy."

"So, what do you say, Knowles? Want to go off grid with me?"

By the time they'd made it down to the beach all of the kayaks and paddleboards had been laid out for use. Mia fidgeted nervously beside her. Maybe Eliza had read the situation wrong. What if Mia would have preferred her to charter a small boat? Or maybe just hide in a grotto somewhere?

"I've never paddleboarded before," Mia admitted. "Do you have any other options?"

"Of course," the man said jovially. He motioned to a group of boards in varying length. "If you're nervous about paddleboarding, let your girlfriend help. Take this board for two."

Mia's skin went adorably pink along her cheekbones and between her breasts. And now *Eliza* was staring at *her* breasts. Eliza swallowed thickly, then entwined their fingers and tugged.

"Come on, Mia. It will be fine. I've got you."

And it was as if those three words held some kind of magic between them.

Eliza didn't have time to overthink it or worry or analyze the potential outcomes. She just locked their personal belongings into a locker and waded into the water after Mia. It wasn't until they were both seated, legs dangling in the ocean, facing each other straddled on the paddle board that Mia asked, "Now what?"

Eliza smirked. "Well, now we stand up and try to see how far we can go before our legs get tired or our arms get tired—or both."

"That all sounds really great, except for the standing-up part." Mia wiggled her hips and the board teetered from side to side.

"It's going to be fine. Watch." Eliza pulled her legs up onto the board and handed her paddle to Mia before standing up. Mia gazed up at her, the sun a halo behind her head. "See? Now you do it."

Mia grimaced. "I'm not so sure you want that. I'm less of a liability when I'm seated. Right here." She patted the board on either side.

"We have to paddle," Eliza said, a small hint of exasperation in her voice. But Mia wouldn't budge. She crossed her arms and raised a brow and pouted at the front half of the paddleboard.

"Fine," Eliza laughed. "You win. For now. At least turn around and enjoy the view."

Eliza didn't get out in nature much, but when she did, she spent time paddleboarding with friends on the Hudson River. Years of summers on the river gave her the core and arm strength to get both of them to the grotto beyond the open waters of the beach.

Mia was adorable sitting cross-legged on the board. She dipped her fingers into the water, letting it flow around her, and often tipped her closed eyes to the golden sun. This was how Eliza was going to remember Mia in the coming months. Smiling and full of wonder, the sun pulling out the smattering of freckles on her shoulders even more.

"Okay, we're here."

Mia opened her eyes. The alcove gave them the privacy Eliza so desperately craved.

Mia looked around the high walls of the craggy rock and the still waters. "Where are we?" she asked softly. She dipped her fingers into the sea, which was now a navy blue.

"Somewhere no one can find us," Eliza said. Her smile spread out across her face. "And now you're going to try this for real."

She leaned down and reached out a hand. Mia grumbled, but she still let Eliza take her hand.

"Don't let go, okay?" Mia asked.

"I promise." Eliza squeezed her hands and centered her weight, ready to be there for Mia if she needed her.

The board wobbled, and they almost fell twice, but suddenly, miraculously, Mia found herself standing on the board. She let out a laugh, disbelief clear in her eyes.

"See, I knew you could do it."

Their bodies were flush against each other. Mia's mouth was centimeters from hers. Her hair was frizzy from the salt in the air. Between the sun and the curls, Mia looked like fire itself. Like life itself dancing in front of her.

Eliza leaned in and closed her eyes.

"Maybe we…" Mia trailed off and Eliza froze. Both of their breaths were heaving. "I just. Maybe we shouldn't?"

Eliza blew out a breath and pressed her forehead into Mia's. She nodded. "You're right. Of course you're right. I'm sorry. I got carried away. It won't happen again."

"It's not that I don't—"

"Mia, it's fine. I promise. Let's get back to the shore. I think we only have seven hours before the bachelorette party tonight and you have to help paddle. We might need all the time we can get."

Mia fixed her with a look. "Very funny, Brewer."

Eliza groaned internally. When Mia used her last name it made her want to take back every promise she'd made herself about this week.

"Come on, let's start planning." Eliza knew they were pushing their luck staying out here so long. She wanted to distract Mia, not make things worse for her with her parents. So they needed to get down to business. "We're going to brainstorm a thousand ways to make sure your conversation with your parents goes the way *you* want it to."

"You'd do that for me?" Mia looked up at her with wide eyes, her lashes a million miles long and something like hope sparking to life beneath the surface.

Eliza's heart clenched. "I'll do that *with* you," she replied. "You've got this."

"Yeah?"

"Yeah."

"Thank you for this. For last night. For today. For helping me get out of my own head. I had a lot of fun. And I didn't even fall in."

Mia turned to face the right direction and looked back; arm outstretched for a paddle. She clutched it in her hands and smirked at Eliza, full of confidence.

And then Mia Knowles fell into the water. And Eliza had no choice but to jump in, too.

CHAPTER TEN

Mia

THE NIGHT WAS a glimmering haze of lights and laughter, spilling from the crowded streets of Taormina. It was as if the whole city had come alive to celebrate with them, a pulse of energy thrumming through the air as the wedding party stepped into the restaurant—a hidden gem on the edge of the nightlife district. Mia felt a thrill of satisfaction with how things had turned out. This was the one thing she'd planned on her own for her friend's wedding, a special gift for Cate and Noah with all their favorite things: delicious food, their closest friends and plans for dancing.

Lots of dancing.

A string of tiny lights twinkled overhead on the terrace, competing with the stars, casting a warm, honeyed glow over tables draped in crisp linens and rich velvet chairs. It felt like the type of place she'd bring a date on her own, secluded and romantic and tucked away.

Eliza seemed to like the place as well. She raised one brow at Mia and gave a nod of approval.

"Well done," Eliza mouthed as she followed the hostess.

A thrill ran down Mia's spine at the compliment. The place felt like a secret kept just for them, a glamorous oasis surrounded by the lively hum of the city.

As they were led to their table on the edge of the terrace, Mia felt the cool evening breeze sweep in from the sea, carrying with it a hint of salt and jasmine. Around her, her friends' voices rose in excitement, bubbling over with anticipation for the night ahead. This was Cate's last night of freedom—*her* bachelorette party—and Mia had worked tirelessly to make sure it was perfect, booking them the best view in Sicily, where they could feel the city's heartbeat mingling with the rush of the waves below.

But it felt a bit like Mia's night, too. Eliza stuck close to her side, a reminder of their day together, hiding away from the world. Eliza had been there for her, protected her the best she could. Mia's shoulders still felt warm from the afternoon sun heating their skin as they floated knee to knee on the paddleboard.

Mia pushed the memory from her mind. She needed to focus on Cate tonight, but she couldn't stop staring at Eliza's toned shoulders beneath her jacket. Now she knew what those shoulders looked like when they were being worked. She only peeked when Eliza wasn't looking back at her and *only* for a few seconds. Ever since Eliza pulled Mia from the water this afternoon, her muscled arms straining to right her on the board, Mia couldn't seem to focus on anything else.

"Mia. I said, did your parents find you?" Beth quirked a brow at Mia and waited. How many times had she asked that question? Was Mia really that distracted? "They were looking for you this morning down by the pool."

Beth's subtle frown and perfect posture gave an air of indifference. But it no doubt brought her joy to remind Mia of how she was constantly under her parents' thumb.

"Oh, really?" Mia responded, nonplussed. "I saw them

for a moment before heading out tonight. I'm sure it wasn't anything important."

It had, in fact, been important. At least to her parents. She'd been trying to shake off the conversation for the last hour. They'd cornered her the moment she returned from her ocean escape and told her she needed to stop seeing Eliza Brewer. Immediately.

"I thought this is what you wanted?" She'd thrown the words back in their faces. "Don't you want me splashing my life all over the gossip columns?"

"Not. Like. *This*. I'm sure Eliza is lovely," her father said. "But she isn't your match. Why don't you date Beth again? Or maybe someone from my board? Brewer Enterprises is not going to expand our family name. She isn't even in our same circles. We don't ask much from you, Mia. And surely you can understand that Eliza is going to bring you down."

How could they say these things about Eliza? They didn't even know her! Anger burned behind her eyes and she tried to keep her voice from shaking. "She was at the Fieldings' fundraiser," Mia interrupted without thinking.

"Yes," her mother finally spoke. But it wasn't to defend her daughter. "I remember quite clearly." Mia blushed at the memory of how their first encounter was interrupted by her mother. Mia wished she could go back in time and restart things with Eliza.

Wait. No, she didn't. There wasn't anything to *start* with Eliza. Was there? She pushed away the thought and tried to process the words of her father swirling around her like likes and comments and shares on her social media.

"This ends now, Mia," her father rasped. "We can talk in the morning. I know you need to get to the party. But please, be reasonable. We need you to be seen with someone who can improve our brand, build on it. She's older than you, Mia. And she seems boring."

"Don't talk about my girlfriend that way," Mia had practically shouted. "I'm leaving."

And then she was out the door. She'd never, never spoken to her parents that way. But the more they talked about Eliza, the more she wanted to burn it all down. Eliza was brilliant. And gorgeous. And generous. She was so many things. Anyone would be lucky to date her.

I'd *be lucky to date her.*

The thought hit her so quickly she wasn't sure what to do. Because technically, yes, everyone thought she was dating Eliza Brewer. But now Mia couldn't stop thinking about what this would all be like if it was real. If Eliza truly did like her in the way they were pretending.

The memory of Eliza leaning toward her on the paddleboard, water droplets glistening on her warm brown skin, came rushing back, sending goose bumps down Mia's arms. Eliza would have kissed her. She'd known it. And there'd been no one there to see them.

A kiss like that? A kiss just between the two of them when it might mean something. Mia couldn't handle that. She couldn't let herself give in to the fantasy that she could actually date someone as accomplished and confident and gorgeous as Eliza Brewer. And God, she *was* gorgeous. So Mia had pulled away.

Even if she really, really wanted Eliza to try again.

And now she had Eliza just inches away from her on the terrace of a romantic restaurant while Beth stared at her from across the table. A reminder of what she once had and no longer wanted.

Mia felt nothing for Beth at all. Not even annoyance, just complete indifference. She didn't want to make her jealous; she didn't want to make her regret dumping Mia. Mia wanted absolutely nothing from her at all.

"Thanks for letting me know, Beth. I appreciate it." Mia gave her a genuine smile and Beth returned it. Even if she looked somewhat confused. "I'll catch up with you tomorrow, at the rehearsal dinner, okay?"

She leaned over and squeezed Eliza's thigh. A silent thank-you for being here that she wasn't sure she conveyed correctly. Eliza looked down at Mia's hand in confusion. And fair. Mia wished she hadn't backed away from that almost kiss on the paddleboard.

Mia wasn't interested in fake kisses anymore. She was only interested in seeing if this thing with Eliza could be real. God, she should have just kissed her. Given in to this desire building in her, even if it could only last a few more days. She was done trying to position herself as the perfect, responsible daughter. Nothing she did was good enough. She might as well do whatever she wanted instead.

A slow, sad song began playing from the other side of the restaurant. A guitar softly strummed while a woman's voice rang out in mournful Italian. The emotion of it hit Mia in her heart. She didn't know anything past conversational Italian, but whatever this woman was singing about, Mia felt it. It was full of want and need and loss.

Mia turned into Eliza and whispered near the shell of her ear, "Dance with me?"

She needed to get her hands on Eliza. Or rather, she needed Eliza's hands on her. On the safety of the dance floor, Mia could show Eliza how she felt even if she couldn't say it out loud. She could give in, just a little, just for the moment. She wanted to bury her face in the crook of Eliza's neck and breathe in her musky scent. She needed to memorize it for later when it wouldn't be so readily available.

Eliza's eyes narrowed as she considered Mia's question. "Later at the club? Sure."

"No. Now." Mia gestured to the makeshift dance floor just inside the restaurant. A scattering of couples swayed to the music, arms draped over each other moving gracefully and slowly.

"No," Eliza said in a hushed voice. "We can't do that. We're finishing dinner and then we have another stop."

"I'm not really interested in what we should or should not be doing." Mia's thumb began a long, slow path up Eliza's thigh. Eliza's breath hitched as she stared at Mia's hand. She sucked her bottom lip into her mouth.

"You're not?" she asked, never taking her eyes away from Mia's hand.

"Dance with me. Please."

Eliza nodded and Mia stood, holding out her hand. Mia's heart thundered in her chest as their friends cat-called and whistled as they walked to the dance floor. Cate was incorrigible, all decked out in her white minidress and vintage veil. Mia gripped Eliza's hand tighter and led her to the center of the room.

Eliza wrapped her arms around Mia and she melted into them. There was just something about being in Eliza's arms. So strong and safe and Mia knew nothing bad could happen if she was in them. She was stronger for it.

They began to sway slowly to the strum of the guitar. After a moment, Eliza's soft whisper broke through. "Why did you ask me to dance?"

Mia rested her head on Eliza's shoulder, breathing in her perfume and the linen of her jacket. "Because I like you like this."

"Like this?"

"Yeah, focused. Concentrating. Like you can't think about anything else because this is taking up too much space."

Eliza huffed. "You're already taking up all the space lately." Mia let the words sink in.

She rested her head on Eliza's shoulder and nuzzled into her neck. She vaguely registered that Cate and Noah were on the dance floor now. And a few other friends, too. She closed her eyes and pressed her hips against Eliza's and pretended for a moment they were together. Eliza's body was rounded and soft and pressed back into Mia, meeting her at every point. The feeling was so warm and delicious and felt so right.

And then it was gone.

"I'm sorry, I can't…" Eliza loosened her grip and stared down at Mia. Her eyes were wide and full of confusion. "I can't do this. I'm sorry."

And then she was gone, retreating out the back door of the restaurant. Panic climbed up the back of Mia's neck. Maybe she'd gone too far. Maybe Eliza was still upset from earlier. *This is what happens when Mia tries. She gets rejected.*

Mia scrunched her nose at Cate in an *I'm not sure* look and pointed toward the back of the building. She mouthed, "I'll check on her."

It didn't take long to find Eliza. She was leaning against the wall in an otherwise empty alley. Her eyes were closed and her hands were fisted at her sides.

"Eliza, what's wrong?"

"Please, Mia. Just leave me alone." The words were quiet and hollow in the small space. Mia fought against her urge to listen, her urge to back off and comply.

"Absolutely not. Tell me what's wrong. We were just in there dancing and then you...you run out?"

"What else was I supposed to do?" Anger flashed hot in her eyes. Eliza's eyes were wide, pupils blown black, and her breath was ragged. "I can't dance with you, Mia. I can't hold you and feel your breath on my neck and your hair in my fingers. I can't do all that and not imagine what it might be like to touch you. To kiss you. To wreck you. I know I said I could do this, but I can't. Not like that."

Eliza took a step forward and placed one hand under Mia's jaw. She threaded the fingers of her other hand through her curls. Mia couldn't move. Couldn't breathe. She was caught in the trance of Eliza's words, her hungry stare, and the way her full lips could barely get the words out. "I can't keep looking at you and pretend I don't feel anything. It's too hard to kiss you, or touch you, and know I can't have you the way I want."

Mia sucked in a breath. Eliza *wanted* her. She could see it in the way her jaw clenched. In the way her eyes were full of heat. The way her fingers were now cradling Mia's face, so gentle and yet so determined. Mia felt drunk with this new information. She hadn't expected this at all. Her own desires mirrored so clearly in the way Eliza was staring at her.

"And what way is that?" Mia whispered. She stared back at Eliza, matching her furious glare, matching her anger and frustration and desire. "Show me, Brewer. How do you want me?"

Eliza surged forward and pressed her mouth to Mia's. It was an angry kiss. Nothing hesitant or tentative. Just pure need as she tugged on Mia's lower lip and pressed their bodies as close as they could be. It was pleasure and pain and Mia felt the drop in her stomach as the inevitable finally caught up with them.

Eliza turned them and pushed Mia against the wall. She liked the sting of the stucco and the way Eliza's arms caged her in. Mia broke the kiss and panted into Eliza's mouth. She needed to be sure. She needed to see Eliza's eyes.

But then Eliza slid one leg between Mia's thighs and groaned before kissing her again.

This time the kiss was slower, but just as needy. And when Mia opened her mouth slightly, Eliza's tongue found hers, sliding along the edge and igniting a storm of desire inside Mia's chest. Mia felt the kiss everywhere, arousal pooling low in her belly, a shiver of pleasure running up her legs to the point where Eliza pressed against her.

There was no one to see this. No one to convince this was real. Just the two of them, in a dark alley, with nothing but the moon, the distant sounds of the musicians and Eliza's mouth asking her for more.

Eliza

Eliza was usually in control. She was good at being in control. She didn't let her emotions get the best of her and she certainly didn't go around kissing beautiful women in alleys. It seemed as if everything Eliza held true to in life was upending itself this week. Her father undermining her work, her employees listening to him even though she was supposed to be the one in charge. Eliza was losing control.

And if everything had already spiraled this far, she might as well enjoy the chaos before she had to right it all. She could spend the next few minutes, the next few hours, the next few days, giving in to all her desires. She could have Mia, in whatever messy way Mia would have her. She was done trying to keep herself stable this week.

"I need to get you out of here," Eliza hummed into Mia's neck. She ran her nose down the edge of her jaw and kissed her under her chin. "I need to get you back to my room. *Now*."

Mia froze, her eyes wide and wild. Eliza had gone too far. Pushed too much. Perhaps Mia didn't want *that*. That *much*. Eliza shook her head, ready to walk back the offer. She opened her mouth to take it back when Mia's fingers dug hard into Eliza's hips and Mia pulled her closer.

Mia let out a low moan, a plea. "Yes. Please." It may as well have been a growl. "Last night was torture. Lying right next to you and not being able to touch you."

God, Mia had a way with words. She was so quiet, except when she wasn't. Eliza wondered if having sex with Mia would be like this, too. Would she ask for what she wanted? Would she tell Eliza exactly what to do? A thrill went down Eliza's spine. And that excitement must have been why her hand trailed up Mia's inner thigh. Mia's words caught in her throat. She swallowed thickly and nodded once, her eyes hooded and dark.

It felt so good to leave Mia at a loss for words.

Eliza's hand trailed higher, under Mia's skirt, and was rewarded with a hitch in Mia's breath when she found the silky softness of her underwear, already damp. Eliza took her time, slowly moving her hand, cupping Mia's sex where she wanted her most.

Eliza pressed her lips to Mia's again, drowning out a moan. Mia opened for her, allowing Eliza to slip her tongue inside and kiss into Mia's mouth. Their kiss on the dance floor two nights ago had been for show. It was hot and rushed and full of fire. Their small touches and brief kisses since then had been a whisper of what was possible.

But this kiss was just for them. It wasn't about convincing their families, or mutually beneficial career moves. This was Mia opening herself up to Eliza, exposing herself in a way Eliza wasn't sure she deserved. But she wanted it—whatever Mia would give her—for the next few days.

Eliza wanted her naked; she wanted to watch her unravel, but first she wanted to see what other moans she could coax out of Mia in this alley.

Mia dropped her thigh to one side, shifting the fabric just enough to give Eliza the access she was so desperately seeking.

"Please," Mia sighed.

Eliza slid her hand higher and was rewarded with Mia's low breaths coming faster and faster. Eliza wanted to take her time. Mia deserved attention and care. But when she began moving against Eliza's fingers, meeting her with each pass, Eliza gave Mia exactly what she was seeking.

A loud smack rang out in the alley, soon followed by the low chuckle that could only belong to Noah Brewer.

"Dammit," Eliza muttered, pulling her hand down and away just in time before she caught her brother's shocked face in her periphery. He likely hadn't seen anything specific, but Eliza definitely had a flushed Mia pressed against a wall. She held her hand behind her back.

"So, we're heading over to the club now." He put one hand on the back of his neck and didn't look Eliza in the eyes. The last time Eliza had a girlfriend, Noah had been a kid. He'd never seen her like this and clearly, he was just as embarrassed as she was.

"We'll be right there." Mia's voice was a squeak.

Eliza flattened out her shirt, which had somehow come

untucked from her pants, and then decided messing with it would only be more incriminating. She dropped the hem and nodded at her brother.

"Yup, we'll be right behind you."

"Sounds good," he said, already turning and walking back toward the restaurant. Just before the door closed, she could hear him mutter, "This is the last time Cate sends me to check on my sister."

The door clicked shut and Eliza closed her eyes. There was a part of her that wanted to go after her brother. She wanted to make sure he would not tell their father and that he wouldn't say anything to Cate. There was a part of her that—

The sound of stifled giggles interrupted her thoughts. She turned to find Mia with her lips pressed together, trying to hold in a laugh.

"You look like you're sixteen and just got caught with a girl in your room."

"Well, good." Eliza blew out a breath. "I *feel* like I'm sixteen and just got caught with a girl in my room."

Mia pushed off from the wall and sighed.

"We can't just go, can we? Skip the rest of the night?" Eliza tried to make her voice calm. But she'd just had her hand up Mia's skirt and she was still breathless.

"Damn, I wish we could." Mia's heated gaze roamed over Eliza. She felt herself go warm everywhere all at once. "We have to go with them, though. I planned tonight." She felt like the entire world had tipped on its axis, and here Mia was promising they'd go back to the party.

"Fine," Eliza huffed.

"It's going to be okay," Mia said. She leaned close and whispered in Eliza's ear. Her warm breath tickled. "But you're going to have to spend the rest of the night knowing how much I want you. And knowing that tonight, when we go back to the hotel, I'll be going to your room."

She walked past Eliza, her skirt perfectly hugging her hips as she pulled the door halfway open.

"Eliza? Are you coming?" Mia asked, her voice completely innocent.

"This night is going to be torture." Eliza rolled her eyes, but followed behind.

"I'm counting on it," Mia said, smirking and lacing her fingers through Eliza's before pulling her back into the party.

CHAPTER ELEVEN

Mia

THE NIGHT HAD in fact been torture. Kissing Eliza in the alley, when no one was there to watch, made something snap inside Mia. Now that she knew, she *knew*, how much Eliza wanted her, it was as if she'd jumped out of an airplane and had to spend the rest of the night in a free fall. The only thing keeping her focused was the knowledge that Eliza had promised, at some point later that evening, to pull the rip cord and open the parachute that would bring them both down together. And she had every intention of holding her to it.

Mia endured knowing looks from Beth, a wink from Cate and Noah's stammering and refusal to look her in the eye. But it had all been worth it, because at precisely 11:02 p.m., Eliza stifled a yawn and claimed, "I can't keep up with you young people. I'm turning in for the night." Then she'd stood, smoothed out her wide leg pants that clung to her generous hips and turned to Mia. "Are you coming? Or should I catch up with you later?"

Mia stood fast, and the edge of her knee hit the table and knocked over an empty glass. "I can come with you." And then she'd had to listen to giggles as they'd made their escape into the night.

It had been so easy, in the dark alley, with Eliza's hand up her skirt making her a useless puddle of want and desire to give in to whatever this was. Eliza told her she wanted her. Not that she had feelings for her. Not that she *liked* Mia. But that she felt the same burning attraction.

She'd told Mia she couldn't be near her and not want this. But it was different now, three hours later, when they'd had a chance to think it all through. Perhaps Eliza had changed her mind? Maybe she really was tired. The ride in the town car was excruciating. A thousand little looks and small touches, but not words. Not anything of consequence. Which was fine. Mia was done talking.

But Eliza's hand never left Mia's as they made their way to Eliza's suite. The small of Mia's back, the edge of her hip, playing with the hairs that had come loose on the back of her neck in the cab. Eliza held onto Mia like she might disappear if she didn't. She held onto Mia like it meant something.

For maybe the second time in her life, Mia was doing something because she wanted to, not because she was supposed to. Kissing Eliza, being with Eliza, was a choice all her own. And it was a good one. It was this realization, even more than the lust stirring in her body anytime Eliza's fingers brushed against her, that made her realize this was the right choice. She felt it deep in her bones. The same feeling she'd had when she'd insisted on going to grad school. An inexplicable knowledge that this was going to change her life for the better.

She wanted Eliza. And she was going to give Eliza anything she wanted.

But Eliza didn't hurry. Nothing about Eliza was ever fevered or rushed. Mia found it both annoying and thrilling that Eliza had so much patience. Eliza set down her bag and took Mia's from her shoulder, gently placing it on the entry table. Mia shivered at the feeling of Eliza's fingers against her shoulder.

Eliza walked toward the expansive wall of windows looking out over the ocean. She pulled open the French doors, letting the late-night breeze fill the room. Mia, feeling emboldened by the kiss in the alley and the tension of the car, approached Eliza from behind and wrapped her arms around Eliza's waist. Mia bit down gently on the edge of Eliza's shoulder and smoothed it over with a soft kiss. A test. A kiss in the privacy of the room. The slight graze of her teeth silently asking Eliza just how far she wanted to take this tonight.

Eliza tipped her head back onto Mia's shoulder, exposing her neck and inviting Mia's mouth to explore. Mia took her time exploring this small opening from Eliza. Eliza who was always so buttoned up, so closed off, was pliant and soft in her arms now. Mia murmured into her neck as she kissed along her jawline.

"You are absolutely beautiful, Eliza. The way you move against me. You've been driving me wild all night."

Mia didn't usually talk like this. So openly about what she wanted. But there was no denying this any longer. She wanted Eliza. And if Eliza wanted this, too, she didn't want to waste another minute.

As if Eliza could read her thoughts, she spun and sealed her mouth over Mia's completely. Eliza pushed Mia against the wall, and nuzzled into her neck, humming. "That." She ran her nose along Mia's jawline. "Was." A kiss behind her ear. "Torture."

Eliza's breath tickled Mia's neck and she giggled. Eliza caught the laughter in her mouth, capturing Mia's lips with her own. All thoughts of confessing her feelings to Eliza

flew out of her brain. There would be time for that later.
Eliza's eyes were hooded and hungry and Mia was intent
on giving her whatever she needed.

"What do you want?" Mia asked, a gasp escaping her
mouth as Eliza continued to explore Mia's body. Her mouth
ran along Mia's shoulder and she bit down at the edge, a
sharp pain that made the soft brush of her tongue that much
sweeter. Apparently, Eliza was great at payback.

"Anything," Eliza whispered against her neck.

That one word sent a thrill down Mia's spine. Eliza had
been reduced to single words, incoherent ones at that. Eliza
could command boardrooms and run entire companies, but
now she was a mess. Her eyes were hooded and desperate. "Please. Anything." She closed her eyes and seemed
to give something up. Hand something over to Mia.

Mia grabbed at one of Eliza's exploring hands and
brought it to her mouth. She kissed her fingertips before
pulling two of them into her mouth.

"I trust you," Eliza said with a hiss when Mia scraped
her teeth along Eliza's fingers.

It was everything Mia didn't realize she needed to hear.
Eliza Brewer trusted her. Wanted her. Mia wasn't going
to waste a second.

"Follow me," Mia whispered. She pulled Eliza into the
bedroom and sat her down on the edge of the bed. She
undid the clasp on Eliza's shoes, sliding first one then the
other from her feet. She ran her hands up Eliza's legs. And
Eliza let her. She watched her, kiss drunk and desperate
to be touched.

Mia took her time. She removed Eliza's watch. Her ear-
rings were next as Mia placed a kiss behind each earlobe.
She took Eliza Brewer apart, piece by piece. Her tank top
was next and the thin black lace of her bra made Mia stum-

ble. God, she was gorgeous, her nipples already straining against the fabric. Mia wanted to capture each one in her mouth, so she did. She laid Eliza back on the bed and teased each one through the lace. Eliza squirmed and sighed and breathed out a "yes" and "more" and "please."

Had Eliza ever once in her life begged for something? Mia wanted to see what else she could get that mouth to do.

"You're doing so well," Mia said. She positioned herself over Eliza's gorgeous body, a perfect blend of softness and strength. She continued kissing her way up from her neck and into her mouth. "I've got you."

And then Mia stripped off her own shirt.

Eliza

Eliza couldn't remember another moment when she'd felt this vulnerable and this safe all at once. Mia looked down at her with adoring eyes as if Eliza was something to be treasured, someone to be treasured. Mia looked at her like Eliza was worthy just by existing. She didn't want anything more from her than that.

Eliza swallowed thickly and pushed back the emotions building inside her. This was just sex. This was Mia blowing off some steam. The sexual tension between them was palpable. It had been for days. It had been since the moment they first spoke back at the Fieldings' fundraiser. Eliza was going to let Mia take her fill. She'd give her whatever she wanted in this bed and ignore everything else.

"What do you need?" Mia trailed her fingers down Eliza's ribs and then leaned down, hovering over her. Her auburn curls blanketed either side of Eliza's face. "I want to make you feel good."

"This—" Eliza's voice broke off, shaking. She closed her eyes and tried again. "This. You. All of this. Just keep touching me."

Mia quirked a soft smile down at Eliza. She must have seen something there because she didn't push anymore. She took her time exploring every inch of Eliza. It felt like seconds or maybe hours before she had Eliza wrung out and begging.

Eliza had slept with other women before. Granted, it had been a while. A long while. But she knew the mechanics. She knew what to do. But Mia made every touch, every caress, feel like something breakable and brand-new. She'd never been with another person *like this*. She'd never felt so all consumed before.

Whatever Eliza had been holding onto, whatever restraint she had left inside her, she let it go. With each touch from Mia, with each murmured word of encouragement, she let her walls fall away. Soon she was trembling and grasping for her and the hot prick of tears took over her eyes.

"Baby, are you okay?" Mia was there in an instant, brushing away one traitorous tear. Her lips were swollen and her eyes were wild with concern. Eliza couldn't speak. She took Mia's face in her hands and kissed her. She could taste herself and the mess Mia had made of her. She nodded into the kiss, deepening it. Mia let her take control. She gave it all back to her.

Eliza knew what to do with this. "Lay back," she demanded. "Please. I want to see all of you. I want to take care of you now."

Eliza practically growled when Mia's mouth dropped open in shock and then snapped closed. Her eyes darkened to a rich umber and she nodded before falling back onto the pillow.

Later, when the light had shifted in the room from darkness to some kind of early-morning gray, Mia draped an arm across Eliza's stomach and nuzzled into her neck. Eliza gripped Mia's hip and ran her thumb over a small mark on her skin.

"What's this?" she whispered into Mia's hair.

"Birthmark," Mia murmured. "I kind of think it looks like an island."

Eliza palmed that patch of skin and considered. "I can see it," she agreed. "Like a tiny Sicily, right there on your hip."

Eliza pulled Mia's leg up so it crossed over hers. "And this?" She brushed her fingers along the edge of Mia's knee. There was a scar there, though she couldn't see it now. She'd noticed it the first night out on the terrace. A small patch of skin that looked healed over ten times.

"Hazard of running." Mia nuzzled in closer and closed her eyes. "I tripped on a rock on a trail near my house. It wasn't pretty. I had to limp back and I was already a few miles down the trail."

Worry flooded Eliza. She didn't like the idea of Mia having to rescue herself. But somehow the image didn't surprise her. Mia wasn't one to shy away from a challenge.

"But you kept running?" Eliza asked. "Even after that."

Mia smiled into Eliza's neck. "You say it like I was hospitalized. Runners get hurt all the time. You should see me after a race. I'm a mess."

"I'd like that."

There was a beat of silence. And Eliza realized she'd said that part out loud. She bit the edge of her mouth. Those words implied a future. A moment after this week when maybe they'd still see each other. She considered taking the words back. Making a joke.

But Mia sat up on one elbow and kissed Eliza. "Only if you run with me." She kissed her again.

Eliza knew Mia was joking, but her heart clenched a little at the idea of waiting for Mia at the end of a finish line with a towel or a water.

"Not a chance in hell," Eliza said against Mia's mouth. "I'll stick to paddleboards, thank you very much."

Mia dug her fingers into Eliza's hip and tickled, distracting Eliza and causing her to yelp. Mia took the opportunity to cover Eliza in kisses from her mouth to her collarbone to the spot between her breasts. It was heaven, watching Mia enjoy her.

God, this woman was everything. Silly and romantic and raw and honest and brave. Mia had crescent-moon indents from Eliza's fingernails just above her hips, a birthmark above her right hip bone and a tiny scar on her left knee. Eliza cataloged each mark of her skin and committed it to memory.

"You're ridiculous," she said when Mia was satisfied with her teasing and collapsed back into Eliza's arms.

"I know," Mia said. And Eliza couldn't be sure if Mia meant it as a joke or not. She pulled her close and tugged the blanket up around them. "But you like it."

I really do.

Eliza trailed her fingers up and down Mia's back in a slow rhythm. Eventually, Mia's breath shifted and Eliza knew she was asleep. She knew next week this would be a memory, something she could look back on when she was still in her office late at night, or hopefully something she could fill her dreams with. So she committed it all to memory.

Because that's what Mia Knowles was. A dream. Someone who deserved the whole entire world. Someone who deserved a partner and a cheerleader and someone who could be with her and be present.

She deserved better than a woman six years older than her who was always at her work's—and her father's—beck and call. Someone who couldn't even admit that she wanted a relationship. What kind of life could she really give Mia? Her fingers stopped mid-motion as her own thoughts echoed back at her. It was the first time she'd admitted, even if it was only to herself, that she wanted *more* than what she'd had the last few years.

Her mother's words echoed in her brain. *His dreams don't have to be yours. And his pressure has no place on your back.* Eliza was used to the pressure at work. She was good at holding that burden. Especially knowing it was not something Noah could handle. Definitely something their mother hadn't been able to handle.

Even if there was a world where Mia Knowles wanted Eliza, wanted all of her, including the messy parts she didn't show to others, there was no one else to take on the responsibilities she had to her family. To her career. This was to protect her brother. Support her mother. Give them stability and draw the attention away from them. She needed to keep her father focused on her and the company.

Eliza blew out a breath as tears pricked at the edge of her eyes. This was for the best. She'd take this week with Mia. This dream week, full of secret kisses, and laughter in the sunshine, and even the godforsaken gondola ride, and tuck them safely away. As far as Mia knew, this was a purely physical attraction. And it had to stay this way.

This ended here. It ended in Sicily.

Eliza pressed her eyes shut tight and let her breaths

mimic Mia's. If she only had this one night, she wasn't going to dwell on what she was losing. She pulled Mia close, pressed a kiss into her hair and fell asleep easily and peacefully, perhaps for the first time, as Mia held her close.

CHAPTER TWELVE

Mia

MIA WOKE SOMETIME before dawn, her mind racing and her body aching for a run. Her shoulders were cold, and the blanket had fallen away as it usually did. She reached, half-asleep, for the covers and instead found Eliza's soft stomach, warm and inviting.

A lump formed in Mia's throat as she pushed herself closer to Eliza. Mia loved watching her exhale soft puffs of breath into the quiet room. She looked so at peace. Mia didn't want to disturb her, but she couldn't help creeping closer and burrowing her face into the crook of Eliza's arm. Eliza turned into her, pulled up the covers and murmured into her hair about *sleep* and *come here* and *it's okay*.

When Mia woke again, Eliza was gone.

Morning light streamed through the curtains they'd left open the night before. Mia stretched, a delicious ache in her muscles from the night before. She strained to hear the click-clack of keys, hoping Eliza was in the next room, but all she could hear was the steady crash of waves. She sat up in bed, eyeing the room for a robe of some sort. Eliza was probably in the living room and Mia would not waste another second. She was going to tell Eliza that last night had been amazing. That she'd developed feelings for her and that maybe they could keep this thing going, whatever this was, even after the week was over.

When she made her way into the living room, she discovered a carafe of coffee, a covered plate of pastries. They were *cassatelle*—pastries bursting with sweet ricotta—along with a pitcher of freshly pressed orange juice. Mia loved *cassatelle*. Had Eliza known? Maybe she saw her enjoying them the other morning, powdered sugar stuck to the tips of her fingers? She bit off the corner of the pastry and picked up a handwritten note.

Mia,
I got called away for an early morning meeting. I didn't want to wake you. Saved you one of those moon shaped pastries with the good cheese I know you like.
xx, Eliza

Mia clutched the note to her chest. The tiny little *x*'s next to Eliza's name shouldn't make Mia's heart flutter, but they certainly did. This was for the best. She really wanted to talk to Eliza, but if she didn't meet her parents for their family brunch on time, they were going to come looking for her. She had just enough time to sneak back to her room, shower and get down to the main restaurant.

Not even their strong desire to be well liked could keep the scowls from Mia's parents' faces. They stared at her pointedly as she sat down across from them and gently placed her napkin in her lap. They didn't speak as the server poured Mia a generous cup of coffee, nor while she stirred in a small bit of cream.

"Well, Mia, I hope you've had your fun." Her father

brought his own coffee cup to his mouth and took a sip. "But you will end things with Eliza as soon as this week is over. We already spoke with the Richardses. They said Beth would be willing to try again, or at least be your date to some high-profile events. Beth is exactly the type of person you need by your side as you move into your new role in this family."

Mia couldn't process all the words coming out of his mouth at once. Her stomach dropped as she replayed the words, trying to make sense of them. Mia didn't know where to start.

"Beth has a girlfriend," Mia blurted out.

Her mom rolled her eyes and her father waved at the air as if to dissipate the words.

"They're not really together," her father chided. "It's just a friend who agreed to be her date to the wedding. Besides, her parents agree that our two families are better off being connected. So you'll at least appear to date Beth over the next year."

"Dad, you can't force me to fake date someone. I'm with Eliza."

The words felt true in Mia's heart and she knew it was what she wanted. She had the sudden urge to stand up and push away from the table and scour the resort, searching for her. She wanted to tell Eliza that she wanted this to be real. It was real. And after last night, after Eliza admitted she wanted her, Mia wondered if Eliza would feel the same way. Mia didn't want to date Beth. She didn't want to date anyone if it wasn't Eliza.

"Don't be ridiculous, Mia. And keep your voice down." Her father relaxed his shoulders and took another sip of coffee. He kept his eyes on her as he carefully set his cup down. A smile crept across his face. "We just want what's

best for you, dear. And you will end things with Eliza. She
has a reputation for being cold and hostile. That Brewer
family is known for drama. Don't get me started on the
tell-all from the former VP of sales. Her father is a tyrant
and she has to be just like him. Ruthless and cold. This
will reflect poorly on you. On us."

"I don't care what the tabloids say about my girlfriend,
Dad. She isn't like that. She's powerful and confident and
I'm not breaking up with her just to create some kind of
perfect family image you want." Mia felt a rush. After so
many years of listening to them, she felt like she was in
control of her life for the first time.

Never mind that Eliza wasn't actually her girlfriend.
But didn't last night change things? She could still feel the
brush of Eliza's fingertips as they pressed into her birthmark, the scar above her knee, the crease of her elbow.

A server approached with multiple offerings. There was
a basket of warm *cornetti* filled with almond cream and
Sicilian citrus marmalades, alongside a platter of juicy figs
and peaches. A wooden board held a rustic *pane cunzatu*,
topped with cherry tomatoes, olives and a drizzle of olive
oil. Small bowls of creamy ricotta and golden honey sat
ready for spreading. In front of her father, however, was a
simple plate of scrambled eggs, just as boring as he liked it.

And pastries. The same pastries that Eliza had left for
Mia this morning. The sight of a *cassatelle* made something ache in Mia's chest. Hopefully Eliza would come
back to the room and see her note, see the partially eaten
pastry and know that Mia appreciated her.

She could think of nothing more in the world she wanted
than to make Eliza feel half as cared for as Mia felt right
now. She reached for the *cassatelle*, but her mother swatted her hand away.

"Mia, dear, have some of the fruit."

Mia's cheeks flushed with embarrassment. Her parents had always told her she could be anything she wanted to be. They doted on her when she was little. But in the past few years, she'd noticed that this love came with strings. And they didn't like when Mia tugged on them. They expected her to stay in line and project perfection. And they weren't afraid to remind her of it whenever she stepped out of line. She didn't want to argue. Not with this strange sense of shame creeping over her. And the niggling feeling that there was something else she hadn't asked about.

"You mentioned my new role in the family?" she asked, trying to keep her voice calm and even. Her parents were keeping something from her, and she didn't want to give herself completely away. If she could stay neutral, maybe they could come to some kind of agreement.

"Ah, yes." Her father grabbed the cinnamon bun she'd been eyeing and took a large bite just to spite her. He didn't even like cinnamon buns. Crusted sugar clung to the edge of his mouth and he wiped it away before continuing. "We know how much you like fundraising. Don't think we didn't know about your little stunt at the Fieldings' fundraiser. Really, Mia. Running off to support another family's efforts and trying to keep us in the dark. Did you really think that would work? You should have come to us. We would have helped. Besides, your mother and I talked it over and we agree."

He paused, relishing the moment. Mia gave a small nod.

"We will let you work with your brother, Parker, on some of our philanthropy efforts, if you agree to our terms."

Mia couldn't help but lean closer. This was it. This was what she wanted.

"Dad, this is amazing. I have ideas. I have so many

ideas. I've been thinking a lot about how we can really elevate the Knowles name—make it about more than just what we have, but what we give." Excitement stirred in Mia. This was her chance. She pulled up the speech she'd been rehearsing for months. "I envision a foundation that champions causes close to our hearts—things like empowering young talent, supporting the arts or even creating sustainable opportunities in places that need it most. We could host elegant events, partner with top-tier institutions, but also keep things real by staying connected to the communities we're helping. It's about creating something meaningful, with impact and grace."

Her father held up a hand to stop her. "Okay, okay, Mia. Clearly, you've been thinking about this a lot. No need to get so excited. We're at brunch." He shoveled a bite of scrambled egg into his mouth and chewed thoughtfully. "So it's settled. You'll end things with Eliza, agree to attend some events with Beth and you can meet with Parker to share these…ideas."

When he laid it out so plainly, anger flared hot in Mia's chest. He was offering her everything she wanted. But at what cost?

"Mia dear, listen to your father." Her mother leaned in close and dropped her voice to a whisper. "Eliza might not want to even date you in a month. You would be foolish to turn down this opportunity and then lose Eliza anyway."

Her mother had a way of crushing Mia's spirit before it even had a chance to fly. She knew right where to push. Somehow, her mother knew that Mia had real feelings for Eliza, and she was determined to smother them. This was the Fieldings' fundraiser night all over again. Her mother ignoring what Mia wanted and pretending not to notice when her daughter was crushed.

Maybe her mother was right. There was no guarantee that Eliza wanted to date her after this week. And even if she did, there was no guarantee that it would last. But her dad wasn't offering her much of an opportunity. It was barely a promise. One meeting, with her own brother. But it was still more than she'd ever been given before.

"If I agree to your terms," Mia said cautiously, "what would my role be? When would I be able to get started?"

Her mother and father exchanged nervous glances. "Dear," her mother said cautiously. "It's uncouth to talk about money at brunch. Best to leave all that for later. Next week, you can meet with Parker and share some ideas. Then your father can decide what happens next."

Her father nodded once with finality and her mother leaned over to pat her hand. They still treated her like she was fifteen. And they were placating her now just as much as they did back then.

It wasn't much, but it was more than she'd heard from her parents in a long time. At least she'd been able to share some ideas. Kind of. But she wouldn't say yes, not yet. She needed to talk to Eliza.

Eliza

Eliza smiled down at the papers in front of her. She'd been doodling on the corner of her yellow notepad most of the morning. She'd just now realized it was slightly in the shape of Sicily. Or maybe Mia's birthmark. Both?

Eliza let out a little breath of laughter.

"Eliza, did you hear what I just said?" Her father let out an exasperated sigh. "Honestly, where is your head this week?"

That caught Eliza's attention. She was sitting next to her

father on a Zoom call with three other board members. This was some kind of emergency meeting to prep for a merger that was still weeks away.

"I'm here," she said curtly. "I just don't understand why we are having this meeting now. Couldn't this wait until after Noah's wedding? When we are all back in New York?" She wanted to ask why her father was sitting in on the meeting at all. Normally, she handled these meetings. She'd been doing it for the past six months since she took over as CEO.

"There was an error on some documents," her VP of sales said as his face filled the laptop screen. "When I called you to review the changes, your phone was off. So I, um, I called Mr. Brewer to confirm."

"I see," Eliza said, narrowing her eyes at the man. They would have to have a conversation when she got back in the office. Eliza was good at her job. One missed call should not be enough to make someone call her retired father. And they all knew it. "Well, we are here now. If there is nothing else, I have a vacation to get back to."

Her father cleared his throat, but it sounded more like a growl. "You mean a girl to get back to," he said under his breath.

A shiver ran down Eliza's spine.

"Gentlemen, I will catch up with you on Monday," she said. She slammed the laptop closed without signing off or waiting for a goodbye. "Father, if you have something to say, please say it."

She expected him to back down. Usually, he was too busy to be concerned with who occupied Eliza's bed, as long as it didn't interfere with work. But apparently he didn't like what was happening.

"Since when do you let emotions get the best of you?"

he said. He sounded more disappointed than angry. Which was so much worse. "You and I have been planning your future since you were a little girl. You wanted this. I built this empire for you. I don't want you to throw it all away on some relationship that won't last. Be sensible, Eliza."

She stiffened. "Father, there is nothing I take more seriously than my work. You know that. Just because I am dating Mia, it doesn't mean I can't be good at my work. She won't get in the way."

"But the dancing. The late nights."

"I am at my brother's wedding. I would do those things either way," she lied. But her father's face fell a bit. "Listen, I know you're worried I'm getting too close, getting too involved. But this is for Noah. I want to make sure he has the best wedding week possible. Part of that is attending events, playing along."

Her father nodded. "And this thing with Mia?"

"This thing with Mia is nothing. A distraction during the week. Come Monday, I will be back in the office, working harder than ever before." Her eyes stung as she said the words. But she'd get them out. She needed to convince herself as much as her father.

Mia had looked so beautiful this morning. Her hair fanned out on the pillow as she lightly snored. Eliza had lain there for a few extra minutes, memorizing the way her chest rose and fell with each breath. The way she still smelled liked citrus and something floral, even after a night of dancing and being wrapped in each other's arms. Dancing and making love. Because that's what they had done. Eliza couldn't deny it.

And now she denied the whole thing. Because she had to. People like Eliza didn't get to have happy endings. She couldn't have Mia and this empire she'd built with her father.

"Good. I don't think I need to remind you that you and I are built differently. Don't lead that girl on. I see the way she looks at you."

"I don't know what you're talking about."

Eliza surreptitiously wiped under her eyes and slid her laptop into her bag. She needed to get out of here. She needed to get back to her room. Hopefully Mia would be gone. And Eliza could take a long shower, rinse away the feel of Mia's mouth on her skin and get her head back in the game.

Her father placed a hand on her shoulder, the way he sometimes did when he dropped his guard and wanted to be sincere. "Eliza." His voice dropped to a low timbre. Eliza felt five years old. "I know this is hard. I know what it's like to choose stability and work ethic over…love. But trust me. It's for the best. For you. And for her."

"Understood," Eliza said. She pushed back her chair and placed her bag over her shoulder. She had to get out of here. She couldn't handle her father being sincere. It was so much worse than when he was tough on her. "You have nothing to worry about."

And with that, Eliza left her father's suite and waited until she was in the elevator to let out the sob building in her throat.

CHAPTER THIRTEEN

Mia

SAND SPRAYED UP behind Mia as her feet dug into the soft area of the beach where the surf had been only an hour before. With each footfall, she replayed her parents' words in her mind. They'd let her *meet* with Parker. She could share some ideas. They were empty words with empty promises.

Even so, she'd never heard them spoken before. Her parents had never given her this much. She so desperately wanted to cling to the possibility of her dream career. But was it worth the cost of not being able to see if this thing with Eliza could really go somewhere?

Either way, Mia didn't have much of a choice. What her parents had offered her was little more than lip service. And Parker would never cross their father. She could try talking to him, but if her dad had already made up his mind, there was nothing she could do. But the idea of posing for pictures with Beth by her side made her skin crawl. She'd practically run away from brunch and threw on her running clothes. She needed an escape.

It was what she had wanted only a matter of weeks ago. To prove to Beth that she had matured, that she could handle long distance. But not like this. And not when there was *something* there with Eliza.

"Mia?" a woman's voice called out from a few paces behind her.

Her heart lurched into her throat, hoping it would be Eliza. But that was just her mind playing tricks on her. She slowed her pace and looked behind her.

A woman in her late forties pushed forward to catch up with her. Her straight brown hair was neatly pulled up in an elastic band and her leggings and tank top were a familiar running brand. She didn't have any makeup on and pulled an earbud out as she caught up to Mia. She knew this woman. It took her longer than it should have to recognize her when she wasn't in a gown or giving a speech.

"Oh. Mrs. Fielding." Mia worked to catch her breath and slowed her pace to a walk.

Mrs. Fielding smiled at her graciously. "Please. Call me Laura."

Her eyes were a clear blue and there were fine lines around her eyes. Mia had always liked Mrs. Fielding. She admired her work with her family, her dedication to funding educational programs,and now the fact that she was running without makeup and didn't seem to mind at all.

"Thanks for slowing down. I can run, but I can't talk at the same time. And I really wanted to talk to you. Eliza told me I could probably find you out here."

Mia's heart fluttered at the idea of Eliza knowing her schedule. And more so knowing she didn't have time for an early-morning run since she'd been…otherwise occupied. Or maybe she'd been watching for her from a balcony somewhere.

"Oh," Mia said, working to keep her voice even. "Is everything okay Mrs. F— Laura?"

She waved her hand at Mia and smiled. "Yes, everything is great. I've been meaning to contact you to go to lunch ever since the fundraiser, but life got so busy. When I saw you at the sunset mixer two nights ago, I knew I had to catch you before the wedding."

Nerves churned in Mia's stomach. Maybe something had happened at the fundraiser? Or maybe she was the one who told Mia's parents that she'd helped in secret. She wouldn't be mad at Mrs. Fielding. She could let that go.

Mia blew out a breath and slowed even more. "Anything. How can I help?"

Mrs. Fielding smiled at her. "I have a good feeling about you. That fundraiser was one of our biggest events ever. When I debriefed with our team, your name came up several times. According to my assistant, you're organized and have an amazing eye for pulling in donors."

A rush of pride ran through Mia when she remembered that night. She'd worked so hard. And it had paid off. The sense of accomplishment she'd felt at the end of that night was unreal. And she'd been chasing it ever since.

"Thank you," she said. "Thank you so much. It really means a lot to me."

Laura nodded. "So, I hope you don't think this is too forward, and if you're already too busy with your own family's work, I understand. But I would love to have you come on board with the Fielding Foundation—in a formal capacity. Eliza mentioned you have a master's in public administration. It wouldn't be a glamorous job, but if this is something you're wanting to continue with, we'd love to have you."

"You're…you're offering me a job?"

Laura's face fell a bit and her mouth formed a thin line. "Once again, dear, I'm not trying to take you away from your family. Especially because we would need you at our offices in Manhattan. You'd need to relocate from upstate

New York. But I just knew I'd never forgive myself if I didn't ask."

Mia felt like she might float away. This was a dream and she was going to wake up any moment. She wasn't expecting this at all. And she'd gotten this offer based on her merits. Her hard work.

"That's very kind of you, but—"

"Please, dear, you don't have to answer right now. Why don't I send you over some details? Let us know next week, when we're all back on East Coast time. We are looking at a few different candidates, but like I said, I have a good feeling about you."

"This means a lot to me. Thank you for finding me and telling me."

"Don't thank me. Thank Eliza. I ran into her in the library a little bit ago. She seemed a little sad, but once we started talking about you, she perked right up."

"So Eliza mentioned me?"

"Well, I may have brought up the fundraiser. It was the last time Eliza and I had seen each other. It was a very natural conversation. I've known Eliza since she was a little girl. She is serious and dependable and goes after exactly what she wants. The other night, at the mixer, that's how she looked at you. You're very lucky."

Mia didn't know what to say. That same feeling came back over her, a sense of calm and understanding. If Mrs. Fielding could sense it, then maybe she and Eliza were on the same page.

Laura patted her on the arm and tipped her head back toward the resort. "I'm going to head back. Promise me you'll think about a position with us."

"I will. Thank you so much for the offer."

"I'll see you at the wedding."

Mia stood in the sand and watched Laura jog back toward the resort. Laura Fielding wanted her. On her own merit. In New York. But at what cost to her relationship with her parents?

And then there was what she had to say about Eliza. Mia went through the conversation in her mind again. Laura had said Eliza seemed sad. Mia reached into her shorts pocket and pulled out her phone. She sent her a quick text to Eliza asking where she could meet her.

If something had gone wrong in a meeting, there was no telling what state Eliza would be in. Mia needed to find her. She wanted to help her the same way Eliza had helped pull her out of her own intrusive thoughts.

She shoved her phone away and started a steady pace back to the resort.

Eliza

The library had been a refuge for Eliza when she first arrived at the resort. She'd turned it into a semiprivate space for a home office when she needed to get work done and required a change of scenery. And then Mia had waltzed in that second day and changed everything.

Now every trace of this library had Mia written all over it. The deep blue velvet sofa where she'd perched that first day. The brown leather book she'd held in her hands as she listened in on Eliza's call. She was everywhere.

Earlier when Laura Fielding had walked in, Eliza thought it might be Mia. She'd been ready to tell her they needed to call this off now. Her father was getting suspicious. Her mother seemed to love Mia and was probably planning to have a second daughter-in-law by this time next year. She and Mia could attend the wedding together, they would be cordial, but they couldn't *be* together again. Not like last night. Then Laura had mentioned her and Eliza couldn't help but smile.

Her phone buzzed in her pocket, but she ignored it. She was too keyed up from last night, and now this morning. She just needed five more minutes before she returned to the real world. Five more minutes in this space that reminded her of the woman she had to say goodbye to in just two days.

God, the room even smelled like Mia. Vanilla and citrus and want. Eliza closed her eyes and rubbed her temples. She needed to pull herself together. This thing with Mia had to stop.

"I thought I might find you in here," a soft voice murmured from somewhere behind her. *Mia.* It was as if she could conjure her just by thinking about her. There was a soft click of the door closing and a lock sliding into place. Or maybe it was Eliza's imagination.

Eliza huffed out a steadying breath and willed her pulse to slow. She didn't turn around; she didn't open her eyes. Maybe this was still her imagination. But then there were fingers brushing along her neck, and hands gently squeezing her shoulders.

"Are you okay?" Mia asked. She leaned down and pressed a single kiss to the top of Eliza's shoulder.

And no, she wasn't okay. But how could she tell this woman, this amazing woman, that this had to stop?

"Rough morning," she said instead. She reached up and took Mia's hands in hers, pulling her down and wrapping Mia's arms around her in a hug.

"No, don't. I just finished a run."

Mia tried to pull away, but Eliza didn't care. She pushed her chair back and took in Mia. She was in the world's tiniest running shorts and a sports bra. Her hair was pulled up in a tangled mess and she was wearing running shoes in ridiculous neon colors.

Eliza bit her lower lip.

"Please don't tell me you're into this sweaty look."

"I am not into this at all," Eliza said, pressing her lips together to hide a smile. "Come here." She pulled Mia down onto her. Mia straddled her lap and gasped.

"Eliza Brewer. We are in a very public library."

"Don't think I didn't hear you close the door."

"And locked it, too." Mia sighed and cupped Eliza's face. "You're going to have to shower again."

Eliza shrugged. "I like you like this. Stay."

In response, Mia leaned forward and pressed a chaste kiss to Eliza's mouth.

"Thank you," Mia murmured against Eliza's mouth. "For talking to Mrs. Fielding. She offered me a job."

Eliza stopped kissing. "Mia, that's amazing. Is that what you want?"

"I don't know." Mia told Eliza about her conversation with her parents. About their empty promises and thinly veiled threats.

"So they want you to be with Beth?" Eliza said, doing her best to hide her disappointment.

"I don't think they know what they want. They want to make all the decisions is all. They want positive publicity. Really, I think they just want to know they can control me. As long as it's their idea, then they're happy."

"But do you think they're right? Would Beth be a good choice for your image?"

Eliza knew Mia was going to date other people after this. She *knew* it. But the idea of approving and seeing photos of her and Beth as early as next month made her stomach turn into angry knots.

"I don't care about my image, Eliza." Mia caught Eliza's face in her hands and pressed their foreheads together. "I am done caring about what my parents think. I want to make my own choices. And if that's dating a billionaire CEO or working for another family or moving to New York, that's my choice."

Eliza felt as though the wind had been knocked from her. Eliza's heart thundered in her chest as she searched Mia's face for any sign she was joking around. Mia was imagining a future for the two of them. As if it would be the easiest thing in the world. The part they were definitely not going to talk about until they had to. Until it was time to say goodbye. Didn't she realize how impossible that would be for Eliza? She shifted in her chair and willed her voice to remain calm.

"Mia, I—"

Mia cut her words off by pressing her mouth against Eliza's again. Harder this time. When she slipped her tongue into Eliza's mouth and ran it along the edge of her tongue, all coherent thoughts fell away from Eliza's brain. She *would* remind Mia—and herself—that this thing between them was still just an arrangement. That it *had* to be just an arrangement.

But not right now.

Eliza Brewer knew when she'd lost a fight; she knew when she'd gotten the best deal and when she wouldn't be able to push anymore. And she'd definitely lost this one. She was once again powerless under Mia's touch. So she sank farther into the chair and let her fingers trail along Mia's stomach. Her fingertips ran over skin, the waistband of her shorts and down each side to her exposed upper thighs. She couldn't let herself think about tomorrow. She could only think about now.

"These shorts are killing me." Eliza grasped a handful of the thin fabric and hissed when Mia kissed down her neck. "I can't think when you're doing that."

"Good," Mia said, her breath hot against Eliza's neck and earlobe. "I don't want you thinking. I want you touching me."

God, they were in a library. The door might be locked, but this was still a public space. This was a terrible idea. Still, her hand twitched, begging her to do as Mia asked. She should say no, but she knew if she didn't get her hands on Mia right then, she would regret it for the rest of her life.

This time was different from last night. Last night was slow, and gentle, a beginning. A conversation between their two bodies where they were teaching each other and taking their time.

But this was need and want and giving Mia relief. Eliza didn't waste time. She moved to where Mia wanted her most. This was fast and hot and Mia's eyes went wide with surprise and gratitude. Mia curved her body over Eliza's. She panted into her ear and closed her eyes and pressed their foreheads together.

"Is this okay?" Eliza asked as she moved her hand in a steady rhythm. Mia gasped and cried out and nodded against Eliza's forehead.

"Don't stop," she said hoarsely. It was practically a sob. Eliza didn't stop.

"You're so brilliant, Mia."

Her words of praise made Mia squirm and whimper. But she needed to say them. She needed Mia to know how amazing she was. So brave and so beautiful and so, so captivating.

"I'm so proud of you for knowing what you want. For asking for it. Take everything you want from me now. Take it all. I can give you what you need."

It was on those words that Mia broke apart against Eliza's fingers. She collapsed into her arms and buried her face into Eliza's neck.

"Oh my God," she said sometime later. "I've ruined your shirt. I've ruined everything."

Eliza smirked and brushed a single tear away from Mia's face. "Maybe you can come back to my room with me and help me shower?"

A small smile creeped along the edge of Mia's mouth. "We don't have dinner for a few more hours," Mia hedged.

"Good, I intend to use them all to our advantage."

Mia stood and helped Eliza adjust her clothing as best they could.

The door clicked open. "Hello?"

"I thought you *locked* the door," Eliza hissed.

Mia shrugged looking sheepish. "I thought so, too," she whispered. "Act casual."

Cate and her entourage of bridesmaids entered the room. Mia's face turned a gorgeous crimson, highlighting the freckles on her face. Her lips were swollen and her hair was mussed. Beth narrowed her eyes and glanced from Mia to Eliza. Eliza gave a small wave, feeling a surge of confidence.

"Hi, Cate. What's up?" Mia said, her voice pitched high.

"We need to steal you away for a spa afternoon, remember? Aren't you checking the itinerary?"

"Oh, I'm so sorry." Mia fumbled for her phone. "You're right. I think I got the times mixed up."

"This was a last-minute add on the group text," Beth said. It was clear she was trying to keep her voice calm. "Maybe keep your phone on?"

"Eliza, do you want to come?" Mia turned to Eliza with a hopeful glance.

But Eliza was in desperate need of a shower and some fresh air. Now that she was coming down from the high of undoing Mia, she needed a few minutes.

"No, you go ahead. Have fun. I'll see you for dinner tonight."

Mia leaned down and gave her a soft kiss on the cheek. "Raincheck?" she murmured into Eliza's hair. Now it was Eliza's turn to feel the familiar creep of heat on her cheeks.

She nodded once and watched Mia Knowles walk out of the library. And Eliza knew, despite what her father had told her, that she was in so much trouble. Walking away from Mia was going to be the hardest thing she would ever have to do. And maybe she didn't have to. She clung to the words her mother had said and hoped it would be enough.

Hoped *she* could be enough.

CHAPTER FOURTEEN

Mia

"Who knows, Mia, you could be next." Hannah, one of Cate's cousins, gave Mia a knowing look from across the spa. "Apparently, the Brewer siblings go from casual to serious in a heartbeat. At least Noah did. Right, Cate?"

Mia looked over at her dearest friend. A creep of pink flushed her cheeks as she pretended to be offended. "Six months isn't a whirlwind or anything. Besides, when you know, you know."

Cate looked down at her ring and smiled. When Mia and Cate were younger, Cate declared she'd never get married. And even if she did, she was keeping her name. Cate had never even dated anyone, at least not seriously, until she met Noah. Mia remembered worrying about her friend in the early months of their relationship. She and Beth were having a rough go of it, and she didn't want the same future for her best friend.

Speaking of Beth, Mia could feel the heated stare on the side of her neck and turned to find Beth, not quite glaring exactly, but not happy.

"What?" Mia asked with exasperation. She kept her voice low so no one else could hear.

"Nothing," Beth said. But she pursed her lips in a way

Mia knew meant she still had more to say. So Mia raised a brow and waited her out. "It's just…you seem really happy. But I didn't hear about you and Eliza dating before this week. And when your mom talked to me this morning, she—"

Beth must have seen the look on Mia's face, and she must have looked wrecked, because Beth cut off her sentence. "You know what, never mind. We can talk about it later."

"Talk about what later?" Hannah asked. Hannah was a few years younger than Mia and Cate. She'd spent summers straggling behind the two friends, wanting to be involved in anything they were doing.

"Oh! Are we talking about Eliza?" Cate asked excitedly. The nail technician had to hold her hands in place to keep them from flailing. "Let's talk about Eliza!"

"We were *not* talking about Eliza."

"Okay, but now we are." Cate turned slightly in her pedicure spa chair, careful not to disturb the freshly applied polish. "Have you been away together before now?"

"No, this is our first real chance to be together in person for any length of time."

"Wow," Hannah said, deadpan. "There is no way I could do long-distance like that. No thanks."

"It's not so bad." Mia shrugged. "You both just have to be willing to put in the work."

Mia stumbled over the last word, realizing too late her mistake. Beth cleared her throat and shifted in her chair, but didn't say anything.

"I bet Eliza will put in the work," Cate teased. If she knew that was Beth's reason for breaking up with Mia, she didn't let on. "I see the way the two of you interact. It's like…electricity. Not to mention what Noah walked in on."

"Oh my God, stop. Please erase that from your brain—and his."

"Come on, Mia. Give me something. We used to tell each other everything." Cate leaned in close and squeezed Mia's hand. She dropped her voice to a whisper. "What made you fall for Eliza? What do the two of you have in common besides sizzling sexual tension?"

Mia spoke without thinking. "I don't think it's what we have in common, but maybe what we bring out in each other. Eliza is bold and confident and asks for what she wants. And it makes me less afraid to do those things, too. Eliza doesn't treat me like I'm fragile. She isn't gentle with me. She knows I can handle hard things and she encourages me to pursue the things I want. And she lets me care for her. She has to be so strong, all the time, for so many reasons. But when it's just us? She lets all those walls down."

Mia stopped speaking and realized the spa had gone eerily quiet. Had the entire group just heard her? Mia's heart thundered in her chest. This whole week these feelings had been building up. She'd been collecting them like miles on her running shoes, the sole slowly wearing down in the same spots as she led up to race day. Eliza had definitely worn her down in places, made her into something softer. But also, something steady. Something she knew she could trust to get her through.

Mia wasn't planning to fall for Eliza Brewer. But when she looked at the facts, it was indisputable.

Mia didn't just want a job working with the Fielding Foundation. She didn't just want her parents' approval. She wanted it all with Eliza. And she wanted to tell her as soon as possible. Before the wedding rehearsal, if she could make it in time.

She wanted to start tomorrow as a couple for real. She wanted a real wedding date, not a fake one.

* * *

Mia stepped into the square, her strappy heels clicking against the cobblestones, a sound that seemed impossibly loud against the gentle trickle of the fountain at its center. The warm Sicilian sun kissed her bare shoulders, the thin straps of her lavender dress doing little to shield her from its touch. She glanced toward the church, its weathered stone looking impossibly quaint, as if it belonged to a postcard rather than the setting for what promised to be the wedding of the century tomorrow.

It was exactly the kind of place Mia would choose for her own wedding. Understated, steeped in history, nestled in between the old and new of the piazza. For the hundredth time, Mia marveled at how Cate and Noah had combined their styles so seamlessly. Her best friend had somehow managed to merge her jet-setting billionaire lifestyle with the quiet charm of a Sicilian village.

"Mi scusi," a no-nonsense voice called out from behind Mia. She stepped to the side, narrowly avoiding someone with a clipboard and a frown.

Mia had been so focused on the cobblestones and the sidewalk musicians across the square, she hadn't noticed the wedding calamity happening around her. The place was swarming with florists, planners and assistants, all buzzing around to finalize details for tomorrow. Yet the church remained untouched, serene in its simplicity, like it had weathered centuries and refused to be cowed by an extravagant guest list or couture gowns.

Mia shifted the small clutch in her hand, catching her reflection in the polished glass of a café window. She looked refined, poised and, to her surprise, not entirely full of anxiety. Ever since she'd made up her mind to tell Eliza how she felt, and to make sure Eliza didn't have a way to brush it off, or skirt around it, and distract her with her mouth, she'd been a bundle of nerves.

Mia sighed, her eyes darting across the square as if conjuring the thought might summon her. She didn't see Eliza yet, but the memory of her muffled laugh against Mia's neck—low and warm, like the morning sun reflecting off the azure sea—lingered in Mia's mind.

What had started as a white lie—Mia insisting she had a date to avoid being interrogated by Cate's family and Beth especially—had turned into something far more complicated.

Fake dating wasn't supposed to feel like this. It wasn't supposed to be catching her breath every time Eliza smiled. It wasn't supposed to be searching the room for her the moment she disappeared. It wasn't supposed to feel like this knot in her chest, part giddy excitement, part aching confusion, every time their fingers brushed.

She shook her head, trying to refocus. She would tell Eliza tonight, but not right now. Not during the wedding rehearsal. Even Mia knew that would be too much. She needed to ignore her feelings, as tangled as they were. The next few hours were about Cate and Noah. Her best friend deserved this fairy tale, and Mia would do whatever it took to help her live it, even if it meant pretending not to notice the way Eliza's touch sent a jolt of electricity up her spine.

A gust of wind stirred the bougainvillea draped over the café's wrought iron balcony, sending a few petals spiraling to the ground. Mia bent to pick one up, absently twirling it between her fingers as she walked toward the church. Her stomach fluttered at the thought of the rehearsal, of Eliza escorting her down the aisle at the end, leaning close to whisper some sly comment in her ear, her breath warm against Mia's skin.

"What are you doing out here?"

Mia looked up from the petal caught between her fingers and saw Eliza. She was in another stunning suit. Charcoal gray with a lavender silk camisole beneath the open suit coat. Those camisoles were going to be the death of Mia.

"We match," Mia said with a giggle.

Eliza looked down and a small smile crept across her face. "You wear it better." She held out her hand to Mia. Mia took it, their fingers interlacing as she stepped to Eliza's side. "It's a good thing you're here. Noah seems off. Really nervous, I think. And no one is listening. Can you do something? Please?"

Mia hadn't realized how long she'd taken arriving at the rehearsal, but she was the last one to walk through the church doors. Inside was absolute chaos. The same woman who had blown past her moments before held a clipboard and looked frazzled. The groomsmen were scattered among the pews scrolling through their phones or chatting with each other. Beth, to her credit, was paying attention and directing her stink eye, for once, on people other than Mia.

And then there was Noah, fidgeting with the cuff of his suit sleeve and looking from one side of the room to the other. She followed his gaze and landed on Cate, who seemed to be trying to calm the group. She was answering questions, signing a paper and trying to make her way over to Noah.

"He just needs Cate," Mia said confidently. "And he needs everyone else to be quiet."

Mia tucked her fingers into her mouth and let out a wolf whistle. Highly un-heiress-like behavior. Her parents would be furious. But her parents weren't here. She could feel Eliza's heated stare as she stepped forward.

The room went quiet and Mia smiled widely. "Well, now that we're all here, why don't we get started?"

Eliza

Eliza watched in awe as Mia took action. She truly was a wonder to behold when organizing something. She handed her clutch to Eliza and began pointing and directing bridesmaids and groomsmen to the front pew on each side of the aisle.

"And who are you?" A woman with a clipboard and a severe bun glared at Mia from the edge of the church.

"Gladys, I'm so grateful you're here," Mia said soothingly. She took the nonclipboarded hand into hers and squeezed. "Since you're in charge this will no doubt be a success!"

Gladys's eyes went wide and Eliza didn't miss the small twinkle in Mia's eyes as she stood her ground. Mia had a way of putting people at ease, making sure they were acknowledged and appreciated, and she did it all without coming off as stuffy or overbearing. She was going to be brilliant at the job with the Fieldings.

As long as she took the job.

Once the group was back on track, Gladys began placing everyone for the ceremony. As each bridesmaid lined up on the left, according to Gladys's directions, the corresponding groomsmen were lined up on the right. Eliza's heart did a funny squeeze when she realized exactly what was coming.

"And Miss Mia, please stand right here." Gladys pointed to a spot on the floor at the front of the church.

Mia rose from her place on the pew, a flush of crimson running up one side of her neck. Eliza wanted to brush her fingertips against it and see if she could make Mia shiver.

Gladys looked to the bench and frowned when she realized there were no groomsmen left to place at the front of the line.

"It's Eliza," Mia said gently, never taking her eyes off Eliza.

"Excuse me?"

"Eliza. She's Noah's best woman. She stands across from me."

"Oh, yes, of course."

Eliza was buzzing with nerves. It was just a rehearsal, for goodness' sake. If she couldn't handle this, what was she going to do tomorrow? But Mia looked stunning, and Eliza wasn't sure how she should be expected to stand across from her and not kiss her. Not want to hold her hand. Not want to promise her the entire world.

When Eliza had been placed in her spot, she looked up to find Mia still staring at her. Mia's eyes were round, and she bit the edge of her lip. "Hi," she mouthed.

Eliza felt her gaze from the top of her head to the tip of her toes.

"Well, there's something you won't see again."

Eliza tried to ignore her father's voice, but he wasn't exactly trying to be quiet. He sat in the second pew, several feet away from Eliza's mother and her new husband. He was grumbling to one of Eliza's uncles.

"What?" Uncle Jonas asked. Jonas was one of Eliza's favorite uncles. He kept his head shaved close and his goatee full and always had sweets in his desk. Sometimes Eliza still sneaked in and grabbed lemon drops from the top left drawer.

"Eliza at the altar."

She saw her dad gesture toward her out of the corner of her eye. Thankfully, Mia was distracted, listening intently while Gladys moved their hands and demonstrated for Noah and Cate the directions they should face for each portion of the ceremony.

"She doesn't have time for dating."

"Isn't she dating the woman across from her?" Her uncle seemed confused.

Just as confused as Eliza. She wanted to drop her hands and walk over to her dad and demand that he stop talking about her life as if he made all the decisions.

"For now." Her father's words seemed so final. "But soon enough, the hours will get to that girl. Eliza will come home one time too late. Or forget her birthday. Miss a dinner. That poor girl will resent Eliza and it will end. It always ends."

"That's a pretty terrible way of looking at love." Jonas rubbed at his chin. "I don't know, they look pretty happy."

Her father harrumphed and crossed his arms across his chest. Eliza felt the hot sting of her eyes burning and blinked back angry tears.

"Eliza is built of something different. Like me. That's why I chose her over Noah. She has what it takes. She can do this. The company is going places with her."

Eliza took a shuddering breath and worked to control her emotions. Her father was talking low and no one else seemed to be paying attention. Mia was absorbed in the directions of the wedding planner. Eliza let out one more slow breath in relief. She didn't want her to know any of this. Dread, guilt and shame spiraled down her throat, burying themselves in her stomach.

"And if she doesn't? What if she stays with Mia? It's Mia, right?"

"She won't. I've seen the way Eliza looks at that girl. She loves her. Too much to give her the same life I had with her mother. A relationship that ends in pain and un-resolved anger. Eliza is too smart to do that to someone."

Eliza's head snapped toward her father, but he was already looking at her. Their eyes connected and he stared at her before saying, "Our legacy is too important. She'll make the right choice."

Eliza couldn't breathe. Her father's words had punched her in the stomach and she gasped. He *knew*. He knew she'd been listening this whole time. Her father put business above everything else. And he assumed she would do the same. He assumed she'd hurt Mia like he'd hurt Eliza's mother. And what if he was right?

She tried to keep her focus on Mia. Her soft curls and determined smile lit up the chapel. But the walls felt like they were closing in. Her father's words echoed in her ears. How long until she hurt Mia?

"Okay. Well done, everyone. We'll save the kissing for tomorrow." Gladys clasped her hands together with finality, but Eliza wasn't sure what had just happened. "Cate and Noah, please proceed down the aisle. Mia and Eliza, you're next."

Gladys's words hung in the air. Mia stepped forward and squeezed Eliza's fingers. Eliza stared down at their joined hands, wishing she knew what she was supposed to do.

"I'm sorry, what?"

"You and Mia. You can exit down the aisle." She gestured to Noah and Cate waiting at the back of the church.

Eliza dropped Mia's hands and backed up. "Oh yes. Yes, of course." But her feet didn't stop moving. "Sorry, I'll be right back. Just need some air."

And before anyone could ask questions, Eliza walked down the aisle, alone, and out the doors of the church into the afternoon sun.

CHAPTER FIFTEEN

Mia

BY THE TIME Mia made it out the door to check on Eliza, she'd disappeared down one of the side streets. Mia had walked the cobblestone path around the fountain, calling out her name before finally trying Eliza's phone.

After two rings, she was sent to voicemail. Eliza needed space. That must be what this was. Her baby brother was getting married and she needed a moment. And so that's what Mia gave her for the rest of the afternoon.

As she dressed for the rehearsal dinner that night, Mia reflected on how much had changed since she'd first arrived at La Piccola Barca. This resort, once a shell of a hotel, was now a bustling and vibrant destination, complete with memories to last a lifetime for Mia.

Mia checked the intricate wooden box for the wedding itinerary. She added the bougainvillea petal she'd caught in her fingers outside the café to the box, along with other mementos she'd hidden away that week. A matchbook from the club where she and Eliza had first kissed, a small scoop of sand in a jar from the day she and Eliza had escaped on the paddleboard to the secluded lagoon, and finally a small black button that had come off of Eliza's tuxedo coat the night they'd first agreed to this ridiculous arrangement. Mia picked up the button and rolled her eyes at herself. *Who keeps the button from a stranger's shirt?* Maybe she knew, even then, that this would turn into something.

Mia pocketed the button for good luck and then shut the box and placed it back on the nightstand in her room before heading to the rehearsal dinner.

The terrace had been utterly transformed, reborn as a lush Sicilian orchard that seemed to have sprung straight from a fairy tale. Towering olive trees in ornate, hand-painted ceramic pots stood sentinel along the balcony of the terrace, their gnarled branches twisted with age and wisdom, their silvery-green leaves catching the glow of string lights above. The deep blue ocean crashed behind the trees.

Everywhere Mia looked, lemon trees stood proudly in large clay pots, their vibrant yellow fruit gleaming like jewels under a canopy of twinkling lights. The trees framed the terrace, their glossy leaves catching the warm glow of hanging lanterns and strings of fairy lights, which seemed to merge with the stars overhead. Tables were nestled among the trees, draped in creamy linens and adorned with clusters of fresh lemons, sprigs of thyme and delicate white blossoms spilling from more of the cobalt blue pottery. The air shimmered with the bright, intoxicating scent of citrus mingled with a hint of thyme and the salty tang of the nearby sea.

She spotted Eliza across the terrace. She was always spotting Eliza across the terrace. Mia waved, feeling ridiculously smitten, and not caring one bit. Eliza nodded back before downing the remains of her champagne glass and heading toward Mia. Her stomach flipped with anticipation as Eliza drew closer.

"All right, everyone, let's all take a seat."

Mia jumped at the boom in Mr. Brewer's voice. It was as if he was trying to keep Mia and Eliza apart. Or at least keep them from talking. Mia found her spot, to the right of Cate at the longest table. Eliza took her own spot, two seats down. All through dinner, Mia tried to make conversation with Eliza, but Eliza seemed to brush her off.

"So, when do you head back?" Noah asked Eliza.

"Tomorrow night, as soon as the reception is over." Eliza's words were like ice over Mia. Tomorrow night?

"Oh, you'll miss the Sunday brunch. Don't go so soon," Cate said. "Mia, are you leaving that soon, too?"

Mia didn't have words. She blinked at them all. "Oh," she said when she realized they were all expecting a response. "I don't… I don't know."

Eliza widened her eyes at Mia in disbelief. They seemed to say *of course you aren't coming back with me*. It made Mia feel rotten.

"Well, when we get back from our honeymoon, we'll have to all get together. Mia, how often are you in New York?"

Never. But no, not never. She had a potential job. With the Fieldings. In New York. "Actually, I think I will be in more often. Laura Fielding offered me a job. And I promised to at least meet with her. If it goes well, I could be in New York quite a bit."

Cate squealed and leaned over, wrapping Mia in a hug. At least one person at the table was happy about the news. Eliza picked up her glass and took a long sip of something warm and brown.

"Okay, so we will all plan something then—it's settled." Noah squeezed Eliza's hand and Eliza winced.

"I'm sure Mia will be busy with work." Eliza shrugged.

"I will be, too. I have a tight schedule once I'm back. And I need to hire a new editor for our sightings page."

"Oh, I heard about that." Noah nodded. "Good for you."

"What are you talking about?" Cate asked.

"I'll be right back," Eliza said. She pushed back her chair and rushed away.

"That was weird. She's been weird since the rehearsal. Anyway, she fired someone for posting those pictures of her and Mia without permission. In fact, she's banned anyone from posting Mia's photograph until further notice."

"Oh, that's so romantic."

"Yeah, Dad was mad. But he's not the one in charge anymore. Which…also makes him mad."

Mia couldn't believe what she was hearing. Not only did Eliza protect her. But she stood up to her father to do it. She pushed back her own chair and blurted out, "I need to go."

She wasn't sure which way Eliza had run off to. But she took a chance and headed to the one spot, beyond the assembled grove of trees, where she thought Eliza might be hiding.

The night had turned cold. Mia wrapped her arms around her shoulders as she stepped onto the empty terrace.

"Eliza?" she called out.

It was dark on the terrace; this area was not meant for guests. But Mia would know the curvy silhouette of Eliza anywhere. She looked especially lovely in the shadowed moonlight, even if she was slumping against the railing.

"I guess you *do* make it a habit of barging into people's private spaces."

A shiver went down Mia's spine at the words. She would know that smooth, low voice anywhere.

"This is twice in one week, Knowles."

Eliza stepped into the light.

"You won't let anyone take pictures of me?"

Eliza shrugged. "It was nothing. The other ones never should have been published."

Eliza barely got the words out before Mia's mouth was on hers. She needed Eliza to know how much this meant to her, how much *she* meant to her. Eliza stiffened beneath Mia's touch, but soon became pliant. Mia took Eliza's bottom lip into her mouth and sucked before Eliza finally gave in and kissed her back.

"No one has ever done something like that for me before." Mia cupped Eliza's face in her hands and searched Eliza's eyes for understanding. "That must have cost your magazine a fortune."

"I don't care about the money, Mia. No one should get to decide how you appear in the media except for you. Not me, not your parents. You."

Eliza cupped Mia's cheeks with her hands and Mia leaned in to the caress. Eliza pulled Mia's hands down and clasped them in hers. Mia curled her fingers around Eliza's and looked into Eliza's eyes.

"I don't want this to end," Mia said. It was a whisper. A plea. Even as she spoke it, she saw Eliza's face change.

"Mia, I—"

"I know you're busy with work. I know you have an entire life. But there's something here. I've never felt this way about anyone before. And I know it's only been a week, but I am falling for you, Eliza Brewer. Somewhere between our ridiculous pact, to the gondola ride, to that kiss on the dance floor. I fell for you."

Eliza shook her head. But Mia wasn't sure if it was a no, or if she couldn't believe what Mia was saying. So she continued.

"I love that you're brave and strong, but you get soft for me. I love taking care of you, even when you don't need it. And I don't want this to end. I want to see where this goes."

Mia's heart was pounding, her pulse thrumming in her ears as the words left her lips. But now, as she watched Eliza's expression, the light of the lanterns flickering in her conflicted eyes, Mia felt her chest tighten with the first crack of doubt.

"Eliza," she said again, her voice quieter now, almost pleading. "You feel the same way. I know you do. You told me you wanted this last night outside the restaurant. Why can't we make this real? Tell me you want to try."

Eliza looked away, her jaw tightening as she gripped the stem of her champagne flute. "Mia…" she began, but her voice faltered. She exhaled sharply, then forced herself to turn back, meeting Mia's gaze with eyes filled with something raw, something almost like regret. "You don't understand. This—what we've had here—it's been perfect, more than I ever expected. But it's not my real life."

Mia stared at her, confusion blooming into disbelief. "What do you mean it's not your real life? It doesn't have to end. We can—"

"No." Eliza cut her off, her voice trembling even as she tried to steady it. "You don't get it. My father built everything we have, Mia. He worked tirelessly to give Noah, and me, a future. And it broke him and my mother. It broke them and she never recovered. This is his legacy. He expects me to do the same. And I can't let him down. I won't. I don't have time for anything else. He's hard on me because he has to be, and I've learned to be just as hard on myself. I don't have time for you. My work…it's my whole life. It has to be."

Mia felt the weight of the words crash over her, but she

couldn't stop herself. "It doesn't have to be," she whispered, stepping closer, her hands reaching out but hesitating just shy of touching Eliza. "You don't have to do it all on your own. You can let someone in. Let me in."

Eliza didn't answer. She didn't have to. The look in her eyes said everything.

"So this was all pretend for you?"

"Don't say that," Eliza practically growled. "I told you. I told you what I can give. What I'm capable of. You don't want me. Don't you see? I don't get happy endings. I don't get the girl. I have work, and I have my family. I have obligations. They need me to make sure everything stays on track."

"I can't believe this," Mia said. Mostly to herself. "Eliza, you can have this. We can figure it out. You're being selfish." Mia felt anger and frustration building in her, causing her shoulders to tense and her eyes to brim with tears. "So you do want this. But you're still saying no. We could at least try, Eliza. You keep telling me to be brave. To stand up to my parents. But what about you? Isn't this worth the risk? Or are you too scared to be happy?"

Eliza scoffed. "Happy? You are the *one* thing I want, Mia. Being with you is the *only* thing I want. But I can't have that. I can't have that and not hurt you. You're going to resent me. But don't for one second think I'm being selfish. I am only thinking of you. I am going to break your heart, Mia."

The words crashed over Mia and she practically swayed with the impact. Eliza thought she was doing this to protect her. Eliza slumped, the fight leaving her, and she reached for Mia. But Mia snatched her hands away. She couldn't feel Eliza's hands on her again, knowing Eliza wouldn't choose her.

"Yeah," Mia said softly. She wiped at another tear, desperate to maintain her composure until she could get back to her room. "I'll see you tomorrow, okay? I'll be the perfect date. No one will know that none of this was real. And then I'll leave you alone."

Eliza

Eliza shut her eyes and leaned over the balcony. She couldn't bear to watch Mia walk away. There was a soft clink on the edge of the balcony next to her, and then she listened to Mia's retreating footsteps.

Eliza looked down and saw one shiny black button gleaming in the moonlight. She recognized it immediately. The button Mia had accidentally ripped off her tuxedo jacket with her bracelet, their night first night here.

She'd kept it.

Eliza let out one quiet sob before picking up the button and shoving it into her coat pocket. This was for the best. Her father had been right. Eliza didn't deserve Mia. She couldn't make her happy. It was better to break her heart a little now, when it was just a hairline fracture, than to wait and break it completely. Mia would come back from this. Eliza knew she would.

Eliza wiped her eyes, straightened her coat and returned to the party. The band was in full swing, and Noah and his groomsmen had started some kind of impromptu dance party.

"Eliza, do you mind getting this guy back to his room?" Cate said, pushing Noah toward her. "I'd take him, but we aren't supposed to see each other until tomorrow. I'm staying with Beth tonight."

"Of course," Eliza said. "I've got him."

"Why aren't you with Mia?" he asked, a lilt to his words. "I like her." He hiccupped and Eliza rolled her eyes, hiding her pain.

"Of course you do. Come on."

Eliza was several years older than her brother and had never had the pleasure of escorting a drunken version of him home. Noah was a sweet drunk. He hugged everyone and everything he said sounded like a song.

"Can you believe I'm getting married tomorrow?" His eyes were wide and his voice was filled with wonder.

"Yes, I can," Eliza murmured. "We've been counting down to it all week." She helped him down the hall and grabbed the room card from his breast pocket. She swiped them into his suite and deposited him on the couch.

"You stay here. I'm going to find you some headache medicine." Eliza did what she did best. She went into fixing mode. She fetched a glass from the counter and filled it with water before locating the pills. "Here. Drink."

He dutifully drank down the pills and handed her the glass. "I'm so happy, Eliza. So, so happy."

She sat down next to him and patted his knee. "I know you are, baby brother. Cate is pretty amazing."

"No."

"No?"

"Wait. No. She is. But I mean for you. Mia is the best. And you are the best. And now the two bests can be happy together. I've never seen you like this, sis."

"Okay, I think you're really drunk."

"Nope. I speak the truth. You two are the real deal."

"Noah, we can't be. Mia and I aren't— We aren't that serious." Eliza's chest ached as she said the words. She wanted to tell her brother everything. She probably could and he wouldn't remember tomorrow. But she'd made a promise to Mia. "I don't want us to end up like Mom and Dad. I need to focus on work."

"Pfft." He waved his hand in the air as if to bat away the words she was saying. Eliza bent down and removed his shoes. He stared at them in wonder and wiggled his toes. "Mom and Dad broke up because of Mom and Dad."

"Come on, into bed with you," Eliza stood and grabbed Noah's hands, but he tugged her back down onto the couch.

"Wait, Eliza. Listen. Mom didn't leave Dad because of work. I mean, yes, that's what they fought about a lot. But work was something they fought about because it was easier to pin her anger there than on the bigger, harder to identify, things. They weren't right for each other. Maybe they never were."

Eliza felt the hot sting of tears at the edge of her eyes. She blinked back the tears, trying to keep them at bay. "It doesn't matter," Eliza sighed. "I'm no good at the girl-friend stuff. The partner stuff. She's going to give up on me eventually."

"You are *the best* at it, Eliza. Cate said she's never seen Mia so happy. And she's finally standing up to her parents? That's huge. And I think it has something to do with you."

"What?"

Eliza turned to her brother, who now had his head back on the couch. His eyes were closed and his breathing was slowing. "Hmm?" he said, only half there.

"Noah?"

"Love you, too," he mumbled. He was definitely asleep. But his words stuck in Eliza's chest.

Mia was happy. And Noah thought it had something to do with Eliza. A zip of pleasure, of hope, coursed through her, pulsing and bright, settling in her chest.

She grabbed a pillow and blanket from his bed, knowing there was no way she could move her brother from the couch now that he was snoring. She tucked him in like she'd done so many times when they were little and kissed the top of his head.

When Eliza returned to her suite, she was overwhelmed with the absolute emptiness of it. She'd spent two nights with Mia in that bed. Two glorious and wonderful nights. The sheets still smelled like her. Citrus and flowers.

Eliza had never felt so alone.

Eliza did not want to admit it, but her brother might be right. She thought about the look in Mia's eyes. The absolute anger and hurt when Eliza put an end to things tonight. No, this was for the best. She needed to protect Mia, even if it meant breaking her own heart in the process.

Eliza closed her eyes, but sleep didn't come. She walked over to the windows and peered out, hoping to see Mia running along the beach. Some kind of sign that she'd made a mistake. But the beach was silent and still. The only movement was the steady lap of waves on the shore and the full moon casting light across the sea.

CHAPTER SIXTEEN

Mia

THE CHURCH WAS dripping in white flowers, lush and opulent. Every surface had been touched since they'd left the night before. Mia looked out the window from the side of the church and to the fountain in the middle of the square. Less than a day before she'd stood there with Eliza, holding hands in the sunlight and whispering to each other.

And now it was all washed away. Mia knew Eliza had feelings for her. She knew it in the way Eliza looked at her and the way she held her. But if Eliza wasn't ready to admit those feelings, if she wasn't ready to be fully present, then Mia had no choice.

"You know—" A voice interrupted Mia's thoughts and she jumped, letting the thin curtain drop from her fingers. "I didn't break up with you because of the long distance."

Mia spun to find Beth standing in front of her. "But that's what you said…"

"Of course that's what I said." Beth rolled her eyes. Like she wasn't almost thirty. "You're an heiress. The sweetheart of the Knowles empire. The life of the party. One look from you would make anyone feel like the luckiest person on earth."

Beth fidgeted with the edge of her dress and cleared her

throat. "But I knew when you looked at me, you didn't feel the same way." Mia wanted to protest but Beth held up her hand.

"It's okay. And I'm sorry I wasn't honest with you from the beginning. But Mia, look at you now. You did so much to help Cate and Noah this week. Your organization, your attention to detail, your ability to somehow convince Eliza Brewer that it's okay to have fun."

Mia's eyes pricked at the sound of Eliza's name. She sniffed and wiped away a tear. "Well, I don't know about that," she said softly.

Beth offered a sad smile. "Look, I don't know what's going on between the two of you. And I don't know why your parents are trying to interfere. But I do know that you've seemed happier this week than I've ever seen you before. And I think it had something to do with Eliza, but I think it might also have something to do with *you*. Something turned on in you this week, Mia. And I hope you nurture whatever it is. I hope you find what you're looking for. And I hope, in some form, we can be friends."

Mia nodded and Beth reached out and squeezed her forearm.

"I'd really like that," Mia said.

Beth didn't have to say any of this, but Mia knew she was right. Even if things hadn't worked out with Eliza, she was different as a result. She was going to meet with Laura Fielding. She was going to take the job. She was probably going to move to Manhattan.

"And I hope you and Eliza are really happy together. I'm rooting for you. No matter what your parents say."

"Wow, Beth. I… I don't know what to say."

"Ladies, it's time. You need to line up." Gladys wielded her clipboard like a sword, and Mia and Beth giggled before falling in line, the last two before Cate.

Beth swatted her words away. "It's fine. Let's get my sister through this wedding, then you can thank me."

They filed into the late-afternoon sun of the courtyard and found Noah's wedding party waiting for them. Her heart clenched as she remembered who she was paired with to walk down the aisle.

Eliza looked gorgeous. She wore a fitted black tuxedo, a strip of black silk running down her leg. It hugged every curve, but the way Eliza brought it to life with her confidence was truly what made her stand out. Her black heels made her a few inches taller than Mia.

"You look beautiful," Eliza said as Mia approached.

Mia's heart clenched. Right. They were still pretending. Putting on a show for everyone else. Mia blinked, the afternoon sun stinging her eyes, and she nodded.

"Right. So do you."

Eliza frowned. "Listen, Mia. About last night—"

"No." Mia shook her head. "Not here. Not right now. I can't talk to you and also make it through this wedding. So please, just stop."

To her credit, Eliza pressed her lips together and nodded once.

"Ladies, over here, please." Gladys motioned for Mia to join the end of the line.

Eliza held out her arm and Mia slipped hers through it. She was glad she could blame the sting in her eyes on the wedding itself. She clutched her bouquet and steeled herself for the ceremony.

"Here." Eliza pressed something into Mia's free hand. A white handkerchief with a trail of bougainvillea embroidered in one corner. Mia dabbed at her eyes and tried to return it.

"No, you keep it," Eliza insisted. "I'm sorry I can't give

you everything. I can't give you what you deserve. You can at least keep my handkerchief."

"I don't want everything, Eliza." Mia would not cry. They were next to walk down the aisle. If Mia didn't say this now, she never would. So even though her voice shook, she said, "I want *you*. I want you to *try*. To take a chance, even though you're scared."

But Eliza didn't have a chance to respond. The doors to the church opened for them and everyone watched as Eliza walked Mia down the aisle.

Eliza

Cate and Noah opted for traditional vows and a simple ceremony inside the stone chapel, which meant Eliza only had to make it through about twenty minutes of awkwardness before she could escape to relative obscurity at the reception. Eliza tried to keep her eyes focused on her brother, but it was too easy to look up and see Mia's wide green eyes staring at her from across the aisle.

She was radiant in the stunning black dress. Eliza had assumed she'd be in lavender, or sage, or some other typical color for a bridesmaid. But all the bridesmaids wore simple black dresses.

Every time Mia dabbed at her eyes with that stupid handkerchief, Eliza's heart cracked open a little more. She knew Mia deserved better than her. But maybe she also deserved better than what she was allowing for herself.

Eliza looked out into the crowd. At her father sitting in the front row. And her mother sitting next to him, her now-husband handing her a kerchief to wipe away a stray tear. Her mother smiled at her and nodded.

Eliza was scared. She was so, so scared. But when she

thought about who she wanted to be a year from now, ten years from now, at the end of her life, she knew she wanted more for herself than a pile of paperwork and a legacy for one.

When Eliza laid it out like this, the answer was so simple. She looked at her mother, at her baby brother, promising to love and cherish Cate. Not promising it would be perfect, or that they would never have to compromise, but promising to love her anyway, even if they didn't know the future.

"And now, the rings." The minister looked to Noah and he turned to his sister.

She reached into her jacket pocket and produced the two platinum bands. As she pressed them into his palm, he squeezed her hand back and mouthed, "I love you."

And then seconds later, Noah and Cate were kissing and the church was applauding and they were all racing back down the aisle.

"I have a surprise for us," Noah yelled above the applause as the wedding party danced into the courtyard outside the church. Just then, the loud sound of chopper blades filled the air and a wicked smile spread across Noah's face. "Even you, Eliza. Please?"

Dread pooled in Eliza's stomach. Noah had always been the daredevil. The one who leaped first and only then made sure he had the parachute. It often worked out for him. He took chances; he took risks. And Eliza was there to catch him if he fell. Not the other way around.

There was no way she was getting on a helicopter. This was worse than the gondola. At least then she was over land.

"Noah! This is amazing," Mia yelled. Her eyes connected with Eliza's for a moment before they moved on to Cate. "I better get one of those microphone things."

Eliza looked over at Mia. She wanted to talk to her; she wanted to get her alone. She was absolutely stunning in that dress. But perhaps the most gorgeous thing about Mia was her confidence. She was so certain about what she wanted. And Eliza was a coward.

"Come on," Cate said as she removed her veil and handed it to the wedding planner. "Down to the docks."

The bridal party took off running. It was the kind of scene that only Cate and Noah could make in the tiny town square. And Eliza, rooted to the spot with fear, didn't follow after. She couldn't do it. She couldn't get on a helicopter. It was too much.

The people on the streets stopped and cheered and clapped for them as they went. Mia trailed behind them, with Beth by her side. It was the exact image Eliza had been terrified of seeing. And she hated it.

She felt a hand on her arm and turned to find her mother.

"I know you're scared," her mother said, "but sometimes we have to do things that scare us."

"Mom, I can't. I could plummet to my death. What if we crash?"

"Oh, I wasn't talking about the helicopter, dear." Her mom gave her a knowing smile. "Is she worth it? Is she worth being a little scared?"

Eliza's heart thundered in her chest. And then, before she could talk herself out of it, she started running. She lost sight of Mia, but followed the sound of cheers and clapping from the crowds. The cobblestone road was tricky with her heels, so Eliza kicked them off and prayed she wouldn't step on a rock.

By the time she reached the helicopters at the dock, the rest of the wedding party had already boarded. She wasn't even sure which helicopter Mia would be in. She spotted Cate's white dress from one window and took a chance.

The pilot waved her in and she leaped into the helicopter. Her heart was pounding, her mind was racing and she was more scared than she'd ever been in her entire life. But there was Mia Knowles, complete shock on her face, looking gorgeous.

"What are you doing?" she mouthed, her eyes wide and nervous.

"I'm telling you I'm in," Eliza practically yelled. It was so loud in this helicopter, she could barely hear her own voice.

"What?" Mia asked.

Cate handed headphones to each of them and pointed at their ears. Eliza obliged, tucking the headphones onto Mia's head before adding them to her own. She felt ridiculous, but at least she could hear Mia now.

"I'm in. With you. I want this. I'm not scared anymore." She cupped Mia's face with her hands and leaned in close. "I mean, I am scared. I'm terrified. But I want to do it anyway. With you."

She didn't care if Cate and Noah could hear her, never mind the pilot. Eliza didn't care if the entire island heard her. She wanted Mia to know that she was ready to be brave.

Eliza crashed her mouth into Mia's. Mia threw her arms around Eliza and Eliza leaned in and kissed her with passion. It was awkward. Eliza had to move the microphone out of the way. Mia was laughing and Eliza felt it against her neck.

She was scared. Terrified. But with Mia next to her, she could do this.

"And I don't care if we have to do long-distance and I don't care if it will be hard. I want to *try*. With you."

"I'm moving to Manhattan," Mia blurted out. "I'm taking the job with the Fieldings. Apparently, we are both doing things we're scared of."

Mia let out a little yelp when Eliza crashed her mouth into Mia's again. She tried to press all her emotions into her kiss. She wanted Mia to know what was in her heart. She wanted to make sure she knew all the things Eliza couldn't say out loud when the helicopter was roaring and her pulse was racing and her heart felt like it was going to beat out of her chest.

"Ma'am, I'm going to need you to buckle up." The pilot leaned back in his seat and pointed at the harness.

Eliza swallowed the lump in her throat and looked from Mia to Cate to her brother. And then she strapped herself in to this death contraption.

Her brother whooped and Cate laughed and Mia leaned over to kiss her again.

They were all given directions through their headphones with mouthpieces and Eliza shut her eyes tight and she squeezed Mia's hand as the helicopter took flight, the pressure of the ascent thrusting her back in her chair.

"Eliza, open your eyes," Mia's voice crackled in her ears. Eliza shook her head. "Babe, please. You don't want to miss this."

Mia squeezed her hand before bringing it to her mouth and kissing her knuckles. Eliza cracked open one eye and peeked at Mia. She was staring back at her.

"Eliza, look. It's so beautiful." Mia pointed somewhere out the window, but all Eliza could see was the absolute joy and wonder on Mia's face.

"Yes," Eliza agreed. "It really is."

CHAPTER SEVENTEEN

Eliza

ONCE THE HELICOPTERS LANDED, guests greeted the wedding party in the open-air ballroom. Eliza didn't regret jumping into the helicopter, but she was grateful to have her feet back on the ground and Mia still in her arms.

An exclusive restored building high above the Sicilian coastline housed the reception; the building blended old-world charm and modern opulence. The Mediterranean stretched endlessly below, its deep cerulean waters reflecting the warm glow of the golden hour. Thousands of flowers—roses, peonies and orchids—cascaded from towering arrangements at the reception, their abundance entwining pillars and spilling over tables draped in shimmering silk. Candles of every size flickered from gilded candelabras and glass votives, their warm light mingling with the soft glow of fairy lights strung in sweeping arcs across the ceiling.

The open balcony, framed by ornate railings wrapped in garlands of jasmine, overlooked the ocean as waves lapped against the cliffs below. The air was heavy with the scent of blooms and the sea, while the gentle strains of a live orchestra set an enchanting rhythm for the evening.

But Eliza wasn't going to remember any of it. How could

she, when Mia was the brightest thing in the room? They moved together across the glowing mosaic-tiled dance floor, the soft candlelight catching the intricate beadwork of Mia's gown and making it shimmer like a thousand tiny stars.

Hundreds of impeccably dressed guests milled around them. Yet to Eliza, the crowd was little more than a blur, the lavish decor a distant hum. Every petal, every flicker of light, every note of music seemed to exist only as a frame for Mia.

Mia was gorgeous like this. She was always gorgeous, always had been, but her gown looked like the night sky as she swayed in Eliza's arms.

"Mind if I borrow my daughter?"

Eliza didn't miss the way Mia's eyes went wide as Eliza's father approached.

"Dad, can we talk later? I'm kind of in the middle of dancing with my girlfriend."

"I don't want to talk. I was hoping we could—" his eyes darted around the room, no doubt noticing he was making a scene "—dance?"

Eliza looked to Mia, and although fear and worry and anxiety snaked up the back of her neck, Mia gave a small nod.

"I'll be over on the balcony if you need me." She kissed Eliza on the cheek and then she was gone.

Eliza and her father fumbled as they joined hands and drifted back and forth on the dance floor.

"Girlfriend, huh?" Her father raised a brow in question.

Eliza huffed. She didn't want to do this. Not now, not at her brother's wedding reception, but she would. "Yes, Dad, my girlfriend. I... I'm serious about her. And she is going to be in my life, whether you like it or not."

Her dad didn't respond for a long time. He was an impeccable dancer. It was a shame he rarely made use of the skill.

"Then I guess I'd better meet her. Officially. Will you two join me for brunch once we're back in New York? I'd like a chance to make a, um, better impression than I've done so far this week."

"Brunch? At a restaurant?"

"Yes."

"Not a working brunch."

Her father let out a short laugh. "Not for work. I'd like to take you out. With your girlfriend. As my daughter."

"Dad, I'd… I'd really like that." She wasn't sure if she believed him, but maybe he was trying. "Did Mom put you up to this?"

"She may have suggested the brunch part. But you put me up to this. You took charge and took a stand—against me—after I approved those photos. Let's just say I might be having a hard time letting go. But I was wrong. And I'm sorry. You've done an impressive job as CEO. You're going to do things I never could. And I know… I know I need to let you do them your way."

"One brunch," Eliza agreed. "And I'm removing your work email account. You won't have access to mine anymore either. You overstepped. And I need to know that won't happen again."

She expected her father to chastise her. Or perhaps make another comment about how maybe she wasn't ready to fully take over. But instead, his eyes glimmered with something close to respect.

"Agreed," he said.

The song ended and Eliza pulled her hand away. "Now, if you'll excuse me, I need to find my girlfriend."

Mia

The fiery pink-and-orange sunset had just dipped into the sea when Mia felt a warm hand on her waist. She didn't have to turn around to recognize the firm yet gentle grip. Her body flushed and her heart raced in a way that only Eliza could elicit.

Eliza, who had somehow fallen for her as well. She'd braved a helicopter for Mia, but she'd braved so much more than that. She'd told her she wanted to try. Eliza had squeezed her eyes shut and wouldn't look down, her pulse thundering under Mia's fingertips, but she'd done it.

"How did it go?" Mia asked.

"Good. He wants to meet you. Properly."

"Sounds…scary."

"Maybe. Probably. But you'll be fine. You're brave."

"So are you," she murmured as she played with the lapels on Eliza's suit coat. "What next? Sky diving? Bungee jumping?"

Eliza huffed, and Mia felt it on the top of her hair. "I don't think so, love. Please tell me that's not a deal breaker."

"Don't worry, you're safe with me," Mia mused.

"I know," Eliza said.

Mia placed her fingertips over Eliza's heart and drummed the beat of the next song playing in the distance. She could get used to this. Eliza under her fingertips, the world fading away around them.

"When I get back to New York things are going to be busy for a while. But I want to make time. I'm going to make time. For this. For us."

Mia's heart squeezed at the sincerity in Eliza's voice. She was under no false pretenses that Eliza was going to stop working as hard or as much as she always had, but she had plans, too. And if the email from the Fielding Foundation this morning was any indication, she'd be just as busy in New York.

"Actually," Mia said, "I'll be in Manhattan next week for a meeting with the Fieldings. Maybe we can start there."

Eliza's eyes went wide with amusement. "Mia, that's amazing. And so fast. Are you sure? Your parents—"

Eliza's eyes flashed with excitement and worry, creating a small furrow between her brows. And while Mia appreciated her protective side coming out, it wasn't necessary.

"Hey." Mia cupped Eliza's face and drew her close. As the song faded, she whispered, "We can deal with my parents later. I *will* deal with my parents later. But for now, can we just enjoy this?"

Eliza pulled Mia close and whispered into her hair, "Of course. I can't think of anything I want to do more than hold you close right now." She kissed her hair, then her temple, and finally her lips, which were quirked into a small smile.

Mia squeezed Eliza at the waist and Eliza's brain went fuzzy with warmth and happiness—and something else, too. Eliza led her out to the dance floor and pulled Mia close. Eliza inhaled the citrus and floral notes that were distinctly Mia.

"Are you sure you want to dance?" Mia giggled when Eliza began tracing kisses along Mia's shoulder. "We do have an entire private suite two floors up. I can think of a million things I want to do to you."

"Later," Eliza murmured. "I'm right where I want to be."

"Good," Mia said.

The song ended and another began. This one was faster and friends and family began filling the dance floor around them. Eliza was going to have to actually dance, not simply sway to the rhythm. Butterflies whirled to life in her stomach.

"You can do this," Mia whispered. She grabbed Eliza's chin and said, "Eyes right here, Brewer."

* * * * *

MILLS & BOON ®

Coming next month

SECRET ROYAL'S NAPOLI REUNION
Nina Milne

Sofia's tummy went into freefall, instincts colliding, fight versus flight, but her feet seemed rooted to the pavement, the two of them caught in an immoveable tableau of shock.

Could it really be Marco? But stood here, looking at him, every bone in her body told her it was. Even though this man was a far cry from the young man of yester year. The overlong hair was now ruthlessly short, his features seemed harder, the jaw more pugnacious, the grey eyes now full of shock, seemed harder. Now her gaze lingered on his lips, set in a firm line. Lips that had given her such joy in that one glorious kiss.

'Marco?' the more her gaze drank him in the more familiar he looked and for once all the years of royalty, of knowing the right thing to say at the right time, the correct smile, the things drilled into her in lieu of an actual education, deserted her and she knew she resembled nothing more than a puffer fish. 'I...'

Continue reading
SECRET ROYAL'S NAPOLI REUNION
Nina Milne

Available next month
millsandboon.co.uk

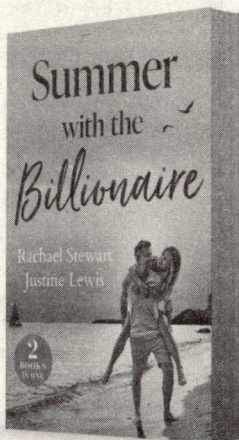

COMING SOON!

We really hope you enjoyed reading this book.
If you're looking for more romance
be sure to head to the shops when
new books are available on

Thursday 25th September

MILLS & BOON

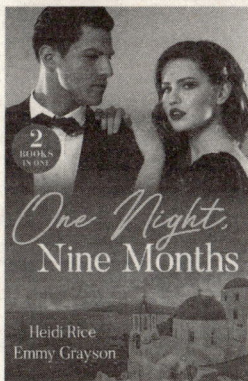

afterglow BOOKS

Afterglow Books is a trend-led, trope-filled list of books with diverse, authentic and relatable characters, a wide array of voices and representations, plus real world trials and tribulations. Featuring all the tropes you could possibly want (think small-town settings, fake relationships, grumpy vs sunshine, enemies to lovers) and all with a generous dose of spice in every story.

♪ @millsandboonuk
📷 @millsandboonuk
afterglowbooks.co.uk

#AfterglowBooks

For all the latest book news, exclusive content and giveaways scan the QR code below to sign up to the Afterglow newsletter:

SCAN ME

afterglow BOOKS

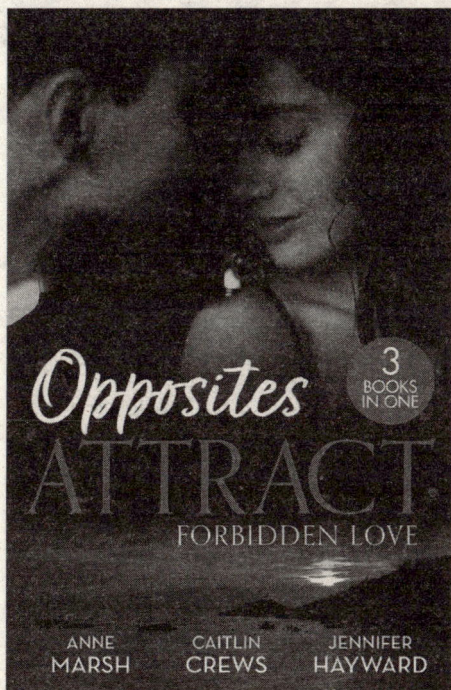